I hope you enjoy my book. A
review on Amazon or Goodreads
would be greatly appreciated!

D0800116

THE

MAD

HATTER'S

SON

Billie
Enjoy!
Helen Starbuck

THE
MAD
HATTER'S
SON

An Annie Collins Mystery

HELEN STARBUCK

Routt Street Press

2018

Routt Street Press

Arvada. CO

info@routtstreetpress.com

Love itself draws on a woman nearly all the bad luck in the world.
—Willa Cather

PROLOGUE

W E HAD BEEN friends for years, until we weren't. I imagined hearing about her secondhand—seeing her in the society pages or in news of a gallery opening or charity function. I imagined being jealous of her and longing to return to our early friendship when our differences seemed meaningless. I remembered her amazing talent. I never imagined her not being there. Now all I can remember is her lying on a gurney surrounded by the familiar, yet strangely discordant, sounds of a hospital ER. I remember being paralyzed by the reality of what had happened and the persistent thought that I was to blame, that I had failed her completely.

 ONE

September, 2000

I STOOD IN THE doorway to my assigned dorm room and looked around. One half of the room was occupied by a small, portable easel with several bound pads of drawing paper leaning against its upright support, fishing tackle boxes stacked around its legs, one open and filled with tubes of oil paint. Leaning up against the wall were several nearly finished canvases. My new roommate was apparently in the Fine Arts program.

The small closet on her side of the room was crammed with colorful outfits, scarves, and shoes. It overflowed, and I couldn't imagine how she planned to close the door. I looked down at my medium-sized suitcase and small carry-on-sized bag and wondered how this arrangement would work out.

"Oh my gosh! I wondered when I'd meet you."

I turned to see a beautiful girl with long blond hair, ice-blue eyes, and freckles across her nose standing behind me. "Hi. Annie Collins," I said, moving into the room. I dropped my bags on the floor by the unclaimed bed.

"Libby Crowder," she replied, following me and extending a hand with short nails and cuticles stained with paint. "I hope you don't mind my taking the side near the window; I need the light for my painting. I won't be doing a lot of that here, mostly over in the arts building, but I like to do my own work, too, not just the assigned stuff."

"No, I just need light to read and it looks like there's enough to do that. Fine Arts major, eh?"

"Yes. I'm so excited, they liked my portfolio, so I'm in the program. What're you here to do?"

"Nursing."

"Wow, that's serious stuff."

"That's what I'm worried about." I laughed.

I was worried. My family lived in Texas and I had chosen to go to college in Colorado as a chance to get away and experience something new, but there were no close friends or family nearby for support. I had chosen Nursing because there were several nurses in my family and I couldn't think of anything else to do. The way I figured it, there are always sick people so I'd always have a job. Assuming I didn't flunk out.

She turned out to be easy to live with, for an artist. She had periods when she was convinced she had no talent, which was ridiculous based on what I saw, and periods of almost mania when she painted at all hours. But mostly she was my friend and expanded my tiny circle of acquaintances to include other Fine Arts students. It was a mixed bag that ran the gamut from just plain weird—pathologically quiet and oddly dressed—to just plain crazy party animals who drank and smoked to excess and had egos so large it was a wonder they could get their heads through doorways. Libby and a few others settled in the middle.

The people I met in the Nursing program were far more normal; some were fun, and all worked hard. Many were oppressively sincere, totally focused on their career choice, convinced they'd been called to nursing to serve the sick. It bordered on annoying and sometimes crossed the border.

We worked our way through undergraduate school, continuing to room together even after moving out of the dorm in our second year. Libby's talent expanded by leaps and bounds, and I loved to watch her paint. She, for the most part, was grossed out at what nurses were asked to do—sometimes I was, too—and we spent a lot of time laughing about it. She had a number of lovers over the four years, some good and some she should have detoured around. I had a few as well, most of whom were mistakes, and relationships for me seemed an endless round of disasters. Between us we shared enough evenings crying on each other's shoulders that it felt like we'd be friends forever.

Libby planned to live a life of ease and grace so she could paint without the tedium of having a day job. I planned to graduate and get a job, tedious or otherwise. Libby went on to get a master's degree in Fine Arts, and I stayed in Colorado and went to work, going back for a master's in Nursing after a few years of practice.

Libby landed a job at the regional arts center restoring paintings, catering to the gentry and the local museum crowd, and painting on the side. I moved slowly through the hospital ranks from staff nurse in the OR to head nurse. In a fit of burnout, I returned to a staff nurse position and opted to work on a per diem basis, and they agreed to let me pick and choose when I would work. It provided me with a higher hourly wage, and I didn't have to be at the hospital's beck and call. It gave me the illusory feeling that I was in control of my life.

Neither of us was wealthy, but Libby moved in a different crowd. She had an innate sense of style that let her fit in with matrons and debutantes in spite of the fact that she didn't earn much. We maintained our friendship despite our differences, and after eleven years we were still close. Then she met Edward Matheisen when he brought in a painting to the arts center to be examined that he was considering buying. He didn't know art and he really didn't even know what he liked, but he knew enough not to get taken to the cleaners.

The effect on our friendship was something neither of us anticipated.

"Oh my god, he's such a babe in the woods." She laughed when she called to tell me about him. "The painting he brought in was atrocious, so I suggested he let me tour him through some galleries until he finds something worth purchasing. He's handsome, too, so it won't be a mercy mission. And he's a widower." Her voice was fairly vibrating she was so excited.

"Sounds like a catch, Lib, but what are you gonna do if you do catch him?"

"I'm sure I'll figure something out." I could almost see her rubbing her hands together.

As I discovered when I finally met him, he was handsome—tall, dark-haired, meticulously groomed. And he had the one quality that most women agree on until they fall in love with a mechanic: He was rich, the CEO of an up-and-coming IT business. He had a reputation as a ruthless businessman and difficult boss. From what I had heard via the grapevine, he was not hesitant to cut people and business associates out of his life if crossed. He personified the *nouveau riche* Libby had always made fun of, and, like them, he wanted to acquire culture. She was happy to help and not long after meeting, they were dating regularly.

Edward was older than Libby, nearing forty, and had been single for about ten years—well on his way to becoming a confirmed bachelor, unless something intervened. Personally, I didn't take to him. I could see why he hadn't managed to remarry; he was not socially awkward so much as just distant. I wondered from time to time if he was a high-functioning Asperger's victim. There was no sense of connection there, and there was a hardness that worried me. When I was around, he tended to disappear or just quit talking. He was unsettling. For the life of me, I couldn't figure out what she saw in him other than his looks and the money.

I was the only one, knowing Libby as I did, who wasn't surprised when she waved a three-carat solitaire in my face. "Look at this!" she crowed, flapping her left hand in my face. "Can you believe how gorgeous this is?"

"It's pretty gorgeous, all right." I laughed; her happiness was infectious. "Do you need a sling to help you hold your arm up? I could get you one."

"No thanks, Annie, I've been lifting weights," she said, smiling like a cat with cream.

September, 2015

LIBBY MATHEISEN reappeared in my life via a voice message that was brief, clear, and typical of Libby.

"It's Tuesday, September first. It's Libby, please call me." She gave me the number. "Thanks." There was a brief pause. "Please call me, Annie, this is important."

It had been twenty-four hours since she'd called, and I hadn't returned it. I didn't really want to because it felt so awkward. Four years and two worlds apart, I couldn't imagine what she wanted. I wasn't sure I wanted to know.

The last time I'd seen her was at her wedding to Edward. Once the wedding had been announced in the society pages, friends who knew that Libby and I had been close bombarded me with questions.

"Are you going to be in the wedding?"

"I don't think so."

"Where's it going to be?"

"St. John's, and then the Denver Country Club."

"Will you take pictures and tell us all about it?"

"If I go, sure."

They finally stopped trying to pump me for details when they could see it was pointless and I wasn't going to give them much information. Honestly, I didn't have much information to give.

My friend, Chip, who worked in the ICU, finally asked, "What's wrong with you? I'd think you'd be excited; this'll be the event of the season, girl."

"It's a long story, but mostly I just don't like her husband-to-be. He's a cold fish and I can't see him and Libby together. She's changed a lot, she's out of my league, and we haven't seen each other much since she met him."

"That's no reason not to go, and I know you're thinking about doing that, don't deny it," he said as we sat down at a table in the hospital cafeteria. "My God, the food will be to die for, and it's a chance to have some fun. You might even meet someone there. They say all sorts of hook-ups happen at weddings, and they'll probably be rich ones at the DCC."

"If you want to go and hook up with somebody, I'll give you my invite."

"You are such a pain. Just do something fun for once."

I got similar advice from other friends who had difficulty understanding why I didn't want to go. My relationship, or lack of one, with Libby was impossible to explain, so I stopped trying. By the time the wedding finally occurred, people were describing Edward's courtship of Libby and their wedding as "fairytale," which always triggers my cynicism. There are people who would say I resent Libby's happiness because it resulted in the loss of our friendship. That is probably true.

I guess I shouldn't have been surprised when we began seeing less and less of each other. I was surprised at how much it bothered me and how resentful I became of each new trinket she sported and every new experience that dating Edward afforded her. It felt as if he were buying her, seducing her with what he could offer, and I was annoyed by how eager she seemed to want it. I wondered what would happen if he grew tired of her. And I often wondered if my reaction to her relationship with him was in part because I had never found anyone special or managed to navigate a successful relationship.

By the time they were married, we hadn't seen each other in several months. I was offered and declined the chance to be in the wedding, asking instead for an invitation to attend. The offer to be in her wedding was a nice thought, but the threads that had held our friendship together had been broken. I hadn't seen her since.

So here I was waffling about calling her. Nursing prepares people to do things they don't really want to do, so after waiting twenty-four hours, I picked up the phone and forced myself to dial the number. The phone was answered on the second ring by a very neutral female voice.

"Matheisen residence."

"May I speak with Libby Matheisen, please?" I asked, using my best manners.

"May I tell Mrs. Matheisen who is calling?"

"This is Anne Collins, returning her call." *Just put her on the phone, I thought. I wanted to get this over with.*

"One moment, please." The phone was put down on something solid, and I waited several moments before I heard Libby's familiar voice and the click of the other handset being hung up.

"Annie?"

"Yep. Long time no see, Lib; how've you been?"

"nnie, could I convince you to come to the house today or tomorrow '" she asked, ignoring my lame attempt at small talk.

I looked at my watch; it was only 10:30. It annoyed me to be eager, but I had to admit I was curious now to discover what was so urgent. "I could come today, I guess. What time?"

She told me and gave me directions to the house. I'd never been to Edward's house, but I had an idea where it was. My idea turned out to be wrong, and I arrived fifteen minutes late. The place was enormous, set back on an elegant piece of property in one of Denver's wealthy old-city neighborhoods. The house was Tudor-style, the kind that had been built in the twenties and thirties in an attempt to recreate the to-the-manor-born atmosphere of an English estate. The grounds were like Edward, meticulously groomed. A black metal fence with arrow-topped spindles surrounded the front yard, and the back yard was shielded from the masses by high brick walls covered in vines.

I approached the heavy front door and rang the bell. I could hear it echoing somewhere in the deep recesses of the house, and it was several minutes before the door was opened by a woman I presumed to be the one who had answered the phone. She looked at me as blandly as she had answered the phone. When I responded to her raised eyebrow with my name, she nodded at me and escorted me through the entry hall and up a large, wide flight of stairs.

I could see the elegant living room from the stairs, and I imagined that the kitchen was on the main floor as well, though I doubted anyone but the help used it. We, however, were going upstairs and I wasn't sure she had heard my name correctly. Most people I knew ate in the kitchen or the dining room. Maybe Libby was different now. Or maybe I'd misunderstood about lunch. I was hungry; I hoped not.

The upstairs hallway was carpeted in a deep, soft gray pile, and the walls were hung at intervals with works of art that said "Libby" all over them. In addition to her artwork, the collection in the hall was a blend of contemporary artists and the occasional impressionist. I doubted that any were reproductions. The woman in front of me stopped at a door near the end of the hall, knocked discretely, then opened it, standing aside for me to enter. I was surprised to see that it was Libby's bedroom and to see her in bed.

Edward rose from a chair at Libby's bedside and walked to me, extending his hand. "Anne, I'm so glad you could come. I'll let you two catch up on old times." It was said in a public voice and as he reached me and took my hand, he said quietly, "Have the housekeeper show you to the library when you leave, I'd like to speak with you."

I responded like I usually do when I am totally baffled: I smiled and nodded at him. I turned to watch him leave the room and heard Libby say behind me, "I was afraid you'd decided not to come."

"I got lost," I said, taking in the room and Libby as I turned and walked toward her bed. I was dumbstruck by the way she looked, pale and thinner than I remembered. I was also surprised at the number of pill bottles on the bedside table. I was about to comment when she cut me off.

"Cora, please bring our lunch up; I'm sure Annie is starving. I'll have some iced tea. What would you like, Annie?"

I asked for Diet Coke, not being much of a tea-drinker.

The phone lady disappeared and closed the door behind her.

Libby motioned for me to sit down in the chair vacated by her husband. Her hand had a fine tremor to it as she reached up and rearranged a lock of hair behind her ear, and I saw her blush when she saw I'd noticed. Her hair had lost its thick, shining mass and her skin looked dry and fragile, like someone twice her age.

"Why *am* I here, Libby?" I blurted out, unable to wait through pleasantries.

She stopped fussing with her hair and glanced nervously at the door, rubbing her fingers with her thumbs as if they felt funny. "I haven't been well. I had a miscarriage almost two months ago and since then I…haven't been well. I just don't…." She kept struggling to put it into words and then gave up. "Oh, for God's sake, Annie, look at me! Something is terribly wrong and everyone tells me it's just in my head! Look!" she cried, and ran a hand through her hair; a surprising amount came out. "My hair is falling out, my hands shake constantly, I get these pains in my hands and feet, and I don't sleep well; this can't be all in my head."

"Have you seen anyone?" I asked dumbly.

"Yes, I've seen my gynecologist and my family doctor. The GYN gave me tranquilizers and a referral to a shrink, and my GP gave me sleeping pills."

"Did you go to the shrink?"

"Yes, for a while."

"Did it help?"

"Oh, don't start, please! Look, I'm not crazy, I'm sick. All he offered was a script for an antidepressant, which I told him I didn't want. I need your help."

"To do what?" I asked uneasily.

"To help me find out what's wrong. I'm scared; what if I'm dying?"

"If you were dying, the doctors would have told you; they wouldn't just refer you to a shrink." At least I didn't think they would. Libby had always been a bit like a first-year medical or nursing student. Every minor illness or symptom was blown out of proportion. She had often used me to reassure her it wasn't serious. I wondered if she wasn't doing that now.

There was a discreet knock on the door and Libby motioned for me to be quiet. The door opened and the phone lady brought lunch in on a trolley. She carefully set up a bed tray with little legs where she assembled Libby's lunch and then placed the trolley beside me and fixed mine. She was efficient and quick and in a few moments Libby and I were alone again.

I wondered how I would feel being waited on hand and foot. I might enjoy it at first, but I think I'd feel a bit bored after a while, maybe even feel as if my every move was watched, but for a while it would be fun. The thought occurred to me that perhaps this was Libby's problem—it had ceased to be fun. Maybe the boredom had become too much, maybe the constant presence of servants had made her just a little paranoid.

"I know you think I'm nuts. You think I've turned into a hypochondriac, don't you?"

"The thought crossed my mind," I replied, looking wistfully at my lunch. I was starving, but it seemed rude to start eating while she poured her heart out to me. I had to ignore the nurse inside my head who was berating me for wanting to eat and for admitting that I thought Libby was nuts out loud. Well, I *was* hungry and I *did* think she might be a little nuts. Libby and I had been pretty straight with each other when we'd been friends. It was hard not to be now. I reached for the sandwich and took a bite while I waited for her to continue.

Libby seemed uninterested in the food. She shrugged her shoulders, picking up the glass and sipping the tea. "You're not the only one who thinks that. But we used to be friends, and I need your help. You're the only one I trust. Annie, please help me."

"What do you want me to do, exactly?" I asked, taking another bite.

"Stay here for a while and take care of me, help me find out what's wrong. I'll pay you double whatever you're making, and I promise if you think it's all in my head, I'll go back to the shrink."

"I've never done private duty, Lib. I don't think this is a good idea. I'm no detective and I'm no doctor. There's got to be a better solution." I had a sinking feeling in my gut and began trying to figure out how to get out of this.

"Please, what can it hurt? If it's all in my head then you've just humored an old friend. If you can discover what's wrong then you've helped me enormously. In the meantime, you've made some easy money. I don't know what I'll do if you don't say yes."

If you want a nurse to do something she absolutely knows is going to result in a lot of trouble, tell her you don't know what you'll do if she doesn't help. It works like a charm.

TWO

ALKING WITH EDWARD that afternoon in the library, I felt
as if I were back in college in the Dean's office discussing the little
prank I had played on a nursing instructor. The discussion had been civi-
lized, but I came away with the distinct impression that the Dean thought
I was a moron and that he was allowing me to remain at school against his
better judgment.

It rapidly became clear that Edward was humoring his wife against his
better judgment, but he wrote out a check for $6,000.00 and gave it to me
without batting an eye. He seemed angry and tightly controlled as he carefully went over details with me. I would stay at the house for six weeks and
care for Libby, he told me in a clipped voice. I could stay in the guestroom
across the hall, and I needn't worry about disturbing him. He informed me
that he was no longer sharing the bedroom with Libby as she was restless
during the night and kept him awake. He was very cool describing his
relations with Libby to me, and I wondered how the Libby I had known fit
into this man's life.

He made it very clear that he believed Libby needed help, but that I
was not the help he felt she needed. "She should be seeing Bill Quentin,
but she refuses."

"That's the psychiatrist?"

"Yes."

"Why did she stop seeing him?"

"You'll have to get the particulars from Libby. She obviously felt he wasn't the answer." It seemed to anger him that I was asking questions. Perhaps no one ever questioned Edward.

"What do you think is wrong?" I asked carefully.

He looked at me steadily for a moment without saying anything. "I don't like discussing private matters with others," he replied at last. "However, you're here at my wife's insistence, and I suppose if you're to be any help at all I ought to be frank." He got up abruptly from the overstuffed couch he had been sitting on when I arrived and walked past my chair to the window. He gazed out for several seconds before he replied. "I think my wife has been deeply disturbed by her miscarriage. I fear, seeing her deterioration, that she may be having some sort of mental breakdown."

He folded his arms across his chest and turned to face me. "I am totally against this ridiculous idea that you can help her, but she refuses to consider any other suggestions. If anything happens to her as a result of this *stupidity*, I will hold you responsible. I expect you to behave like a professional. If you feel her life is in danger because of this foolishness, I expect you to see that she gets the appropriate help. Is that clear?" He stared at me and again, there I was back in the Dean's office.

"As glass," I replied, feeling small and angry. I needed to get back on an equal basis with him and establish some authority for myself, or I could see being blamed for things over which I had no control. "I think you need to hear me out as well, since you've been so frank with me. Libby was a very close friend of mine until recently," I said, pausing so that he knew what I meant. "I have no intention of letting anything happen to her. If you have serious doubts about this idea of hers, Edward, then you better do whatever you think is appropriate. I'll give you back your check and you can continue with your life. Otherwise, you can put that talk about holding me responsible where it belongs. If I take this on, you can be sure I'll do it with the same seriousness that I care for any patient. Is that clear?"

He looked taken aback and had the grace to look almost embarrassed, and it gave me a little satisfaction. I didn't feel quite so small anymore.

"I understand," he said shortly. "You can keep the check and continue as planned." He turned back to the window. Apparently, I had been dismissed.

"I'll let myself out. I told Libby I'd be back in the morning."

He didn't respond or turn from the window, so I let myself out of the library and closed the door behind me. On the way home I felt the anger slowly subside as I replayed the episode in my mind. Edward was like a few surgeons I had had the displeasure of working with over the years. He'd wanted to impress me with how powerful, rich, and well-positioned he was compared to me. He wanted me to be very aware of how benevolent he was being by humoring his wife's request. And just like those surgeons I knew, he enjoyed bullying people. He liked to push and he enjoyed seeing people squirm. I learned early on with people like that it's always a power play you couldn't walk away from. I hoped I hadn't lost the first inning.

I LIVE in a small duplex in Washington Park, known as Wash Park to the natives, and it felt good to get home. The sun was shining as if it knew winter was creeping up, so I decided to take heed and spend some time in my garden. I changed into jeans and an old shirt and gathered up my gloves and spade. I wondered, as I worked pulling out weeds and dying plants and turning the soil, what life with Edward must be like. The thought that Libby might be in a postpartum depression had been planted in my brain by what her doctors had suggested to her and reinforced by Edward's opinions.

It had been a while since I'd spent any time with Libby. I didn't remember children being high on her list of priorities, but perhaps that had changed. I could easily see her experiencing a major depression or hypochondriacal episode as a result of being married to Edward. But I had to admit that my opinion of him was biased.

I didn't know that much about postpartum depression; it wasn't my area of expertise. I wasn't sure if a woman could experience it after a miscarriage, or only after a full term pregnancy. I didn't know much about obstetrics except what I remembered from school and what most women know about pregnancy and childbirth. More to the point, I didn't know for sure whether this was Libby's problem. Her physicians and her husband certainly seemed to believe it was.

I knew something was wrong, which didn't make me much more insightful than any of the other people involved. I took out my frustration on the weeds, hacking away with the sharp end of the spade, letting my mind drift. It had to be painful to lose a pregnancy you'd hoped for, assuming that Libby had wanted the child. But I imagine that even if a pregnancy was an accident, I would be sad that it was gone in some deep, personal place. I tend to project my feelings on the world at large and assuming that Libby felt as I did was probably a mistake.

I do know that the mind is very powerful. Perhaps, if you lost one important thing, you might want to replace it with something that would get your husband's attention; illness was something that would get as much attention as the pregnancy. I could see that I would have to get Libby's permission to speak with the physicians she had consulted.

I didn't know how to approach this plea to take care of her. If you know you're dealing with a psych problem, you deal with it quite differently than if it's a medical problem. I had to know why her physicians could only recommend tranquilizers, sleeping meds, and a shrink. It was an easy prescription to make and one that's used too often, in my opinion, but perhaps in this case it was warranted.

I stopped terrorizing the weeds to wipe away the sweat threatening to run into my eyes. It was late afternoon and the air was cooling off as it does in Denver in late August and early September once the sun begins to set. I'd put off the inevitable long enough. I had shifts coming up at the hospital this weekend that I had to try to get rid of. It wouldn't be easy. Working twelve-hour shifts on Friday, Saturday, and Sunday was ideal for me. I got paid for forty hours and had the rest of the week to myself. I didn't have much hope that I'd be able to get rid of all the shifts, but I wanted to give it a shot. If I had to work, I could always use the opportunity to get answers to some of the questions I had about Libby's condition.

I was stowing the garden spade in the garage when Angel Cisneros hailed me from the back door of the adjoining duplex. Angel, Angelo to those who didn't know him well, was very appropriately nicknamed. He looks like a fallen angel. His large dark eyes are framed with the kind of lashes that God only gives to men. He has a lush lower lip that begs for attention and a playful flirting attitude that's hard to resist. He tries, with no great success, to comb his loosely curled hair off his forehead, but it insists on waving and an occasional curl always manages to escape to dangle invitingly over his eyes.

There had always been an attraction there and I was sure it was mutual. I had never encouraged or acted on it out of self-protection. His record with women was to meet, enjoy, and then pass on to the next one. That wasn't what I wanted. I was much happier with him as a friend. I wasn't sure how he felt about that, but he never pushed the issue. I didn't want to have a fling and then lose his friendship.

"How's the garden going, *chica?*"

"Not bad," I replied, closing the garage door. "How goes the fight for truth, justice, and the American way?"

He laughed. "The usual: lies, injustice, and some kinda way. I'm not sure it's American." Angel worked in the district attorney's office. He was a fledgling star who imagined, after a few years of hard work, that he'd be the next Colorado Supreme Court judge. He was a welcome sight now as I noticed the beer he held out to me. "So, I have my eyes on a new law clerk; will there be another crop of strawberries? I got the champagne on ice."

"The strawberries are done for the year, I'm afraid, you'll have to go to the grocery store. Don't you think that approach is a little predictable?"

"Yeah, but I'm not using it on you. You, I'd have to work on for a while." He settled into a lawn chair and indicated I should have a seat in the one next to him.

"I can't, Angel, I gotta try to get rid of my shifts this weekend."

"You can sit and drink a beer. Sit down and tell me what you've been up to. I haven't seen you in days."

I've never claimed that I couldn't be distracted, and I managed to spend half an hour sitting on the patio telling Angel all about Libby and Edward. Angel's final comment was the kind that sticks with you and needles you, even though you dismiss it initially.

"Rich people live different lives than we do, Collins, and they think the rules apply to everybody but them. You keep your eyes open and if you see anything weird or suspicious with this chick, let me know."

The sense of something not being quite right about Libby had been nagging at me, although I'd been trying to dismiss it. At this point, there wasn't any backing out; I had committed to caring for her.

In an effort to lighten things up and help relieve my discomfort, I said, "You've been with the DA too long, Angel. Every situation isn't an indictable offense, you know." He shrugged and I stood up. "I gotta go; I'll keep you posted if you're interested."

"Do that," he replied, giving me a casual salute with his beer bottle.

THREE

I WAS ABLE TO get rid of all but my Sunday evening shift and Libby didn't complain when I explained I would have to work. I arrived on Thursday afternoon and was shown the alarm system and how to work it, given a key, and escorted to the room across the hall from Libby's. After I unpacked, the phone lady took me for a tour of the house. I had to keep reminding myself that her name was Cora or undoubtedly I would slip and offend someone.

I soon realized it was a huge house, built for people with the money to indulge their whims. All the usual formal rooms were present: dining room, living room, and library. The house had all the normal family rooms, too: kitchen, informal living room, bedrooms, and baths. The difference, I realized, was that whoever had built the house had had the money to play.

There was a sunroom that was large enough to be a small public arboretum, and Libby had filled it with a riot of everyday and exotic plants. The air was warm and heavy with the scent of loamy dirt and growing plants. There was a tiny reading room with its own ornately mantled fireplace and floor-to-ceiling shelves filled with every kind of book. Two huge, soft chairs with ottomans sat facing each other, flanked by reading lamps.

There was a second floor studio for Libby. It was a bit dusty at the moment, but it held a collection of easels and tables where she obviously spent a lot of her time. I leafed through a standing rack of paintings and saw with pleasure that she still had the ability to capture people and places on canvas. There was one painting that caught my eye that I remembered from when we were students, a poignant study of two old women on a park bench surrounded by pigeons. It took my breath away then and had lost none of its power. Libby had always been talented and her talent had just continued to grow.

I was given a brief glimpse of the nursery. Cora explained with some discomfort that the room had been built as a nursery originally and that Libby had begun to redecorate it to her own taste when she realized that she was pregnant. The room looked as if workmen or decorators had just stepped out for lunch and would return shortly. The impression lasted as long as you didn't look closely enough to see the dust. I had a brief, uncomfortable mental image of Libby covered in cobwebs, ensconced in the center of this abandoned nursery like Miss Havisham, in maternity clothes rather than a wedding dress. I frowned to rid myself of the thought and followed Cora as she closed the door and started back down the hall.

We passed a stairway leading up to the third floor which Cora apparently had no intention of showing me. "What's up there?" I asked, stopping and looking up the stairwell.

"The third floor is Mr. Matheisen's private floor. No one goes up there," she replied coolly.

"No one? Not even to clean?"

"No one, miss."

"Does he spend a lot of time there?"

"I don't make it my business and that is how Mr. Matheisen likes it. If you're curious, why not ask him?"

"Maybe I will," I said and smiled at her.

My smile was not returned, and I watched as she turned and walked hurriedly off toward the stairs to the main floor. I wondered how you lived with servants and their constant presence. I got the feeling that Cora didn't like my being here any more than Edward. Perhaps it was the additional person adding to her responsibilities or maybe she felt the same as Edward did about my helping Libby. Libby mentioned that Cora worked 7:00 AM to 5:00 PM and that I should feel free to ask her for whatever I needed.

It seemed unlikely that I would, and it was a relief to know she didn't live here and I wouldn't have to be under her scrutiny after hours.

I glanced up the stairwell to the third floor and had to fight the urge to sneak up to Edward's private domain. Now was not the time to alienate Edward, or anyone else, by trespassing. It was time to check in with Libby. I reminded myself that I was being paid to be Nancy Nurse not Nancy Drew and that even Edward deserved his privacy.

LIBBY WAS sitting up in bed when I returned to her room. A *Vanity Fair* magazine lay open on her lap with a reprise of famous deaths that raised suspicions about the cause like those of Marilyn Monroe and Sunny von Bulow, and strewn across the bed was an *Art World* and *Elle*.

"So, d'you think he did it?" I asked.

"What?"

I pointed to the magazine, "Klaus von Bulow, do you think he killed Sunny?"

She laughed. "God, for a minute I didn't know what you were talking about!" She glanced down at the opened page showing photos of von Bulow and photos of his then-wife. "It wouldn't surprise me if he did. People with money and privilege can be very cold when it comes to getting their way."

The thought seemed to stay with her and she slowly ran a finger across the page of the magazine.

It was an awkward moment, so I changed the subject. "Have you got any plans for today, Libby?"

She looked up at me blankly. "No."

"Well, I for one think you ought to get out of bed. It's beautiful outside; why don't we go out in the back yard for a while?"

"I don't know, Annie. I don't have much energy these days."

"And you won't have any if you stay in bed. Come on." I found her bathrobe and helped her into it and fished under the bed for her slippers. I pulled out a pair of kitten-heeled satin slippers with bows. "Libby, do you have any real shoes? Tennis shoes or something that you won't break your neck in?"

"In the closet, over there," she replied, pointing to a door.

When I opened it, I discovered a small room with a dressing table, vanity, and racks of clothes. Shoes of all sorts were placed carefully on shelves against the far wall.

"What did you say your name was? Marcos?" I asked as I searched through the shoes.

I heard her giggle from the other room. I found an expensive pair of running shoes that didn't look like they had any miles on them, and I returned to the bed with them. "These ought to be good," I said as I knelt down and began to help her put on the shoes.

She reached out to steady herself and put her hand on my shoulder. I looked up at her and smiled, then returned my attention to the shoes.

"Thanks Annie."

"No problem, just remember, I don't shine shoes and I don't do windows."

"I wasn't talking about the shoes. It's good to have someone to laugh with."

I stopped and sat back on my heels. "Yeah, it is."

The moment confused us both and then it passed. I helped her out of bed and let her stand for a moment before we set out for the back yard.

The house had an old service elevator in the back hall that led to the kitchen; Libby used it to get from one floor to the other. We sat on the patio in deeply cushioned teak chairs around a teak table. Libby had asked, or rather told, Cora to bring drinks out to us, and we sat under the umbrella and watched birds flit from the trees to a bird feeder in the yard.

The yard was filled with flowers and shrubs; climbing vines covered the high brick walls that enclosed the back yard. It was like a secret garden; there was no way to tell that people and traffic were on the other side of the walls.

"It's lovely out here, Lib. I'd spend every day out here gardening and enjoying the space if I lived here."

"It is nice. It's one of the things I've always loved about the place."

"Remember that little house we shared in college?" I asked. "I loved that yard."

"Yeah, you always kept it so nice. You know me, I'm not much of a gardener. I have the plants in the sunroom, but I have a plant service care for them. I never knew what to do with the outside. You always did. All I really know is painting."

"Well, that's a pretty amazing talent. Almost anyone can garden. I don't know many who can paint like you do."

She smiled and turned her face up to the sun, which emphasized her paleness. "You always were my biggest fan. I've missed you, Annie."

"I've missed you, too," I said.

 # FOUR

I WAS SURPRISED TO find that Libby was taking Ambien to sleep, an assortment of vitamins, Valium for anxiety, and a pain reliever on an as-needed basis. A quick glance when she was in the bathroom the following day confirmed that she had gotten them from different physicians. I wondered why that was all they could offer her.

I asked her to let me examine her, which felt weird to both of us. Her reflexes were good, and although she could be a little unsteady on her feet, I couldn't find anything alarming. I did a quick neuro check and questioned her about the migrating pains in her hands and feet. I looked at her feet carefully, thinking that it might be possible that her neuropathy was diabetes-related.

"No one said anything about diabetes at the OB-GYN's office," she said. "Do you think that's possible? I mean I'm not overweight and I don't know anyone in my family that had it."

"I don't know, Lib. It's a possibility; it can cause peripheral neuropathy, which is a fancy term for what you're feeling in your hands and feet. Your circulation looks good. After I talk to your docs, I may have a better idea of what they looked at and we can go from there. Are you willing to go back to your GP and let him follow up?"

"No, not really, but I guess I'd consider it."

Oh good, I thought, she's relying on me to figure this out. *This was a really stupid idea,* I told myself. I was already flailing and felt totally out of my comfort zone. I could stitch up a wound, hell, I could probably take your appendix out if I was the only choice available, but private duty nursing was just not my strong suit.

"You're not eating well—why's that?"

"I'm just not hungry."

"Well, tell me some things that would appeal to you and I'll ask Cora to fix them." I remembered our college years and laughed. "Maybe I should get you some weed; that always perked up the appetite."

She laughed. "God, do you remember that ice cream binge after that one party? I couldn't look at ice cream for months."

"Unfortunately," I said, patting my backside, "I was just fine with ice cream even after that."

"Do you ever wish you could go back?"

"To college?"

"Yeah, things seemed easier, less complicated than the way things are now."

"Oh, I don't know, it always seems easier when you look back. I'm not sure it was. Maybe less complicated in terms of life experiences, but we had our share of difficulties."

Libby laughed. "True, but getting out of them seemed simpler then."

It felt so normal, so easy being with her again. It saddened me to think that we had wasted four years, that I had let my frustration and envy ruin our friendship. And a small hurt part of me was angry that she had let me and hadn't tried to stay friends. Love and friendship were not easy roads to travel.

I asked Libby to sign releases giving me the permission to speak with her physicians about her medical treatment, and I made appointments over the phone to speak with two of them. The shrink was proving hard to reach. Libby signed the permission forms, but did it hesitantly. I couldn't blame her; reading through a person's medical history is the ultimate invasion of privacy. Unfortunately, it's just an illusion of privacy when you stop and think of all the people who have access to the information.

I spent Friday and Saturday getting used to the routine of the house, readjusting to being around Libby, and staying out of Edward's way. He didn't make many appearances during the day, although he always sat with

Libby in the mornings and talked to her for a while before he left for his office. He would often eat dinner with her at the bedside, and I found those small gestures touching. Perhaps they had more of a relationship than I had credited them with. I was trying hard not to let my encounter in the library further color my judgment of Edward.

SUNDAY WAS a zoo at the hospital. There had been a multicar roll-over accident on the Interstate, and we spent the evening in the OR cutting, stitching, drilling, plating, screwing, and casting the trauma patients who had been brought to our emergency room. I'd been on my feet since noon, and by the time I arrived at Libby and Edward's, I could barely think. I'd been standing so long I was having an out-of-body experience with my feet. It was almost one in the morning, and much to my surprise, I found an insulated covered dish with a sandwich and a plastic-wrap-covered glass of milk sitting at my bedside when I turned on the light. It had been sitting there a while, but was still welcome. It had to be Libby's idea; I was sure that the phone lady hadn't thought it up. I was beginning to think that she disliked people in general. She didn't display any affection to either Libby or Edward that I'd seen.

I ate half the sandwich and drank the milk before I fell into bed. A shower would have been nice, but it was too much trouble. I hadn't had an opportunity to talk to any of the docs I knew at work about Libby, and I had an appointment with her gynecologist at ten. I was trying to sort out the questions I had for him when I fell asleep.

I have an internal alarm clock that is pretty reliable as long as I don't expect it to wake me up at too preposterous an hour. I woke the next morning at 8:45, which wasn't bad considering the day I'd spent at the hospital. It didn't leave me much time to get to the appointment with Dr. Gerald, though.

I arrived at his office on time and had to wait for twenty minutes. The office was newly remodeled, low-key, tastefully done, and fully staffed. I was shown at last into his office, after a brief detour to one of the exam rooms where I had to explain that I had an appointment to speak with the doctor and wasn't a patient.

Gerald stood and motioned to a chair that sat opposite his desk. He looked briefly at his nurse who had no chart to offer him and then held out his hand.

"Ms…?"

"Collins, Anne Collins."

"How can I help you?" His hand was warm and smooth, his nails well cared for, all good qualities in a gynecologist, I mused.

"I've been asked to special duty Libby Matheisen for a few weeks, and I thought it would help me if I could speak with you." I lay the permission sheet on his desk. "I have Ms. Matheisen's permission to speak with you and to review her chart so I have a better idea what's been going on."

He read the note and I could see his brows draw together. "They've hired you as a private nurse? Why?"

"Libby doesn't seem to be bouncing back from her miscarriage. Can you tell me when you last saw her and a little bit about the miscarriage?"

He leaned over, picked up his desk phone, and punched a button, "Beth, bring Libby Matheisen's chart in, will you?" He hung up without waiting for a reply, content, it seemed, that all would happen as he had requested. "I believe I saw Libby about four weeks ago; she seemed depressed, but otherwise fine." There was a discreet tap on the door and Beth deposited the chart on Gerald's desk, leaving without any acknowledgement from him. He leafed through the chart, pausing here and there to read an entry. "Yes, she was here in August. She was complaining of depression, insomnia, and a few other vague complaints."

"Such as?"

"Hmmm…yes, here it is. She claimed that she had pains that came and went in her hands and feet and that she was losing her hair."

"Did you examine her?"

He looked up from the chart and smiled. "I examine all the women that come to see me no matter how insignificant their complaints."

"Did you think her complaints were valid? Did you find anything out of order?" I could see he wasn't going to volunteer anything, and I hoped I could think of the right questions to ask.

"She seemed tired. She was losing some hair, but that can happen after a pregnancy from hormonal shifts. I couldn't elicit any real reason for the pains in her hands and feet, although I recommended that she start taking a B complex vitamin. Sometimes B-12 deficiencies can cause peripheral neuropathy. After talking to her, she said she was anxious and wasn't sleeping well; I gave her the name of a psychiatrist and an anti-anxiety medication. I wanted to see if the Valium would help with that."

"Did you do any lab work?"

"I ran a CBC. Her hematocrit and hemoglobin were a little low, but not low enough to be alarming. Her blood glucose levels were fine and there wasn't anything abnormal about the other values."

"It's just hard to reconcile how she looks with depression," I said in frustration.

"Ms. Collins, all you have to do is visit one of the mental health facilities around town and take a look at the people who've been hospitalized to see the effect depression has on people." He sat back in his chair and folded his hands across his chest. "I think Libby needs to see Bill Quentin. I don't think there's anything seriously wrong, but I'll be happy to see her again if you think it's necessary." He stood up and offered me his hand. "I have patients to see, but if you want, you can remain here and look through her chart. Please don't copy or remove anything from it, but I have no problem with you looking at it."

I assured him I wouldn't copy or steal anything, and he left me alone to peruse the chart. I hate looking at old charts. You get an idea of what happened, carefully couched in language that the author feels will look good if the chart ever ends up in court. It's not like reading a good book where there is a narrator to fill in the blanks and explain things. You have to go day-by-day, entry-by-entry, and hope you can piece together what happened. I always thought the best entries were the ones written by social workers or psych nurses, but this was written by an OB-GYN who just put in the facts.

Libby was ten weeks pregnant when she came in for her first OB appointment. The chart contained an ultrasound photo of a gestational sac with a tiny creature in it lost in the general TV static blur of the ultrasound field. *Pretty amazing, really,* I thought. Things had looked good according to Gerald's notes, and Libby was supposed to return a month later.

The next entry noted a call from Edward wanting information about amniocentesis. Gerald's entry stated: *Patient's husband told that amnio not worth the risk or expense in a 32-yr-old female unless routine triple screen shows a possible abnormality. Husband insistent on amnio. Will discuss with both at next appt.* The next entry documented an exam that revealed, as Gerald put it, a *15-wk uterus, no complications. Triple screen within normal limits. Husband again requesting amnio. Risk/benefits explained. Will schedule consultation for end of week with George Henry.*

The name Henry rang a bell. He was one of a breed of docs who seem to be able to read the collective unconscious and be in the right place at the right time with whatever turns out to meet the needs of the latest trend.

The latest trend was women putting off having children until the last possible moment and then being terrified of having a defective child. George Henry steps in with his "Reproductive Technology Corp" and either confirms their worst fears or gives them the peace of mind that people used to have to wait nine months to get. The couple can then enjoy the rest of the pregnancy complete with the knowledge of the child's sex, if they want to know it. If there was something wrong, they could prepare for the difficulties that come with raising a disabled child, or they could terminate the pregnancy.

It was a tough call for me. On one hand, it seemed a little cold-blooded, and on the other, I couldn't imagine willingly giving birth to a seriously damaged child. I'd worked at a major children's hospital for a long time before finally getting out of pediatrics, and I know the reality of caring for those kids. It isn't a life for the kid or the family. Life, as usual, offers no easy solutions.

But I was curious why Edward was so insistent on an amnio. The test isn't considered routine unless the woman is over thirty-five. Edward had been the one to broach the subject first, and I wondered why. Libby was healthy, and so was Edward, but I knew next to nothing about either family, and maybe there was some history of congenital problems that prompted the request.

The report from Henry's office was the usual chromosomal gibberish about the number and description of each chromosome and the baby's blood type, but the final line indicated that there appeared to be no abnormalities in the female fetus that Libby carried. The amnio results were documented in Libby's chart at about her nineteenth week, and two weeks later she miscarried. It's a misnomer to call it a miscarriage at that date; it's much more of an extremely early delivery. A few weeks along and a couple could watch their life savings disappear into a newborn intensive care unit.

I briefly wondered if the amnio had precipitated the miscarriage, but it seemed unlikely since the two were separated by several weeks. Gerald's notes were brief and clinical on Libby's preterm labor that had not responded to the usual treatment to halt it and the subsequent delivery of a stillborn child. There were no comments on the possible cause or the repercussions of the loss. A life had begun and was lost; end of story, I guess. It left a lingering sadness even in these curt, clinical pages. I could only imagine how it had felt for Libby.

I sat back in my chair and sighed as I rubbed my neck. It seemed pretty cut-and-dried. There was a brief follow-up note regarding Libby's subsequent visit and complaints: *Pt. complaining of tiredness, difficulty sleeping, some slight hair loss, and depression. Physical exam unremarkable; labs notable only for mild anemia. Referred to Bill Quentin for psych eval. Prescribed anti-anxiety med.* I couldn't fault Gerald for his referral, but it irritated me. Men get tests and women get psych referrals. I flipped through a few more pages, and found nothing that would indicate anything other than depression in a normally healthy female.

I got up and took the chart out to the front desk and gave it to Beth. "Please see that Dr. Gerald gets this back and thank him for his time," I said.

FIVE

BILL KELSEY'S OFFICE was busy. The family practitioner, like most of his generalist colleagues, was just keeping his head above water. Managed care is not a nice business, it doesn't care about anything except the bottom line, so health professionals and patients get screwed routinely. Docs have to work harder, see too many patients, and get paid a pittance. Patients get less time with their physicians and less careful scrutiny from them. It's a recipe for disaster but nobody is willing to rebel, yet.

Kelsey's nurse ushered me into his office and replied that he'd be there as soon as he could and said she hoped I wasn't in a hurry. I settled in and picked up a *JAMA* that had fallen on the floor from his overburdened desk. The chair was reasonably comfortable, the office was quiet, and the reading matter wasn't stimulating enough to keep the previous night's workload from sneaking up on me. I got a good forty-five minutes of shuteye before the opening door startled me awake.

"Good heavens, I haven't kept you waiting that long, have I?" A tall, distracted-looking fellow held out his hand to me as I tried to regain some dignity. "Bill Kelsey. You must be Anne Collins."

"Yes, thanks for seeing me," I mumbled, taking his outstretched hand. It was firm and warm. "Sorry I dozed off; I put in a long night in the OR last night."

"The multi-car roll-over that was on the news?" he asked. When I nodded, he replied, "SUVs. I keep telling myself I ought to sell mine, but it's paid for finally and it's hard to gear up for new car payments again. Well, what can I do for you?"

"Libby Matheisen asked me to take care of her for a while and I wanted to speak with her physicians before I got started. I understand that you're her primary care doc?" He nodded and I handed him Libby's signed statement, which he looked at carefully. "I wonder if you could tell me what you make of her current illness?"

"Not sure what to make of it, really. I've known Libby for several years, before she met Edward, actually. Just saw her for the usual things—colds, UTIs, had a bad bout of the flu several years ago, but generally she's always been pretty healthy. I didn't see her regarding the pregnancy at all, until after the miscarriage."

"Why'd she visit then?"

"She wasn't happy with the psychiatrist she'd been referred to and came to see me. She felt that no one was listening to her and that everyone, including her husband, was attributing her symptoms to depression from the miscarriage."

"What did you think?"

"That I was walking into a mine field," he said with a laugh. "I hate getting caught between a patient and another doctor. She had vague symptoms, fatigue, some hair loss, and migrating pains in her hands and feet. There wasn't anything that I could put my finger on. No diabetes, no odd eating habits that could cause a vitamin deficiency, no real reason for the neuropathy I could determine. There are so many things that can cause symptoms like that, and some of them can be psychological—like depression or even chronic fatigue syndrome. I took some blood and gave her a script for Ambien, but when I suggested it might be helpful to talk to someone she blew up and left. I ran the blood work, which was unremarkable. I left several messages about her blood work and asked for her to at least call me and we could try to sort out what she felt was wrong, but she never returned my calls." He looked unhappy about it.

"That's it?" I asked.

"That's it. I can't make people return for treatment or further evaluation. I treat the people who are here as best I can. She wasn't here and wouldn't return my calls, so I dropped it. How is she?"

"Not good, in my opinion. She looks awful. She's 'taken to her bed' as my grandmother called it, and she wants me to find out what's wrong. I've agreed to care for her for a while, mostly to humor her. Edward isn't pleased; he thinks I'm a threat to his wife's health. And I'm not happy about the whole thing, either."

"I'm sorry to hear that."

"Do you think there's any reason to run her through any further tests?"

"Honestly? I will if you can get her in here, but based on what I saw when she was here I don't think so. If you think there's something else that needs to be looked at, please let me know."

"Okay, thanks. If I need to run anything medical by someone, can I bother you with it?"

"Sure. Here's my cell number. If you use it you won't have to go through the gauntlet out there." He wrote the number on the back of his card and handed it to me.

He got up and offered his hand to me again and walked me to the door of the office. "I'd like to help if I can, but Libby was pretty upset with me." He seemed to hesitate at the door.

"What?"

"I don't know. It's bugged me ever since she stormed out of here. She needs help and I couldn't provide it. Maybe you can. Good luck."

"Thanks," I replied.

THERE ARE a lot of things that occur to the body that evade definitive diagnosis and treatment. Mostly, they seem to affect women. I have a theory that women repress more and their bodies make them pay for it. Then there's my other theory that if the majority of doctors weren't men, these problems wouldn't be so prevalent in women or so hard to diagnose. I try not to dwell on things like that; it makes one bitter and hard to live with, and I'm hard enough to live with as it is.

I went home and riffled through my nursing texts in frustration. They were more than fifteen years old and in health care that's like trying to use the Dead Sea Scrolls to research a medical problem. I hadn't been able to contact Dr. Quentin, and I was annoyed and imagining a lot of reasons why he wasn't responding. Based on my experiences so far, I wasn't sure I'd get any more information from the shrink than I had from her GYN or family practitioner. If her shrink didn't return my calls, I figured I'd just let him go for now.

I was stuck. I didn't know what I was doing and I didn't know who to talk to or how to get out of the situation I was in. I was getting the distinct feeling Kelsey had described—like I was walking in a minefield.

How do you know you've gone in the wrong direction until things blow up in your face? In retrospect, I should have listened to the warning bells that kept tolling, but Libby had been my friend. It's hard to know when to back out when it's someone close to you. Maybe that's why they recommend you don't provide care for those you know and care about.

SIX

I WAS ON MY way home to check on things and have some quiet time before returning to Libby's when I decided to call a friend and see what she thought. Mary Alice Doyle's initials had amused me when I first met her in nursing school and resulted in my giving her the nickname "Maddie." She was from a large local Irish Catholic family. I had informed her that she needed to get a name that wasn't such a stereotype. I was a bit of a pain in the ass when I was younger, but the nickname had amused her and, much to her parents' dismay, she had kept it. Now no one except her immediate family ever called her Mary Alice. Maddie had become an OB nurse practitioner after a few years of working in labor and delivery. Perhaps she could answer some of the questions I had about what had happened to Libby.

The duplex was quiet when I let myself in and I let out a sigh of relief. It wasn't easy staying at Libby's. I was in her home and felt like I was trespassing most of the time. No feet up on the coffee table, no raiding the cupboards or fridge when the need arose, no familiar things in familiar places, and little privacy until Cora and the other help left in the evening. It was good to be home. I kicked off my shoes and called Maddie's number. I had to leave a message and hope that Maddie would call back before I had to go back to Libby's.

It was a little after one and I hadn't had breakfast or lunch, so I rummaged through the pantry and fridge and found something to eat. Once that was done it hit me just how tired I still was from the night before, so I lay down on the couch for a little nap. *Just an hour*, I thought, then if Maddie hadn't called, I'd return to Libby and Edward's.

⌒⌒

SOMEWHERE A phone was ringing and my first thought was "Oh, God, they want to add another emergency case," when I realized where I was and what was happening. I glanced at my watch and was horrified to see that it was 5:00 PM as I grabbed the phone.

"Hullo?" I croaked.

"Annie?"

"Yeah? Who is this?" I felt like I was emerging from a cocoon and a sticky one at that.

"It's Maddie. Are you okay?"

By then I had surfaced a bit more. "Oh, hey…Maddie…thanks for calling back. Sorry I'm so out of it. I was asleep."

"Didja work last night, or just have a hot date?" she asked, laughing.

"You'll have to remind me what that is; unfortunately, I was working. Seriously, thanks for calling back. Could we get lunch or something? I need to run some stuff by you."

"Sure, I'd love to see you. When do you want to get together?"

"Soon, whenever works for you. I really need to talk to you." I must have sounded tired or discouraged or like someone in distress. I could almost hear her knitting her brows.

"Annie, is everything all right? You're not in trouble, are you?"

I had to chuckle then. It was so Mary Alice. "I'm not pregnant, Maddie, if that's what you're thinking, but I have some questions I need your expertise on."

"Well, okay. I'm glad you're all right, though. You don't sound too good."

"It was a tough night, but I'm fine, just exhausted. You know how it is."

"Yeah, I do. How about tomorrow? I break for lunch at one; we'd have an hour unless the office goes down the tubes. Or I could meet you after work at six for dinner. Then we'd have longer to catch up,"

"Let's do that. I don't know how long this'll take."

We made our plans and talked for a bit longer before hanging up. I sat on the couch after hanging up and stared vacantly at the room in front of me. I was exhausted and my nap hadn't helped. It had left me foggy and weighed down with an odd sense of uneasiness. I couldn't put my finger on what it was; it just felt heavy. Sometimes you get feelings about people and situations and you have no way of knowing where it comes from or why you feel it. I just couldn't shake the feeling that I was missing something and so was everyone who had seen Libby. There was an undercurrent of unhappiness that seemed unrelated to her miscarriage but I had no idea what it was; things just felt off. That's the problem with intuition—sometimes it's just too damned vague.

I rested my head against the back of the couch and closed my eyes. Everything about them felt off. Edward was alternately distant and then at least peripherally involved, and Libby puzzled me. She was clearly unhappy and depressed. One moment she was friendly and the next she was irritated and demanding with everyone. Sometimes people reject therapy when that's what they need the most. If I knew what was under that unhappiness, maybe I could convince her to talk to someone. Maybe.

I wondered, yet again, what the reality of Libby and Edward's marriage was. Outwardly, they seemed to live a charmed life. But there was also this slight disconnect that seemed to hover about them. Edward wasn't sleeping with her because her restlessness "kept him awake." The comfort of a husband, presumably your lover, would seem to be sorely needed after losing a child, and Libby's husband was sleeping elsewhere.

Alone? I wondered.

When she and Edward had first begun dating, he seemed to dote on her; nothing was too good for her, and he squired her around like a jewel on his arm. I think that was when the wedge between us first appeared. I admit I was envious. She was being taken to parties that I couldn't attend unless I hired on with the caterer. Edward was handsome and rich—what more could you ask for? Libby's talent as a painter had finally been officially noticed, and she was getting commissions and doing very well. I was slogging away working twelve-hour shifts in a hospital OR. It was work that was fascinating and had its fun moments, but it's not glamorous and there weren't a lot of prospects, romantically speaking.

I think I tried for a while to believe that we had just drifted apart as friends, found other interests, or that Libby had just risen too far above me to stay friends. But the reality was I withdrew because I felt awkward around them and felt like an outsider. I was hurt that Libby appeared to have moved on and angry that Edward had taken her from me. So we stopped being friends. And now here we were. I had no idea what to make of the situation.

I sat there a while longer until I realized that I just couldn't bear to stay at their house tonight. I wanted my bed and my sanctuary, so I called Libby and told her that I'd be by in the morning to see her. She sounded tired, too, and said that was fine. I showered, got into my jammies, ate a cheese sandwich accompanied by a cheap glass of wine, and then crawled into bed with a favorite book. It was a book guaranteed to entertain and keep me on the edge of my seat (so to speak), but it was also guaranteed to create unreasonable fantasies about what could be had in a relationship and a certain amount of disgust with life as I knew it. Still, a strong, adventurous, handsome, funny, sexy, loving, faithful main character was a man to be admired. Not found in real life, unfortunately, but a girl can dream and so I did halfway through the first chapter.

SEVEN

T HE NEXT MORNING, rested and feeling less oppressed, I drove to Libby's house. When I arrived in her bedroom, she was on the phone with someone explaining my presence and talking about what she had asked me to do.

"I want someone to help out here. I'm tired of sitting in this bedroom alone and I'm hoping she can find out what's wrong with me." She paused and listened for a minute. "Well, that's not your decision, is it? I don't know how you found out, but I can guess and you can tell Karen I don't appreciate her blabbing this around."

She waved me away impatiently and seemed both uncomfortable that I was there and annoyed with what appeared to be all the questions she was being asked. I ducked out and went across to my room and gave her a few minutes to finish the conversation.

When I returned she'd hung up and was fussing with her hair, running her hands through it restlessly, agitated. I apologized for walking in on her call.

"It's fine." She frowned, rubbing her fingers together, which seemed to have become something of a nervous tic with her. "One of my girlfriends visited the day I hired you and I made the mistake of telling her. You can't trust people to keep their mouths shut. She told several people and the friend who called heard it by chance. He thinks that you being here is silly, like Edward does. I told him it was my decision and he didn't like it, which is just too bad."

She watched me with a frown on her face as I gathered up the pill bottles and sat down next to the bed. "Edward's always pushing me to go back to the shrink and Cora's always pushing me to eat, and you're always trying to get me to do things I don't want to do. I just wish everyone would stop telling me what to do," she said irritably.

"I'll try to remember that," I said, causing her to roll her eyes at me. "But that's part of why I'm here, remember?"

That seemed to break the mood and she smiled and apologized. "I'm glad you're here, Annie. I'm just out of sorts."

"Let's talk about these pills," I said, gesturing to the containers I held.

I asked her about the vitamins, and Libby said she'd bought them on the recommendation of the friend who'd just called. I suggested that I get a specific B complex vitamin for her on the off chance that a deficiency was causing the neuropathy and that maybe she should cut back on the others. I figured the fewer meds going in her, perhaps the easier it would be to sort out what was going on. We talked about the other meds, and it didn't sound as if she was abusing any of them. If they helped her sleep, be less anxious, or relieved the discomfort in her hands and feet, that was a good thing.

She seemed in a better mood so I insisted that we get out of the house and do something. She needed the fresh air and a change of scene regardless whether whatever was ailing her was physical or emotional. I suggested we go to the botanical gardens that were a short drive from her neighborhood. The day was lovely and the gardens were always beautiful, peaceful, and soothing even in the worst weather. She agreed but seemed hesitant, saying that she wasn't up for all that walking. I reassured her that we would only walk a bit and then find a place to sit and enjoy the surroundings.

I was surprised to find that the gardens were hosting an exhibition of Deborah Butterfield horse statues—breathtaking creatures that appeared to be made of driftwood. These slightly bigger than life-sized horses were cunningly tucked into unexpected places—a mare and her foal resting in a nook surrounded by trees and flowers, a lone stallion standing by a reflecting pond. They charmed Libby and me.

She steadied herself by holding onto my arm while we walked to a spot near one statue where we could sit comfortably in the shade for a bit. She had insisted on a hat and sunglasses, and I suspected she was embarrassed about anyone she knew seeing her. Libby had always been very careful about her looks and somewhat vain. *She had a right to be*, I thought: *even ill, she was beautiful.*

"Aren't they amazing? You forget they're not real," I exclaimed.

"They are real in a way. All art has life, if it's really good. That's how you know it's good, it speaks to you, becomes real."

I thought about her art. I remembered her painting of two old women sitting together on a park bench and it seemed to echo us sitting here. "When I was given the house tour, I saw that painting of the old women. I always liked that."

She smiled. "I always liked it, too. I guess that's why I never sold it." She paused, watching a squirrel chatter and flit through the branches of the tree across the path. "I'd forgotten about it, though. I haven't been up to the studio in a while. When I found out I was pregnant I got distracted redoing the nursery and then…then there didn't seem to be much I wanted to paint."

"I can imagine."

We sat quietly and listened to the birds for a bit.

"I always wondered where the ideas came from," I said. "They say humor often comes from a place of pain, and I guess maybe it's the same for other artists, but I would think it would be hard to be creative when you've been through what you have."

"Not so much hard, really, sometimes your best work comes from difficult places. I just didn't care anymore. I had been feeling odd, not like myself, then I lost the baby, and that has turned into this, whatever this is. I know everyone thinks I'm depressed or crazy, but something just doesn't feel right. I don't see how it could all be psychological."

"So what do you think it is?" I asked cautiously. She was opening up a little, and I didn't want her to retreat into herself and stop talking.

"Oh, hell, who knows? I can't paint with this tremor; I just can't do the fine work. My hands and feet feel like there are pins and needles in them, and I'm tired. Maybe it is all in my head."

Again we sat in silence.

Finally, I said, "Tell me about your life since we stopped hanging out together. It's been quite a while and it's like I don't know you anymore."

"Life has changed for both of us, hasn't it?"

"It doesn't feel like my life is a lot different from when we were close. It's just the same old, same old."

"No, your life's moved on, too, but it's true mine is quite a bit different these days." She fiddled with the Butterfield brochure she had been handed as we entered the gardens. "How come you haven't married or found someone special?"

I laughed. "I work twelve-hour days in the OR with surgeons. A social life is not easy to find when you're isolated in an area that's out of bounds to the public and most of the hospital, you're dressed in weird clothing, and covered in hats and masks. You have a choice—you can get involved with a surgeon, a huge mistake in my opinion, or hope you connect with someone on the outside." I watched a small group of kids wander by on a nearby path. "Mostly I haven't had much luck finding anyone, or anyone who'd stick around."

"Like the art world, it's pretty closed and insular, too. And artists can often give doctors a run for their money, depending on the artist."

"Yet you found Edward; he isn't an artist."

"No, he isn't." She paused. "I think that's the fatal flaw in our relationship."

"Meaning what?"

"Only that women always go into a new relationship thinking it will be different from the last one, the new relationship is the one they have been searching for, the new person is perfect. But all relationships have a fatal flaw that shows up eventually, when you take the blinders off and start to really look at the other person. Once you see it, that usually spells the end to things, unless you can tolerate it."

"Wow, I thought I was cynical. Is that really how you feel?" I was surprised; Libby just didn't seem the type to be that disillusioned.

"Don't you think it's true? Tell me you've never been totally in love and then woken up one morning and looked at that person and thought, *What am I doing here?* Have you ever been in a relationship that ever lasted or worked out?"

"Well, I'm probably not a good one to ask. I've experienced far too many of the 'What am I doing here?' scenes. I just figured I was too attracted to the commitment-phobic bad-boy types." I looked around at the beautiful setting and sighed. "Boy, you sure know how to make a girl feel optimistic, Lib."

She laughed. "Sorry. I just look around and it seems to me that's the way it is."

"Is that the way it is with Edward?"

She frowned and seemed to be searching for something else to talk about. "It wasn't in the beginning," she said at last.

"What's changed?"

"Nothing and everything. Maybe he hasn't changed at all, maybe I can just see him more clearly now and he isn't who I thought he was. I'm probably not who he thought I was, either. Sometimes I think people should be serial monogamists—you know, faithful while it works, and then move on to someone new when it doesn't."

"Jeez, Lib, this sounds like something I would say, not you. I'm the aging single woman who can't seem to keep a partner for longer than a year or two. What's changed between you two?"

"Oh, he's just very caught up in his work. Techies are pretty logical and linear and artists aren't, and techies aren't touchy-feely types at all. My work," she said, using air quotes around "work," "is just a hobby to him, not work. It adds to my curb appeal and it has some glamour that rubs off on him, but to him, it isn't really work."

She stopped and thought for a bit. She seemed to be debating whether to continue or not, then said, "He's gone a lot and it gets lonely, when he's here he's absent, too. When I became pregnant, it was hard to tell how he felt about it. After the amnio he seemed better, but to be honest, after the miscarriage I wasn't sure how he felt about it. As soon as he knew I was pregnant, he seemed to pull away. He kept saying he was surprised by it and needed time to adjust but that he was happy. I don't know, I just didn't think he was. Babies are pretty disruptive; maybe he wasn't sure he could cope. My illness or whatever it is, was all the excuse he seemed to need to move into the upstairs area where his personal space is."

"Yeah, what is it with that space? Is it really off limits, even to you? The ph—Cora said no one was allowed up there."

"Oh, she makes a big deal out of it; it's just his space and he doesn't like anyone messing with it. He keeps a lot of his prototype stuff up there." She held up a hand as I took a breath. "Don't ask, I have no idea what that means, I'm not a computer person. He's never really told me I can't go up there, he's just made it clear he doesn't want anyone up there. He's sort of a control freak, and it's easier to leave him to his little world than to intrude and upset him. And honestly, I don't care enough to look. Cora's not allowed in my studio, either, and there's no mysterious reason other than I don't like people messing with my stuff."

What a difference four years can make, I thought. It didn't seem like enough time to travel from fairytale wedding to this. "Are you happy?" I asked. It was a stupid question, clearly she wasn't, but I guess I wanted to hear her say it and try to figure out just how unhappy she was. She didn't reply.

"Were you two trying for a child?" I asked, trying another tack. I had such a hard time seeing Edward as a parent, and the Libby I knew had never seemed all that anxious for kids. Kids took more selfless devotion than I had ever seen Libby expend on anything other than her art.

She frowned and began shredding the exhibit brochure. "No, we weren't, we'd never talked about it, really, and I always had the impression children were not high on Edward's 'to do' list. I never really thought about it, either. I honestly thought that I couldn't have kids, I don't know why, other than I had never had any 'mistakes' happen before I was married. And it was a relief, I guess, that I never got pregnant. I'm not sure either of us are parent material. We used precautions, but they're not foolproof and the pregnancy really was accidental." She had an odd look on her face, slightly wary and slightly embarrassed.

"Are you happy?" I asked again.

"Aren't we all?" she replied with a forced smile and, then, before I could answer, she said, "Oh, don't mind me, I'm just in one of those moods. Would you mind if we went back to the house? I'm very tired all of a sudden."

LATER THAT day I made a run to Whole Foods to pick up a few things Libby had requested after we returned to her house. I had always called it Whole Paycheck because it is expensive, but they carried things that couldn't be found elsewhere. When I did shop there, I had to stay away from their dessert section to avoid being trapped in my bed and needing a crane to extract me, but they had a lot of prepackaged food that was easy to keep a single person fed without a lot of fussing. Apparently, Libby insisted on most of the shopping being done there because it was natural food. *Glad she had the money to do that*, I thought.

I got what I needed, checked out, and headed out to the parking lot. The Cherry Creek Whole Foods parking lot was always packed to the gills, and traffic was a nightmare. I stepped off the curb and began walking toward where my car was parked, fishing in my purse for my keys, when I collided with a guy who had his ear buds in place and was fiddling with his smartphone; clearly neither of us was paying attention. The collision made me lose my grip on my bag and it crashed to the ground, spilling the contents in the way of approaching cars.

He dropped to his knees, pulling out the ear buds and began scrabbling for my groceries. "God, I am so sorry, did anything break? I'll replace it if it did. Are you okay?" He was babbling and putting things back in the bag as a driver laid on his horn behind us.

"Hey!" he yelled, standing up and addressing the driver. "Give us a minute here!"

"I'm fine," I said, replacing the last item in the bag and standing up. "We should move before Mad Max runs us down," I said, stepping back on the sidewalk.

He laughed. "Yeah, drivers down here are insane. Hey, I'm sorry about that, I wasn't paying attention. My name's Ian Patterson. What's yours?"

"Annie Collins." He was very attractive: tall, dark-haired, blue-eyed, and had a great smile. He was nicely and expensively dressed. "Well, thanks for helping me get it all back in the bag, hope your day goes better from here on."

"How about letting me buy you a coffee? There's a coffee place across the street. It's the least I can do."

"Umm, okay, that'd be nice, thanks."

We walked through the parking lot and across the street to the coffee shop, ordered, and I found a table. He paid and brought the drinks, sliding into a seat across from me.

"Again, sorry about that. You sure your groceries are undamaged?"

"They're fine," I said, smiling. He was kind of cute with his apologies, and I was glad he'd suggested coffee.

"Well, that's good. I feel like an idiot. I don't usually run into pretty women in grocery store parking lots, well, not literally anyway," he said, smiling at me.

"What were you listening to that was so enthralling?"

"I was looking for a Maroon 5 song I thought I'd purchased. I can't find it, so I'm thinking I didn't do the purchase thing right. Shouldn't let myself get so caught up like that and ignore the world around me. Although this is a nice outcome."

He flirted shamelessly throughout the conversation. He was amusing and persistent and I ended up giving him my phone number. He didn't volunteer a lot about himself other than that he was a real estate broker. He spent a lot of time asking about me and seemed very curious and interested in what I did. It surprised me; most men's eyes glaze over when I start talking about what I do, but it was nice to be listened to. We agreed to have lunch that week. *Not bad for a grocery run*, I thought, as I headed home.

I returned to Libby's to drop off the items I'd bought for her and left the house at five to meet Maddie for dinner, telling Libby I'd return later. She'd gone into a quiet, reflective mood after the trip to the Gardens and I hadn't been able to continue our conversation. She'd been irritable and short with Cora and Edward, but she told me to have a good time as I left.

I met Maddie at an old Capitol Hill neighborhood restaurant that had been a favorite during nursing school. It was poorly lit, which was probably a good thing as nothing had changed in all the years we'd patronized it. We were seated at a duct-taped, leatherette-covered booth at the back of the restaurant. Besides us, there was one older couple eating at a table across the room. I watched them as they ate. They never seemed to look up or carry on a conversation with each other. I couldn't tell whether they were a couple or related in some way, but it seemed unlikely that friends would sit so quietly intent on eating without interacting.

Maybe Libby was right. Maybe humans didn't have it in them to go the long haul as couples, or maybe it had been easier when we didn't live so long. Being married for a few years before your wife died in childbirth or you died of an accident or illness made it easier to say *"til death do us part"* and mean it.

Aside from Libby's views on relationships, I had been feeling like time was running out for me. The relationships I'd been in had pretty much been disasters. I chose poorly and spent far too much time trying to be whatever I thought the current significant other wanted, which of course never worked. I wanted just one lasting relationship before I died, I thought morosely, but so far, no luck.

If nothing else, this job caring for Libby was depressing me.

Maddie and I perused the menu and then, when the waitress reappeared, we ordered what we had always ordered. We laughed about that; it had been a standing joke in school. While we waited for our meals and sipped on house wine, we got caught up on each other's current status.

"Well, one bright spot is that I met a guy. Ran into him, literally, at Whole Foods in the parking lot. He's pretty good-looking and he seems like a nice guy. We're meeting for lunch later this week."

"Good. You need some fun in your life." She waited until the waiter deposited our plates before continuing. "Is he anything like your last nice guy?" she asked.

"Oh, who knows? He seems nice, seems interested. I guess I'm just going to have to wait and see."

"Otherwise, you're sure everything's all right? You just look so down."

I told her about the odd job I was tackling. Maddie knew Libby from college although they had never been friends. For reasons neither would elaborate on, they had never liked each other.

"There's nothing like hanging out with a depressed, unhappy person to make life a joy, is there? I just can't figure out what's going on. She's clearly not well, she's depressed, and her marriage doesn't sound like it's on firm ground, but he does dote on her in some ways and she seems to care about him. I don't know what to think."

"Marriage and pregnancy can sometimes be a bad combination—not that pregnancy without marriage is any better." She laughed. "Relationships change fundamentally when the reality of a pregnancy sets in. People can be thrilled, happy, scared, and overwhelmed. But they can also be unhappy and feel trapped. Some people, mostly women, think getting pregnant is the cure for all that ails their relationship, when in fact it rarely is. We're so brainwashed about what it 'should' be that no one is prepared for what it is."

"It seems to me that Libby was surprised but okay with it, not sure about Edward. There's one thing that bugs me: Why would he be so insistent on an amniocentesis? Libby isn't old enough for it to be necessary."

"Are you sure it was his child?"

That question hit me out of the blue. "Why would you ask that?"

"An amnio would be one way to find out whether the baby was his without coming out and saying he thought it wasn't. He would have to provide blood for testing but that could be easily and quietly done. It doesn't sound like there was any other familial history or reason to have it." She rotated her wine glass back and forth. "I just wondered. You say he's gone a lot, not particularly attentive when he's there…maybe she got bored or lonely and found a substitute and then got pregnant by accident."

"I have no idea about that; Libby and I haven't been close since her marriage. But you think these symptoms could be legitimately tied to the pregnancy and miscarriage?"

"Sure, based on what you've told me. Unless there is some test result that would indicate otherwise, they could all be tied to it."

I sighed and we ate silently for a bit like the old couple.

"Why do you think it might be something else?" she asked.

"I'm not sure I do, but Libby thinks so. She thinks she's being handed an easy excuse for what's going on and being fobbed off on a shrink. I've looked at her records and talked to her docs, and I can't find anything to indicate that it's anything else. I don't know where to go with this."

"Honey, if it walks like a duck and quacks like a duck, it's probably a duck. You know it could be as simple as she got pregnant to try to reanimate her marriage, then lost it, and is making a play for her husband's attention by being sick. Having said that, it can be hard for women to recover from pregnancy loss, especially if there are other relationship issues tangled up in it. And some women don't know how to get attention any other way than being sick."

"I feel like I'm just babysitting her. I never know what kind of mood she'll be in. One minute she's friendly and the next moment she's not. To tell the truth, I don't really know what to do for her. I don't like this type of nursing. I like the OR; it's direct, and to the point, and the patients are under anesthesia."

Maddie laughed. "Annie, you need to put an end to this situation; it's not good for either of you. Take care of her for a week or two more and then get out."

Easy as getting out of quicksand, I thought.

EIGHT

"PUTTING AN END to the situation" was a lot like ending a relationship that you wanted out of but the other person didn't. Not anywhere near as simple as it sounds. I had no idea how to get out of it gracefully or without seriously damaging the fragile relationship Libby and I had started to rebuild.

To be honest, though, I wasn't sure how I felt about the relationship. Whatever we had had, it wasn't the same anymore, and the added responsibility of caring for her made me think of her as more of a patient than a friend.

Based on her behavior, there were times she clearly thought of me as her employee. It made being there hard. At other times we were close to being the friends we had been, able to talk and laugh about the past. And at other times I wasn't sure who she was. I'd gotten her the additional vitamins and was working with her to get her out of bed and up and around again, but nothing seemed to have much effect.

After talking to her GP again and getting no real help, I'd suggested acupuncture and massage for the neuropathy, which didn't go over well.

"I'm not a flake, Annie; I asked you to help, not just suggest diversions."

That annoyed me. "It's not a diversion," I said in exasperation. "I know a lot of people who've gotten pain relief using both, including me."

She snorted at that and picked up a magazine from her bedside table.

"What do you want me to do, Libby? No one can identify anything other than postpartum issues. I spoke with your GP and he had nothing to suggest other than what I've been doing, which hasn't been much. I thought the massage might make you feel better. I think the acupuncture would, too."

"When I want to go to the spa, I'll let you know."

At that I gave up and left her to her magazine. It was beyond frustrating; it seemed that all she expected of me was to provide company. I had no idea why I was there or how to help her. Libby was subtly different than I remembered her. She had always been self-centered—nothing was as important to her as her art—but there had also been a core of integrity and goodness. Now there was just unhappiness and irritability.

Unfortunately, her unhappiness was attaching itself to me. I had enough issues with this particular emotional landscape on my own, I didn't need help to get there nor did I want to get marooned there, but if I ended the arrangement, as Maddie had suggested, I felt like I was abandoning Libby. And so I went back and forth and back and forth in my head and got nowhere. *Sometimes,* I thought, *if there was an identifiable part in my brain responsible for guilt and waffling I'd have it destroyed.*

It was my second week at the house, and I decided to see if I could improve her mood by taking her to the nearby farmers' market. It occupied a fairly small corner of the parking lot at a nearby mall so it wouldn't require a lot of walking. Her walking was improving, but she tired easily. She again insisted on sunglasses and a hat despite it being an overcast day.

Things were going well, and we were laughing at some of the oddball offerings that show up at farmers' markets—what do "mood rings" have to do with farmers? As we made our way back to the start of the market, a man walked past and bumped Libby's shoulder. The glancing blow threw her balance off and as I made a grab at her to keep her from falling, the man's arms went around her from the side to steady her. There was a sharp intake of breath as he let go, and I looked up to see Libby with her mouth open and looking very pale.

"Libby, it's so good to see you…. How are you? I heard you were ill," he babbled, taking her by the shoulders and scanning her face.

She seemed stunned. "I-I'm fine. I, uh, this is my friend, Annie," she managed at last and turning to me, she said, "This is Jeff; he and I used to work together."

She seemed to be getting her face under control, but was still visibly shaken by the encounter. I could hear Maddie's question and I wondered who exactly this person was. Someone she cared about or just a co-worker she was embarrassed to see in her current condition?

"I'm so sorry about your loss," he said, and I thought I saw a brief but quickly concealed flash of pain in his eyes. "I called and left a couple messages on your cell. I didn't know what to say or whether I should keep trying to get in touch. I…I never heard from you. Are you okay?"

"I'm fine, Jeff, I just haven't bounced back very well. It's just as well you didn't pursue things; it wouldn't have helped anything."

I was shocked at the brusque response and he was clearly embarrassed.

"Libby, let's go find a place to sit down for a while—" I began to say.

"I don't need to sit down, I need to get out of here. Stop fawning over me, both of you."

She turned and started to push her way through the crowd toward where we'd left the car. Jeff closed the distance and made to grab her arm; I heard him say something to her and was shocked when she pulled away and slapped him. She began forcing her way through the crowd, leaving the two of us standing together, mouths agape, watching her difficult progress.

I picked up her hat that lay at my feet, and said, "I'm sorry, I should go with her. She's not been well, but that was rude and uncalled for."

He grabbed my arm before I could walk off, and asked, "Is she okay? Really? I hear rumors and gossip and I don't know what to believe."

"She's not well, but I don't think it's serious. I really can't discuss it and I need to go."

He scrabbled in his pocket and pulled out his wallet. After a brief search he pushed a card into my hand. "Please, if I can do anything, let me know." He walked off.

What the hell? I thought as I made my way back to the car. I had had just about enough of the prima donna behavior to last me a good long time, and while she was not well, I wanted an explanation.

As I got to the car, I could see her leaning against the passenger side looking flushed and out of breath. I used the remote control and unlocked the car. She opened the door and sat down. I sat in the driver's seat and looked at her. It was hot and little air was moving. I could feel the sweat sliding down the side of my face from the quick walk back. The car doors hung ajar and we sat there silently.

"Want to explain what that was all about?" I asked, tossing her hat into her lap.

"No. Please take me home."

I hit the steering wheel with both hands. She jumped. "You cannot treat me like a servant, Libby. That was just weird. I deserve an explanation. Who is he?"

I saw her mouth tighten and her brows gather like storm clouds and knew she wasn't going to relent. "Well, you're not going to get one, so let's go."

We drove back to the house in silence and she allowed me to follow her into the old service elevator in the hallway that took us up to the second floor. She walked into her bedroom and sat on the bed for a moment. Looking up at me standing in the doorway, she said coolly, as if talking to Cora rather than a friend, "Why don't you take the afternoon off? I'm exhausted and I'd like some time to myself."

"You're really not going to explain anything?"

"No," she replied, as if talking to the hired help rather than a friend.

"Fine," I said and left.

I WENT back to the farmers' market and bought some things for dinner after leaving Libby's. Still fuming, I stopped and got two bottles of wine. At home, I put the food away and poured a glass of wine, then took it and the bottle out into the yard with me. The shade of the large linden in the back yard beckoned, so I dragged a lawn chair under the tree and flopped into it. I must have been a sight, glass in one hand and bottle in the other. I tipped my head back and closed my eyes. It was hot even in the shade; summer's last hurrah, I guess.

This bizarre caretaking-weirdness needed to stop. The whole scene at the market and afterward seemed like the actions of an entitled, spoiled brat.

I'm not sure I even tasted the first half of the glass, but eventually I stopped gulping and calmed somewhat. I really did need to end this. My life could be crazy, too, but I didn't need more of someone else's craziness lumped into the mix. I began to wonder if Maddie was right and this was all manipulation on Libby's part. Maybe it *was* the only way she could get attention.

Having decided to tell her I wouldn't be back in the morning, I got up and went inside to make the call. As I went to get my cell phone, the doorbell rang. It was Angel with a grocery bag in hand. I must have looked like a homeless person standing there with rumpled, sweat-damp clothes holding a wine glass in one hand and a half empty bottle of wine tucked under my arm. All I lacked was an overloaded grocery cart and a cardboard sign.

"Rough day?" he asked, clearly taken aback.

"I was sitting out in the yard drinking," I said, gesturing with the bottle. "Come in, just don't get too close." I held the door and he walked into the living room. "What's in the bag?"

"I stopped by to see the folks and Mama sent me home with a pot of posole and quesadillas. Her posole is to die for and she gave me so much I'll never finish it alone so I thought I'd see if you wanted to share it."

"Sure."

He followed me into the kitchen. I set my bottle and wine glass down on the counter and handed him a clean wine glass.

"Give me a minute." I sprinted for the master bath calling, "Make yourself comfortable," over my shoulder.

When I finally emerged, he had poured two glasses of wine, was heating the soup on the stove, and had the quesadillas warming in the oven.

"This looks good," I said as he ladled the soup into bowls and put the quesadillas on a plate.

IT WAS a pleasant evening, it had cooled slightly, and we ended up sitting out on the patio finishing the wine and talking about our jobs. When he finally asked about my day and what had happened, I told him about the earlier encounter and Libby's reaction and that I was debating about resigning the job, if that was the right word.

"Makes you wonder why she wouldn't explain it to you. Any idea who he is?"

"No, only that they worked together at some point. He gave me his card and insisted that I call if there was anything he could do. It seemed to me that he had a more serious interest in her than a co-worker would have. She seemed very surprised to see him, upset by it, and flustered that I was there." I ran a hand through my hair, which had finally dried. "Then she refused to explain who he was. Dismissed me like I was her lady's maid and she was done with me. I'm totally fed up with the weirdness and the pointlessness of my being there."

I sipped my wine. "I can't figure out what's going on; she seems sick, but there's nothing to indicate that anything's wrong physically other than recovering from the miscarriage. I would never have pegged Libby for a hysteric or hypochondriac—well, that's not entirely true; she had those tendencies even in college. She used to say that's why she loved having a nurse for a roommate. But it never got to this level before."

"You think she was involved with him?"

"No idea, but you're the second person who's asked basically the same question. After this morning, I don't think Libby's going to tell me anything. I'm not sure it's any of my business, even if she was involved with him."

Angel stretched out his long legs and yawned. "It might go a long way to explain what she's going through now, though. Think about it: you cheat on your husband but finally end the affair. In trying to repair the marriage, you get pregnant and then lose the baby. Some would see that as divine punishment for the affair, which would just add to the loss."

He sipped some wine and rested his head against the back of the chair. "Or, you have an affair, accidentally get pregnant, and have the prospect of a divorce loom in your face. Faced with that, you end the affair and go quietly back to your husband and let him think it's his child. Then lose the baby and realize you've lost both the person you were involved with and his child, too. Either way it's a recipe for lots of guilt and lots of self-recrimination." He laughed. "But hey, I was raised Catholic; we're ruled by guilt. May not apply here."

"Maybe that's why you're a lawyer, able to see all potential scenarios. I never suspected her of having an affair until Maddie brought up the possibility, and the market incident makes me suspicious. It would explain a lot. Maybe I should have a chat with Jeff. He wants to help; if I had some idea what the heck was going on I might know what to do. As it is, I just feel like a servant."

"How about not doing anything and letting it all sort itself out? You said yourself taking care of her wasn't what you wanted to do anymore."

"I didn't really want to do it from the start, but I let her talk me into it. Now it's more curiosity than anything." I watched the moon hanging over the yard, casting its soft light on the garden. "Who am I kidding? She's pissed me off and I just hate it when someone won't answer my questions."

"Ah, *chica*, remind me never to piss you off." He laughed. "Sometimes it's best to leave things alone. If you talk to him and it gets back to Libby, she's going to be pissed and it really is an invasion of her privacy. If it were me I'd give notice and walk away. The whole situation seems ripe for disaster."

"It does, doesn't it?"

We sat comfortably in silence for a while until he sat up and picked up the empty glasses and wine bottle. "Thanks for sharing dinner with me; it's been nice. I've got an early day tomorrow, so I'm gonna head home." We walked into the house, deposited the glasses and bottle in the kitchen, and said good night as he headed for his side of the duplex.

NINE

I N A SNIT, and because I couldn't decide whether to resign or not, I called Libby the following day and told her I needed a day or two to cool off. I also told her that if I was to continue, we had to be honest with each other. She agreed, but whether that extended to explaining what had happened at the market wasn't clear. Not wanting to press the issue over the phone, I told her I'd be there the day after tomorrow and ended the call.

As I sat there trying to decide what to do about Jeff Davies, my cell rang. Ian of the parking lot collision was checking in to set up the lunch date and we agreed to meet later that day at a nearby restaurant. When we got there, we sat on the patio enjoying the late Indian summer weather. We ate and laughed about our run in at Whole Foods, and he played the intro to the song on his smartphone that caused our unexpected introduction.

"So this is the one that caused the collision?" I asked as Maroon 5's "Sugar" started to play.

"Yep, this is the one."

"I love this song; it always makes me want to dance."

"Then we should go dancing sometime."

"Well, I mostly dance around the apartment in my underwear without an audience. I'm not good at dancing in public."

"I'd like to watch that," he said, laughing. "Next time I'm over, you can demonstrate."

"So what do you do again?" I asked.

"Real estate broker to the rich and famous." He took a drink of water. "High-end real estate, mostly."

"Really? That sounds like fun."

"You'd think, wouldn't you? It's more like babysitting spoiled, petulant kids."

"There must be something about it you like." He looked around as if thinking and thinking hard, and I laughed. "Oh come on, it can't be that hard to think of something."

"Okay, okay, what I like is the freedom to set my own hours, that's if you don't count all the accommodating clients' schedules. I like seeing how the other half lives, and of course I can make a good living."

"Yeah, they do live differently, don't they?"

"They do for sure." He picked up his glass and watched me over the rim. His eyes were a beautiful blue that had a spark of mischief in them as we talked. "So, what do you like best about your job?"

"You'll either laugh or be horrified."

"Promise I won't, tell me."

"I like seeing what's on the inside, knowing how the body works. I like figuring out what's causing the problem and helping to fix it. And I like patients who are asleep 'cause I don't have a lot of patience with sick people. So the OR works really well for me."

"How did you end up a nurse if you don't have patience with sick people? I thought nurses were supposed to minister to the sick," he said, brushing a lock of that black hair out of his eyes.

I have to admit, he didn't laugh and he didn't seem horrified, so I continued. "I'm not a nurse I guess, philosophically, anyway." I laughed. "I didn't enter nursing with altruistic notions; I wanted a profession where I'd always have a job. Plus, there were several nurses in my family. Nursing sort of felt familiar, since I was exposed to it my whole life." I frowned. "The weird thing is I'm doing exactly what I hate at the moment and taking care of a former friend. It's turning out to be catering to her neuroses and trying to stay in her good graces rather than any nursing."

"Really? What's going on?"

"She's ill, or more accurately, not recovering from a recent experience, but she's convinced something's wrong and all her docs say otherwise. She wants me to help her find out what's wrong."

"It's going to be hard to do that if nothing's wrong with her, won't it?"

"No kidding."

"Well, now you have me curious. We'll have to go out again so I can hear how it turns out," he said, smiling at me and then changing topic. "Is your family here?"

"No, Texas; yours?"

"Arizona. I guess we're both transplant orphans in a way." We ate companionably for a bit before he said, "My folks and both brothers live in Arizona, and I have a sister in California. I don't see the family much these days. They're busy and so am I. How about you?"

"My folks have passed and my sisters live in Texas. I don't get there much—every now and then over the holidays. I was glad to get out of there and come to Colorado. I guess that's why I stayed."

"I think it's good to get a fresh start away from family and all their expectations. You have a chance to make yourself up as you go that way."

"I guess; I never thought of it that way."

I DECIDED to go through with setting up some sort of meeting to talk to Jeff Davies. It was underhanded going behind Libby's back, but her reaction and refusal to tell me about him kept gnawing at me. I found my purse and rooted around in it until I found the business card "Jeff Davies, Art Consultant" had given me, and sat looking at it for a bit, trying to think what I would say if I called. I couldn't really begin with "I want to know if you and Libby were having an affair," which is what I suspected. Finally, I called the number. The receptionist told me he was busy but routed me to his voice message and I asked him to call me when he got a chance, telling him it was about Libby. I hung up and was on my way to get dressed when my phone rang. It was Jeff already on the other end.

"I got your message; sorry I wasn't here to talk. I'd be happy to meet with you. When did you have in mind?"

"I'm at loose ends today and tomorrow. Is there a time that works for you?"

"I go to lunch at twelve. Could we meet at the little place across the street from the gallery, would that work?"

I agreed and got the directions. He seemed pretty eager to talk, which had to be a first since I'd taken on this job.

I ARRIVED at the restaurant a little before twelve; Jeff was waiting at a table. I sat down, reintroduced myself, and thanked him for meeting with me.

The waitress arrived with menus and water and when she departed, he put his menu down and asked, "What's going on with Libby?"

I took a deep breath. "I can't really discuss the particulars, she miscarried, you knew that, and she's having a hard time recovering. That's really all I can tell you. But perhaps you can tell me more about her. We were close friends at one time, but I haven't been in contact for quite a while, and I'm having some problems figuring out what's going on with her."

The waitress put in an appearance, we ordered and, after she left, I waited for what he was going to say.

He twiddled the paper band that had held the silverware and paper napkin rolled together and his eyes drifted off as if in thought, then he sighed. "What do you want to know?" he asked at last.

"I'm not even sure. How do you know her, how long have you known her, what's your connection to her? I don't know really. You're the first person I've met who knows her other than her husband and the housekeeper, and they're not saying much. I need someone who can give me some background."

"Libby and I worked together until recently. I've handled her art sales through the gallery for several years. She stopped working earlier this year. The last time I talked to her was over the phone regarding some sales about six or seven months ago. That was before the miscarriage, I think."

"How did you hear about that?"

"The art world grapevine, which lives to discuss dirt. People who knew her told me about the pregnancy and the miscarriage."

"But not Libby?"

"No. As I said, we hadn't talked in a while."

He frowned and cleared his throat, eyes darting around.

He clearly wasn't happy. "Jeff, was your relationship close? Would she normally confide something like that to you?"

"We were partners. We've known each other for years, and I was the only one who handled her art sales for her. I thought she considered me a friend; I did of her. It was like something changed. The pregnancy was the cut off and the miscarriage sealed it."

I took a deep breath and with some misgiving I asked, "Was the baby yours?"

He looked stunned and his face paled. "Why would you think that?"

"You seemed pretty upset when you ran into her the other day, as did Libby, and you seem upset talking about her now. You say you were close to her and yet you're completely shut out. Libby refuses to discuss what happened at the market or explain who you were to her. Maybe I'm wrong; if so, you have my apologies."

The silence hung heavy about us, and I figured I had blown my only chance to get any information from him when he said, "I have no idea if the baby was mine. I didn't even know she was pregnant. She ended our affair abruptly, and I only heard about the pregnancy and miscarriage by chance. I have been out of my mind since she left, wondering why she left, wondering how she was. When I heard about the pregnancy, I wondered if the baby was her husband's or mine and if that was the reason she left. We worked together for almost five years and had been lovers for almost two and all of a sudden she called it quits, no reason, no chance to fix anything, just gone."

"I'm sorry," I said for lack of anything else to say.

"So am I. I guess love, at least I thought that's what it was, can't compete with money and privilege. I don't know if that's why she dumped me; I hope she wasn't afraid to leave him. Several weeks before she ended things with me, she'd been very distracted and seemed to always be cancelling our arrangements. There was a point where I honestly wondered if she'd found someone to take my place."

"You said you hoped she wasn't afraid to leave him. Did she seem afraid of Edward?"

"No, not really, just totally bored and unhappy. I guess that's why we ended up together. At first I was a shoulder to cry on, then it became… more. I keep trying to figure out why she went back to him. I really thought she'd leave him and we could be together. I'm an idiot."

You and millions of other people, I thought. "What was she unhappy about?"

"Everything. I never understood what she saw in him to begin with. He was her total opposite, not an artistic bone in his body, it was all computers and tech stuff and money." He paused and ran a hand over his mouth and frowned. "So of course that was a lot of what she was unhappy about. He didn't understand her creative drive, especially if it interfered with what he wanted to do. He wasn't able to talk about anything except computers and his business and investments and tech challenges and the latest software, which was like a foreign language to her. And he was gone a lot. He worked long hours and then came home and worked some more up in his little world upstairs. I gathered that they weren't very well matched intimately. She never gave me specifics, but she gave off very unsatisfied vibes."

"They seemed to be in all the right places, parties, and so on. It seemed to me she liked that."

He sat there clearly remembering past events before he said, "Edward went to all sorts of society events to hobnob with potential investors and he'd insist that Libby go along. She enjoyed it, too, don't get me wrong, he wasn't forcing her to go. But when her art really took off, she'd get a lot of attention at the events and often get commissions for paintings. She thought it annoyed him, distracted potential investors, I guess."

He looked at me with a sort of lost expression on his face. "I always figured it was his money that was the attraction. She gained access to a house and a social position and money that she wouldn't be privy to otherwise. Edward made it so she didn't have to worry about paying rent and she could concentrate on her art."

I started to respond, but he interrupted. "I wasn't a leech, you know," he said earnestly. "I make a good living from commissions; I never asked Libby to pay for anything. I could have taken care of her; I wanted to. I guess it's hard to leave that kind of money, though." He rubbed his hand across his mouth again and let out a huge sigh. "I can't imagine life without her, and I can't stand her for breaking off with me and going back to that arrogant bastard. What a fucking mess this is."

"It is that, all right," I said.

The pain in his face was nearly unbearable to look at. Lunch had arrived and gone cold, and neither one of us could think of anything to say to return to a less uncomfortable conversation, so I laid money for my half of lunch on the table and got up to go.

"Jeff, I'm so sorry about what happened between you and Libby, but I appreciate you talking and being straight with me. I know it's been painful and I have no idea if it helps her, but it explains some things."

"You won't tell her we talked, will you? I'd very much appreciate it if you wouldn't."

"No, I don't see any point in mentioning it."

"Thanks," he said, staring at the plate of congealed food on the table in front of him. Not knowing what else to do, I touched him briefly on the shoulder and left him there.

I DON'T know why I was surprised or why I was so angry with Libby. I'm not naïve; I know people cheat on each other all the time. I just couldn't seem to get my head around a Libby who would play with someone's affections like that, then go back to the husband she supposedly was so unhappy with. It seemed so cold and calculating. Her reaction to the accidental meeting at the market and now the story of her relationship with Jeff infuriated me. She was acting like such a heartless, entitled bitch. I didn't know what to think; I didn't remember Libby ever being like that. That was a long time ago, I reminded myself, a long time ago. On the other hand, every story has two sides; I had heard Jeff's and at some point I might hear Libby's version of it. Whether it would change my opinion of her, I had no idea.

TEN

I INVITED IAN OVER for dinner that night. He arrived with a bottle of wine and flowers in hand and helped prepare dinner. Not being a great cook myself, I was surprised at how easy he was in the kitchen. He teased me about my cooking skills, doing a silly impression of Julia Child with her high-pitched warbling voice and then offered to cook the entire dinner if I'd dance to Maroon 5 in my underwear. I declined, for the moment, much to his dismay. Despite not dancing, dinner turned out well.

"So tell me where you learned to cook like that?"

"I like to eat so I went to a couple of cooking classes. Took a week-long course in Santa Fe, which was fun. I think I must have some aptitude for it; it just comes easy," he said as we moved into the living room.

"I love Santa Fe; the food is amazing."

"It is. I'll have to make some of what I learned to cook for you sometime."

"It's a deal."

As the evening progressed, he related being hit on by a rich client's wife earlier that day. It was an amusing story about getting caught in a walk-in closet as the husband wandered down the hall, but it apparently had its drawbacks.

"It's not the first time it's happened. The hardest thing is to deflect their advances without upsetting them and causing problems with the husband I'm trying to sell a house to. It's usually the husband who has the deep pockets; offend him and you're screwed."

"Seriously? That happens?"

"Seriously." He laughed and ran his hand through his hair.

It was thick, black, shiny, and on the long side. It was hair that made me want to run my hands through it, and made me want him to run his long-fingered, strong-looking hands over me. For a moment I lost track of what he was saying.

"They're alpha predators, regardless of how helpless they may appear. It's interesting to see them in the society pages and know that more than one of them has trapped me in a pantry or up against a wall and snagged a feel or a kiss before I could extract myself gracefully and before the husband walked in on us."

"I would think a single guy would enjoy that, minus the getting caught by the husband part."

"I don't like to be manipulated or used to relieve boredom," he said, sounding annoyed. "I like to pick my own partners. I guess it might be flattering to some, but mostly it makes my job harder."

In the course of the evening the conversation came around to Libby, and I explained that I thought she was just unhappy about life in general.

"Unhappy enough to make herself sick?"

"Maybe. She had an affair then cut it off abruptly, and the guy is broken up about it and wants to get back together. I can't find anything wrong with her, really, and neither can her docs." I took a drink of my wine. "I should have known better than to get involved with her from the start. I'm not sure why I let her talk me into it."

"Friends and family are hard to resist. My brothers have dragged me into more harebrained schemes than I care to remember. It's partly why I moved here." He sat back with his glass of wine, watching me with a quizzical look on his face. "You've done your best and it's not working; that's not your fault. Sounds like her life's pretty messed up. I'm not surprised she's depressed. Maybe it'd be a good idea to quit and let her sort things out."

"It probably would be." I sighed and then remembered this was supposed to be a date, not therapy. "Sorry to dump this on you; you didn't come over to listen to my sob stories."

"It's okay, sometimes you need a sounding board. I don't think you're going to solve your friend's problem, though."

"Me, either." I got up and dished out the ice cream I'd bought earlier that day and brought the bowls over to the couch. We ate in silence until I finally said, "Would you like some coffee or something?"

"I have a better idea." He put his bowl on the coffee table and leaned in close and kissed me, his mouth tasting sweet and cool from the ice cream. He had lovely lips. He was hesitant as his tongue touched mine and then more insistent. I fumbled my bowl to the table and reached up to take hold of the curve of his skull, my fingers weaving through his soft, dark hair and returned his kisses.

We were in a bit of an awkward position sitting next to one another on the couch. He leaned against me, gently pushing me sideways, so we could recline next to each other. His body was long and lean and relaxed, and he kissed me and took his time, exploring my body as I did his, pulling away periodically to watch my face. He was smiling and his eyes were a lovely blue, heavily lashed with black and topped with expressive black brows.

"You're very lovely," he said, touching my face and tracing the line of my jaw. "Very lovely and very close to being ravished unless you put the brakes on and tell me to stop."

I smiled. "Don't stop now." I pulled him down to me.

WE BEGAN on the couch and ended up in the bedroom, and I didn't regret the decision. He was thorough and gentle and considerate, and at times rough and demanding, and I found myself responding in ways that hadn't happened in a long time. It might end as other relationships had, but I was hungry for the closeness and once again willing to take the risk. In the end, we fell asleep in each other's arms, and waking up the next morning to find him beside me sleeping peacefully, instead of gone, was lovely. I reached out and touched his hair and smiled as his eyes fluttered open.

"Morning, Sunshine," I said.

"Mmmm," he said, stretching. "Morning."

We lay there quietly for a bit before his eyes flew open and he cried, "Oh, God, what time is it?"

"About six. Are you due at work?"

"Yes, I have a showing at nine. Thank God, I don't think I can move just yet. I didn't get much sleep last night," he said with a smile.

"You poor boy, working so hard, not sleeping. How about some coffee?" I got up and grabbed my robe from the back of the bedroom door.

"Ah, that would be wonderful. I'm going to hop in the shower, if that's okay?"

"Towels are in the closet in the hall. Cream or sugar?"

"Both, please." He sat on the side of the bed and stretched, then rose and walked unselfconsciously into the bath. He was lovely to look at, tall and athletic with a dark dusting of fur across his chest, arms, and legs, with a bit more in all the right spots.

When he reappeared in the kitchen his hair was wet, he was warm and slightly damp, and had a towel wrapped around his waist. He accepted the coffee cup and took a deep swallow. "Ah, perfect. I'm starting to feel restored. How are you this morning, madam?"

"Wonderful, thank you. And you?" I felt absurdly as if I were chatting at a tea party instead of the two of us standing partially clothed in my kitchen. He returned to the bedroom with his coffee and me in tow.

"Couldn't be happier unless I was spending the day here. But I need to get going. I've got a bunch of showings today. How about doing something on Wednesday? We could go out to dinner or a movie, if you'd like," he asked as he gathered up his clothes.

"I'd like that."

"Great, think about where you want to go and I'll call you later," he said, pulling his slacks on and doing them up.

He had put on his shirt, socks, and shoes and finally stood up. He gathered me to him, undoing the belt on my robe and slipping his hands around my waist. "Lord I could take you again right now, but I'd never make it to the showing." He nuzzled my neck and gave me coffee-fla-vored kisses.

Things were getting serious and certain bits were making their opinion about what to do quite obvious.

"Darlin', if you keep this up you will never make it to your showing," I said, kissing the tip of his nose.

He stepped back, then leaned in and snatched another kiss. "I wish I was unemployed at the moment. Mmmm, you are delicious. I'll call you later. Go back to sleep so that I can imagine you sleeping and think of all the things I'd like to be doing with you."

"Go or I won't let you leave." I took his hand and dragged him to the front door. "Last night was unexpected and lovely."

"It was and I don't intend for it to be the last lovely night."

I watched him walk to his car and wave. *Me either,* I thought.

I PICKED up a weekend shift in the OR to take my mind off Libby and Jeff and all the other nonsense. It was a quiet one for a change, a few add-on cases that hadn't made it onto the Friday schedule, but no real emergencies to handle. While I was sitting in the OR staff lounge on break, Natalie Gould, one of the hospital pathologists, came in, poured some coffee and found a spot on one of the couches. She was waiting for a specimen that required some urgent, special handling and was killing time until she was needed for its transport and evaluation.

Natalie was the only female pathologist at the hospital. Some of the surgeons had initially maintained she was a politically correct hire so the hospital could avoid the appearance of hiring only male pathologists, but she was good and had gradually won them over. She was also friendly and social, not something you always saw in pathologists. As I was sitting there, I wondered if she could help me figure out what, other than miscarriage or mental illness, might cause Libby's symptoms.

"Can I interrupt your reading?" I asked.

"Sure," she replied, putting down the months old *People Magazine.*

"What would cause hair loss, tremors, peripheral neuropathy, mild depression, and irritability? I have a friend who everyone thinks is just experiencing the aftermath of a miscarriage or depression.

I just wondered if there could be another cause that may have been overlooked."

She laughed. "It's not you, is it? People often preface inquiries like that by saying it's for a 'friend.'"

"No really, it's a friend of mine."

She sat there for a minute and let her eyes wander. "Lots of things, actually. Those symptoms are vague and can be attributed to a number of conditions, including postpartum symptoms, depression, vitamin deficiencies, diabetes, hypochondria. The tremors and neuropathy, that's a bit odd, but if she was deficient in B vitamins or a diabetic that would account for that. What springs to mind, other than what she's been told, is exposure to heavy metals, pesticides, herbicides, slow-acting poisons. In rare instances, radioactive material exposure, like that Russian, Litvinenko, in London ten years ago? He was exposed to polonium 210."

She paused, looking as if she were thumbing through an invisible textbook. "That's highly unlikely, though; it's way beyond the normal person's ability to find or pay for or be accidentally exposed to. Serious exposure to radiation is also pretty rare unless you work in the nuclear industry or live somewhere an accident has occurred. Lupus might be a reasonable explanation. Other than that I'd have to do some research."

"Oh, that's probably not worth the time or trouble. I'm just grasping at straws anyway. All her docs say there's nothing really wrong, her husband thinks she needs a shrink, but she's convinced it's something more serious than that. Based on what you just mentioned, I can't think how she'd be exposed. She doesn't garden, so that kind of eliminates pesticides and herbicides. And I have no idea where she'd come in contact with heavy metals; poisons are just too out there to consider. She's taking a lot of stuff, OTC vitamins and pain relievers, and then on top of that she's using Ambien to sleep and Valium to get through the day."

"That's not a great combination of drugs; she should be careful not to add alcohol to the mix."

"She's never been a big drinker, even in school. She's a tea freak, though. Can you overdose on tea?" I asked jokingly.

"Unlikely, might get a little jittery from the caffeine, though. Might contribute to shaky hands but not to the extent you said." She thought for a bit, then said, "It's been my experience that people often have an intuition about these things. But in the face of being evaluated by several docs, it seems unlikely that it's more serious than a case of postpartum depression—not to downplay that, it can be pretty debilitating."

"I don't know what to think or how to help."

"Probably the best thing is to let her docs handle it. I'm not sure what you could do, anyway. It's unlikely you can talk her out of what she believes. If you support her and they're not real, then you haven't helped. Kind of like alcoholics; no one's going to be able to force them into treatment or recovery until they decide to do it themselves. Either she'll listen to her docs and hopefully get better, or she'll get worse and they'll have something more to go on. It's an uncomfortable position to be in."

"No kidding."

The intercom snapped into life and a voice announced: "Dr. Gould. Ready for you in room four."

"Thanks," she said to the intercom as she got up. "It's interesting, though. Keep me posted, okay? Sorry I couldn't be of more help."

"No, it's been helpful, thanks. I will keep in touch, if you don't mind."

"Of course not."

COLLINS, YOU are grasping at straws, I thought as I walked back to my room's scrub sink. Heavy metals, poison, or pesticide exposure were just too farfetched to believe. Lupus, though…maybe her GP should screen for that, if she'd go back to see him. It seemed unlikely she would, based on her behavior. I put a new mask on, scrubbed, and returned to my room to finish the case, my conversation with Natalie Gould rattling around in my head. When the surgeon had to ask for a suture for the second time and gave me bug eyes over the top of his mask, I realized I had to let it go and pay attention to the here and now, stop playing Guess What Libby's Got.

WHEN I arrived at her house on Monday, Libby acted as if nothing had happened. She asked how my weekend had been, what had I done, what did I want to do today? I closed her bedroom door and turned to face her. She was sitting in a chair by the window, and when I turned, she looked like a trapped creature. The expression on her face made me hesitate to say what I had planned, then the anger from our last confrontation returned.

"So here's the deal, Lib: I want an explanation about who Jeff Davies is to you or I am done. If you can't or won't explain what happened the other day, that's your choice, but I have no intention of playing games like this or continuing to babysit you. What's it going to be?" I stood there and waited as the minutes passed.

"I have no intention of explaining anything. It's none of your business," she replied at last.

"Okay, then. I hope you get better, I hope your life is wonderful, but I quit."

I turned to open the door and she blurted out, "Annie, please, can't you just let this go?"

"No," I said my voice rising in frustration. "There is too much weirdness going on. I feel like I'm in a maze with a blindfold on. There's something more complicated going on than you just not feeling well and I don't think it's physical. You need help, Libby, help I can't give you. Go see someone, for God's sake, maybe not the shrink you saw, but someone. Go back to your GP and ask him to run more extensive tests. I don't know what to do, and it feels like all you want is company on your own terms. I can't do this anymore." I jerked the door open and went across the hall to gather the few things that remained in the guest bedroom. Libby followed me into the room.

"Annie, you can't just leave, you said you'd help me. What am I going to do?"

I felt pressured and nearly on the verge of relenting, which made me mad. "You won't let me help you. Everything I suggest, you reject. So you can do just what you've been doing, keep playing poor little rich girl and gathering sympathy and concern from me and everyone who cares for you and shutting them out when it suits you, when the reality is there's very likely nothing wrong with you except you're depressed."

Her eyes flashed and I saw a brief glimpse of the Libby I had known years ago. "How dare you say that? I'm sick. What's the matter with you? You've never treated me like this! I thought I knew you."

Our voices had been rising, and I heard footsteps in the hall as I said, "I thought I knew you, too. Guess we were both wrong." I pushed past her toward the door and stopped.

Edward stood in the doorway.

"Is everything all right, Libby? What's going on?"

"I'm fine," she said in a subdued voice as Edward turned to me.

"Libby and I were just discussing the fact that I can no longer provide care for her. She's not happy about it. That's all that's going on. Now if you'll excuse me…."

I stepped toward the door and he backed into the hall. As I walked down the hall, I heard him saying something to her, and then realized that he was following me.

"Anne, if you will wait a moment?"

I stopped at the top of the stairs and waited for him to catch up.

"Why are you leaving?"

"Because I don't think there's any need for me to be here. I think Libby is depressed about a number of things, which she won't talk to me about, and can't or won't admit that she needs help from a therapist. I think she's using me to avoid it, and I don't want to be party to that. I was asked to help; I can't help, so I'm leaving. I will figure out my hours and let you know if I need to return any money."

"Keep the money. You're sure about leaving?" he asked, with an almost desperate expression on his face.

"I'm as sure as I can be, not being a physician or a shrink. You said I was to tell you if I felt she was in danger or needed other help, so that's what I'm doing. I won't take responsibility for her any longer." I turned and started down the steps, then stopped and turned back to him, "I would suggest you try to convince her to see someone." I couldn't resist adding, "And I think you should pay more attention to your wife."

❧

TUESDAY I got a call from Jeff. "I thought you said you wouldn't tell Libby about our conversation," he said when I picked up the call.

"I didn't."

"Then why did she call me and give me hell for causing such a scene at the farmers' market? She said it had caused a fight between the two of you and you'd quit caring for her."

"We did get into a fight and I have left. Part of the reason I contacted you was because Libby wouldn't explain what happened that day, wouldn't even talk about it, or you, and still won't. I didn't say anything about talking to you."

It was quiet on the line for a moment. "She acted like you'd told her what I said."

"Did you tell her we talked?" I rolled my eyes, waiting for the inevitable answer.

"I said we talked, not what about. She was furious. I told her I just wanted to know how she was, that I loved her, and wanted her back, that I didn't know what had happened between us."

"And?"

"She calmed down a bit and we agreed to meet this afternoon. She said she couldn't talk at the house, so I said we could meet. I just needed to know what you might have told her."

"I didn't tell her anything at all about our conversation. Jeff, she's very…I don't know, not really unstable, but she can't handle a lot of drama with you or with her husband. I know you love her, but don't cause problems for her. Not now, at any rate."

"I have to see her at least once more. I have to know about the baby and why she left. I can't leave it like this."

Love doesn't make the world go round, it makes people go round the bend, I thought as I disconnected.

ELEVEN

I T WAS A weight off my mind knowing I was finished with taking care of Libby, and yet it bothered me. I needed to talk to someone and called Maddie. I told her what had happened at the farmers' market and Libby's reaction.

"I talked to the friend and it turns out they were an item. A serious item, at least on his part. She ended the affair, with no explanation when she discovered she was pregnant. He didn't know about the pregnancy until he heard about the miscarriage from other people who knew her. He's heard nothing from her since she broke it off, and he has no idea if the baby was his or not."

I sighed heavily. "When I went to see her, she refused to explain anything. It just infuriated me and I quit. She's treating this guy horribly and acting like a spoiled brat. I guess they're meeting this afternoon. I'm not sure what about but I suspect he wants to get back together."

"Wow, be glad you're out of it."

"Do you think there might be anything to Libby's idea that something else is going on?"

"Not really, why?"

"I don't know, she's so insistent. I don't know what to think. I happened to talk to Natalie Gould. Do you know her? The pathologist?"

"I know of her, but I don't think we've met."

"She suggested some other things that could cause some of the symptoms, like heavy metal or insecticide exposure, or some other toxin. Does that sound plausible?"

"Well, I suppose it could be any of those things, but it's not likely she'd be exposed to any of those, is it?"

"As I told her, she's not a gardener, so unless it was some accidental exposure, I can't see how she'd come into contact with pesticides, and poison just seems like sci-fi. I suppose some of the oil paints she uses might contain heavy metals—do they allow that anymore?"

"I thought some of the colors artists use were still toxic; they used to contain all sorts of nasty things like arsenic and such. There are colors like white that are made with lead, and I think cadmium and cobalt are considered toxic, but you'd have to *eat* them to get poisoned that way. The solvents they use, I guess would be toxic. I have a cousin who works in pastels and artists are told not to breathe the pastel dust because of its content. A lot of them use gloves or hand sealants when they work with them."

"Well, the solvents might be a source of exposure, but surely an artist would know that and take precautions, right? And Libby isn't going to eat her paints. Not sure about the other stuff."

"That assumes she's been exposed to something, which seems kind of farfetched when her symptoms would suggest otherwise. You're really struggling with this, aren't you?" Maddie asked.

"That's a nice way to put it; obsessing is more accurate. I'm sorry, just tell me to shut up and I'll try my best to do it."

"I'd never tell you to shut up, but Annie, you quit. Seems like it's time to just let go of this. There's not much you can do about it, anyway."

TWELVE

IAN AND I spent Sunday together. We passed the evening watching
Netflix, and he spent the night. I brought him up to speed with my
experience with Libby and Jeff.

"Yeah, they were having an affair; unfortunately for him she wasn't
all that serious. As a result, she and I had a blow-up when she wouldn't
explain about the farmers' market, and I quit."

"That should help you get back to normal, don't you think?"

"Yeah, I guess."

"What's the 'I guess' about?"

"Oh, people. After our blow-up, she called him and read him the riot
act about the farmers' market, and he arranged to meet with her the next
day. He wants to get back together with her, I think. I'm not sure that's
even possible, but who knows?"

"Doesn't sound like it," he said.

The following week we were both busy. He called several times to touch
base. Then he called Friday morning to remind me about our Saturday
"excursion," which he'd talked about on Sunday night, but still wouldn't
say what it would be. He was a little distracted, said he was snowed under
with paperwork.

I WORKED the 12:00 PM to 12:00 AM shift that day, which can either be a quiet shift or an insane one depending on the phase of the moon. At least that's what we attribute it to; no one really knows what triggers the waves of calamity that we periodically saw. No doubt researchers would tell you there's no significant difference in the number of catastrophes during those time periods and others, but that wasn't the way it felt.

In any event, the early evening was calm, and it looked like it would be a good night. I was transporting my last patient to the post-anesthesia care unit with the anesthesiologist when the charge nurse hollered to us to stop on our way back. Ten minutes later we stopped at the front desk to find out what she wanted.

"They're bringing a trauma patient up from the ER, and since you just finished, you get the case. Denver Health was on divert, the usual Friday night knife-and-gun club, I guess, so he was sent here. The patient's ETA is about twenty minutes. My understanding is it was an assault of some sort, multiple facial and head injuries," she said, looking at her scribbled notes. "Let's see…a blowout fracture of one of his orbits, probably a fractured jaw, and a subdural that's continuing to bleed, so the neurosurgeon will go first, then the other surgeons will follow. I'm going to find some folks to help set up; environmental services is turning the room over now."

"Okay, thanks," I said, and headed back to my room while the anesthesiologist headed for the ER.

The OR is a fascinating place. It can look chaotic, and truthfully some people are easier to work with than others, but at the best of times, especially when it's urgent, we work like a well-oiled machine. People show up to help without being asked, and everyone does their job or whatever needs doing. When I got to the room, there were two people already setting up and opening the supplies, someone had retrieved the neuro headrest, put it on the table, and brought the instrument sets and drills to the room. My scrub tech was out scrubbing her hands and getting ready to go in and set up for the first procedure. The anesthesia tech was checking the anesthesia machine and setting up IV lines. He had brought the difficult intubation cart into the room and put the crash cart outside the door. Ten minutes later, the intercom buzzed and the charge nurse said the patient was on his way up to us. I checked to see what else was needed and then left to meet the patient at the front desk.

His neck was stabilized with a collar, and his face was barely human. His right eye was swollen shut, his face was bruised and swollen, and it was clear he was in pain and scared. I walked up and picked up the chart, leaning close to say hello.

"My name's Annie; I'm your nurse. I know you're in pain and moving your jaw to speak hurts, so I want you to take my hand and I am going to ask you a couple of questions. Squeeze my hand once for yes and twice for no, okay?" He squeezed once. It was an emergency and his level of consciousness was compromised, so the usual lengthy nursing assessment had to be short and to the point. I needed to know whether he had allergies and was the correct patient; the other information I would need to gather from the chart. The anesthesiologist and surgeon listened in; no point in making this man repeat things multiple times.

I picked his wrist up to read his ID bracelet and stumbled over the first question, "Jeffrey Davies?" He squeezed once and I took a very close look. "My God, Jeff?" He squeezed again.

The anesthesiologist looked up. "You know him?"

"Yes, socially."

"Do you want us to find another circulating nurse?"

"No," I said shortly. "I'm fine."

I finished my questions and readied the chart as I struggled with what had happened to him and tried to keep track of Jeff's squeezing responses. When that was finished, I turned to collect the chart and take him to the OR when he reached out and grabbed my hand. Tears were leaking from the sides of both of his eyes and he looked a little frantic.

He pulled me close and moving only his lips whispered, "Be careful."

"We will, Jeff, we'll take good care of you, please try not to worry."

He squeezed twice and pointed at me, mouthed "Be careful" and pointed at me again.

"What do you want me to be careful of?" I asked, but he couldn't say with gestures or squeezes and he didn't have the strength to try to talk. He dropped my hand and kept his eye on me.

Will, the anesthesiologist, looked at me with raised eyebrows and then at Jeff. "We need to get started. Are you ready?"

I nodded and noticed that Jeff's good eye was closed; he had drifted away.

"Let's get this show on the road," Will said, and we made our way back to the OR.

INTUBATING HIM was not easy but when it was accomplished and Jeff was under, the OR ballet began, positioning, prepping, draping, and hooking up the equipment so the team could begin the surgery. Once everything had begun, I asked what had happened.

"I heard it was a mugging, near where he works," the surgeon replied as he made the incision in the scalp. "Raney clips," he said to the scrub. "Someone nailed him near his car in the parking lot, the EMTs said. Another driver found him. He was unconscious but regained consciousness when he arrived in the ER. He's been in an out of consciousness since then. He hasn't been able to provide any information about what happened. It makes you wonder; smashing someone's face to bits is a pretty up-close and personal type of violence."

"Will he be all right?"

"No telling for sure at this point. Cautery, please. If we can't get the bleeding stopped or limit the brain swelling post op, or if he has a more extensive brain injury, that could complicate things. He was in pretty rough shape when he got here. Drill, Carol. His Glasgow score wasn't great but he wasn't bottoming out." He paused to use the drill to create the bone flap. "But he kept going in and out of consciousness. Sometimes it's just easier for them to check out for a bit when these things happen. Hopefully, he won't check out entirely. Irrigation, please."

My thoughts raced as I did the computer charting. The mugging could have been, most likely was, random, but his entreaty for me to be careful was unsettling. What did I need to be careful of? Or was it someone I needed to be careful of? Was the beating somehow connected to his meeting with Libby? I suddenly wondered.

"Annie, can you bring the crash cart in the room?" Will called, bringing me out of my thoughts. "His vitals and EKG are a little worrisome. Get some defibrillator pacing pads and let's get him hooked up, just in case." We did so, but things settled down, and Will seemed happier with the readouts. I helped him draw a blood gas and get it to the lab and then hung out near him in case he needed help.

"What do you want to do for post op airway management?" Will asked the neurosurgeon.

"I think we'll need to leave him intubated for a bit 'til the swelling goes down and he's out of the woods. They're probably going to have to plate his jaw and wire it shut, so he's going to need a stable airway. Do you want to leave the nasotracheal tube in or should we trach him?"

"Depends on how stable he is when everyone's done. If it looks like an airway is going to be needed for a while, then we ought to trach him. Or we could play it by ear for a day or two and see how he does. I hate to trach unless we have to."

"Same here, let's let it ride for now."

The surgeon went back to his work and time passed, accompanied by the beeps, hisses, suction noise, the sound of the drills, and requests for things. By the time we finished, near midnight, the subdural had been evacuated, and the neurosurgeon was hopeful there would be no further bleeding. The maxillofacial surgeon had repaired and wired Jeff's jaw, and the plastic surgeon had repaired the blow-out fracture of his eye and the cuts to his face.

Jeff's face looked appalling. He was more swollen and bruised, the nasotracheal tube was taped in place, and his head was wrapped in bandages; his lips were swollen and his right eye and the tissue around it was a huge, purple mess; both eyes were lubricated and his left eye was taped shut. I knew we had fixed the damage, but looking at him, it was hard to tell we'd fixed anything.

We wheeled him to the ICU and saw him settled and report given. My shift was over, but no one had been waiting for Jeff to come out of surgery. He was apparently alone or the powers-that-be hadn't been able to contact or find family members. So when the ICU bunch had stabilized him and were through with their admitting process, I drew up a chair and sat by the bedside, holding his hand. I squeezed it once, and said, "I'm here, Jeff, I'll stay with you tonight."

I thought I felt a slight twitch of a finger, but perhaps I imagined it.

I FELL asleep a little after two, my head resting on the edge of the ICU bed. I felt someone wrap a blanket around my shoulders and dim the lights in the cubicle. I was vaguely aware of people's periodic movement in and out of the ICU cubicle, but was otherwise untroubled by the staff. My dreams were troubled, though: snatches of panicked OR scenes, sounds of ambulances and flashing lights, interwoven with appearances by Libby, Maddie, and Ian. Through it all, Edward stood at the edge of my dreams, watching and waiting, for what I didn't know.

I felt a hand on my shoulder. "Annie, wake up, you need to go home."

I squeezed my eyes tightly shut and then opened them to look around. I tried to raise my head off the bed but my neck muscles were frozen in place and very unhappy at being expected to move again. I sat up slowly and saw my friend, Katy, standing there.

"There's nothing you can do right now; he's stable and he's doing as well as can be expected."

"Yeah, I should go home. Let me know if his condition changes, will you?" I stood up and stretched. It was almost 6:00 AM.

"Of course."

I walked to the OR and changed. Heading home, I realized that Ian had planned on coming over for breakfast before we spent the day together, but I was exhausted and needed some sleep.

"Annie? What time is it?" Ian asked when he answered my phone call.

"It's a little after six, hope you don't mind, but I need to bail on breakfast. I spent the night in the ICU with Jeff Davies. He was assaulted and is in pretty bad shape."

"I didn't think you knew him."

"I don't really, he's my friend Libby's lover, the friend I've been babysitting, but there was no family and I felt like someone should stay with him."

"Going a bit above and beyond, don't you think?"

"Maybe. It seemed to make sense last night. Ian, I'm beat. I'm going to go home and get some sleep. Maybe you could come over later."

"I could come over and sleep with you," he said.

"Okay, as long as it's just sleeping." I laughed. "I'm really tapped out."

I WOKE up around noon to find Ian next to me. Still groggy I was momentarily confused, then the previous night came back to me slowly. I slipped out of bed, found my purse and cell in the kitchen, and called the ICU. Jeff was holding his own, still sedated and in rough shape, but in no immediate danger, so I thanked the nurse and hung up. I wondered if I should call Libby. Would it help or just create more problems? What if the mugging, or whatever it was, was somehow connected to her?

"Be careful." Jeff's warning came back to me and I decided to err on the side of caution. With my usual misgivings and second-guessing, I made coffee and took both cups into the bedroom, setting them down on the bedside table. I took mine and eased into bed.

After a few minutes, there was movement next to me, and a groggy voice said, "I smell coffee, does that mean you've retuned to the land of the living?"

"I'm awake. That's progress."

"Is there a cup for me?"

"Yes, but you have to sit up. I'm not going to give it to you if you're lying down."

"Mmmm," he said, snuggling into my hip. "Maybe I'll just stay here for a bit longer."

"Well, stay as long as you like; it's Saturday, no rush to get up other than the prospect of cold coffee." I took a sip and then remembered I had cancelled breakfast and he had planned on a surprise outing, which was probably not going to happen now.

"That was a heavy sigh." He pushed himself up and leaned back against the headboard as I passed him his cup. "What's the matter?"

"It's Saturday."

"So you said." He took a sip and all was quiet for a second or two. "Ah right, Saturday, picnic day. Your friend's lover has thrown a bit of a monkey wrench in that, hasn't he?"

"I'm the one who threw the wrench. I'm not sure why I stayed; I just felt so sorry for him; no one was waiting for him. He's a mess after what happened, seemed like someone should stay with him last night, and I feel responsible for what happened to him."

"Why? How could you possibly be responsible for what happened?"

"I don't know. I keep wondering if his attack was connected to my meeting with him and then him and Libby meeting day before yesterday. Don't look at me like that," I said irritably. "I am not paranoid. Before I took him to the OR, he told me to be careful, and he was quite clear that it was me he was talking about."

"Annie, you said he was pretty badly hurt. It's possible he didn't know who he was talking to." He watched me as I sipped my coffee, avoiding his gaze, so he tried another tack.

"Please don't take on problems that you don't have to."

We sat silently drinking our coffee. I knew what happened to people with traumatic injuries: the brain shuts out memories of the event, distorts perception and memory, and sometimes the memory of what happened never comes back. Jeff had seen me and then Libby within days of each other, both meetings pretty upsetting in and of themselves, then he'd been assaulted. Maybe he'd confused me with Libby, maybe the "Be careful" had nothing to do with either of us. I would probably never know, and when he returned to consciousness, he might not even remember what he had said.

I closed my eyes and rubbed my forehead. Five hours' sleep after being awake for nearly twenty hadn't been very restorative. I yawned expansively with a hand over my mouth and just sat there for a bit.

"You're beat," Ian said, "and for some reason so am I. Why don't we just sleep for a while longer and then we can decide what, if anything, we want to do today?"

"Okay. Seeing Jeff's injuries and taking care of him and having him act like that before surgery has thrown me a curve. You're most likely right; I shouldn't be so fixated on this. I'm just exhausted."

"I can tell." He sat his cup down on the bedside table and relieved me of mine. "Lie down; it won't hurt either of us to get a little more sleep."

WE SURFACED around two that afternoon, feeling somewhat more human.

"Still feel like doing something or not?" he asked.

"I feel like breakfast at the moment, or maybe lunch, something to eat anyway, then let's talk about it. The day's nearly over, so I'm not sure what we could do." He was seated at the peninsula in the kitchen, and I was searching the refrigerator to see what I could make. "I could do eggs and bacon and some toast, how about that?"

"Perfect." He watched me pull a pan out of the cupboard and food from the fridge. "I've got someone covering my clients for me this weekend, so if you aren't booked for tomorrow, we could go somewhere, stay the night and spend tomorrow having our picnic." I didn't respond, distracted by trying to get the burner to light. "Or," he said, backpedaling, "we could just stay here and maybe go take in a movie, or we could drive up to Boulder and hang out."

"I would desperately like to get out of Denver. Boulder would be fine, I guess, and we could stay the night somewhere, I suppose. Why don't you just pick something and let me know what the plan is. My brain is on overload right now."

The eggs were cooking, toast was in the toaster, and the bacon was frying in another pan on the cook top. It smelled warm and homey, and I realized I was starving. Ian sat silently at the peninsula bar and watched me cook. He looked at home sitting there shirtless and shoeless in his blue jeans, but there was a frown playing around his eyes.

"Annie, do you want me to go home? Things between us have moved pretty fast and I probably overstepped by coming over, instead of giving you some space. Maybe we should put the picnic on hold for a bit."

I dished out the food and took it to the bar top, handing him a plate and sitting next to him with mine. "It has moved fast," I said. "But it moved fast because that's what I wanted the other night. You're not overstepping.

When, if, you do, I'll let you know. Right now, I'm starving and I just want to be away from here and pretend that the last few weeks never happened, that I don't know anyone named Libby, and that Jeff isn't lying in the ICU half dead. So eat up, Prince Charming, and then let's figure out what to do before the entire weekend disappears."

THIRTEEN

WE ATE, CLEANED up the kitchen, showered, and dressed. I packed an overnight bag and we headed to Ian's place in his car. I realized I had no idea where his place might be, and a little judgmental voice said, *Too fast, too soon.* I told the voice to mind its own business. Things were what they were and there was no undoing them; more to the point, I didn't want to undo anything.

He lived in a townhome off Speer Boulevard in what was dubbed the Golden Triangle. It was west of the art museum and on the periphery of the area around the Denver Country Club. Not the area with the huge, expensive country club estates, but the odd little area surrounding it that contained small bungalows and rundown duplexes and, in spots, renovated buildings, new apartments, and townhouses. His townhouse was a row house attached to three others. They were contemporary, tall, narrow, adorned with metal, and required climbing a steep flight of stairs in the front. The garages sat to the right side of the staircases and constituted the entire street level of the townhouses, everything else resting on top.

The living room had floor-to-ceiling windows that faced the front of the house. It was filled with an eclectic selection of good furniture. I sat on the couch and took it all in as he headed up the stairs to assemble an overnight bag.

"Wow, between the car and this place, I guess high-end real estate must pay well," I remarked.

He stopped on the stairway and laughed. "It does and that sort of makes up for the crappy jobs I had before I got licensed and for fending off the rich wives."

"What kind of jobs?"

"Well, let's see, I worked at a medical supply company for a few years, managed a Vitamin Cottage/Natural Grocers for a while, those type of jobs. Then I got tired of working with bosses and staff who were less capable and less intelligent than me, so I decided on real estate. I can set my hours pretty much, although I do have to cater to clients. It pays well and I don't answer to anyone but myself." He started back up the stairs, saying, "I'll go get my stuff, be right back."

His townhouse looked comfortable, if a bit austere; it seemed men gravitated to that look. There was a bookcase along one wall that ran from floor-to-nearly the ceiling that was crammed with books and other odds and ends. A fireplace and a couple of nice pictures on the wall completed the room. It looked like a show home.

I could hear him upstairs on the phone, a quick business-like call, then I heard drawers opening and closing and a door closing. When he returned, he had a small leather valise in hand and had changed into clean clothes. He set the bag down, walked to the fridge and pulled out a couple of water bottles and some fruit and cheese, which he loaded into a small cooler.

"Ready to go?" he asked.

I nodded and we departed.

We headed out of town and then eventually headed north on Highway 93, which ran to Boulder along the Flatirons, a range of startlingly sharp foothills that looked as if someone had taken slabs of stone and shoved them into the prairie at an angle. I assumed we were headed for Boulder, but we passed through it and continued northwest on highway 36.

"Where are we going?" I asked.

"Estes Park. I got us a room at the Stanley, as luck would have it. I've always wanted to see the place and spend a bit of time in Estes. It's supposed to be a really beautiful old hotel. Sound okay to you?"

"Sure as long as we're not in room 217 or on the fourth floor."

"Why? What's wrong, are they falling apart?"

"No, they're haunted," I said, staring out the window as the beautiful mountain scenery whipped past.

He was quiet for a few minutes, then said, "Okay, I have to ask, you don't believe in ghosts and hauntings, do you?"

"I've never had any psychic experiences myself, but it runs in my family." I laughed at the look on his face. "I take it you don't?"

"Not really. It seems like it's often a hoax or a way for someone to run a con, or just plain hysteria."

"All I know is my mother was amazingly prescient about things that she couldn't have been aware of, and of things that would happen. It made being a teenager difficult because she always seemed to know if you'd been up to something. There were times when I thought she was just good at guessing." I shrugged. "She probably was, most mothers are good at that, but there were other times that were downright unnerving." I watched the surrounding foothills become more mountain-like and covered with pines and aspens.

"That must have kept you on the straight and narrow."

I snorted. "For the most part, but teenagers never figure adults know anything or will figure anything out, so it wasn't a complete success as a deterrent. It did keep me from really extreme nonsense."

"You said it runs in your family. Are you the only one who doesn't see things?"

"Apparently. My youngest sister experiences things and has premonitions, I guess you'd call them." I hesitated, and then laughed. "My grandmother ran a nursing home and had a cat that would sit outside a resident's room, and when he did, the resident usually passed within twenty-four hours. Itchy—the cat, not my grandmother—would sit there in the hall until the person died and then he'd go about his business as if it was no big deal."

I'd rolled my window down and was letting my hand drift on the passing wind current. "I had a very strange childhood in that respect. So, while I don't know if the hotel is truly haunted, I do not want to stay in a room that has freaked guests out for many years."

He looked at me, raised an eyebrow, and replied, "Our room is in the Lodge, used to be called the Manor House. I'm not sure, but it sounds like it's not part of the main hotel."

"Good."

WE ARRIVED around six; it was still light but edging toward dusk. Ian had called ahead before we left his place and told them we'd be a late check-in, so the room was waiting for us. I teased him about assuming we would stay over before he was sure. To which he replied that reservations at the Stanley were hard to get on short notice and could always be cancelled if plans changed. Apparently, he had been hoping when he made the reservation.

The Lodge was lovely and looked very similar to the main hotel, which was nearby. With white siding, red roofs, white railings and porticos, it was quite elegant and welcoming. Smaller than the main hotel, it was advertised as a bed and breakfast and, while in the midst of the main hotel complex, had that cozy feel. We were welcomed, and after checking in, were escorted to our room with the usual "Where are you from? Is this your first visit?" chat on the way.

The room had a small dormer alcove with a two-seat table and a view into the back garden. There was a small sitting area with a TV and couch and chair. The bed was piled high with pillows and came with a down comforter and a memory foam mattress. *The room would make the visit a success even if nothing else did*, I thought.

After showing us how everything worked, and being discreetly tipped by Ian, our escort left and we had a chance to look around.

"Not bad at all," Ian said, opening the door to the bath and then looking out the dormer window. "And not a ghost in sight."

I gave him the evil eye. "So is this what makes you decide you've walked into something you weren't bargaining for and after we get home, you quietly disappear and tell people I am a little unhinged?"

He raised an eyebrow at me. "Really? Bit of an overreaction to being teased, isn't it?" He grabbed my hand and pulled me to him. "You wouldn't have lasted a minute in my family; teasing was the name of the game."

"I wouldn't know, since I really know nothing about your family."

He pulled me over to the couch and sat down, pulling me onto his lap. "Seems like neither of us really knows the other very well. We need to remedy that. What would you like to know?"

"Whatever you want to tell me."

"Well, let's see, I'm the oldest of four, three boys one girl, grew up in Phoenix, public school all the way through high school, then came to Colorado for a business degree at CU." He shifted me a bit on his lap and continued. "My folks are both alive and still live in Arizona." He paused and thought for a moment. "I have a married sister who lives in California, two kids. My two younger brothers live in Arizona. The older one is in grad school and the younger one is a jack-of-all-trades, master of none, who is currently bartending and living with his latest girlfriend. I think that's a pretty complete synopsis about me—now it's your turn. First, though, you're going to have to sit on the couch and let my leg get some feeling back or I'll need help getting to dinner. Oww!" he cried as I knuckled him in the arm.

"You've already heard about the family weirdness," I said, moving onto the couch beside him. "I'm the oldest of three girls and there was a lot of teasing in my family, but it was always two against one, so it was relentless and, because it involved girls, sometimes it wasn't very nice. People should have two kids or four, but never three; it's not a good number.

"I grew up in Texas, outside of Austin. I got my undergrad nursing degree and a master's here, and like you, I just stayed, too." He didn't look totally bored, so I went on. "Dad passed some time ago and Mom passed a couple of years ago. Next younger sister lives in California, has been through two husbands. My youngest sister is married with two boys and lives in Austin." I took a deep breath; it seemed like an unflattering synopsis, but family is family.

He nodded. "Feel any better?"

He looked so solicitous it made me laugh. "Yes, it feels a lot less like a one-night stand. How about you?"

"It felt like confession, but at least I know you a bit better."

"You're Catholic?"

"No, are you?"

"No."

"Does it matter?"

"Not really, as long as you're not into devil worship or some other weirdness like Scientology."

"You have family members and pets who are psychic and you think Scientology is weird?" He quirked an eyebrow at me and shook his head.

"I'm starving," I said abruptly. "How about you?"

"Done with the background checks, are we?"

"Yes, for now. I'll let you know what the private investigator tells me. Do we need reservations somewhere? I haven't been in Estes since I was a kid."

"I made one for us in the main hotel so we wouldn't have to go wander around in the dark looking for something to eat. We can wander around tomorrow."

"Boy, you had this all planned out, didn't you? Would've been a huge let down if the other night hadn't happened, eh?"

"I'm a Boy Scout at heart, always prepared. But whether it had happened the other night or not, it would have happened eventually, had I anything to say about it and you didn't object." He leaned over and kissed me on the end of my nose. "Come on, let's go downstairs and see what's on offer. We have to go over to the main hotel; maybe the restaurant will be haunted."

"I will never live this down, I can see that now."

FOURTEEN

THE RESTAURANT HAD a patio and it was still warm enough at night, with the help from patio heaters, that we could sit there and eat dinner. For a Saturday night it wasn't crowded, and like a lot of higher-end restaurants, there was no rush to get you out the door and get other diners seated. Both of us were hungry so there wasn't a lot of talk over dinner, but afterward over the remains of the bottle of wine we had a chance to talk. The wine was adding a rosy glow to things, and I was truly enjoying myself.

"It was so nice of you to bring me here. I haven't been to Estes, well, as I said, since I was a little kid. I don't remember much about it. Most of what I remember is that Estes was where my folks came on their honeymoon. Stayed in a cabin somewhere around here. My mom must have been in love to do that; she was never big on camping."

"And would you have to be in love to do that?"

I laughed. "I would have to be dead drunk and head-over-heels in love, if that was my groom's idea of a honeymoon hotel. As a way to spend a weekend, though, it would probably be fun as long as there was hot running water."

"It would be fun, and I think most of the cabins around here have all the mod cons. I've never camped out in the wild, I'm too much of a city boy to do that, but a cabin up here for a while sounds quite nice." He sat back with wineglass in hand and watched me. "So what else would you have to be dead drunk to do?"

"Well, let's see, go to a baseball or football game," I said and thought for a minute. "Water skiing; I've tried it and even with alcohol it's just a high-speed enema, in my opinion."

Ian choked on his wine. "God, I wasn't prepared for that. I promise never to ask you to water ski. Anything else I should be wary of?"

"Not really, I'm not terribly adventurous." He was staring off toward the grounds on the other side of the patio looking lost in thought. "So what would *you* need vast quantities of alcohol to be persuaded to do?"

"Ballets and operas. I don't think even vast quantities would be able to make that an option." He paused to think for a moment. "Oh, and I would have to be bordering on the edge of acute alcohol poisoning to watch the TV shows my brothers watch, or play video games."

"Yeah, there's a lot of drivel on the TV these days." I looked at the wine bottle and tipped the last of it into our glasses. "We are either going to have to get another, which personally speaking I don't think is wise, or we could stagger back to the room and settle in. Just FYI, if you order more wine, you'll need to call the concierge and ask for the bell boy's luggage cart to take me back to the room."

"I say we stagger back to the room." He swallowed the last of his wine.

He signaled the waiter, paid the bill, and waited patiently for me to disentangle my purse from the chair back and get up. *Maybe a luggage cart was in order*, I thought, but he was steady on his feet and we walked back to the B&B arm-in-arm. The bed had been turned back with chocolates left on each pillow, and the two small bedside reading lamps cast a soft light on the room.

"You know, I could live like this," I said and then remembered Libby's house and the sense of being under scrutiny all the time and the lack of privacy. "Well, maybe not. It's sure nice once in a while, though."

"Yes, it is," he said, helping me out of my jacket as he kissed me. It seemed one thing led to another—kissing, clothes somehow coming off and being carelessly dropped on the floor, finding myself in bed in his arms—and in the light of the lamp that he couldn't reach, we became reacquainted and slowly explored each other. We were slightly more cautious; the rush and exhilaration of our first few times had become a slower, more thorough exploration. Rather than the blind physical need to connect, this time it felt like we were finding a path to the other person, and we made our way slowly but surely.

I lay in the low light of the remaining bedside lamp and watched him. He was warm and solid, his face relaxed and eyes closed, his eyelashes fanned on his cheeks. There was a trace of sweat on his chest where my hand lay, and beneath it, I could feel his heart beating and his chest rising and falling. I felt his breathing drop into the deep rhythm of sleep and I was content to stay wrapped in his arms, my head on his shoulder, peaceful.

FIFTEEN

TOWARD MORNING, I woke with a start. I wasn't sure what had awakened me. I was anxious and it felt as if there were a weight on my chest. The room was dark, but it was clear from the lighter gray seeping around the window blinds that dawn was on its way. I lay there, with Ian spooned around me, and listened. The hotel was quiet and outside I could only hear the occasional birdcall.

I couldn't place where the vague sense of unease had come from. I'd had no unsettling dream or worry that had floated up into consciousness. *Probably just an accumulation of the stresses of the past month*, I thought. It would pass, the day awaited us, and, for now, all was quiet and peaceful. At last I fell back to sleep feeling Ian's warmth surrounding me, the comforting touch of his arm around me, the occasional prickle of chest hair against my back and the feel of his legs, curled up shrimp-like, against mine.

I woke to the sound of the shower being turned off abruptly and felt the vacancy in the bed next to me. I lay there listening and enjoying the sound of him rattling around the bathroom. He emerged sometime later toweling off his hair, a small shaving nick on his jaw.

"Awake, I see. Did you sleep well?" he asked.

"I did."

"I did, too."

"You're like sleeping with a teddy bear, very cuddly," I said as he came and sat on the bedside.

"I wouldn't call you a teddy bear, with all the hairy implications that calls to mind, but you're soft and squishy and very comforting to cuddle with."

"Not sure that's a compliment—soft and *squishy?*" I asked, my voice squeaking upward on "squishy."

"Definitely a compliment. I cannot imagine trying to cozy up to a bag of bones like some of the women you see these days, nor would I want to." He leaned over and kissed me, setting the towel aside and stretching out alongside me. "Check-out is noon, so we can discuss what to do today over breakfast, check out, and then go do whatever you want. If we're home by six or seven, will that do?"

"That'll do. I'll go shower." I got up and went to the bathroom, relieved my bladder, and turned on the shower. The sense of unease was inching back, which annoyed me. I wanted to enjoy this brief respite from the daily grind, so I decided firmly not to give into it. The shower was hot and went a long way to dispelling the doom and gloom. When I emerged into the room, I felt much better.

We packed and left the bags in the room to go get breakfast. A few couples were eating at the tables in the dining room, but for the most part it was evidently a low-traffic weekend. It was near the end of September and the mountains were heading toward winter; maybe fewer people came to stay this time of year. We finished breakfast and retrieved our bags from the room. I waited near the lobby entrance while Ian went to check out and was surprised when an older woman approached me.

She touched my arm and leaned toward me to say, "I'm sorry for your troubles. Your friend is going to need your help."

"Excuse me?" I said, baffled by her physical familiarity toward me and by what she had said.

She looked uncomfortable and then fluttered her hand in the air. "Ah well, it's not easy to explain. Things are not what they seem. Please be careful, dear." She walked away.

I stood there with my mouth open, watching her go out the door and felt the anxiety engulf me again. It wasn't as if people didn't say bizarre things to each other in my family, but this was just weird.

"Wait a minute!" I called, finally coming to my senses. I started after her, but she had left quickly and was nowhere to be seen when I emerged from the hotel's front door. I stood there scanning the entrance area and couldn't see anyone who looked like her.

"There you are. I wondered where you'd taken off to," Ian said, coming out of the door. "Anxious to get going?"

"Yeah," I answered, still scanning the area in hopes of seeing the woman. "Yeah, let's go."

He must have noticed the odd look on my face and my hesitancy. "Everything okay?"

"I…I'm fine." I did not feel like sharing what had just happened. I was not in the mood for more teasing, and the creeping sense of anxiety and oppression had returned, along with the urgent need to go home that her comments had triggered. We walked to the car and put the bags in the trunk. Ian was talking and joking about something, but I couldn't concentrate on what he was saying.

He stopped and looked carefully at me. "You don't look fine to me; what's the matter?"

"I don't know, would you mind terribly if we just went home? I'm so sorry to ask, I just…I don't know, but I think I'd like to go home."

"Okay, sure. Are you not feeling well?"

"No, that's not it. I'm sorry; it's not you or the time we've spent here. It's…the last forty-eight hours have been pretty overwhelming for me— please, I just want to go home."

He gave me a long look, then frowned, and said, "Okay, let's go." He opened the car door for me and then went around and got in the other side.

The first half hour or so of driving was very quiet. I wasn't sure if he was disappointed or pissed off. Ian put a CD in and set the volume low. He watched the road with occasional glances in my direction, and I stared out the window. After a couple of glances, he turned off the CD player and asked, "Are you going to tell me what the problem is or do I have to play twenty questions?"

"I don't know what's wrong or I'd tell you. I just need to go home."

"Oh, God, it's not Itchy the cat, is it? He wasn't outside our door in the middle of the night was he?"

"No, it's not, and this isn't funny," I snapped.

I turned back to the window and after a while he turned the CD back on and we drove home to the soft voice of Van Morrison.

WE REMAINED silent throughout the ride back to Denver, and the longer it went on the harder it was to think of something to say to break the silence. We arrived at my house and he helped me bring my bag to the door, setting it on the porch while I found my keys.

When I finally got the door opened I turned to him. "Ian, look, I didn't mean to cut our weekend short, I just—"

He interrupted me by putting a finger on my lips. "It's okay, you don't need to explain. It's true you've had a rough couple of days and I think you need to have some time to yourself. I'll be in touch." He leaned in and kissed me chastely and then turned and walked to his car. The headlights came on and he drove away.

I stood on the porch watching morosely as his taillights disappeared and then heard Angel's door opening as his porch light came on.

"Oh, it's you," he said. "Thought I heard someone. Where've you been?"

"Estes Park," I replied, picking up my bag.

"I'm glad to see you. A package came for you late yesterday; I had to sign my life away for it. Do you want me to bring it over?"

"Sure," I said wearily. I didn't really care about packages at the moment, but it seemed rude to refuse.

I went in the house, leaving the door ajar for him and dropped my bag by the couch. I could hear him struggling with something and went to investigate. The package he was manhandling was about four feet by five feet, and while awkward, it wasn't heavy when I took hold of a corner.

"What in the world is this?"

"No idea, I can't tell from the packaging."

"Did they say who sent it?"

"I didn't ask."

"Help me get it undone."

We managed to open the package and to my surprise it was Libby's painting of the two old women that I'd admired for so long. I sat back on the couch and stared at it, then saw that an envelope had fallen out of the frame at the back. I opened it and read,

> *I'm sorry for the trouble I've caused. I hope this makes up for it. I've enclosed a bill of sale so you'll have it as proof that I gave this to you if Edward or someone questions it.*
>
> *Libby*

I got up and kicked my bag out of the way. "God, I am so tired of this! What the fuck does she mean 'if Edward or someone questions it'? How the hell would I get one of her paintings if she didn't give it to me? And what business is it of his what she does with her paintings?"

"I sense a disturbance in the force, Collins. What's wrong?"

"Oh, don't fucking Yoda me, everything is wrong! Libby is a hysterical lunatic, her husband is a creep, her boyfriend is a fool who just got his head bashed in and is in ICU and that may or may not be related to Libby and her husband," I ranted, pacing in front of the couch.

"I woke up early this morning and just couldn't shake this sense of anxiety and then some nutcase at the hotel told me she was sorry for my troubles, whatever the hell that meant, that things were not what they seemed and my friend would need my help, and I have no idea if she meant Libby or Jeff. I ruined a weekend with a guy who I really like by insisting on coming home. And nothing's wrong here except I have a very expensive early Libby Crowder painting sitting in my living room. I feel like I'm being jerked in a million directions and I don't have a clue why." I burst into tears and flopped down on the couch.

"Wow, bad week eh?" He sat down next to me and hesitantly patted my shoulder.

Angel had grown up with a couple of sisters and a number of female cousins, but mostly what they had taught him was that when a female is wound up and on the verge of exploding, it's best to keep your distance and if you were fool enough to approach, you had to do it carefully.

"Can I get you something? A drink? Some Advil?"

"I am not premenstrual, I don't need Advil," I snapped at him.

He retracted his hand slowly, as if any sudden movement on his part would trigger an explosion, and got up and went in the kitchen where I could hear him opening the fridge. He returned a few minutes later with two beers and handed one to me.

"Want to tell me about it or would you rather I went home and left you alone?" he asked.

"Oh, stay for a bit, drink your beer, and then go home, I guess."

He laughed at that and sat back on the couch and drank his beer for a bit. "So what's up, the rich people get to you finally?"

"Yes, and it didn't take long." I drank some beer. "Angel, you have friends in the Denver police department, right?"

"Yeah, why?"

"The man Libby was having an affair with, and who's most likely the father of the baby she miscarried—yeah, I know, it gets worse," I said when he rolled his eyes. "He's in the ICU after being beaten to a pulp not long after he and Libby met to discuss the whole mess. They hadn't had any contact in months and for the beating to happen after they met makes me wonder if the two events are related. I'd like to know what the police know about the attack and what they think happened. Can you find out for me?"

"I could probably find out, but my guess is they don't know much. These things often happen for no obvious reason, and sometimes they never find the person who did it. But I'll ask around, see what I can find out."

"Thanks, I appreciate it."

"Annie?" That worried me; Angel almost never called me anything but Collins or *chica*. "You should stay out of this or at the very least be careful and not tell a bunch of people you're curious about it."

"If *one* more person says that to me I am going to scream. What am I supposed to be careful of? What?"

He shrank away from me, holding his hands up and looking worried. "All I meant was that if you get too nosy and too loud about it, and the person who assaulted the guy isn't just some random, drug-addled criminal, it could stir up all sorts of problems for you. It could be dangerous for you. Maybe just cool down and let the police handle this. That's their job, not yours."

"I suppose, but I would still like you to see what you can find out, please?"

He sighed in exasperation and swallowed the last of his beer. "Okay, but I don't think there's much to find out. Will you be okay by yourself? I could camp out on the couch if you're worried about being alone. No funny stuff, I promise." He grinned at me.

"Thanks, but I'm fine, just really tired and fed up."

"Okay, sleep well, *chica*."

"Thanks for hanging out and for signing your life away for the delivery."

"Kind of a disappointing gift," he said, heading for the door. "Wonder why she sent you a painting of a couple of old women?"

"You wouldn't understand, and I'm too tired to explain."

I SHOULDN'T have insisted on coming home. The sense of urgency and anxiety was gone now, and I felt foolish. I didn't want to check in with Libby but at some point I had to call the ICU about Jeff. I took my bag to the bedroom and emptied it and then returned to the living room.

I leaned the painting up against the wall. It was probably a $15,000 painting what with Libby's talent and her current popularity and there it sat, the most expensive thing in the house. I had no idea what to do with it. Part of me wanted to return it because the gift felt like a bribe, and the rest of me was as thrilled as a kid at Christmas. I had always loved the painting. For now, I left it leaning up against the wall. I would figure out what to do with it tomorrow.

I got undressed, put on some pajamas, and heated up some leftovers. Sitting at the kitchen peninsula I remembered Ian sitting there yesterday morning and wondered whether he was pissed off or disappointed by my insistence on coming home. He had seemed okay when he deposited me at my door, but the ride home had been uncomfortable. Time would tell, I guess. I picked up my phone and dialed the hospital and was put through to the ICU. A friend of mine answered the phone.

"Chip, it's Annie. I wondered how Jeff Davies was doing?"

I heard him sigh. "Well, he's stable. I probably shouldn't be discussing it with you, since you're not family."

"I'm not some random nosy neighbor, I'm one of his caregivers. It's a professional inquiry. Did any family members turn up?"

"No, not yet. I thought maybe you were friends. Katy said you'd spent the night of his surgery at his bedside."

"I know him, but we're not friends. I just felt sorry for him. He was really scared before surgery and I just felt someone should be with him."

"He's not much changed, really, but at least he's not deteriorating. They keep running scans on him; no telling what the final outcome will be. You know how it is with head injuries."

"Yeah, I do. I know a friend of his. I may bring her by tomorrow. Would that be okay?"

"Sure. I'll be here seven to seven tomorrow, so come when I'm here and it should be fine. As far as we know, there's no family to object to the visit, and it might be what he needs to keep him from drifting away from us."

"Are you worried about that?"

"I always worry about that, sweetie; ICU is a place where a lot of people decide they don't want to stay and it can happen anytime. People they care about, that's what they come back for."

"Thanks, Chip. I'll see you tomorrow."

At the moment, the anxiety I'd felt and the woman's comments seemed pointless. Jeff's situation wasn't great, but it wasn't desperate. *We should have stayed in Estes*, I thought angrily.

SIXTEEN

I CALLED LIBBY THE following morning. I thanked her for the painting and asked her if she was sure she wanted me to have it. She said she did, and that she was sorry things had ended the way they had between us.

"I'm calling to see if we could meet today? I could come pick you up and we could go somewhere, have lunch or something. I don't like leaving things the way they are. Are you up for it?"

I didn't want to say anything about Jeff on the phone. It was deceptive and she'd probably be furious when she found out. I didn't want her to refuse to meet. *Better safe than sorry*, I thought.

"I'm feeling a bit better," she said. "When do you want to pick me up?"

I picked her up around noon, and she did seem slightly better; perhaps her illness was psychosomatic. She was still a little unsteady on her feet and hiding her hair under a scarf she had cleverly tied around her head and wearing her signature sunglasses. I stopped at a little deli, we got sandwiches, and I drove to Wash Park and found a shady spot to sit. The weather was still remarkably warm for the end of September, but that was often how it was in Denver. After settling in and allowing her to eat for a bit, I took the plunge.

"I'm sorry things ended badly between us, but we need to talk. I know about you and Jeff, and I want to hear your side of the story. I hope you'll talk to me."

I waited. She was upset with me and clearly felt that it was none of my business, but she was pretty much stuck here with me. She couldn't walk home, and I was her only transportation.

"I don't see how that's any of your business. But since you say you already know, I'm not sure there's any point in trying to keep it private. I figured Jeff had talked about us; he said he hadn't said anything to you about us when you talked, but I know him, he spills his guts at the drop of a hat."

I had to bite my tongue to keep from saying he wasn't doing much talking now. "So tell me what happened."

"We'd been friends for several years because he was the one who handled my art sales. I've been pretty unhappy as you guessed and I spent a fair bit of time talking to him about it. We had a lot in common and he was a sympathetic listener. One thing led to another and we became lovers."

She stopped talking and I wondered if she would say anything else.

Finally, she took a deep breath and then exhaled. "I was so tired of being married and ignored. He offered me something different and forbidden; it seemed harmless. And then I got bored with him and felt pressured. He kept wanting more, more commitment, more time, more everything." She paused for so long I wasn't sure she would continue. "I'm ashamed to admit, I met another man quite by accident at a housewarming party, and we got involved while I was still involved with Jeff. When I discovered I was pregnant, I called it off with both of them and neither took it very well." She blushed. "I have no idea who the father was, which is incredibly embarrassing, and I was scared that Edward would find out and divorce me. We had a prenuptial agreement. If he found out what I'd done he could divorce me and I'd get nothing but a small lump sum."

The look on her face was as if Edward would take her children from her, rather than divorce her and leave her with a tidy sum. Perhaps access to his money was that important to her.

"I couldn't stand that. And I didn't really want to be divorced because then Jeff would start pressuring me to marry him and I thought the other man might want to take up where we left off. He was really upset when I told him the affair was over, and he still calls every now and then." She put a hand up in front of me and said, "And please don't ask who he is; you've already been intrusive enough about Jeff. Let me have at least some privacy."

I sat back as if slapped in the face. I guess I deserved it, and Angel had warned me. I wondered, briefly, whether the man was the "friend" who'd called Libby and tried to dissuade her from hiring me.

She continued. "The pregnancy sealed it. It gave me a reason to end things with both of them and go back to Edward. We still had a sporadic sex life when he was home and not distracted, but I slept with him several times so he'd think the baby was his. You probably think I'm a selfish bitch, and I guess I am, but I had a lot to lose. And then I lost the baby."

"Doesn't sound like you loved Jeff or your other lover. Do you love Edward?"

"I don't know anymore. I liked Jeff immensely, and, at first, my relationship with the other guy was pretty intense and exciting, but no, I wasn't in love with either of them. They gave me the attention and the excitement that I wasn't getting at home, but it wasn't love. I thought I was in love with Edward, and I do care about him, but what I really love is my work. I wanted to be able to keep working without worrying about bills and Edward offered that. Jeff offered what he could, but it would never have worked for us, and"—she almost slipped and said the second name but caught herself—"and I don't think the other one had any intentions in that direction. I know I didn't."

I sat and watched her. For the life of me I couldn't reconcile this Libby with the one I remembered, and my heart broke for Jeff. I wasn't sure a visit from her would help, but by God she was going to see him and she was going to make an effort for him.

"Well," I said, "I'm not sure it'll matter, but Jeff was assaulted and is in the ICU. No one knows what actually happened. He's on a vent and he's not doing all that great."

She looked stunned, but said nothing, so I continued. "We can't determine if he has family. Do you know if he does or how to contact them?"

"He was an only child and his parents passed away several years ago, so there is no family to contact."

"I want you to come with me now to see him and talk to him."

"Why?"

"Because he needs something to hold onto, a familiar voice, something. Unfortunately for him, you're it. So as one last favor to me, you're going to visit and tell him you love him and you want him to get better. The only thing you can't tell him is that he's wasted the last few years of his life because you were bored."

She had the grace to blush at that. I wondered about her and I wondered if there was any point to this, but I felt like Jeff needed something from her. It was the least she could do.

A short time later, we walked into the ICU. I saw Chip and motioned him over. I introduced Libby and explained that there was no family. He walked us to Jeff's cubicle and opened the sliding door, allowing us to enter. The lights were low, and there was the usual background noise of monitors with their beeps and constant read-out of his vitals. Jeff lay on his back, arms at his sides, head still wrapped in gauze. The tube exiting his nose was taped to his face and attached to the ventilator that sighed with every breath it pumped into him. His face was still puffy and bruised but the swelling had gone down some. He looked as bad as you would expect someone to look after a serious beating, but Chip and I were used to seeing things like that and Libby was not.

"Jesus," she whispered and brought a hand to her face. "Will he be okay?"

"We hope so," Chip said. "He's relatively stable, but not waking up like we hoped he would." He left and returned with a chair, which he placed at the bedside. "Take your time. People in this state often hear well and have an awareness of the people around them, so hold his hand, if you want, and talk to him. With the exception of touching his face, you can't hurt him; the contact will do him good. No upsetting conversations, please. If you need me I'll be at the nurse's station."

He looked at me and quirked his eyebrow as he left, indicating he wasn't sure this was a great idea, but was willing to see how it went, and he wouldn't be far away.

Libby sat down hesitantly on the chair and just watched Jeff. After a few moments she reached out and took his hand, stroking his arm with her other hand. "Jeff…it's Libby." Interestingly, his pulse rate picked up. She turned and looked at me, slightly panicked. "I don't know what to say."

I went closer, leaned over and whispered in her ear, "Tell him you love him. I don't care if it's true or not, and tell him you're hoping he'll get better. Then sit and hold his hand and talk about whatever you two used to talk about, just keep it simple."

I stepped back by the sliding door of the cubicle and waited. I was torn, I felt like they deserved privacy, but after our conversation earlier, I had no idea what she might say to him and I wanted to be close enough to put a stop to it if it seemed to be going badly. She did her job, she was a good actress, I will give her that. There were even tears at one point.

Suddenly she stood up, and said, "I can't do this anymore."

"Then say goodbye, tell him you'll be back later." She shook her head no and I grabbed her arm and held it tightly. "Tell him, now."

I released her arm and she turned toward his bed. She did what I'd asked and then abruptly left the cubicle. As I followed her she turned on me and said, "Don't ask me to do that again, you understand me? I am not coming back." Her voice was rising and from the cubicle I could hear the beeping of the pulse monitor increasing, which worried me. Clearly Jeff could hear her. I took hold of her arm again and marched her toward the door of the unit, with a glance at Chip and a head jerk in Jeff's cubicle's direction. He rose and headed that way as we exited the unit.

"I don't intend to ask you again, in fact, I don't intend to contact you at all if I can avoid it. I'll call you a cab; I have things to do."

We rode the elevator to the first floor, and I took her to the concierge at the entrance and asked him to get her a cab. Before I left, I asked her, "If he dies, do you want to know or not?"

She stared at me and said nothing for a moment and then nodded, so I left her and went back up to the ICU.

Chip was still with Jeff. "Is he okay?" I asked as I entered the cubicle.

"Well, his vitals are okay, pulse was pretty high for a bit after your friend left. My guess is he recognized her voice or heard what she said, but he's settled down now. You gonna stay for a bit?"

"Yeah, I will."

"Okay, let me know if anything changes. I'll check back in a few."

I spent the afternoon there, talking to him, holding his hand, helping Chip when I could and staying out of his way when I couldn't. Jeff seemed to have settled into his unresponsive norm. No spikes in pulse, no nothing. I was discouraged and angry. I had hoped that Libby could help, and after talking to her, I had hoped that she would continue to make an effort to help him, but I knew now that she wouldn't.

Why do nice people waste their time on assholes? I wondered. Considering who he had wasted his time on and how devastating the breakup had been for him, there was part of me that felt perhaps it would be easier if he didn't survive. But who could say what was easier? The outcome was beyond my control, in any event. The problem was I liked him and felt sorry for him, a lethal combination.

There was little any of us could do. I couldn't even pray, didn't know what to ask for. I have always thought that it must be a great comfort to Catholics to have a saint to pray to for every situation, but I felt a bit lost. Before I got up to leave at six, I leaned in close to him and said, "Jeff, please don't give up."

I DROVE around aimlessly because I couldn't bear to go home to an empty house and I didn't know where else to go. I finally picked up a soda at a fast food drive-thru and drove over to Ian's townhouse. I sat out front debating about whether to go up and knock on his door or just go home. I wasn't even sure if he was home. We had parted on uncertain terms and I had yet to hear from him. If he was home, I didn't know whether he would welcome a surprise visit. So I sat and drank my soda and debated. Half an hour later, my phone rang.

"You gonna come in or just sit in your car?"

"Would you mind?"

"Of course I mind, that's why I called you. I mind you sitting out there by yourself, when you could come in and we could talk or eat or drink or whatever you want to do. So get your butt up here."

I got out of the car and walked up the stairs to his door, which opened as I reached for the door handle. We looked at each other, a bit awkwardly, and then he stepped back and ushered me in. Getting out of the car and walking up to his door had resulted in an urgent need to pee, which was a little embarrassing. "Um, could I use your bathroom? I've had a lot to drink sitting out there."

He laughed at that and pointed me in the desired direction. "First door on your right down the hall." When I returned from the bathroom, he motioned to the couch, where I sat down. "Can I offer you something? I haven't had dinner yet; have you?"

I shook my head and lay my head on the back of the couch. "I'm not sure I'm hungry and I'm swimming in soda. Maybe I could just sit with you for a bit, then I'll head home."

"Why?"

"Why what?"

"Why go home? You're welcome to stay, you know."

That was all it took for me to start crying. I might have been able to hold it in if he'd still been upset with me. He sat down next to me and took me in his arms.

"For God's sake, Annie, tell me what's going on. I don't know what happened in Estes, but if I've done something, if it's my fault, just tell me."

"It's not you."

"Just tell me what's going on or what's happened, please."

So I told him, everything, the uneasiness, the weird woman at the hotel, the painting, Angel's warning, Libby and Jeff and her mystery other lover, and the fiasco in the ICU.

He replied at last. "Several lovers at one time is pretty cold-blooded, slutty behavior. Did she say who the other one was?"

I was a little taken aback at his characterization of Libby, but cheating on your husband with multiple simultaneous lovers and having no idea who the father of your child was probably did qualify as slutty behavior.

"No. She told me I'd intruded in her life enough by talking to Jeff and not to ask about the other guy. Apparently, she cared for Jeff, but for her it wasn't serious; it was for him. I don't know about the other person, she didn't seem that involved." I had stopped crying and took a couple of ragged breaths. "This is someone I liked and thought I knew. We were friends, at least until Edward showed up. Now I wonder if I was just someone who amused her or that she wanted around until she didn't. That's what she did to Jeff, all because she was bored with her marriage and then she left without explanation because she was afraid of losing Edward's money and not having the freedom to paint her damn paintings. Who does that?"

"Evidently, Libby does. My experience? People in her class with his money do that pretty commonly." There was an undercurrent of anger in his voice. He'd said the attentions of his clients' wives annoyed him, when a lot of single guys would have been amused or taken advantage of the opportunity. Maybe his annoyance with the behavior of rich bored wives had become something more to him than annoyance.

He still had his arms around me and he stroked my hair. "You know there's nothing you can do about this, right? You can't fix Libby or Libby and Jeff, and Jeff will either get better or he won't. And the other guy is probably relieved to be done with her. I know it sounds harsh, but whoever he was, if he knew about the pregnancy he's probably glad she miscarried. He's out of the relationship and home free. However the situation resolves, it's out of your hands."

"That's what is so frustrating. I feel like I should be able to fix something."

"I'm not surprised, they don't call them helping professions for nothing. One thing you can fix, though, is to go wash up; your mascara needs fixing." He smiled at me and pulled me up off the couch. "In fact, I have a great bathtub that almost never gets used. I think it's calling your name. Go sit and soak for a bit, and when you're finished, we'll eat. There are towels in the closet outside the bath and feel free to use my bathrobe, it's on the bathroom door."

⌒

I EMERGED a half hour later, rosy from the bath, enveloped in his robe, and feeling less fragile. He had been busy in the meantime and had dinner ready. We sat at the table and ate, not talking much, but it seemed our impasse on the way home from Estes had been resolved. After dinner we watched a movie and finished the wine from dinner.

"So do you still want to go home or do you want to stay?" he asked as he turned off the TV and gathered up the wine glasses.

"I don't think I should drive, I'm too relaxed and a bit tipsy, so if it's okay, I'll stay."

"Stop asking if it's okay. Jesus, Annie, if it weren't okay you wouldn't be here. I want you here and I'm glad you came by."

"I'm having a little trouble figuring out what's happening with us, and after a day with Libby, I don't want to intrude. I don't want to be with you if you don't want me here."

He looked at me for a long moment. "Why would you think I didn't want you here? I've wanted you since the day I met you, and I've felt like a puppy dog following you around ever since." He stroked my cheek and my heart performed a flip. "I will promise you one thing: If I don't want to be with you, I will tell you. That's highly unlikely, so stop worrying about it. It's late and I have to meet a client in the morning, so if it's okay," he said with a raised eyebrow, "let's go to bed."

SEVENTEEN

WE BOTH LEFT early the next morning, Ian to work and me to my house. Back at home, I stood looking at the painting, trying to figure out where to put it. I had wall space in the bedroom, but I wasn't sure I wanted two old women watching what went on in the bedroom, although it would probably amuse them. I finally chose a spot in the dining room that I used as an office, and found a hammer and picture hanger. The painting looked good once hung up. It had always been beautiful, but it was slightly tarnished by the recent revelations about Libby.

I spent the afternoon cleaning house and thinking about what had happened both with Libby and Jeff and with Ian and me. *Nothing like cleaning house to get your brain moving*, I thought. The phone rang and it was my boss wondering about my taking a shift later that day and one the next. At loose ends, I agreed. It would take my mind off all this nonsense and while there I could pop in and visit Jeff.

Ian called while I was on my dinner break and we chatted for a while. He was going to spend the evening catching up on paperwork, and we agreed to meet up after I got off the next day at seven. During a lull in the evening that looked to go on for quite some time, I told my scrub nurse, Carol, I was going to ICU to check on a patient and to call me if she needed me for anything, otherwise I'd be back in about twenty minutes.

Katy was on duty caring for Jeff when I got there and she reported no improvement. I saw the docs had finally removed the nasotracheal tube and performed a tracheotomy. That told me they didn't hold out much hope for a quick recovery.

"They're worried there may be more bleeding, so the doc has ordered a CT. We're just waiting for word that radiology is ready for him," she told me. "But you can sit and visit until we have to take him for the CT. Are you doing okay? You're the only person who visits him. It's so difficult to see friends like this and it's difficult for me to see how hard it is for you when you visit."

Katy and I were work friends, and it was nice to know she was worried about me. "We're not really friends. Just acquaintances, but it breaks my heart to know he's here alone. He's a really nice guy who got involved with the wrong person. It's sad, really."

"The woman you brought in the other day?"

"Yeah, it didn't work out like I hoped." I sighed. "I'll keep him company 'til you're ready to transport him."

Katy nodded and returned to the nurses' station.

There is something almost womb-like about an ICU cubicle, especially in the evenings when staff keeps the lights low and try to keep the monitor sounds low enough to hear but not so intrusive that they bother the patient. Patients lie in ICU beds hooked up to IVs and catheters and endotracheal tubes and ventilators. Like a child before birth, everything is done for the patient; next to nothing is expected of him or her except to heal. Everyone hopes to see the patient emerge healthy and whole at some point. Sometimes, though, it doesn't matter how good we are at mimicking life; hope slips away and life leaves with it. I felt that hope for Jeff starting to slip and it scared me.

He was turned on his side and propped with pillows, so I sat next to the bed and took his hand. "Hey, Jeff, it's Annie, come to visit again. They're a little worried about you not waking up. They're going to take you to radiology and do a CT to see if anything's changed since the last scan. I figured you'd probably want to know where they were taking you." I watched his face and glanced at the monitor, not a blip and no facial changes. Maybe he was already gone. "You know there are days when I wish I could check out, too, and checking out for a while is fine, but it's time for you to come back and join the rest of us."

There was movement at the sliding door, and turning, I saw Katy.

"They're ready for him Annie, I need to ask you to leave."

"Sure," I said. I squeezed Jeff's hand and leaned in close to say, "Hang in there, Jeff," and left the cubicle.

As Katy and the others disentangled lines and hooked them up to portable equipment and prepared to move him to the radiology department, I went back to the OR. Things were still quiet, so I sat in the lounge with other staff members half listening to the TV and the others talking and joking with each other.

THE CT was puzzling, no new bleeding, but Jeff wasn't waking up. I spoke to the neurosurgeon when I saw him in the hallway the next day. He shook his head and frowned.

"He's not recovering the way I hoped he would," he said. "We're doing everything we can, but I just don't know at this point. His Glasgow score is low, you know that's not good. He doesn't respond to commands, he's not moving on his own, not opening his eyes; whatever happens, he probably won't be teaching at Harvard." He looked frazzled and sighed heavily. "We should have some idea where this is heading in a few days." He looked at me. "I seem to recall you know him, right?"

"Yes, but not well. He was close to a friend of mine until recently. He has no family so I've been stopping by and letting him know I'm here. Probably silly to do; I feel sorry for him, though."

"Hmmm, no family, broke up with your friend, I assume?" He raised an eyebrow at me as I nodded. "Well, keep visiting him 'til we have some idea where this is going. It doesn't sound like he has much to wake up for. I don't like to get all touchy feely, but family and friends are important."

I thanked him and returned to the OR. I didn't like being a lifeline, if that's what I was. At least for now, though, there didn't seem to be much choice. I repeated the mantra that Jeff would recover. It had been going through my head at intervals, now I started adding please at the end. I wasn't sure who I was talking to. I smiled and remembered Maddie saying years ago that Saint John of God was the patron saint of nurses, physicians, and the sick. She seemed to know a saint for every occasion and sent prayers their way routinely, so I added a request to him as well. It might not help, but it couldn't hurt.

EIGHTEEN

IAN ARRIVED THE following evening with pizza and beer in hand and we planned to binge-watch a series on Netflix. Midway through the pizza, someone knocked at the front door. When I opened it, Angel was standing on my doorstep.

"Hey," I greeted him. "Come in. You want some pizza?"

"Sure, thanks." He entered, saw Ian sitting on the couch, and stopped.

Ian rose and stuck out a hand. "Ian Patterson," he said, giving Angel the once over with a polite, but not very welcoming look on his face.

"Angel Cisneros," Angel replied, offering his hand and giving Ian a similar measure of scrutiny.

It was like watching two dogs sizing each other up, Ian wondering if Angel was some kind of threat and Angel giving him the eye like a protective older brother. I snorted in amusement, and they both turned to look at me. "Ian, this is my next door neighbor; Angel this is a friend of mine. You can both back off and be nice to each other now."

Ian had the grace to blush and Angel looked slightly chagrined. Ian returned to claim the couch as his, thus relegating Angel to an armchair on the other side of the coffee table. If the territoriality continued I could imagine them getting up and peeing on things to establish what was theirs. Shaking my head, I walked to the fridge and retrieved a beer for Angel, and offered him a plate and napkin, pushing the pizza box closer to his edge of the coffee table. I took a seat next to Ian.

"So, what's up? Just being social?" I asked.

"Uh, yeah, plus I wanted to tell you what I found out."

I really didn't want to discuss this in front of Ian but the cat was out of the bag. "What? Have they found the person?"

"No, and they're pretty much where I thought they'd be. No suspects. They've got a security tape that shows Jeff heading toward his car but the rest happened out of camera range. Other than establishing a time, it's not very helpful. There seemed to be someone who entered the periphery of the video about the same time, and he may be the perp, but there is no way to identify him. So they're still at square one, which is par for the course on things like this unless someone who saw something or knows something comes forward."

I happened to glance at Ian. His elbow was resting on the couch's arm and he was absently stroking his forehead. His brows were knit into a frown and his lips had thinned. I had enough experience with him by now to know that either he was annoyed that Angel was here or he was unhappy with what Angel was telling me. I suspected there would be words about whatever it was. Twenty minutes later, when Angel said his goodbyes and I closed the door on him, I turned toward the couch and stopped at the look I was receiving.

"What?" I asked.

He took a deep breath. "At the risk of being told to mind my own business, who the hell is this guy and why are you pumping him about a police investigation?"

"*This guy* is a lawyer in the DA's office and my next door neighbor. I wanted to know where the police were with the investigation into Jeff's assault, that's all. I asked him to see what he could find out."

"Why do you care? He got mugged. It happens."

I was put off by his callous attitude toward Jeff, and he seemed almost angry that I was curious about what had happened, which I couldn't quite figure out, but continued to explain. "I care because he's someone I know and I feel sorry for him. I also think it's a little too coincidental that Jeff's beating happened a few days after his meeting with Libby. I think it's connected. I just don't know how yet."

"Oh, for God's sake. This isn't any of your business. I thought you quit taking care of Libby."

"I did."

"Then why are you pursuing this? Did it ever occur to you that people get mugged every day and there's no conspiracy involved? It's not connected to anything; it's just bad luck." He paced in agitation. "If you go to the police to tell them your suspicions, you'll have to tell them about Libby's relationship with Jeff and the other guy as well, and they'll go talk to her and her husband. You think she was pissed that you talked to Jeff? Wait and see how she feels if *that* happens." He stopped pacing and looked at me in astonishment. "You're butting in where you don't belong and causing trouble for other people when it's none of your business. In addition, it could put you at risk. Did you think about that? Is that what you want?" His voice had risen as he spoke and his words hung in the air.

"I think you and Angel are being overly alarmist," I said.

"Oh, so he said the same thing, did he? You consult with him about this kind of stuff?"

"Sort of. What're you so upset about? Angel and I are just friends, and I don't think there's anything to worry about by my asking to be kept up to date on this." I watched him and when he didn't reply, I said, "Ian, this isn't that big of a deal. Talk to me, why are you so upset?"

"You spend every waking minute thinking about this and all your spare time at work sitting at that guy's bedside and worrying about him. Why wouldn't it upset me? I feel like I'm competing with a guy in a coma," he shouted at me. I was taken aback, stunned that he would feel that way. "And then you've got your neighbor feeding you police information while you're dreaming up conspiracy theories. It just pisses me off. Why can't you let this go?"

"Ian, I had no idea you were this upset about what I'm doing."

We stood staring at each other. He shook his head at last, walked to the coatrack, and retrieved his jacket. "I'm going home. I hope you'll stop this; it's becoming an obsession." He put his jacket on and reached to open the door. "I'll talk to you later." He left.

Hearing him drive off, I got up and walked out onto the shared porch and pounded on Angel's door. When he opened it I pushed past him into his living room and turned on him. "You have all the subtlety of a toilet seat," I shouted at him. "Why would you tell me all that in front of someone you don't know?"

"I thought you wanted to know. I didn't think it was that big a deal, and I figured you'd say something if you didn't want me to talk about it."

"Oh, right, what was I supposed to say? 'Gee, Angel, don't talk in front of people you don't know'? After you said you wanted to tell me what you found out in front of Ian, what was I supposed to do?"

He looked a little sheepish and shrugged. "Who is he anyway?" he finally asked.

"The two of you were like dogs in a turf war, posturing and eyeing each other. He asked the same thing about you. He's a guy I like, not that it's any of your business."

He held his hands up. "Just asking. You know much about him?"

"Enough to know he's a nice guy."

"How'd you meet him? It wasn't online, was it?"

I looked at him in annoyance. "What? Do I have to screen my dates with you now? You're acting like a guard dog and Ian's pissed about my looking into Jeff's assault and quizzing me about you."

"You don't need to clear anything with me, I just wondered how you met him. He seems a bit territorial and wasn't happy to see me at all."

"He was unhappy about what you told me, not you. God, men! I don't know why I have anything to do with any of you."

He looked at me with a goofy smile on his face and said, "'Cause you can't live without us?"

I turned and started for the door, then changed my mind, turned around and slapped his face. I left.

MY HAND stung and I felt like an idiot. I couldn't remember ever slapping anyone, but Angel's comment had pushed me past the limits of my patience. The evening's plans with Ian were clearly over, and I didn't want to watch TV alone. In a bout of frustration I finished the remaining slice of pizza and opened another beer. Maybe they were both right and I should just stay out of it.

Ian would be much happier if I just stopped with my worrying over Libby and Jeff and let it go. I felt up to my neck in it, though, *and* responsible. Ian had dismissed that, was actually pretty upset about it, apparently, but perhaps if I hadn't pursued the issue—meddled, I suppose could be another word—about Jeff and talked to him, Libby wouldn't have gotten in touch with him, and, if this was connected in some way, maybe Jeff wouldn't have been beaten half to death.

I sat on the couch and drank my beer…and like a search and rescue dog, went back to the trail, unable to let it go no matter the havoc it was creating in my life. I wondered whether Edward was the connection. How likely was it that Edward would go to such an extreme if he found out Libby had cheated on him when he could just divorce her? With the prenuptial agreement she'd signed, Edward would come out with his assets pretty much intact. It made no sense. It seemed unlikely that Edward would have committed the assault himself. IT guys were not a very physical group of people as a rule, but they were smart; he could have hired someone.

That took me back to the original question, why bother? Why risk it? Was Libby, or Edward's wounded pride, that important to him? I could easily see him feeling anger, betrayal, outrage, embarrassment, maybe even hurt feelings, but assaulting someone or committing murder, if Jeff died? It just seemed over the top to me. I didn't know all that much about Edward and had never really wanted to. I had no idea whether he was capable of assaulting Jeff or hiring someone to do it for him, and had no idea how to find out.

I could see where this train of thought was heading and it made me squirm. After debating for a few minutes, I poked my head out the front door and could see that Angel's living room lights were still on. There was going to be a lot of crow eaten tonight.

I knocked on his door.

Angel opened it and, seeing me, asked, "Come back for another swing?"

"I'm sorry," I blurted. "Are you okay?"

"You aren't the first woman to slap my face, Collins. I'm fine. Usually, though, I get slapped for reasons that are a lot more fun than talking out of turn," he massaged his face. "You've got a pretty decent swing on you, stung like crazy. Come on in for a minute, if you want."

I walked in and turned to him. "I shouldn't have done that; I'm really sorry. Your comment was just the icing on the cake. The last few weeks have been one frustration after another and now Ian is pissed at me for pursuing this with you."

"Are you serious about him?"

"Yes, but now he's mad about all this, so I'm not sure it matters how I feel about him."

"Men don't give up easily if we're interested, and he seems interested." He ushered me to his couch where I sat down. "Sounds like we're both worried about your involvement in this. Any chance you'll give it up and let the police handle it?" I stared at him and shook my head no. "Figured as much. You are like a dog with a bone, Collins. Was the apology all you came over for?"

I blushed. "No, but that was important. Can you find out about Edward? Do a background check or something?"

"Why?"

"Because he creeps me out and I think he might be involved with all this. He's got every reason to be: cheating trophy wife, specter of divorce, the embarrassment of having someone like Libby cheat on him and get pregnant, and the social repercussions of that. I don't know, he just seems to have a lot of reasons why it would make sense for him to have Jeff beaten up. Maybe as a warning to both Jeff and Libby to knock it off?"

"You're assuming he knows about the affair and Jeff, and that he would take it that far for payback. Literally thousands of people go through this on a daily basis and don't try to off their spouses or the person they're cheating with." He laughed. "They think about it, a lot sometimes, but they rarely follow through on it."

"I know that, and there are other people who do go off the deep end for all sorts of reasons. I'd just like to know who he is and what he's capable of."

"You make me nuts." He scrubbed his face with his hands. "Keep in mind, you don't like Edward at all and could be trying to pin this on him because of that. I know he has reason to be furious with her, but it's a stretch to think he'd have her lover assaulted, assuming he even knows about the affair. It's far more likely Jeff was mugged." He watched me and I could see him give in. "What do you want to know?"

"Anything you can find. What's he like, does he have a lot of enemies or people who think he's an ass? What happened to his first wife? How ruthless is he? I don't know...what kind of background checks do you do on people who are suspects?"

"He's not a suspect, Collins, except in your mind. I hope you know I could get in a lot of trouble for this."

"Well, if it's that risky, forget it, I'll just Google him and see what I can find."

"Oh my God, you sound like my mother: 'Well, if you won't help me I'll try to figure it out on my own, Angelito.' Do they teach women to do that?"

I laughed. "No, we just learn quickly that it works. Seriously, if it's that risky for you, forget it. I don't want you disbarred or anything."

"It's okay, I'll poke around cautiously. If I don't find anything alarming with a cursory look, then I won't proceed. If something jumps out, I'll let you know." He showed me to the door and opened it. "For God's sake don't come up with anything else, okay? I like being a lawyer."

"Thanks, Angel, I really appreciate it."

"Right," he said, closing the door after me.

I went back to my side of the duplex and locked up for the night. I tidied up and shut off lights before heading to bed. Once there I couldn't sleep and lay in bed with my brain spinning in the dark.

Giving up on sleep, I got up and found the book I'd been reading in snatches over the last week and took it back to bed. It took reading several chapters before I fell asleep with it lying on my chest. Sometime later a ping from my phone woke me. I fumbled for it on the bedside table, and saw there was a text from Ian.

<Are you awake?>

<I am now. What woke you?>

<Never went to bed. What were you doing?>

<Dozed off reading a book in bed.>

Things were silent for a bit before the phone pinged again.

<I'm sorry.>

<Me too.>

<I'm serious. I'm sorry I took off. I was really upset.>

<I know this upsets you but I feel responsible and I need to figure out whether that's legit or not. If Jeff's attack was random then I'm not at fault. If it's connected to my conversation with him and his meeting with Libby then I am. I owe it to Jeff and myself I guess to try to find out.>

There was no reply for several minutes. More minutes went by, and I began to think he was gone and wouldn't be coming back.

He replied at last. <Sleep well; I'll be in touch.>

<OK> I replied, even though it wasn't.

NINETEEN

TALKING TO CHIP the following day at work was depressing. There had been no improvement in Jeff's condition, and the docs were debating about whether it was from brain contusions, diffuse axonal injury, or secondary injury to the brain, most of which meant all they could do was provide life support, manage his symptoms, and wait to see what happened, but it didn't look good.

According to what I knew, the first twenty-four hours were a crucial indicator of outcome for coma patients with a traumatic brain injury and we were long past that. Low Glasgow coma scores usually meant a poor outcome, a medical euphemism for death, or severe disability if the patient woke up.

I came on breaks when I could and sat with Jeff for short periods of time, hoping to see his eyes open or some movement of an arm or leg, but saw nothing. I sat with him after my shift was over and watched his face, with its gradually resolving bruises and swelling, and wondered what, if anything, was going on inside.

I had run out of things to talk about and finally leaned over close to his ear, and said, "Jeff, you've been through a lot and I know you're probably tired of all this. It's okay if you don't want to stay here. I get it, and it's okay to let go if that's what you want."

No response at all.

I decided as I made my way to the door of the unit that I had to let go as well. Ian was upset about my persistent visits to Jeff and my worries about him, and I knew he didn't want me involved in the investigation of Jeff's assault. He was clearly frustrated and feeling like he was in competition for my attention. No doubt he was heartily tired of hearing about it. I would probably feel the same way if the tables were turned. Perhaps I would tell Angel to just forget my request. If the police had found nothing, it was pretty presumptuous for me to assume I would come up with anything.

Chip stopped me on the way out to let me know that a family friend had been located who had provided the name of Jeff's attorney who was his power of attorney and the executor of his will. Libby hadn't been back. A couple of the people he'd worked with had visited, once, and not returned.

I figured the docs would attempt to wean him off the vent and see what happened. It was anyone's guess. If taking him off the vent was successful, there was a small possibility he would wake up, eventually, and almost certainly with disabilities. He could also die, or he could go on in this twilight state indefinitely. I hoped more than anything that he would die if he couldn't recover. Otherwise, it was painful to think about. I asked Chip to let me know if anything changed drastically and went home.

I ARRIVED home in a low mood. I stretched out on the couch and let my mind drift. I ought to let Libby know about Jeff, I supposed. I wasn't sure she'd care, but I'd told her I would let her know if he passed. It seemed like the current state of affairs warranted her notification. Perhaps she'd want to say goodbye. After mulling that over for a bit, I got up and drove over to her house and rang the bell. Cora answered, cold as ever, and I asked to speak with Libby. She told me Mrs. Matheisen was in her room, could I show myself up? I could and knocked on the bedroom door when I arrived. I heard a muted "Come in" and opened the door.

Libby was propped in bed, looking a little less well than when I'd last seen her. She seemed surprised at my appearance, so I just rushed ahead.

"Jeff's not doing well. It's entirely possible he's not going to make it. I thought you might want to know, maybe to say goodbye, provide both of you some closure, if that's possible."

"What's happened?"

"Nothing, unfortunately. He hasn't woken up and he's probably not going to. If he's lucky he'll die and if not, he'll be like you saw him the other day for however long it takes for his body to shut down."

She stared at me and her mouth opened and closed as if she were trying to say something and couldn't find the words.

"That's all I came for. It's up to you if you go see him. I don't want to be involved; I just thought you should know. I'll see myself out."

"Annie?"

I turned back toward her and was surprised to see tears on her cheeks. My first instinct was to revise all the horrible things I'd thought about her and then my rational mind took over and thought how convenient the tears were. "What?" I asked.

She sighed, raising her hands palms up as if in supplication, and said, "I'm sorry. I'm sorry I'm not who you thought I was, and I'm sorry I couldn't be who Jeff wanted." She laughed bitterly, swiping at the tears on her face. "I'm not even who Edward thinks I am. I'm not sure I know who I am anymore." She stared down at the coverlet. "I appreciate you letting me know. Take care of yourself, Annie."

That hit me unexpectedly and my voice caught as I said, "You, too." I left.

WHEN I got home I found Ian sitting on the front porch steps, tossing pebbles from the walkway out into the street. I got out of the car and closed the door, looking over the top at him. "Keep that up and I'll have to charge you for gravel replacement."

He laughed and pitched the last of his rocks. "Hey," he said.

I sat down next to him on the porch.

We sat there without speaking for a time and then I asked, "Still pissed at me?"

"Not as much, just some." He sat with his long hands dangling over his knees, looking down at his feet.

He didn't sound as if he were happy about being on my front porch, which made me wonder why he'd come. I was tired of trying to figure people out. I felt like I was dealing with a multiple personality trying to take care of Libby. Edward was just a cypher; he had been more visible to me than ever before, but that coldness prevented me knowing him any better than I ever had. And Ian? Well, I hoped he was just feeling annoyed and unattended to. Personally, I was just tired.

At last he looked at me. "What're we going to do about this?"

I leaned against the porch railing and looked at him. "It's been a bitch of a day, Ian. Jeff is probably dying and I just left Libby with the happy news."

His eyes narrowed. "That's what I'm talking about. I ask what are we going to do about this, and the first thing I hear is a status report on Jeff and Libby. You wonder why it pisses me off." He returned to staring at his feet.

"Well, it's part and parcel of my shitty day and it affects how I feel about 'doing something about this.' All I know is right now I don't have any plans to do anything about anything; I'm just too tired." I watched him as he studied his feet. "What're your plans? Going to stay if I promise not to involve myself any further with Jeff or Libby or are you bailing now?" I was surprised to hear the bitterness in my voice. I hadn't expected that.

The remark seemed to have hit a nerve. "Is that what you want?" he asked and I could see the flare of anger in his eyes.

"No," I said quietly. I reached out and touched his arm, "Ian, I like you…a lot…and I'm sorry if you feel like you're competing for my attentions. You can't ask me to stop what I'm doing; I need to find out what happened to Jeff. But that doesn't mean you're superfluous; you're not competing with Jeff or Angel."

"But that's how I feel." He tilted his head and looked at me. "I'm sick of hearing about Jeff and Libby, and honestly I'd like to not have to worry about whether I'm in competition with your next door neighbor. At the very least, couldn't you just stop pursuing this Jeff thing? I worry about what you're getting into."

"No, I can't just stop pursuing this. And I don't know how to reassure you about Angel. You need to quit worrying about that. We've never been more than friends."

Dusk was falling and the air had chilled. The end of September and October are lovely months in Denver, bright clear skies, falling leaves, and increasingly cool days toward the end of October. It was the first week of October, though, and nights were growing considerably colder. As happened most years, the kids would be Trick-or-Treating in their flimsy costumes covered by heavy winter coats, trudging around in the snow come Halloween. At the moment, it was just cold and getting darker.

"Have you had dinner?" I asked. He shook his head. "Well, let's go in before we freeze and I'll see what I can come up with. Maybe we'll both feel better with some food in us." I held a hand out to him and as he took hold I leaned away from him balancing against his weight as he pulled himself up.

Dinner was a quiet affair that felt strained by the silence between us. Neither of us seemed to know how to resolve it, so we ate, commenting periodically on inconsequential things and then lapsing into silence. He declined to stay over and left shortly after dinner. I struggled with wanting to promise him that I would stop involving myself and resisted it. It would not bode well for us if the only way he would stay was for me to cave on this. I had caved on things in other relationships and it had never helped. Once that expectation took hold, it was a slippery slope. But I kept asking myself if what I was pursuing was worth ending the relationship over. *Fatal flaws, indeed,* I thought.

"Arrgh!" I yelled and pounded the back of the door as I closed it. If I didn't enjoy sex, there really would be no point in associating with men at all.

TWENTY

THE NEXT MORNING, I drove by the gallery where Jeff had worked. I parked across the street and watched it for a while, noting who arrived and left, then drove down the alley and looked at the parking lot. It was a wonder anyone had found him. The parking lot was blocked from street view by the building itself and the one across the alley. Without the person who found him needing to access his car, Jeff would not have been found until morning and would probably have died. That brought me up short. Perhaps that had been the intent—murder, not just assault.

Jeff had said the art world grapevine was notorious. I wondered how much the participants knew about Jeff and Libby and whether they knew anything about Edward. Having watched the traffic in and out of the gallery for a bit, it was clear that the patrons were not short of money, if their clothes were evidence. Most of the women wore outfits that would have cost me two weeks' pay. I snorted, more like a month's pay. The few men I saw were much less flamboyant, but it was clear they were expensively dressed.

It surprised me to discover that I was actually contemplating going in and asking around. If I did, I would have to play the part or I would get nowhere. That presented a problem: aside from the whole "Be careful, stop intruding" issues Ian and Angel had, I had no clothes like the women I'd seen and had no idea how or where to get them. I put the car in gear and drove away. I found a small café and went in for a late breakfast.

I let my mind wander while I ate, turning over all the reasons not to pursue this and all the reasons why it might not be a bad idea. During this convoluted process I remembered that a friend's daughter worked at a designer outlet store and was pretty good at dressing her mother, when she could convince her to wear expensive clothes. Back in my car I called the friend, and she arranged for me to meet her daughter later that morning at the store where she worked.

On arrival at the store I felt as intimidated as I always did at upscale stores or restaurants. Like Julia Roberts in *Pretty Woman*, the saleswomen were never nice to me and I could feel their condescension. My friend's daughter spotted me before I could make a break for it and took over the transformation.

"So what're you looking for? Mom said you needed an outfit," she asked, sizing me up.

"Not sure. I need to pass for someone with money, but I can't afford these prices. I don't even know what to look for."

"Well, casual or more formal?"

"Umm, casual, I guess. It's an art gallery."

"Shopping or a gallery party?" she asked. She was tiny and very pretty and dressed to the nines. How did someone who was only twenty become that self-assured?

"Shopping, I guess? It's a fishing expedition, actually. I want to find out some stuff about a dealer there."

"Well, first off, it'd be better if you didn't sound so hesitant. Just remember you're convinced you're the most important person on Earth and everything is about you. If you can do that, with a little help in the clothes department, you should fit right in."

I laughed. "It's all in the attitude, I guess."

"You better believe it," she said and dragged me over to several racks of clothes. "You know women like that have a lot of money, but they're just as insecure as we are; more so, sometimes. They're just better at bluffing their way along." She pulled out several pairs of pants and an armful of tops from the racks and escorted me to a dressing room. "Okay," she said. "Try these tops with each pair of pants and see which combination you like best. I'll go find you some jewelry, a pair of shoes, and a bag."

"I don't think I can afford this, at least not all the accessories. Maybe we could limit it to just a top and pants?"

"You forget, this is an outlet store—the same clothes, just less expensive—and I get an employee discount, so just pretend you have all the money in the world. We'll sort out the details later."

Maybe this is how Marie Antoinette lost her head, I thought, *pretending she had nothing to worry about and listening to her dressmaker.* The outfits were really pretty though and when put together with the accessories were amazing. I looked at myself in the mirror and loved them all; Marie had nothing on me. I hoped the outcome of my scheme worked out better than hers had.

My personal shopper appeared at the dressing room door and poked her head in. "So which one is it going to be?"

"I like them all. Why don't you pick based on what you think looks best on me? I kind of have stars in my eyes right now."

"I'd go with this one." She pulled out the navy slacks with a gold pattern running through them, a caramel-colored jacket and a navy blouse; combined with the shoes and a purse it was perfect. She had found a couple of large ropy necklaces with stones in them and a pair of earrings that I would never have chosen, but which looked perfect. I made it out of the store for slightly under $500.00. It left me breathless, but it would have been far worse without her employee discount. I thanked her and slid a hefty tip into her hand. "Maybe you can teach me how to dress one of these days?"

She laughed. "That's what my mom says but she reverts to jeans overnight. Happy to help, though, if you're serious."

AT HOME, I showered, did my hair, and dressed in the new outfit. Generally being someone who went to work without makeup, I drove to a shopping mall near me and had one of the makeup saleswomen fix me up, and then, to feel less guilty, bought some of the makeup that I thought I could remember how to use. I looked at the time and drove to the government building where Angel's office was. I nearly lost my nerve when riding the elevator to the DA's office, but the doors opened and I was faced with either letting them close and giving up on this idea or continuing to bluff my way through. I walked up to the receptionist's desk and asked for Angel. She put in a call and indicated I could take a seat and wait.

Ten minutes later Angel walked out, talking to someone who headed off in another direction as Angel came toward me. "Angelo Cisneros," he said, holding out a hand. "How can I—Annie?" His mouth had fallen open and he looked a bit dumbstruck.

"Does it look that bad?"

"No. What have you done to yourself? You look incredibly hot."

"Thanks, I think. I was going for more of an independently wealthy look. Is there someplace we can talk?"

He led me down the hall to a small office with an overburdened desk and closed the door. "Somebody lifted my extra chair; I haven't seen it in a week or so." He pulled a chair from behind his desk and offered it to me as he leaned against the desk. "So what brings you here dressed to kill?"

"I need a favor. Can I borrow your car?" Angel drove a Lexus and I didn't think I could carry off the charade driving my beat-up Ford Fiesta.

"My car," he repeated. "Why do you want to borrow my car?"

"I need a nice car for a few hours. I'll have it back before you need to leave."

"What're you up to?"

"You'll have a fit if I tell you."

"I'm gonna have a fit if you don't. Spill." He folded his arms across his chest and waited. After explaining what I had in mind, he covered his eyes with his hand and sighed. "You're going to do this no matter what I say, correct?"

"Correct."

He said something unintelligible in Spanish that I didn't think I wanted translated and then looked at his watch. "Come on, I'll go with you. Maybe I can keep you from getting in any real trouble."

"Wait, you don't need to come. I just want to use your car."

He looked at me in exasperation. "You're going, so I'm going, or you don't get the car."

"Fine."

∽

TWENTY MINUTES later we pulled up in front of the gallery. Angel got out, slipped into his suit jacket, shot his cuffs, and closed the door. He came around to the passenger door and opened it for me. "We make a pretty good-looking couple, Collins. If you get tired of your new boy toy, just let me know."

"Very funny. How am I going to explain you?"

"You're my wife and we're here to find a Libby Crowder painting, just roll with it."

I rolled my eyes as he took my arm under his and we made our way to the gallery door.

A tiny bell rang as we entered. It was cool and quiet in the gallery. Huge expanses of wall were covered in paintings and the gallery seemed to favor only a few artists. The carpeting was soft and helped keep things quiet. There didn't seem to be anyone around as Angel and I began to make our way around, looking at what was on the walls.

"May I help you?" She had materialized seemingly from nowhere, and, were it not for Angel's arm around my waist, I probably would have squeaked in surprise.

"Yes," he said smoothly. "My wife and I are looking to purchase something by Libby Crowder. I understand that your gallery carries her work."

It felt strange to hear her maiden name, but that's what she used professionally.

"Why, yes, we do, exclusively." You could almost see the dollar signs appear in her eyes. "My name is Shelby. Which one did you have in mind?"

"I don't know, what do you think, baby? Shall we just look at whatever is here or did you have something in mind?" Angel was clearly enjoying himself; me not so much.

"Why don't you show us what you have?" I suggested, having no idea what else to say.

She led us into a separate room that was filled with Libby's work. Varying sizes, varying subjects, all amazing. Once in the room she followed us around, providing running commentary on the paintings.

Angel began acting bored, or at least I thought it was an act, and finally said, "I'm going to leave this up to my wife; I have to run an errand. Baby, why don't you look around and see if you find anything you want. I'll be back in half an hour and we can decide then." He pulled me to him, planted a kiss, and nuzzled my neck, taking the opportunity to whisper, "It's all yours, Miss Marple."

He had the nerve to pat me on the bum as he pulled away and walked out of the gallery. I planned to kill him when I had a chance.

"My, what a handsome man." The woman sighed, watching him walk out the door. Then remembering where she was, she said, "Anything appeal to you?"

"All of it, really, but my husband won't be happy if I tell him I want to buy them all."

"Well, point out several you like and we can take them into the viewing room. The light's better and you can see them by themselves without the distraction of the other paintings."

I pointed to a couple that I would have been ecstatic to own, and while I waited she took each one into another room and propped them on easels.

"They really are lovely," I said. "I wonder if Jeff Davies is around? He gave me his card a few weeks ago and told me to come in and he would show me her work. I feel a bit disloyal not working with him."

"I'm so sorry, Mr. Davies was in an accident a few days ago and isn't working at the moment." She hesitated, and I raised my eyebrow a tad. "It was really quite shocking; he was assaulted in the parking lot around the corner."

Apparently, I was now hooked into the art world's grapevine. "My goodness, I had no idea, what happened?"

"No one knows, really. I think it was a mugging; there are so many homeless people on the streets these days, you never know what might happen. It was after the gallery closed for the night and he had worked late, so no one really knows."

"Were there any security cameras?"

"No, not once you leave the area immediately around the building. I guess there was one pointed on the parking lot, but I don't know if there was anything helpful on it."

"These paintings are all several years old. Is there anything newer?"

"No, not at the moment. Ms. Crowder usually only produces two to three canvases a year, and her last was a year ago."

"Really, why?"

"Well, these things take time to create and then an artist's life can interfere with the process. I gather she had a miscarriage and isn't well. I don't know how Jeff's assault will affect her. They were friends and he'd handled her sales for years."

"Just friends?"

"There were rumors, but there are always rumors when people work closely together. It's a shame with Ms. Crowder not working and now Jeff out indefinitely, there won't be any new stuff for a while."

"Good heavens, will this drive up the prices on her work?"

"Well, you know supply and demand; if she doesn't resume painting, then the ones that are available will become harder to lay hands on. It would be a very good investment, for you and your husband."

"That's true, it would be." I looked at the paintings up close and then wandered around viewing them from different angles. I had no idea what I was doing, but it apparently didn't strike Shelby as odd. "I seem to recall she's married, right?"

"Yes, to Edward Matheisen."

"Is he an artist, too?"

She laughed. "Well, not with anything but money and computers, but he's pretty good with those."

"Seems like an odd couple, not much in common."

"Oh, it's a bit of an unusual pairing. She's very pretty, though, and very much in demand in the art world; not many men find that off-putting. His first wife was quite the looker, too, and came from money. They say that's how he financed his initial software company."

"Really? I had no idea he was married before. Did they divorce?"

"No, he was a widower when he married Ms. Crowder."

"What was her name, do you know?"

"Beth Stanton, originally. They met and married in LA, and he moved back here after her death."

It amazed me how much information Shelby had to offer and did offer. "What happened to her?"

"She was in a car accident and died of her injuries. I heard that he was driving, and there were some rumors about alcohol contributing to the accident. He was injured, but she died at the scene. I guess her sister was convinced he had caused the accident intentionally. You know how families can be. I guess his wife was thinking about a divorce, and, from what I heard, she had been having an affair. But nothing ever came of the sister's accusations."

Interesting, I thought. I heard the tinkle that announced someone entering the front door and turned my attention back to the paintings. Angel walked back to where we were. "How's it going, babe? Find anything that'd make you happy?" he asked, sliding his arm around my waist and giving it a squeeze.

"Oh, honey, I just can't decide," I cooed. "Shelby here has been so helpful; it's between these two, but I need to think about this for a bit."

He sighed loudly, as if severely put upon. "Okay, but you're going to have to come on your own next time, I have work to do." He let go of me and held his hand out to the salesperson, and taking her hand in his said, "Thank you so much. Have you got a card so my wife can call you when she decides?" The woman handed him a card from her pants pocket and watched in dismay as we left.

We walked to the car and got in. "Pouring it on a bit thick, don't you think?" I commented as he pulled out into traffic. "And why'd you leave?"

He grinned. "*Chica*, it can never be too thick. Besides, I figured Shelby would spill the dirt faster if I wasn't there. What'd you find out?"

"I got Edward's first wife's name and that she funded his software ventures and died in a car accident, which her sister thought he was responsible for. The rumor was the first wife wanted a divorce and had been having an affair, so it's sort of similar to the situation Libby is in, if it's true. Sounds like there were rumors about Jeff and Libby, but I couldn't get anything more than that out of her."

"Still, not bad for a first effort at detective work. You happy now?"

"Not really. I don't know if what I found out is anything helpful or why I thought it would be; it's just rumor and innuendo. Obviously, the police didn't feel he was to blame for the first wife's accident, I mean it wasn't intentional." I watched out the window as we moved through traffic toward Angel's office. "I would really appreciate it if you wouldn't say anything to Ian about this."

"He's not on my speed dial, Collins. I won't say anything." He looked at me and was silent for a bit. "I think we'd both prefer it if you'd stay out of this."

"Neither of you seem to get how upsetting all this has been or why I want to know what happened." I tucked a stray lock of hair behind my ear. "It would help if you didn't say anything."

"The only thing not telling him is going to do is to piss him off royally when he finally hears what you've been up to. There's no point in concealing information 'cause somebody always finds out, at the worst possible time, usually, but Ian won't hear about it from me." He let it drop and we remained silent until we reached his office building. "Where's your car?"

"Second floor, near the elevators."

When we found it, I opened the passenger door just as my phone rang. I looked at him and he indicated I should go ahead and answer. "Hello?"

"Annie? This is Chip."

I squeezed my eyes shut and did not want to have this conversation. "What's happened?" I asked, knowing what the answer would be.

"We took him off the ventilator. He lasted about half an hour and stopped breathing. His lawyer had provided a DNR, so we didn't hook him back up. He's gone. I'm so sorry."

I sat silently holding the phone. I hadn't really known him, but I had made some connection and now he was gone.

"Annie? Are you there?"

"Yes, thanks for letting me know, Chip. I can't talk right now, but thanks." I ended the call and just sat there with the car door open and the phone in my hand.

"Annie, you okay?" Angel asked, reaching out and putting a hand on my shoulder.

I shook my head no and watched as tears fell on my hand. Angel reached over and drew me to him, holding me as I cried. "What's happened? What can I do?"

"Nothing, Jeff's dead," I managed to say between sobs.

He held me, patting me on the back and sat with me until the worst was over. He retrieved his phone from his jacket and hit the green button when he found the number he was looking for. "Hey, Patty, it's Angel. I got a client who's a bit upset so I'm gonna drive her home. I'll be back in about an hour. Any calls, take a number and tell them I'll get back to them. If it's an emergency, you know how to reach me."

He disconnected and turned to me. "Give me your keys; I'll drive you home."

"That's not necessary, I'm fine," I said between hiccups.

"You're not fine, just close the door and quit arguing with me. I'll bring your car back later."

I shut the door and rebuckled my seat belt and handed him my keys. I sat back and rested my head against the headrest and closed my eyes. "Fine," I said. It occurred to me that I had been saying that a lot lately.

HE OPENED the door and let me into the house, walking in behind me. "You want me to call anybody? Ian maybe? Maddie?"

"No, I'll be fine. Thanks, Angel."

He gave me quick kiss on the cheek. "I'll bring your car over after work. It may not be 'til six or seven though, that all right?"

"Yes."

"Okay, you need anything, you let me know, promise?"

"Sure."

He looked worried, started to say something, and then left, closing the door behind him. I stood in the living room and had no idea what to do. It occurred to me after a few minutes that I probably should let Libby know. I'd told her I would, but she was the last person I wanted to talk to. Didn't seem to be a way out of it, so I punched in her cell number and waited.

When Libby finally answered, I was not kind. "Jeff's dead. I said I would let you know. They took him off the ventilator and he didn't make it." There was a long silence from her end. "Do you even care?" I shouted into the phone. "Are you so self-involved that this is just a problem solved for you?"

"No, I…I just don't know what to say. God, I never thought it would turn out like this. I never wished him ill, you have to believe me, Annie."

"I don't have to believe anything you say." I hung up and threw the phone on the couch.

WHEN ANGEL showed up later with my car, he found me sitting on the couch fairly well stewed in Scotch. I had managed to work my way through three, or was it four, glasses. I couldn't remember.

"I think you've had enough, *chica*."

That annoyed me. If I wanted to drink myself under the table it was my choice. But I really didn't want an audience for it; it was embarrassing.

"God," I blubbered. "I just keep making a mess of things, don't I?"

"It's okay, it's one of your many charms." He reached down and picked up my phone from the coffee table. "What's your unlock code?"

"Who are you calling?"

"Ian. I can't check on you tonight; seems like someone should keep an eye on you."

"No! I'm fine. I don't need a damn babysitter and I don't want him here." I knew Ian wouldn't want to hear about Jeff and having Angel call him would just further strain things between us. I'd just go to bed and sleep it off. I lurched up off the couch, "Oh, God," I moaned, clamped a hand over my mouth, and raced to the bathroom.

Angel wisely stayed in the living room until I managed to make it to the bed. I heard him come to the doorway. I lay with my eyes closed to keep the room from spinning and felt an overwhelming desire to sleep for a long time. "Ugh, I smell like vomit," I said sleepily. "Please just let me sleep and don't call Ian or anyone else. I'll be fine."

"I won't. Go to sleep, Annie."

TWENTY-ONE

CHIP AND I went out for dinner on Sunday evening so he could bring me up to date. Jeff's body had been taken to the medical examiner's office. Since it was now a murder rather than an assault, an autopsy was needed.

"I'm not sure what they'll find that the docs haven't already documented but I guess it's standard policy in this kind of situation," Chip said.

"Poor Jeff. Does anyone know whether there will be a funeral or some kind of memorial service?"

"I doubt anything will be set up until they release his body." Chip sighed.

"I just hope the police can figure out what happened."

"I'm not sure whether they'll be able to identify who assaulted him; that's not always possible."

"True. I don't think they have enough information to do that, either. I know I have a lot of questions that need answers."

"I'm sorry, Annie. I wish Jeff's situation had turned out differently."

"Well, you know what they say, life's a bitch and then you die. Some days are more of a bitch than others."

Angel popped in later to let me know what he'd discovered about Edward. There wasn't much. He'd gotten his start from funding supplied by his first wife, which I knew thanks to Shelby, but had managed quite nicely from there. There didn't seem to be any scandals attached to his first marriage other than the accusations made by his wife's sister, which were never deemed legitimate.

He didn't appear to have any suspicious debts or income, the insurance policies he and Libby had were not out of the ordinary, and other than that, no one had much to say about him except that he was good at what he did for a living. He wasn't very well liked, apparently, and had lots of former employees and associates who were happy to badmouth him, including his sister-in-law, but that didn't make him a criminal.

"I think this is pointless," I said. "I didn't get anything of any real value from the gallery saleswoman, and you haven't found anything earth-shattering, either."

"No, I haven't."

"You're probably right, I'm letting my personal feelings about him interfere. And Ian's probably right, as well, that this was just a random mugging."

Angel hesitated for a minute, then said, "Apparently, his first wife's sister lives in Denver. I suppose if you're going to pursue this, you could see if she'll talk to you. Her name's Judith Stanton Moore. I have her address and phone number if you want it."

"Why are you being so helpful? I thought you didn't want me nosing around. Why the one-eighty?"

"I don't like it, but trying to talk you out of doing it hasn't worked. I figure if I give you the little I found out, you'll see it's not worth the time and energy and drop it." He laughed. "That's probably wishful thinking. Just promise me if you talk to this woman, don't push it, and don't share your suspicions about Edward. You can never tell where someone's loyalties lie, regardless what they tell you."

He leaned forward from his place on the couch and rested his forearms on his thighs, looking down at the car keys in his hands. "Honestly, I wish you'd drop it and try to accept that whether this was an accident or not, it's not likely to be solved, especially by you."

I sighed. "I'm not sure if there's any point in pursuing it. Maybe it's not Edward; maybe whoever it is will never be identified. Ian thinks I'm paranoid and keeps pointing out that people get mugged all the time and it isn't a conspiracy."

"He's right, but just because you're paranoid doesn't mean you're wrong. At least not all the time." He laughed.

"Tell him that. Anyway, I appreciate what you've done." I smiled; he was such a doll once he dropped the playboy persona. "Thanks for looking out for me Friday night. I guess God takes care of idiots by giving them friends."

"Well, God is a busy person, according to my mother. She always warned me, *'Don't push your luck or He'll forget about you and then where will you be, Angelito?'* So remember that, okay?"

I laughed, he always repeated his mother's words with a Spanish accent in falsetto. "Your mama would tan your hide if she could hear you."

"She would, but I'm not dumb enough to do that in front of her. Keep me posted, Collins, okay?" He stood up and collected his coat.

There was a knock on the door, and when I opened it, Ian stood there with a bottle of wine and what smelled like dinner.

"I was in the neighborhood and thought I'd see if you wanted to eat." He walked in and then saw Angel standing by the couch and stopped. "Am I interrupting anything?"

"No, come on in," I said.

Angel said, "I was just leaving; Annie and I were talking about Jeff Davies. He passed yesterday and I wanted to see how she was doing."

It was annoying to hear Angel explaining his presence so carefully, but then I saw the look on Ian's face and realized he wasn't happy to find Angel here and Angel didn't look happy to see Ian. Men, it was always a pissing contest. I wondered if these two would ever be friends.

Angel left and Ian and I had dinner, during which he not so subtly fished for information about Angel.

"He seems very fond of you," he said at last.

"He is fond of me, I'm fond of him, too, but that's as far as it goes. We keep an eye out for each other, that's all." I had no intention of mentioning the ongoing attraction between us. We hadn't acted on it and weren't going to.

"I think he's more than fond of you, and he seems to be ever-present. I wish you'd called me and let me know about Jeff; I could have come and kept you company."

"No point in burdening you with it. There was nothing anyone could do. My solution was to drink too much and then go to bed." I smiled at him. "You don't need to worry about Angel. He likes to play the field. That's a field I don't want to play in; I don't like being one of many."

"That's nice to hear," he said.

I had my doubts that the reassurance was going to put the Angel issue to bed. It was something Ian was going to have to figure out for himself. There wasn't much more I could say.

BY TUESDAY there was no word in the obits about a service for Jeff and I had no one to ask, so I called the gallery in desperation to see if his co-workers knew anything. Shelby, to whom I did not introduce myself, said that it had been planned for Wednesday but had been delayed because of the autopsy. She told me it would be Saturday at 1:00 PM, and I thanked her and hung up. I asked Ian if he would go to the memorial service with me and he reluctantly agreed.

I called Maddie and told her about Jeff. "I'm so sorry to hear that he passed. Boy, Libby is not a very lucky person, is she?"

"I'm not sure it has anything to do with luck or the lack of it. She's made a number of bad choices and they're coming home to roost."

"Still, heavy consequence for a bad choice. I'll try to come to the service. I've got a couple of moms who are ready to pop so I can't promise. I'll call if I can't make it."

"No need to make yourself crazy; you didn't know him. But maybe we could spend some time together after the weekend."

We made plans for lunch for the next week. In the meantime, I'd taken the rest of the week off. I didn't want to deal with ill or injured people, not yet, at any rate. I looked at the piece of paper with Edward's former sister-in-law's information on it and wondered whether there was any point in trying to talk to her. I Googled her and didn't find much, then checked Facebook and the *Denver Post*.

All concerns about privacy aside, the Internet is a vast source of information about people. Judith had been educated well, she'd married well, divorced well, and was currently between husbands. She had no real job, as far as I could tell, but was a member of the Junior League and a few charities around town and seemed to live a full social life.

One of the charities she was a board member of was having a wine tasting on Friday to raise funds for the Children's Hospital. I checked the website; there were still a few tickets left. I purchased one and decided I could probably get some more mileage out of the new outfit by going and perhaps I'd find a way to talk to her.

I debated about asking Angel to go with me but decided against it. He was not very low-key where women were concerned, and I didn't want to attract undue notice. In the meantime, I decided not to say anything about it to Ian or Angel; there was no point in adding fuel to the fire.

Ian called and asked me over for Friday night, but I lied and told him Maddie and I were going out to dinner, so he suggested a movie on Saturday as a way to relieve the post-memorial lows. He had been somewhat distant after arriving to find Angel and me talking, and there was still an undercurrent of strain over my insistence on pursuing answers to Jeff's assault. We had not made love since that night and it seemed to me he was holding back, as if further intimacy with me was somehow a risk he wasn't sure he wanted to take. I wondered fleetingly if his aloofness wasn't an attempt to manipulate me into giving up my inquiries about Jeff, and then dismissed it.

I would pursue this attempt to talk to Judith, and if nothing came of it, I was through. I would talk to the police and tell them what I did know, assuming I could do so and they wouldn't tell Edward who'd given them the information, but the rest was up to them. Sometimes as much as you want them, answers are not available.

FRIDAY EVENING found me at the Denver Country Club. I took a taxi to avoid using my car, and was helped out of it by a uniformed valet and instructed where to go. I wandered around in the room where the event was being held, looking at the silent auction items and put a low bid on a few, hoping to look like I belonged. There was a buffet table of food and a table of different wines to sample.

I continued my progress around the room, excusing myself to get around people and smiling until I felt as if my face would fall off. The food and the wine, which I was nursing along, were really very nice. People talked in clusters, obviously familiar with each other, the subject being either what a great job the hospital did or relating personal experiences there. I accidentally bumped into a woman and was apologizing as she turned toward me and I froze: It was Shelby from the gallery.

"Oh, my goodness, it is you! Mrs. Cisneros, right?"

I nodded dumbly, trying desperately to think of a way out of this.

"Wow," she said, giving me the once over, "you must really like that outfit." I nodded and gave her a frosty smile, but she seemed unconcerned. "Is your husband here?" she asked, scanning the crowd.

Angel attracted women like moths to a flame.

"No, charity functions aren't his cup of tea."

"Oh, that's too bad. So did you decide on a painting?"

"No, my husband and I are on opposite ends about which one to get and he refuses to buy both, such a miser," I pouted.

"Well, you know, we could let you take them home overnight and see which one looks best in your home, if that would help." I felt sorry for her; she was so eager and I was such a dead end, she just didn't know it.

"I'll mention it to him and let you know," I said.

"Well, here's my card again, my cell is on it, so call anytime."

As she said that and handed me her card, a woman walked up to us, and smiled. "Shelby, you agreed, no business deals or sales pressure tonight."

"I know, Judith, I'm sorry. I just happened to run into Mrs. Cisneros. She and her husband came into the gallery to look at Libby Crowder pieces, and I wanted to touch base with her about that. I promise no more business." She grinned sheepishly and wandered off toward the buffet table.

The woman turned to me and extended a hand. "Judith Moore. I'm the event organizer."

"Nice to meet you. Anne Cisneros." *Sometimes the stars align*, I thought; now how to bring this around to Edward? "So, no talking business, eh? I thought this would be quite the schmoozing opportunity."

"Well, it often deteriorates into that, but we're hoping to keep folks, especially those with deep pockets, focused on the charity and not their latest business deals. It's not easy. Are you enjoying yourself?"

"Yes, the food and wine are excellent, and I placed a couple of bids here and there."

"That's great." She rotated her wine glass between her thumb and fingers, looking around the room, and then asked, "So you're interested in Libby Matheisen's work?"

"Yes, it's amazing. Do you know her?"

"Not personally. I know her husband."

"Edward? Do you work with him?"

She laughed ruefully. "God no, computers and I do not understand each other. No, he was my brother-in-law at one time."

"Divorce?"

She looked uncomfortable. "No, my sister died."

"Oh, I'm so sorry."

"Well, it was some time ago, so it's not as fresh as it was. Still painful, though."

"I can imagine. I just lost a friend to an accident."

"It never seems to end does it? What happened to your friend?"

"He was assaulted about a week ago and died of his injuries. You may have heard about it, Jeff Davies, he was Libby's agent."

"Yes, I had heard about it. Do they know what happened?"

"No, not so far."

"That's a shame. The police don't seem to have much luck solving some crimes." She looked around the room and smiled as a waiter brought around fresh glasses of wine and replaced our empty glasses. "It's funny what you hear about people. Society is never without its gossip."

"Really, what have you heard?"

"Lots of rumors about him and Libby, for a start. That they were having an affair and then broke up, and then I heard she was pregnant and miscarried." She continued in an amused voice: "I heard that it might have been Jeff's, couldn't have been Edward's. I wonder how he felt about that?"

"Why couldn't it have been his?" I asked, my heart speeding up.

"Well, to be fair, he didn't know it when he married my sister, but when she couldn't get pregnant, they found out he was sterile. It was one of the reasons she was filing for divorce."

"Wow, that makes for a pretty unpleasant situation if it's true."

"Yes, it does. Libby's a talented artist. I never understood what she saw in him or what my sister saw, for that matter."

"No accounting for taste, is there?" I didn't know how to put it, then just blundered on. "I don't know him personally. I wonder how he took the news of the pregnancy?"

"Edward is like a computer; he only works if you do things right. He doesn't take things that upset his life well, and I suspect this was quite an upset. I know he was quite upset when my sister filed for divorce. Makes me glad I'm not Libby; she should be very careful."

She seemed to be remembering something, and I wondered if it was what had happened to her sister. Then she suddenly became aware what she was talking about and that she was talking to a stranger.

She turned to me, blushing. "I am so sorry to air dirty linen like this. Please just chalk it up to my being overworked with this event. I hope you enjoy your evening." And she was off to visit with other groups.

IN THE taxi home, I pondered the bombshell Judith Moore had dropped and wondered what to do with the information. It certainly gave Edward a motive for the attack on Jeff, but it wasn't proof of anything except that he hadn't been honest with Libby. He knew the baby wasn't his, assuming Judith was right about the sterility. It was one thing to deal with a cheating spouse, quite another to deal with one who was pregnant and passing the baby off as yours. If he'd go so far as to have Jeff assaulted, assuming that's what he'd done, what would he do to Libby?

His behavior toward her was odd. Why would you be solicitous and concerned over a wife who had cheated on you, gotten herself pregnant, and tried to pass the baby off as yours? Most men would have shown her the door and filed for divorce, and he could do that with few consequences because of the prenuptial agreement.

So why was he allowing this little charade to continue? I found it hard to believe that he cared so much for her that he couldn't bear to lose her. Perhaps what he didn't want to lose was the image of the wealthy man with the beautiful, talented wife, who lived in a world where all was well.

I was still tossing and turning at midnight, plagued by the information and what to do with it. Probably the best thing would be to tell the police, but if Edward had been responsible for the assault, I didn't want him to find out I had provided the information. I was about to get up and find something to do when my phone rang.

"Hey," Ian said, "did I wake you?"

"No, how come you're awake?"

"My neighbor's lunatic dog wouldn't shut up and I couldn't get to sleep. I wasn't sure if you'd be home from dinner, but I thought I'd call." There was silence for a bit. "How was dinner?"

"Nice, good food, good company," I replied vaguely.

"I've missed you," he said.

"Missed you, too. You're welcome to come over if you want."

"Oh, that's okay, I don't want to wear out my welcome."

"You're in no danger of wearing out your welcome. It's up to you."

"You're sure?"

"Of course."

⌒

I FELT guilty about going behind his back. I didn't want to upset him or us any further, so I stuffed the guilt back in its hidey-hole and figured what he didn't know wouldn't hurt him.

When he arrived we talked for a bit about our day, then we curled up together in bed. He wrapped himself around me, kissed me on the neck, and whispered, "This feels better." A few minutes later, I felt him relax and drop off to sleep. Not long after, I followed him to sleep.

Early that morning I woke to the sensation of his hands running over me and turned toward him. He watched me and leaned in to kiss me. He was aroused and became more insistent in his kisses and his explorations and finally, after what had seemed like an eternity, made love to me. It was a gentle wordless reunion, both of us making amends. I had missed the connection with him and vowed silently not to let anything screw this up.

SITTING AT the very back of the chapel at the funeral home, I realized I hadn't thought things through very carefully and in all probability was heading for a blowup with Ian. I never thought my little charade at the art gallery would ever come to light and I had asked him to accompany me to the memorial before I had attended the charity function.

I hadn't noticed Shelby the gallery saleswoman so far, but I imagined she would be here. I could see Libby seated in one of the front pews of the chapel, unaccompanied by Edward. Ian had insisted that we sit at the back of the church and I had agreed. I was hoping that sitting in the back would help me escape any inconvenient social encounters.

The chapel wasn't full, but more people had turned out than I expected. The urn with Jeff's ashes sat on a small table at the front, flanked with flowers and music playing quietly in the background. The little service card that I'd been handed as I walked into the chapel was pretty bare, Jeff's name, birthdate, date of death, and the formulaic Lord's Prayer inside with a picture of the Good Shepherd on the front. Not much to mark his life or his passing.

I sat through the brief service, noticing at one point that a small group of people got up and left through a side door. I hadn't seen them clearly, only noticed the movement out of the edges of my vision. One of them looked vaguely Shelby-like, but I was on edge and figured it was my imagination. I scanned the crowd and found Libby; she wasn't among the ones who had left. Watching her, I wondered if Edward knew she had come and, if he did, what he thought of it. He couldn't really object; she had known Jeff for a long time and not to come would have caused more of a stir than to be here.

Ian sat quietly by my side, his elbows braced on his knees, head down, alternately fiddling with his car keys or his cell phone. There were clearly better things he could think of to do on a Saturday afternoon and I imagined he was thinking about them, not meditating on the shortness of life. As it turns out, I wasn't, either; I was meditating on how to make a quick exit.

The chaplain finished his homily and explained that there would be a reception following the service at the art gallery; he invited everyone to come and share his or her memories about Jeff. The music began and people began standing and moving toward the exit. I stood up and pulled Ian along with me, making for the door. Stepping out into the cold, bright day, I started off toward the parking lot when I heard someone behind me call "Mrs. Cisneros!"

God, some days I had the worst luck. I ignored her and continued walking, but I heard her shoes clattering on the pavement behind us. "Mrs. Cisneros, are you coming back to the gallery?"

"Who's she talking to?" Ian asked.

I shook my head and kept going. We reached the car and he opened the door and got in. Shelby caught up to me and grabbed at my arm.

I turned and walked her to the back of the car and hissed at her, "What do you want?"

"I, uh, I just wondered if you were coming to the reception."

"No, I'm not. I need you to go away, please."

"Okay," she said sounding offended. "Sorry to bother you." She looked at me and the car and Ian and then said with a smirk, "No husband today, either?"

I ignored her and turned and got in the car. Ian pulled out and we rode in silence back to the house; thunderheads had clearly formed over his head.

As we went into the house, he snarled, "Mrs. Cisneros? Want to explain that?" He waited a moment and said, "That's Angel's last name. Why the hell did she call you that?"

The proverbial jig was up. "I went to talk to that idiot who stopped me in the parking lot. She works at the gallery where Jeff worked. I thought I might find out something about the night he was attacked. I didn't want to use my own name so I used Angel's."

"And why does she think you're married?"

I hesitated, and then said, "Because I took him with me and that's what we told her."

"And didn't say anything to me about it."

"No. I didn't want to upset you."

"Well, that didn't work out very well, did it?"

No it hadn't. It was very clear he was furious but working hard to control it. "Ian, I'm sorry. Now that Jeff's dead, I feel like no one cares what happened to him. I just…I don't know, I'm sorry, I know you don't want me involved."

"I don't, but that doesn't seem to matter at all. More importantly, I don't want to be lied to."

"I didn't lie to you!"

"You may as well have; you didn't say anything about it. What did she mean, 'No husband today, either?'"

I knew I was screwed, so I just blurted it all out and waited for the blowback, which wasn't long in coming.

"So you did lie to me. You said you were going out with Maddie on Friday. Do you even have a friend named Maddie?" He grabbed my arm and shook me. "Do you lie to everyone or just me?" He was furious and a little intimidating.

I pulled away and said, "I lied to you about going out with Maddie, but she really is a friend of mine, although at this point you probably don't believe much of what I say. I lied because I didn't know what else to do. I knew you'd be pissed about me continuing to meddle in this. I just wanted to talk to the ex-sister-in-law and see if she could shine any light on Edward and his relationship with Libby." I sighed, knowing I was just digging a deeper hole. "She told me that he's sterile, which would give him plenty of motive for going after Jeff."

It was the wrong thing to say, clearly.

"You are the most infuriating woman!" he shouted. "God, you just won't listen, you just won't stop, will you? This is not your job or your responsibility. Let the goddamned police do their job and stay out of it! Why can't you do that?" He was getting louder with every sentence, and I knew there wasn't much I could say.

"Your involvement is maddening enough, but I will not tolerate being lied to. You can do as you like, it's your life, but don't lie to me!" He stopped for breath and when he resumed he had stopped shouting and was working hard to get himself under control. "I can't do this. I just can't do this!" He turned and opened the front door so hard it rebounded against the wall as he stormed through it and left.

I felt the bottom drop out of my stomach. I was so tired of trying to navigate this relationship while trying to do what I felt I needed to do. Part of me wanted badly to just drop all the meddling and placate Ian.

What *did* it matter what had happened to Jeff or might happen to Libby?

For things to settle down between Ian and me all I would have to do is wash my hands of this.

But it did matter.

TWENTY-TWO

SOMEONE WAS KNOCKING at the door. I had cried myself to sleep and it was early evening now. I went to the door and looked through the peephole: It was Angel. I leaned against the door, trying to decide if I wanted to open it, but he knocked again, so I did.

"How was the funeral?"

"How do you think? It was sad and boring and miserable." I turned and walked toward the couch to sit down, leaving Angel at the door. "What do you want?" I asked rudely.

"Nothin' really, just wanted to check on you, see how you were."

"I'm fine, just fine. Seeing Jeff as a can of ashes is so much less alarming than seeing the aftermath of his beating, or watching him lie there in the ICU and die by inches, or going to a funeral that could have been about anyone it was so generic, and then having a major blowup with Ian; everything's great and I'm just fine."

He raised his eyebrows at me. "What happened with Ian?"

So I told him. "Do not say I told you so or I will personally beat you to a pulp," I warned him.

"Wasn't planning on it. Anything I can do?"

"No."

"I got pizza next door and you're welcome to come share it. Kinda seems like you could use some distraction. What d'you say?"

I sat there, debating.

"Oh, come on, you need to eat, so do I. Come eat and then you can go home and cry some more."

"Sometimes I really hate you."

He shrugged. "That's how most women end up feeling about me. Mama's the only one who still loves me. At least, I think she does." He laughed and pulled me up off the couch. "Just promise me you won't throw up on me if you get drunk."

"Oh, for God's sake, you deserve to be thrown up on for that comment," I said as he towed me over to his side of the duplex.

IN THE end, I was glad he'd insisted. I was hungry. It's funny how the body goes on and requires its usual needs to be met regardless of what's happened. His company was familiar and undemanding, and we finished the pizza and a couple of beers sitting on the couch. He turned a movie on, and we sat in the darkened living room and watched it. There was no discussion about Ian, Libby, Jeff, the funeral, or any heartfelt conversations about how I was. Being around a guy at times was pretty easy: They didn't ask, and you didn't have to share. I felt like Scarlett O'Hara, I put Ian out of my mind and would think about him tomorrow.

I woke up on Angel's couch covered in a fleece blanket with a pillow I didn't remember seeing last night. I remembered falling asleep in the middle of the movie and then nothing else. He'd left a note on the coffee table.

Had to run by the office, I know it's Sunday, had some stuff to catch up on before tomorrow. Didn't want to wake you last night, hope you feel better.

Maybe the only way to have a good relationship with a guy was to be friends and keep the romance and the sex out of it.

There really wasn't anything I could do to repair things with Ian, but I called and, when he didn't answer, I left a message, apologizing. I told him if I could undo the damage I wanted to and that he should let me know. Before I hung up I said, "I care about you and I shouldn't have lied to you. I hope we can figure out a way to mend things." Having seen the look on his face when he had said he couldn't do "this," I didn't think any apology I offered was going to help.

It would break my heart if he was gone for good and it pissed me off because I had a right to do what I'd been doing. I wasn't sure how to reconcile the two; I wasn't sure I'd get the chance.

I went out for a walk to get out of the house and to try to walk my way out of the frustration I felt. While walking, I thought about what I knew and what I should do with it. I could always go to the police, speak to whoever was in charge of the investigation, hand the information I had to them, and walk away. A day late and a dollar short, as my dad had always said. Too bad I hadn't thought of that before I'd blown up things between Ian and me. I wondered what, if anything, I ought to tell Libby. If Edward was sterile and Libby stuck to the story that the child was his, what would he do?

Mostly, I wondered if there was some way to turn off the endlessly circular thoughts that crowded my brain. The walk helped, but I was loath to return home. Life goes on, though, whether you want it to or not, so I went home and called the hospital and signed up to work a lot in the coming week; nothing like work to anesthetize you.

It looked as if Angel had returned, so I knocked on his door and waited for him to answer. "Hey," I said when the door opened, "do you know who's handling Jeff's case now that it's a death not an assault?"

"I can find out. Why?"

"I want to talk to whoever it is and tell them what I know and what I suspect. Then I'm going to butt out. I've done enough damage."

"I'll find out tomorrow and get you a name and number." He looked at me closely, and asked, "You doing better?"

"Yeah, I guess. I appreciate the company last night, and your couch is pretty comfortable."

He grinned. "Never slept on it, but that's good to know."

"Well, thanks, Angel."

As I turned to go back to my side of the duplex, he said, "Annie? This business with Jeff should be left for the police to sort out. I get why Ian might be pissed off, and relationships take work, but the work shouldn't be all one-sided. You shouldn't have to cater to his ideas about what's okay for you to do to keep him around."

"Relationship advice from the guy who plays girl-of-the-month?" I asked sarcastically.

"Okay, I deserve that. I admit I'm not crazy about him, but I care about you. If he makes you happy, that's great, but it's not okay if he puts you through the wringer." He shrugged. "Just don't want to see you hurt."

"He's not putting me through the wringer, I'm putting myself through it," I replied and went home.

AFTER DEBATING for the rest of the day about whether to talk to Libby, I decided that she should know about the sterility, if for no other reason than to decide whether to proceed with her charade or confess. I called and when she answered I wasn't sure exactly what to say, but I didn't want to see her in person.

"It's been a rough week, hasn't it?"

She sighed. "No kidding. So what did you call about?"

"I'm just sorry about Jeff and the way things ended for both of you."

"I am, too, but nothing to be done about it now except feel bad about it."

"I was pretty hard on you. No one knows what goes on between two people in a relationship other than the two involved. I should have just stayed out of it." She didn't respond so I continued. "How are you feeling, any better?"

"No, not really."

"Libby, I need to tell you something, I'm not sure how, really, but I think you need to know. I believe Edward might be sterile. Has he ever told you that?"

There was silence on the line. "Why would you say that? Where on Earth would you have heard that?"

"His ex-sister-in-law told me."

"Judith?"

"Yes."

"Oh, for God's sake, she hates Edward. She's badmouthed him for years. She's insane, she thinks he killed her sister, for God's sake."

"Well, I thought you should know. If he is, it makes passing the baby off as his pretty awkward. Maybe I'm wrong, but I thought you should know."

"Well, you are wrong. You should just stay out of other people's business."

"Yeah, I've been hearing that a lot lately. Look, I'm sorry. I'm sorry about what happened to you and to Jeff, and I am sorry I couldn't help you. Take care of yourself."

She responded by hanging up. What did I think she was going to do, thank me? What a fucking mess. I made up my mind that I wasn't going to talk to the police, I wasn't going to talk to Libby again, and I wasn't going to keep picking at this. I undressed, crawled into bed, and pulled the covers over my head. I planned to stay under them until I grew old. Depressed, discouraged, and significant-other-less (I snorted at that; what kind of a word was that?), I had made a huge, seemingly unfixable mess of things.

TWENTY-THREE

WORK IS BETTER than lidocaine for numbing pain and it temporarily takes your mind off things and makes you focus on the tasks at hand. I felt comforted being around the people I'd worked beside for the last several years and listening to their banter and gossip and was grateful to have something else to focus on.

Maddie and I spent an evening together. We hadn't seen much of each other since before Jeff's funeral.

"So why's Ian upset with you?" she asked as we ate.

"I didn't tell him about visiting the art gallery with Angel and pretending to be married to find out what the gossip was on Libby and Jeff. And I told him I was going out with you instead of telling him about attending a charity function to try to meet Edward's ex-sister-in-law. He found out the day of the funeral and was furious. I haven't heard from him since." I shifted on the couch, and said, "I have no idea whether this is repairable or not."

"You want to repair it?"

"Yes, I really like him, but this Jeff and Libby thing just keeps surfacing and causing problems for us. He's totally sick of hearing about it and wants me to stop involving myself in it. The other problem is he and Angel don't like each other at all. It annoys the crap out of him when he finds Angel at the house 'cause Ian thinks Angel wants to be more than friends."

"He does, if you'd give him the slightest encouragement. I've never understood why you don't."

"I know he does, I'm not stupid. I don't want to encourage him."

"Why not? Why spend your time with someone who's so touchy when you and Angel get on so well together, and he isn't trying to control what you do?"

"'Cause Angel's like a bee in a flower garden; he tastes every flower he finds and doesn't stay with any of them. I like Angel, I really like him, but I don't want to be just another flower and then lose the friendship and have to move if things blew up in our faces."

"Well, personally I'd welcome being one of those flowers even if it was temporary. A little of that Latin love would be fine with me. He makes my heart flutter every time I see him, just don't tell my husband that. But I haven't met Ian, so maybe there's more there than what you've told me." She watched me and sipped her wine. "This obsession with Libby and Jeff would try the patience of a saint. I can kind of see why he'd be pissed. If Ian's what you want, then I hope the two of you can figure things out."

"It's not an obsession," I said petulantly as she rolled her eyes at me.

ANGEL HAD given me the name and phone number of the homicide investigator assigned to Jeff's case, and I'd put it in the kitchen junk drawer. I thanked him and told him I didn't plan to speak to the investigator. I told him what I had found out about Edward and how badly the conversation had gone with Libby.

"Playing detective has caused nothing but problems for me, Jeff and Libby, and Ian. So I don't think I'm going to talk to the guy."

"I'm not sure what they'd do with the information anyway; it's not really damning. It's interesting about the sterility, though. If it's true, it's weird that he didn't throw her out and file for divorce. Sounds as if she didn't know anything about it."

"I don't think she did, but I've caused enough problems. She doesn't believe me anyway. It's up to the police to sort this out. I just wish I'd figured that out a long time ago. Finding out who assaulted Jeff isn't going to bring him back, so what's the point?"

"You're asking an assistant DA that?" He laughed and then saw that I was not amused. "It's okay, Collins, I think you're doing the right thing. It'll all work out; truth, justice, and the American way will win in the end."

"You're an ass, Angel, but I love you." I closed the door on him.

THE FOLLOWING day I got a call from Angel. "Sorry to bother you at work, but I thought you'd want to know. They found a guy they think might have had something to do with Jeff's assault."

"Seriously? How'd they find him?"

"Well, he sort of found them. He turned up dead and had Jeff's wallet and credit cards on him."

"Dead? What happened?"

"A jogger stumbled over him early this morning on the path that runs along Speer Boulevard by the river. His head had been bashed in, not a pretty sight."

"And they're sure he's the one who assaulted Jeff?"

"He's all they've got. His hands looked like they'd been pretty beat up at some point recently. They were nearly healed, but he'd apparently broken his right hand, which was casted. They're checking hospitals to find out when and where he was treated to see if it connects with the beating, but they're pretty convinced the hand injuries are from Jeff's assault, and he had the wallet and credit cards, so they think he's good for it."

"Why would someone kill him and leave the wallet and credit cards?"

"Who knows? Maybe he got into it with one of the homeless who live around there, you know, said the wrong thing and triggered someone's psychosis. Maybe the voices told the assailant not to take the wallet. No way to tell. To be honest, if he were alive they'd have a hard time prosecuting him based on old hand injuries and a wallet he could have picked up anywhere, but he's dead and he's all they've got. I thought you'd want to know."

"Thanks, I appreciate it. Let me know if anything else turns up, okay?" And then before he could hang up I asked, "What was his name, do you know?"

"Didn't ask, but it'll probably be in the news later today." I thanked him again and hung up.

I stopped at a Starbucks on the way home to peruse a newspaper to see what might have made the news about the death. I scanned the front section of the paper while nursing a coffee at one of their tiny tables and found a short article on Jeff's attack and the recent death of a person of interest in the assault. The story revealed that a jogger on the river path near the Speer and Grant Street bridge had found his body that'd been tentatively identified as a petty criminal by the name of Jimmy Scott. Over the last few years he'd been charged with a variety of crimes: breaking and entering, assault, and check kiting. He had served some time for some of the charges and been plea-bargained out of a couple.

It struck me as odd that someone like that would be either out jogging *or* interacting with the unfortunates who lived along the Platte River. What possible reason could he have had for being there? I stopped. I was doing it again. Libby might need help, but apparently I did, too. Enough was enough. I put the newspaper back in the stand, picked my coffee up, and drove home.

IT WAS a surprisingly quiet few days, nothing more than routine cases. Chip, Katy, and I connected over dinner in the cafeteria one night, and it was good to talk to people who knew me and knew Jeff.

"You know, sweetie, you weren't the one who assaulted Jeff, and you were one of the few people who sat vigil with him."

I nodded. "It's just so discouraging. I really hoped he'd recover."

Katy nodded, "I did, too. We do the best we can, but the results are out of our hands, you know that."

I did and it helped, but I wondered if I would ever stop feeling responsible.

No word from Ian, so I had to assume that our connection was irretrievably broken. Moving on wasn't going to be easy, but as with Jeff, the outcome was out of my hands now.

I spent my time in a fog, whether working, eating, or sleeping. Maddie and Chip kept in touch by phone, and Angel checked in periodically. Sometimes he brought take-out or sat and chatted about his day and asked about mine. He passed on anything he'd heard about Jeff's homicide. Apparently, there were two homeless people who'd provided information about the attack under the bridge, but they had enough issues between them that the police felt their stories were unreliable despite both being fairly consistent. I finally had to tell Angel I didn't want to hear anything about it and he agreed to stop.

TWENTY-FOUR

I T WAS FRIDAY and I had gotten home at midnight, crawling into bed with relief. It had been a twelve-hour funfest at work and all I wanted was oblivion. Sometime later, my phone pinged and I groped for it. I wasn't on call so I couldn't imagine who would be texting me at 1:30 in the morning. I hit the center button and entered my code and saw a text from Libby.

<I'm sorry Annie> and nothing else.

I'm sorry? Sorry about what and why at 1:30 in the morning? I quickly texted back

<Libby what's wrong?> Nothing.

<Libby?> No response.

I had a very bad feeling about the text and got out of bed. I threw some clothes on, grabbed my coat, purse, and keys, and headed out the door. I arrived at Libby's fifteen minutes later; the front porch and security lights were on, but the house itself was dark. I walked up to the door and turned the handle, surprised to find it unlocked. I walked in, expecting to have to turn off the alarm, but it was silent, too. A small voice kept telling me this was a bad idea, that I should call 9-1-1 and wait until the police arrived, but I needed to find Libby.

I made my way up to her bedroom, pushed the door open, flipped the light on, and saw her splayed across the bed on her stomach. Her face lay to the right and she had her cell phone in hand. Her thumb rested on the screen as if she were still trying to type something.

"Jesus, Libby!" I ran to her and felt for a carotid pulse. She had one, but her breathing was very slow. I grabbed the bedside phone and dialed 9-1-1.

"Nine-one-one, what is your emergency?"

"This is Anne Collins," I said, giving her the address. "I'm with a friend who's attempted suicide. I need an ambulance."

"Please repeat that address."

I did while pulling Libby off the bed and onto the floor to begin CPR.

"Is the person breathing?"

"Yes, but not well. Look, I'm instituting CPR, I'm a nurse, so just send an ambulance and EMTs and let me get started. I'll keep the line open but I can't talk to you right now." I dropped the phone on the bedside table and bent over Libby, made sure her airway was clear, and extended her neck. I pinched her nose closed and began to breathe for her, periodically checking her carotid pulse. There was alcohol on her breath, which struck me as odd, but I was too busy and frantic to think more about it. Her heart continued to beat, but she wouldn't breathe on her own.

I had never done this anywhere except a hospital where there was a team of people to help. *Please hurry, please hurry, please hurry* I kept praying with every breath. Her pulse seemed to be slowing, so I stopped briefly for a couple of quick compressions, then back to breathing for her. It was hard work and I was tiring. There was no ambu-bag, no meds, no help—*oh God what had happened?* I was aware of a commotion in the hall and then hands pulling me away and feet stepping in and people taking over.

I crawled out of their way and sat against the wall with tears running down my face. A few minutes later, a policeman bent over me and asked if I could step out into the hall and tell him what happened.

I explained and he asked to see my cell. I handed it over and told him the code. He looked at it carefully and handed it back to me. "What made you come over?"

"The text. It was weird and she didn't answer me."

"How did you get access to the house? Are you a relative?"

"No, the house was unlocked and the alarm was off when I got here."

"Didn't that seem odd to you?"

"Well, yeah, but I needed to find her."

"Was she having problems?"

"She'd had a miscarriage and wasn't recovering well. We were friends."

"Why do you think she would try to kill herself?"

"A close friend died recently and she has been unhappy in her marriage, then lost the baby. Maybe that was enough. I never thought she was that depressed. I don't know," I said helplessly.

"Any idea where the husband is?"

"No, I have no idea."

He took Edward's name and mine, and he took my phone number, saying they'd want to talk to me further at some point. I stepped aside as the EMTs wheeled a now-intubated Libby past on a stretcher, one EMT bagging her and the other steering the cart.

"What hospital?" I called after them.

"Denver Health," one of them called.

I turned to the police officer. "I have to go with her, please." He stepped aside and I hurried down the stairs and out into the night, following the ambulance as closely as I could to Denver Health. It was probably the best place to take her; it was the closest and it was a level 1 trauma center. I wasn't an employee, however, and had no right to access the ER. I had to sit in the waiting room and wait, one of the hardest things I had ever done. I let the admitting clerk know who I was and whom I was waiting for, and asked that I be allowed to see her as soon as she was stabilized.

An hour passed before anyone came looking for me. A young, harried-looking and grim ER doc scanned the waiting room and settled on me. I felt a wave of fear clench my stomach as I rose from the hard plastic waiting room chair. "Ms. Collins? I understand you found the victim?"

"Libby Matheisen, yes. How is she?"

His face told me before he got the words out and I only half heard the "I'm sorry, she didn't make it." He saw the look on my face and continued. "You did a great job of keeping her going 'til the EMTs got there. We did what we could when she got here, but she became arrhythmic and we couldn't get her to convert to a normal sinus rhythm. After half an hour working on her, we stopped. I can take you back to see her, if you want."

I nodded numbly and he shepherded me back to the ER cubicle where Libby lay on the gurney, saying as we arrived, "You can stay as long as you like, we're pretty overwhelmed at the moment. We've put in a call to the medical examiner's office and the police. I'm just not sure when they'll get there."

I stood there looking at the room with its resuscitation detritus strewn across the stretcher and floor. It was chaotic in the ER, multiple people were coming and going, I'd seen an ambulance's flashing lights through the automatic doors, and somewhere I could hear a man shouting and cursing and other voices trying to calm him down.

With other more urgent patients to deal with, no one had taken the time to clean things up or make her presentable. It appeared as if the team working on her had just stopped and disappeared, and most likely they had; there was nothing more to be done here. The endotracheal tube was still in her airway; her blouse had been cut away to get the EKG leads on and access veins.

Someone had failed to shut off the EKG, and a flat green line traced its way across the screen over and over again. The O_2 saturation monitor's alarm was beeping. I moved automatically to shut both off and moved closer to the gurney.

Her hand was still warm, her nail beds were blue, and her eyes were closed. She had an unearthly paleness to her. Her hair was spread across the cart, tangled in the EKG wires. She looked peaceful. Her hair seemed to be the only thing with any life in it, and noticing a pair of bandage scissors that lay near the IV line, I reached for them and without thinking I cut off a piece of it close to her scalp at the back of her head to be less visible. Some bizarre need to have something of her to keep made me slip it into my pocket.

"Libby, what happened? Why didn't you talk to me?"

And then I stopped—of course she wouldn't talk to me, I had turned my back on her. She had reached out at last, but too late. I pulled a rolling stool up that had been pushed against the wall and sat next to her, picking up her hand and holding it against my cheek. I lost track of time, but the young doctor returned eventually and asked if I would like to get a cup of coffee. There were two morgue attendants standing at the cubicle entry, and I could tell they wanted to get her ready for transport to the hospital's morgue. I rose and followed him out into the hallway.

"I think I'll pass on the coffee," I said. "I'm just going to go home."

"I don't think driving's a great idea, you've had a terrible shock. Is there someone I can call to come get you?"

I stared at him blankly. "No," I replied at last. "Have they found her husband to notify him?"

"Not so far; I guess he's out of town?"

"I wouldn't know." I stood there for a moment. "I'm really tired, I'm going home. Thank you for all you tried to do."

"I really wish you'd let me call someone...." His voice trailed off.

"Thanks, I'll be fine."

I found my way out of the ER and the hospital and to my car, and slowly, as if in a dream, made my way home. It was nearly seven when I let myself in, dropping my coat and purse and keys on the floor and making my way to the bedroom. I passed the office area, saw the painting, and stopped. We would never be two old ladies in the park, and there would never be any more paintings. I slumped to the floor and broke down and cried, curling into a fetal position, unable to move.

I APPARENTLY gave Angel the fright of his life. I'd left the car in the driveway with the door open and had left my front door open as well. He'd left for work very early that morning before I arrived at the house and was returning home when he saw the open car door and my front door standing ajar and burst into the living room calling my name.

I really didn't see any point in responding. I was fine, a little cold, but just fine.

"Annie, for God's sake what happened?" He gathered me into his arms and was checking me over. "Are you hurt or sick?"

I could feel his heart thumping against his chest and wondered in a detached sort of way why he was upset.

"I'm fine, really, I can drive home. There's no one to call."

"What? Jesus, what the fuck happened?" He grunted a little as he picked me up from the floor and carried me into the bedroom. He laid me on the bed, removing my shoes and jeans and covering me with the sheet. "It's fucking freezing in here. Did you know you left the front door open?" He pulled the comforter up around me and turned the bedside lamp on. "Annie," he said, tapping me on one cheek and then the other. "Annie, wake up and tell me what happened."

I looked up at him and smiled. "I'm fine, just a little cold." And then let my eyes close; sleep seemed preferable to answering questions.

I HEARD voices. They sounded familiar, but I couldn't be bothered to figure out who they were. I felt a warm hand on my wrist, checking my pulse, then a stethoscope on my chest moving carefully and a beep in my ear that I assumed was a temp monitor indicating it was time to read it. Seemed weird; I didn't think I was in a hospital. I had been earlier, but I couldn't remember why. And why was I so cold? I started shivering and couldn't stop.

"She's okay, just pretty cold. Are there any other blankets around?" I heard someone ask, it sounded like…Maddie?

"I'll see what I can find."

Angel's voice, I thought hazily.

"Crank the heat up while you're at it."

I felt someone stroke my cheek and the touch was comforting. "Annie, can you wake up a bit? I want you to drink this." I felt myself being lifted up against pillows and opened my eyes.

"Maddie, what are you doing here?" I asked, completely baffled to find her sitting there.

"Trying to get you warmed up. Here, can you take a drink of this?" She held the cup to my lips; it was hot tea with lots of sugar in it and it tasted wonderful, so warm.

"I'm fine, really, just tired and cold." I was glad to see her, but nothing seemed real. I felt several blankets piled on top of me and more tea offered. "Why are you here?" I asked again.

"Because Angel called me. What happened to you?"

"Everyone keeps asking me that," I said irritably.

"I know, and we have yet to get an answer," said another voice. I looked around and saw Angel hovering behind Maddie, his face haggard.

I sat there blinking at the two of them and then like a movie playing in my head I saw the dark house, Libby on the floor, could feel myself breathing for her, and then saw her in the ER cubicle. "Oh God, it's real, isn't it? She's gone." I began to weep and turned away from both of them pulling the comforter up high around my face. "Please go away, please," I cried.

"Annie, who's gone?" Maddie pulled me back over toward them.

"Libby," I whispered. "She's dead."

"What? When? What happened?" Angel's questions sounded frightened.

"It doesn't matter, she's gone."

I turned away and closed my eyes. After some low-voiced conversation, they left the room. I could hear the conversation continuing in the living room, but it seemed pointless to try to follow it. I hoped they'd go away and leave me alone. I didn't want to talk about it or think about it. The conversation died and I slept. At some point I heard the phone ring and heard Angel answer it. I thought I heard him say he was my attorney and that I wasn't available to talk at the moment. Finally things quieted down.

A while later, I heard someone come into the room and heard the rattle of china. Heard it being set down on the bedside table and felt someone sit on the side of the bed. I felt a hand on my back and heard Maddie's voice. "Hey, how about waking up for a bit and having something to eat?"

"No, thanks."

"No seriously. If you keep this up, I'm calling an ambulance and having you taken to the hospital. Do you want to do that or sit up and at least drink something?"

She sounded serious, so I rolled over. She was sitting there, and when I looked up, she quirked an eyebrow and indicated the tray. "Eat or drink or go to the hospital. What'll it be?"

"Why can't you two just go home?"

"Angel has."

"Then you should, too."

"Not happening. So do I call an ambulance or not?"

"Oh, fine," I said, sitting up and leaning back against the headboard. I felt weak and shaky. I took the cup of tea and wondered vaguely why they always gave tea to people.

I heard someone come in the front door and Maddie got up to see who it was. When she returned a little bit later after a bunch of mumbled conversation, Ian walked in behind her.

"Angel called me on your cell. He asked me to come over."

"He shouldn't have."

"Well, he did, and I'm here."

"I don't want you here because Angel talked you into coming over."

"Do you always try this hard to get rid of people who care about you?" he asked. "You scared Angel half to death, and you're lucky he found you when he did. You were pretty hypothermic. A few more hours and you'd have been a Popsicle. It's nineteen degrees out, did you forget that?"

"Look, you're here because he called you, and I appreciate that, but you've done your duty and now you can go. You wouldn't be here otherwise. I don't see the point of you making a courtesy visit, acting all concerned, and then disappearing on me."

"You would try the patience of a saint."

"Well, apparently I try everyone's patience, either that or they die. I'd go while the going's good."

Maddie interrupted the conversation long enough to say that since Ian was there, and I was doing better, she was going to head home. I nodded, gave her a hug and watched as she left.

"You want to talk about what happened to Libby? Maddie said some policeman called earlier wanting to talk to you. I guess Angel told them he was your attorney. He told Maddie he would call the police station in the morning and arrange a time for you to talk to the investigator." He waited for me to respond and when I didn't he said, "It might help to talk about it."

"It won't help. She's dead. She committed suicide. She sent me a text saying she was sorry, and when I got there she was barely alive and died in the ER. There, I've talked about it and it hasn't helped." I glared at him, trying to bluff it out and not start crying.

He stared back for a bit, then took the tea from my hand and gathered me into his arms. "Come here. I'm so sorry you had to go through that."

His arms were where I wanted to be, but I knew that he wouldn't stay and I would never see Jeff or Libby again and I cried my heart out for all of us.

WHEN IT seemed as if I had cried more than I ever thought possible, he made me finish the tea and eat the toast. "Maddie said your temp's almost back to normal, and that you just need to rest and stay warm. I'm going to stay, in case you need anything. I'll take the couch, so you can rest."

"You don't have to…."

"I know, I don't have to stay, you're fine," he said in an irritated sing-song voice. "I'm staying in case you're not."

"Okay." I sighed, giving up.

He turned the bedside lamp off and left, and I heard him moving around the living room, shutting off lights and settling in. I scooted down on the bed and turned away from the door. He hadn't let me finish. I was going to say that he didn't have to sleep on the couch. I wished he had offered to stay with me rather than sleep on the couch, but I wouldn't beg. I wanted to, but I wasn't going to. I stared at the wall on the other side of the bed, and wished more than anything I had never returned Libby's call that day so many weeks ago.

I slept, but without rest. My dreams were unsettled. I saw Jeff in the ICU damaged and attached to life support and then Libby and Jeff standing together holding their hands out to me as if wanting me to do something, but what? I woke with a start, and then, when I realized that it was a dream, I drifted back to sleep. I was back in the bedroom with Libby trying to breathe for her when she opened her eyes and grabbed my hand and wouldn't let go. She kept mouthing the word *help*. I was frantic and I couldn't get her to let go.

I cried out and sat up with a jolt, my heart racing, my breath coming in gasps, and heard Ian get up and come to the doorway.

"You okay?" he asked.

"I keep having dreams. They won't stop." I held my head in my hands then looked up at him. "I need you to hold me, to stay with me, even if you have no intention of resuming our relationship. I can't do this alone tonight."

He stood there and I thought he would refuse, but finally he moved to the bed, got in next to me, and took me in his arms. "I'm here, see if you can rest." Having him hold me didn't stop the dreams, but when I'd startle awake, he'd wrap his arms around me and tell me it was just a dream and I could fall back to sleep. I had no idea what I would do when he left, but for now, it was all I needed.

ANGEL SHOWED up the following morning while Ian was making breakfast. He took Ian up on the offer to eat and sat down next to me at the peninsula.

"Sure glad to see you up and around, Collins. You scared the bejeezus out of me. Please don't do that again." He awkwardly patted my back with one eye on Ian, and said, "I'm sorry about Libby, must have been a horrible experience for you."

I nodded as he accepted a cup of coffee and stirred in cream and sugar. "I talked to the detective who called yesterday, told him I was your lawyer. They want to interview you later today, around two. I was surprised they'd do it on Sunday; I guess they have no lives, either. So I'll come pick you up and go with you."

We accepted plates of food from Ian, who then sat down with his own.

"I don't need a lawyer, Angel. I didn't kill her."

"Spoken like a true innocent. You're not talking to them alone, Collins, that never ends well."

"I think you should listen to Angel and let him go with you, Annie. It can't hurt."

"Okay, but I just don't see why it's necessary."

"You be the nurse and let me be the lawyer, okay?" He had shoveled his breakfast in and finished his coffee in several gulps. "Gotta go," he said and gave me a quick kiss on the cheek and shot Ian a rather smug look. "I'm sorry all of this had to happen, but we'll get through it."

The "we" made me smile.

I picked at my breakfast and sipped the coffee, while Ian ate quietly. He looked as if he had no intention of staying; he was dressed and ready to go. The elephant in the room sat squarely between us, but neither of us would admit it was there.

Finally, after trying out several sentences in my head and discarding them, I said, "I appreciate you staying last night. I'm sorry Angel involved you, but obviously he was a little freaked out."

"It's okay. I'm glad he called."

I let several minutes go by. "I am sorry, you know. I wish more than anything I could go back and change so many things, but I can't."

He sat there quietly stirring his coffee and finally said, "It's taken me a while to figure out that your involvement in this is unlikely to change. It's damned inconvenient and frustrating as hell for me, and I expect it is for anyone who cares about you, but it is what it is. I'm glad Angel called. I had been trying to figure out a way to call and couldn't. I guess what I'm trying to say is I'm yours, if you'll have me back."

I leaned my head over and rested it on the top of his shoulder. "I'll have you back."

TWENTY-FIVE

WHEN WE WERE on the way to the police department, Angel gave me a lecture on what to do and what not to do. "Answer their questions, if you don't know say so, don't volunteer anything, and if I say not to answer, then for God's sake don't decide to answer anyway."

"Angel, I didn't kill anyone. I don't understand why you're so wigged out over this."

"No, you didn't kill anyone, but you were the only one on the scene of a suicide, based on a text you received. A text that really didn't indicate Libby was going to do away with herself. All she texted was she was sorry and gave no indication what she was sorry about." He glanced at me briefly. "What looks odd is you were in a house where you don't live, and, according to you, it was unlocked and unalarmed, which is highly unlikely in that neighborhood. Do you see what that looks like? It's odd at best and the police investigate deaths like this to rule out homicide. They like to jump on oddities and go fishing. I don't want you to bite, so please listen to me, okay?"

"Okay. Thanks for going with me. I didn't really want to come by myself." I sat in the passenger seat and wondered what they'd want to know. I was apprehensive, but I wanted to get it over with. "Should I tell them about Edward and my suspicions?"

"Let's see how it goes. If I think it'd help I'll ask for a moment to speak with you and then we can decide what to say about it. Just remember, don't volunteer anything."

"Thanks for being there yesterday and for calling Maddie and Ian," I said suddenly. "I appreciate it. I know you don't like him much."

"I don't like him much, but if he makes you happy, then I'll deal with it. He came over and he stayed with you; those are points in his favor," he said, giving my hand a squeeze.

We pulled up to the building and found a parking place, entered the front door and had to pass through a metal detector before being allowed to continue. Angel talked to the officer at the front desk and we were instructed where to go. The elevator was what you would expect in a police building, old, not well cared for, and smelled like a combination of sweat, pee, and weed.

When we exited the elevator, a Detective Frost and his partner were waiting. He looked like he was in his fifties, not seriously overweight but accumulating that middle-age spread. He had a pleasant but somewhat homely face. His tie was askew and his brown hair was thinning. He introduced his partner as Detective Miller. She was much younger and much less friendly looking—hair skinned back in a ponytail, wearing a cheap shirt and pants, and a frown. They escorted us to an interview room.

I was getting nervous. I'd seen too many TV shows. It doesn't seem to matter how innocent you are, around the police, you always feel guilty of something.

We sat at the table, the detectives on one side of the table and Angel and me on the other. Detective Frost indicated a camera at ceiling height. "We record all conversations that take place in here; it's for your protection and ours." He aimed a remote at the camera. He stated the name of everyone present, the date and time, and what the interview pertained to, then turned to look at me. His partner just sat and watched.

"So, Ms. Collins, can you tell me what happened night before last?"

I looked at Angel and he nodded, so I began. "I worked until midnight at the hospital and came home and went to bed. At around one-thirty I got a text from Libby Matheisen that said, 'I'm sorry, Annie.' She didn't respond when I texted back, so I texted again asking her what was wrong and got no response. Libby hasn't been well and she'd lost a close friend recently. I just figured I should check on her.

"I drove to her house and the house was dark. The outside lights and security lights were on, but nothing else. When I tried the front door it was unlocked and when I went in the alarm was off."

"That didn't seem odd to you or concern you that it might not be a good idea to go in?"

"Yes, I guess, but I needed to find her and make sure she was all right. I went upstairs to her bedroom and found her face down on the bed, holding her cell phone. She had a pulse, so I called 9-1-1 and pulled her onto the floor and started CPR. I don't know how long it was, but the EMTs arrived and took over. I spoke briefly to a police officer there. He looked at my cell phone to see the texts and then returned it to me. I followed the ambulance to Denver Health and waited and then a doctor finally came out and told me she hadn't made it."

My voice caught in my throat and I was afraid I would cry. Angel put a hand on my shoulder and asked if I was okay to continue. I nodded.

"Did you think Mrs. Matheisen was depressed or at risk for suicide?"

"I thought she was depressed; she hadn't been well. I didn't think she was suicidal, but we hadn't parted on the best of terms right before her friend passed." I felt Angel nudge me with his knee, apparently I was volunteering information, so I shut up.

"And who was this friend?"

"Jeff Davies. He was assaulted about three weeks ago and died of his injuries; you probably know that."

"And did you know him?"

"Not well. I only met him twice before his accident, but I took care of him when he had his surgery."

"And what was Mrs. Matheisen's relationship to him?"

I looked at Angel.

He said, "Can I have a moment with my client, please?"

The detective stopped the camera, and they both got up and left the room.

I turned to Angel, "What do I say?"

"I guess you need to come clean about what you found out. Just keep it simple, okay? No speculating about Edward. If they ask, then answer."

He got up and opened the door and the detectives reentered and we began again.

Frost restarted the camera. "I'll ask again, what was Mrs. Matheisen's relationship to him?"

"They had worked together for some time; he was the agent who sold her artwork."

"That's it?"

"No, I found out he and Libby were having an affair." I chose to say nothing about the other lover. I had no name, no idea where they had met, nothing, so I decided to keep it to myself. No point sullying Libby's reputation any more than necessary.

"How long had that been going on?"

"I'm not sure, a couple years, I guess."

"Was she still involved with him?"

"No, she broke it off when she discovered she was pregnant. He didn't know about it until he heard about her miscarriage."

"Was the child his?"

I looked at Angel and he nodded. "Jeff seemed to think so, as did Libby."

"Any idea how her husband felt about it?"

Angel interrupted, "I don't see how my client would know that; it would be speculation on her part."

"Okay," he said watching me. "Did Mrs. Matheisen say anything to you about whether her husband knew about the affair or that the child might not be his?"

"She told me she didn't want to be divorced, so she made a point of sleeping with her husband several times and then told him the baby was his. She didn't say anything to me about whether he knew or was suspicious about her having an affair."

"You said you and the deceased hadn't parted on the best of terms, can you explain that?"

I sighed. "Libby and I were friends in college. When she met Edward we drifted apart. I hadn't seen her in four years when she called me and asked me to come take care of her. She hadn't been well. She'd miscarried and her doctors thought what she was experiencing was attributable to post pregnancy issues, but she felt there was something more serious going on and wanted me to take care of her and help her figure out what it was."

"Do you normally do that kind of thing?"

"No. I work in the OR."

"Then why would you decide to do it?"

"She was an old friend and she seemed very upset, so I agreed."

"What happened?"

"I spoke with her doctors, with the exception of the shrink she saw, who never called me back. Neither of them felt there was anything seriously wrong with her. The more time I spent with her the more I felt the docs were right and that I was feeding into her ideations. I didn't think that was a good idea, so I quit."

"That doesn't sound like bad terms to me. What happened?"

"While I was caring for her, we ran into Jeff Davies by chance and both of them were upset by it. Libby was very angry. She refused to explain what their relationship was or why she was so mad and I was frustrated, so we had words and I decided it was time to stop working for her. I talked to Jeff later and he told me about their affair; Libby wouldn't talk to me about it. While I was taking care of her, she blew off everything I suggested and then she wouldn't explain about Jeff, so I quit. That was the issue."

"Okay. We had a hard time tracking her husband down. Did you know he was out of town?"

"No. Edward and I really don't speak with each other."

"Why is that?"

"I never cared much for him and didn't make any effort to get to know him, so we don't really have any reason to talk."

He sat there for a moment as if trying to think of something else to ask, then said, "I want to thank you for coming down and making a statement. We investigate every unexpected death to rule out homicide, but based on her text to you and the fact she was alone in the house, it looks like a pretty clear-cut case of suicide. We're waiting for the medical examiner's report and if he rules suicide, then the case will be closed."

"What happens now?" I asked and felt Angel nudge me again.

"You'll need to come in and sign your statement. I'll call you when it's ready and the ME will release her body to her husband, probably by midweek. The husband plans to cremate her, so we keep the bodies a bit longer in case something turns up and needs to be followed up on."

"I just wondered."

He spoke to the camera to note the interview was over and shut it off. "I appreciate your being willing to talk to us, and I'm sorry for what you must have gone through."

"Thank you."

Angel stood up, gathered his briefcase, and held my coat for me. Detective Frost asked if we could find our way out. Angel assured him we could.

We walked to the elevator without speaking and when its doors had closed he let out his breath. "I'm glad that's over. It sounds like they're satisfied it was a suicide, and they don't have anything that might make them wonder about your involvement. But you never know. They're like cats; they like to play with their catch before they kill it."

"Jesus, Angel, scare me to death why don't you?"

"Sorry. Look, you did well. I'll run you home and then I have to get back to the office; I've got a shitload of work to get through. Will you be okay?"

"I'll be fine. Between you and Ian I feel like I have two guardian angels. I'm very grateful for the both of you."

"So did you two work things out or not?"

"I think we did. He was pretty upset when he found out about the gallery and the charity function, but I think we've patched things up." I made a face.

"Like I've always said, stick with the truth and you'll be fine."

"Says the man who wants to guard everything I say to the police."

"Talking to the police is a whole other subject, *chica*."

TWENTY-SIX

I WENT BACK TO work on Monday. Ian had spent the nights at my place since Libby's death, and I was grateful. I was still dealing with the dreams. I couldn't seem to shake them, and having him close when one woke me in a panic helped enormously. I was doing laundry the evening before resuming work and checking pockets when I found the lock of Libby's hair. I stood in front of the washer looking at it and wondering what to do with it. I ended up putting it in my jewelry box.

Edward had returned home and according to what I saw in the news, a memorial service would be held on Saturday at a local funeral home. I planned to go. There was no visitation because, like Jeff, Libby would be cremated. As much as I believed in it and wanted to have my body cremated when the time came, it was hard to think of Libby as ashes. All that creativity and talent turned to dust. But I guess that's what was in store for all of us: "...*ashes to ashes, dust to dust.*"

I ran into Natalie Gould at the hospital the following day in the OR's unrestricted area and thought about Libby's hair. "Natalie, you remember the friend I asked you about?"

"Sure."

"How would I go about having her hair analyzed to see if maybe there was something affecting her that no one was aware of, like the heavy metals you mentioned?"

"Are you doing it to reassure her?"

"No." I paused. "She committed suicide a few days ago."

"Oh, lord, I'm sorry." She reached out and squeezed my arm. I never could figure out how someone so relational could spend her waking hours in a lab with specimens, and slides, and tissue. "So what's the motive for pursuing this?"

"I don't know, honestly, I just feel like I need to make sure that there wasn't something more going on. I'm not going to feel great about that if there was, but maybe it would resolve some of the questions I have."

"Well, you need to be clear about what you intend to do with the information. If you think someone intentionally exposed her to something toxic, you should probably turn the hair over to the police department and let them handle it. If you get someone outside the police do the evaluation, the results could be questioned because of the chain of custody issue. Otherwise, I can give you some resources to contact. Do you think she was intentionally exposed?"

"I have no idea, really. She overdosed, so even if she was exposed to something, it didn't cause her death. I don't know what to think. When I was caring for her it seemed like her docs were right and it was just depression or a bid for attention. And maybe it was, but she wasn't getting better. Then again, this may just be a way for me to absolve myself for not sticking with her and getting her some help."

"I'd take it to the police and let them handle it. Better yet, if they still have her body, ask them to take some hair and run the tests. If it's for your information only, here's someone to call." She grabbed a Post-it from the OR desk and scribbled a name and phone number on it.

"Okay, thanks. Would something like hair analysis be done in an autopsy of someone who commits suicide?"

"Most likely not unless there was some reason to suspect foul play, or some condition or reason to do so."

"Okay, thanks again."

"Let me know what you find out," she said with a smile.

MAYBE IT was time to just come clean about what I knew, give them most of the hair, and let them take it from there, I thought, as I walked back to the OR lounge. For some reason, I wanted to keep some of it. Angel would be pissed if I didn't run it by him first, but I was afraid he'd talk me out of it. Maybe I should divide the hair sample into two segments, give one to the police, and keep one and have my own tests run on it. In the end, I decided to call and talk to Angel. He wasn't happy.

"Annie, I don't think this is a good idea for a lot of reasons. They're going to wonder why you didn't say anything when we talked to them before. I know you've got this bug about her husband and his possible involvement with Jeff's death, but it's a stretch to think he'd poison her."

I could tell he was annoyed with me.

"If you tell them all your suspicions and they take them seriously, it's going to cause problems. If they question Edward, whether he's innocent or guilty, he's not going to be happy. If he's guilty and he finds out it was you who set the police on him, you could be his next target. Even if she was poisoned, it didn't kill her. I know that sounds a little harsh, but it won't bring her back. I just don't see any advantages to doing this."

"What if I have part of the hair analyzed on my own and if it's positive for something, then go to the police?" He sighed and I could hear his frustration. "Angel, I need answers. If her hair doesn't show anything, then I didn't ignore her pleas for help. If her hair shows something toxic, then maybe someone gave her something, and if so, that person needs to be punished. Aside from that, I need to know."

"*Madre de Dios!*" He swore softly and then continued. "If you're intent on this, then I'm going with you. I'll call and arrange something. Do not do anything until you hear from me, do you understand?"

"I promise."

"For what that's worth," he muttered as he hung up.

NOT LONG afterward, he called me back and said we had a meeting the following afternoon and he would pick me up. When we arrived at the police station and exited the elevator, Detective Frost was waiting patiently for us. His partner showed up after we'd gone into the interview room.

We went through the previous routine and when everything was running, he asked, "So what brings you back, Ms. Collins?"

Angel spoke, instead. "My client has further information to provide you, which because of the emotional issues surrounding her finding Mrs. Matheisen, she forgot to mention."

"Okay, what information?"

I took a deep breath and began. "Libby met with Jeff Davies after I spoke with him and two days later he was assaulted and then died of his injuries." I stopped momentarily and looked at Angel and he nodded, so I continued. "It seemed odd to me that the attack happened so close to his meeting with Libby. I went to a charity function after Jeff had died and by chance ran into Edward's ex-sister-in-law who, in the process of talking about him and Libby, revealed that Edward was sterile. According to her, he wasn't aware of this until he and his first wife couldn't get pregnant. That's when it came to light. If it's true, my guess is he never told Libby, otherwise why would she have tried to pass the baby off as his?"

I stopped again and looked at Frost; his expression was impassive. I hoped I was doing the right thing, but in for a penny in for a pound. "I think if he is sterile, her pregnancy, combined with Libby's affair gives Edward a motive for both Jeff's attack and for maybe staging Libby's suicide."

"You do." It wasn't a question, and his face stayed impassive as he watched me. I remembered Angel's cat comment and felt like an unfortunate mouse.

I nodded. "Early on, before Jeff's assault and death, I spoke with a pathologist about Libby's condition and asked her if there could be any other explanation for it and she mentioned exposure to heavy metal and pesticides or other toxins. She told me if her doctors hadn't found anything, I should assume Libby was okay. I thought she was. I couldn't think of any reason for her to be exposed to those things and I thought Libby was milking the situation for some reason, so I quit taking care of her."

I sat still for a minute, looking at my hands and wondering whether I was wrong about this, too. I took a deep breath and began again. "But since her suicide, I wonder if maybe her illness was engineered and maybe her suicide was, too."

And here's where it gets sticky, I thought, but I continued. "When I was in the ER after she'd passed, I took some of her hair. I wanted a memento. But now I'd like to give it to you and ask that you run some tests on it to see if I'm right. If I'm not, I'll just go away. If I'm right, then she was exposed to something toxic that caused her illness. Her illness may have been the reason she committed suicide, but if the exposure wasn't accidental and it caused the illness then…." I didn't know where to go so I stopped talking and waited.

He sat back and looked at me for a few minutes and I felt sweat collect under my arms. I could easily imagine why a guilty person might suddenly confess—I wanted to and I hadn't done anything wrong.

"Well, that's quite a lot to have forgotten to mention."

Angel interrupted. "My client found an old friend who had overdosed and she had to try to resuscitate her alone in a dark house until the EMTs got there, and, despite that, the friend died. I think that's adequate reason to have forgotten a lot. My client is trying to help you, not cause problems."

"I can see that, Counselor. Do you have the hair with you?" he asked me.

I fished in my purse for the plastic sandwich bag I'd put part of Libby's hair into before we came. "Here," I said. "Do you believe me? Will you test it?"

"I plan to investigate what you've told me."

"He's going to have her cremated; the memorial is Saturday. If that happens and the hair tests positive for something, will that be enough?"

"Enough for what, Ms. Collins?"

"Enough to pursue investigating her being poisoned and her suicide being a possible homicide."

"Ms. Collins, despite your concerns, the ME has ruled the death a suicide and I see no reason to doubt that. He plans to release her body tomorrow or the following day and then her husband can proceed with the cremation. I can't prevent the next of kin from proceeding with whatever plans they have for the body based on one person's suppositions, especially if I have nothing solid to prevent them from claiming her."

"If you've any question about the hair I've given you, ask the medical examiner to take a sample of her hair before you release her body. Maybe it would be better to do that anyway so the chain of custody isn't questioned."

Frost smiled slightly at that but waited for me to finish.

"Ask for it to be tested and for any other tests that might be helpful. Will you pass on the information I've given you?"

I was feeling a bit frantic; he just sat there looking at me. "Please, if she was being poisoned, don't you want to know?" I felt Angel take one of my hands and squeeze it, but I couldn't stop. "Isn't that what you're supposed to do?"

"We intend to follow up on what you've told us," Frost said.

Angel stood up. "My client is upset and this interview is over. I hope you'll take the information in the spirit in which it was volunteered. I trust whatever you investigate you'll leave her name out of it for her safety." He pulled me up and helped me into my coat and led me out of the room and down finally to the car.

"He's not going to do a damn thing, is he?" I asked.

"I don't know, but honestly Annie, it's all pretty circumstantial. It's a lot of work for a pretty circumstantial theory. He said he'd follow up, and my bet is he will at least look into it." He drove carefully and silently through the rush hour traffic, and finally said, "I need a drink and some dinner, how about you?"

"I'm not very hungry, but if you'll take me home I'll get some takeout and fill you with beer or something. If you're particular about what you want to drink then we need to swing by a liquor store. All I have is three quarters of a bottle of Scotch, a six-pack of beer, and a bottle of red wine."

"Well, that should do it." He laughed. "Is Ian coming over? Maybe you should call and ask if he minds me hanging out. He never seems all that keen on it."

"It's my house; you can stay if I want you to. I don't think Ian will care in any event. He's glad you're unofficially representing me."

Ian had eased up slightly where Angel was concerned. Angel was making an attempt to be friendly with Ian, but I knew he didn't like him much. The effort on his part was solely because of his friendship with me.

"Hey, it's not unofficial; I'm just not charging you for it. You wanna order Chinese?"

"Sure."

⌒

I INVITED Ian over and ordered Chinese. I told him what I had done and he scratched his head in a distracted sort of way, and finally said, "Well, at least you took Angel with you and gave the police the hair and aren't playing private investigator on your own." He ate a few more bites, then added, "I think I'm going to take up meditation or maybe just take medication. One or the other ought to help."

Angel snorted at that and I gave them both evil looks.

"Try praying to St Jude, he's the patron saint of lost causes, and I think dissuading her from doing this is pretty much one of those," Angel offered helpfully.

"Probably." Ian sighed and went back to eating.

TWENTY-SEVEN

I DISCOVERED THAT GETTING hair analysis results could take anywhere from a couple of weeks to six months depending on who was asking for it, why they wanted it, and how unfunded they were. The other variable was how backed up the testing lab was. The one Natalie Gould told me about said a week, but the person I spoke to didn't sound convincing. I didn't want to ask Detective Frost whether he was pursuing it or how long it would take him to get results. In any event, neither of us would have results until after Libby's cremation. So I forked up the money and left the ninety strands they required, kept the rest, and hoped the test would help me lay the issue to rest.

I wasn't sure what to hope for, but anything would help. No sign of toxins or heavy metals and Edward was off the hook, and I might be able to accept that things had been both simpler and much worse than I'd believed and Libby was depressed enough to have taken her own life. Life lessons are often hard, but this one had taught me a lot, primarily that getting involved with caring for friends was a very bad idea.

If the results showed something unexpected, then I didn't know what I'd do. I could take the results to Frost, but I had no idea if he had followed through and talked to the medical examiner or had the hair I left with him tested. I had no idea if they'd even be able to use the sample I was testing. It seemed to me they now had two unsolved homicides, and a possible poisoning and suicide, and they were going nowhere fast. I needed to know what they were doing and whether they had released her body.

As I walked into the elevator at the police station, I knew that Angel was going to kill me. When I stepped out, Detective Frost stood there like a perfectly trained guard dog, waiting for me to make the wrong move.

"We meet again, Ms. Collins. What can I do for you?"

I think what he was doing was smiling, but it was hard to tell.

"I wondered if we could talk off the record. Is that what you call it?"

"Sure, do you mind if my partner sits in?"

"No, I guess not." His partner never seemed to talk, and it was easy to forget she was there as she watched and listened and took notes. Already the second thoughts were occurring, but it was a little late to change my mind. He walked us into an office, motioning to his partner to follow and closing the door after she arrived. I sat on the chair in front of the desk, he slumped into the other behind the desk, and Miller leaned against the door with her arms crossed over her chest.

I felt a bit trapped, but it was a trap I had set myself, so I blundered on. "I wondered where you were with releasing Libby's body to her husband and whether you decided to follow up on the hair sample I left with you."

He didn't respond immediately. He never seemed to rush into any-thing, unlike me. "I discussed what you told us last time with the medical examiner, and he said he'd follow up and take some samples himself before he released her today."

"Oh, that's good. Do you know when you'll hear the results?"

"Not before her funeral, if that's what you're asking."

"No, I just wanted to know. I didn't figure you'd get them back before then." I sat and fiddled with the strap on my purse, not knowing where to go with this. "If for some reason her hair comes back with something in it that shouldn't be, what happens?"

"We'd take it from there and try to figure out why it was there and whether someone intentionally exposed her to it." He watched me fiddle with the strap and finally asked, "How about telling me what's on your mind, Ms. Collins?"

I kept seeing cats playing with mice and it made me very uncomfortable. "Okay, here's what's on my mind," I said, making up my mind to stop walking on eggshells. "I think it's very coincidental that Jeff, Libby's lover and most likely father of her child, gets beaten to a pulp after meeting and talking to her, and then the guy who supposedly beat him up is found dead under a bridge by the Platte. Why would he be there and why, if it was an unplanned attack, would the attacker leave Jeff's wallet and credit cards on the guy?"

He sat there listening, but made no comment, so I went on. "Then, after all that, Libby commits suicide. She never stuck me as suicidal, depressed certainly, but not to that extent. I remember tasting alcohol on her lips when I was trying to resuscitate her. I never saw Libby drink; she was taking Ambien and Valium and knew not to. I mean, obviously, if she wanted to commit suicide, she might. But more importantly, how could she have texted me fifteen minutes before my arrival, and then be so out of it when I got there that I couldn't rouse her and she could barely breathe for herself? That doesn't happen in fifteen minutes. None of it makes sense to me unless none of the events were accidents."

I looked at both of them. They sat there waiting as if I had more to offer. "Um, so, that's what's on my mind."

"That's quite a lot to have on your mind. Not bad points, however. Where did you hear about the guy under the bridge?"

"It was in the paper."

"So it was, but the bit about the wallet and credit cards wasn't." He twiddled a pencil that had been lying on the desk, and then asked, "Where did that information come from?"

"I'd rather not say; it's a confidential source."

He rolled his eyes at me. "Okay, we can have that conversation another day. I assume you think it was her husband behind all this?"

"He has good reason to be, don't you think?"

"If what you say about him is true, he certainly has reason to be upset with his wife. Most men who get cuckolded, though, don't kill their wives and their lovers or hire someone to do the dirty work for them, and then, if I'm following your thoughts correctly, kill the hired gun. They just divorce them. What makes you think the husband, Edward, that's his name, right?" His partner nodded. "Yeah, Edward. What makes you think he'd go off the deep end like that?"

"Why not? None of it really makes sense. If he were sterile, why would he go along with Libby when she told him it was his child? He insisted on an amnio, but if he's sterile he didn't need that to tell him the child wasn't his, so why do it?" I took a deep breath. "This whole thing feels like revenge to me. Punish Jeff for sleeping with his wife and getting his wife pregnant. Punish Libby for the affair and pregnancy by hurting Jeff, which would punish her again when he died, and then get rid of her and be done with it."

I wasn't sure, looking at Frost, whether he thought I was insane or was listening and trying to decide what to do with the information. But I kept talking.

"And, if he had someone else beat Jeff up, maybe the guy came back when Jeff died and threatened him or something and he killed that guy, too. No more cheating wife to deal with, no blackmailer, no ex-lover. And while we're on the subject, exposing someone to toxins would be a great way to cause a miscarriage, so no bastard baby to deal with, either."

I stopped and thought that I did sound insane. "Look, all I'm saying is there are too many loose ends to just chalk everything up to a random assault or suicide. I may be totally wrong, but she was my friend and I owe it to her to see that these things are followed up on. I can't really investigate it or I would; I need you to do that."

"It's a lot to consider, but I want to be clear: you need to stay out of this, got it?"

"I don't want to be in it, okay? I just want someone to take me seriously and investigate it. Will you do that?"

"We will look into all of it."

"Will you let me know what you find out?"

"We're not in the habit of consulting with members of the public during an investigation," he said, giving me an exasperated look. "But when we're done, I will touch base with you if you promise to let us handle things. Okay?"

"Okay." I sat there for a moment longer. "She was a friend of mine and I liked Jeff. I want to know what happened and if someone is responsible, I want that person to be held accountable."

"And if it turns out it was a random assault and she did commit suicide, then what?"

"Then life sucks, doesn't it?"

TWENTY-EIGHT

WHEN I GOT home I poured myself a glass of wine and got out my phone. In the interest of being honest with both of them, I sent a group text to Ian and Angel that said,

<I talked to Detective Frost, without a lawyer, and told him ALL my suspicions. He will look into them. I also had my part of the hair tested and am waiting for results. I'm telling you at the same time so you can both get pissed at once and we don't have to do this multiple times. If he arrests me, I don't expect either of you to post bail.>

A few minutes later a reply arrived from Angel <You're the most annoying human being I know. I'll bail you out and represent you in court, now please let the police do their job.> Then almost immediately he texted <And when they arrest you, don't say fucking anything without me being there.>

It made me laugh, and then I heard another ping and looked at what Ian had texted. <I feel sorry for Frost and Edward. God help them both.>

I texted Ian privately, <I hope you're not totally pissed.>

<No, now that you've done it, maybe you'll stop. How about dinner at my place at 7?>

<See you then.>

When I arrived we sat on the couch and talked. He had dinner in the oven and it was cooking while we relaxed.

"What made you decide to go back to the police?" he asked, pouring us both a glass of wine.

"I just wanted it all off my chest and it's probably not smart, but I didn't want Angel editing everything I said. Maybe now I can let them deal with it and not feel like I'm the only one who can take care of it."

"How'd they respond?"

"Ha! You haven't met Detective Frost. I have no way of really knowing how he takes anything. He listened and seemed to take everything I said into consideration. At least he didn't tell me I was nuts and throw me out. For all I know, though, he may have the men in little white coats on their way now to pick me up, so I'm glad I'm here and not at my place."

I sipped at the wine, and then said, "He told me they would look into it all and when they knew anything they'd let me know. But they released her body today and the funeral is still on for Saturday."

"It sounds like he took you seriously."

"Maybe." I sighed. "I'm really tired of going to funerals. I haven't been to this many in recent memory."

"Yeah, funerals are the pits," he said and then blushed.

I laughed. "Did you just say funerals were the pits?"

"Pretty poor choice of words, eh?"

"Very. Are you up for another one?"

He nodded and went to check on dinner. "Any idea how Edward is taking all this?" he asked from the kitchen.

"No idea. Frost won't tell me anything and Edward and I aren't friends."

"It sounds like Edward is at the bottom of all this. I just hope Frost doesn't mention you if he questions him." He removed a covered dish from the oven and set it on the kitchen island along with plates and silverware. "Dinner's served."

"I don't think he'd involve me like that, at least I hope not. What are you worried about?"

"If you credit your theories, then Edward is someone who doesn't scruple to get rid of people who cause problems for him. That's the definition of you in a nutshell, and I don't want you assaulted or dead under a bridge somewhere. Please just assume the worst and be careful, okay?"

"Okay."

"I mean it, Annie, please? You've done your job and he's in their bull's-eye, so let them go from here."

"I will be careful, I promise." I squeezed his hand. "I'm relieved to have spoken with Frost and told him everything I think may have happened. I'm handing it off to them. They can do what they like with it. Either something will turn up or it won't. If it doesn't then it doesn't matter what I think, it'll be over. It won't bring either of them back no matter what Frost finds out."

"No, it won't. And you need to be prepared for this to end up being a random assault and a suicide and nothing more."

TWENTY-NINE

THE FUNERAL WAS nicely done; Libby would have been pleased. I had no idea what Edward intended to do with her ashes. Part of me wished I could have some, just to take them somewhere and have a private farewell, but that wasn't going to happen. Edward stood at the door and spoke with each person who had attended the service.

When we reached the door, he took my hand and said, "I appreciate what you did for Libby, she always thought well of you. Will you come back to the house for the reception?"

"No. Thank you, though. I'm sorry for the way it turned out."

"I think we all are." He let go of my hand and Ian and I left.

"Sure you don't want to go to the house?" Ian asked.

"No, all I can think of is how unhappy she was and her lying on that bed, dying," I said, tears welling up. He put his arm around my shoulders and gave me a squeeze. He seemed relieved that I hadn't wanted to go.

"At least you were there and tried to keep her alive."

"You know, I told Frost I could taste alcohol on her lips when I was giving her mouth-to-mouth. Libby didn't drink. I don't think I ever saw her drink, even in college. And she was taking Ambien and Valium, she knew not to drink, but she had. Maybe she did commit suicide," I said as we walked to the car.

Getting into the car, I continued. "The thing that bothers me the most is the state she was in when I arrived just seemed too far advanced to have happened in fifteen minutes. How could she text me, and then fifteen minutes later I couldn't get a response from her and she was barely breathing? That just doesn't make sense."

I could see the worried frown on his face and the crease between his eyebrows. "I'm not medical, Annie, I have no idea, but it seems to me that the ME would have been able to determine that. I know you feel guilty about her, but at some point you just need to let this go."

"I told Frost so he could investigate it. I don't plan to get any more involved. It just bugs me. I hope he can find some answers."

"I hope so, too." He started the car and then turned to me. "Would you like some company tonight or do you want some time to yourself?"

"If I'm alone I'm just going to beat myself up about all of this, so some company would be nice."

"How about dinner out, and then we can find something good on TV and zone out?"

"Sounds like a plan. We're dressed up, might as well make the most of it."

WE ENDED up at an Indian restaurant and then came back to my house. It was a quiet evening. I'd closed the door to the office before Ian picked me up to go to the memorial service so I wouldn't have to see the painting. It might have to stay closed for a while. We made love and despite how comforting it was, I ended up crying in his arms, for Jeff, for Libby, for their baby, and for me and the friend I had lost.

THIRTY

IT WAS HALLOWEEN and I was assembling the candy for the night's little goblins, when the doorbell rang. It wasn't yet dark, so I was surprised that kids were out this early. I opened the door to find a man in a suit standing on the porch.

"Can I help you?"

"I'm hoping you can. I represent Edward Matheisen and after conducting an inventory of his wife's paintings, one is missing. It's a painting of two women on a park bench. I am here to determine whether you have it or know where it might be."

"I'd like to see some identification." He handed me his card and I closed the door on him. I called the number and the law firm's secretary answered the phone and confirmed he was a partner. I used my phone to Google the name on the card and the phone number and they were legitimate. I opened the door and allowed him to enter.

"Do you have the painting?" he asked.

"I do. It was a gift from Libby Matheisen."

"A very valuable gift. Do you have some proof that it was a gift?"

"As it happens, I do." I went into my office, returning a few moments later with the letter from Libby. I handed it to him.

"I will need this to show Mr. Matheisen."

"You don't need the original bill of sale. I'll make a copy for you." I said, holding out my hand.

He reluctantly handed it back and I went in to make a copy. I returned and handed him the copy.

"It's Halloween," I said. "I guess all the ghouls are out. Was he afraid I'd stolen it? Perhaps tucked it into my handbag after I tried to resuscitate his wife?"

The man's face reddened; then he put the copy in his briefcase, turned, and left. When Angel arrived home from work I went over to tell him.

"You know, it's like getting gum on the sole of your shoe. I don't think I am ever going to be free of Libby and all the chaos she brought into my life. It's a damned good thing she enclosed that letter with the painting."

"Yeah, it is. I would suggest that you put that in a safe deposit box, just in case. You don't want it to disappear. As valuable as the painting is, without proof of ownership, you could be charged with a felony. In the meantime, I have a small safe, give it to me and I'll keep it until you can get a box."

I handed it to him. "Edward is such a bastard."

Angel sighed. "He would no doubt say he was taking care of his wife's estate. If the painting was missing, he did the right thing. The way he went about it was tacky, but it's valuable and its whereabouts needed to be confirmed. If he or anybody else shows up that's connected to Matheisen, don't let them in. Tell them if they want to talk to you they can call me and set something up."

"Okay."

"Personally, I'd get a chain lock so no one can force the door open."

"Are you serious?"

"Yes, I'm serious," he said in frustration. "You've got a valuable painting on the premises. Keep your doors locked and frankly I'd get an alarm system."

"I guess opening the door for kids and handing out candy is out of the question?"

"It is for now. Don't open your door unless you know who it is."

Leave it to a lawyer to create paranoia. In this case, perhaps it was warranted. The following day I made a trip to Home Depot and picked up a chain lock for the front and back doors. And I contacted an alarm company that would send a technician out the day after and install an alarm system. I installed the chain locks on both doors and went to work later that afternoon.

IT ACTUALLY took a month for the hair results to come back, so much for promises. I had almost forgotten it, and Ian and I had slipped into a comfortable routine without Libby or Jeff's constant intrusion. The test results unfortunately opened that door again.

I showed it to him when he came over.

"I will be damned," he exclaimed.

"I know, right? Thallium, since right about the time she found out she was pregnant. I'm taking it to Frost tomorrow. You do not accidentally come into contact with thallium. I Googled it. People used to poison rats with it. It was odorless and tasteless so it could be mixed with grain or something and the rats would eat it and die. But thallium was banned in the US some time ago, so somebody is responsible for this."

"Where would you get it, though?"

"Edward's a computer geek; there are probably any number of ways he could find and purchase it. Apparently there's this thing called the dark web, where all sorts of illegal stuff goes on and it's very hard to trace who's involved. It could also be as simple as the fact that it's an old house they lived in, it was built in the 1920s, and any number of things could be in the basement or garage or attic. Who knows?"

"Where did you hear about this dark web thing?"

"After I got the results this morning I called Natalie Gould and she mentioned it. Then I talked to Chip, my nurse friend in ICU. He's a computer nerd, too, and he verified what she said."

"Well, you were right about her illness not being psychological."

"I just wish I'd believed her, she might still be here."

"Or maybe not. It was hard to believe when all the docs were telling you it was all in her head, and knowing this might not have prevented her suicide."

"Do you think her GP could get a copy of the autopsy?"

"Why would you want it?"

"I want to know what they found. I guess maybe it would help me sort some of this out. What else can I do?"

"We both know what else you're capable of doing."

"Well, this is totally out of my depth; Frost is going to have to handle it."

"Thank God."

THE FOLLOWING day, when I told Angel about the results of testing Libby's hair he cautioned me that when Frost had requested further testing before releasing Libby's body, higher-ups weren't happy. The ME had declared it a suicide and they wanted to be done with it. They were wary of upsetting someone in Edward's position and a previous investigation had blown up in Frost's face, so he wasn't in good favor. When the hair results came to light, there would be more pressure for Frost to make doubly sure there was concrete evidence before proceeding. Angel warned me Frost wasn't going to be a happy camper after getting the results.

Frost, as usual, was waiting as the elevator doors opened. "To what do I owe the pleasure?"

"I have some information to give you."

"Come with me." He sounded resigned as he led me to the office where we'd previously talked. His cohort was not in evidence today. He ushered me in and closed the door. "What's up?"

I handed him the hair analysis report. "What's this?" he asked, putting on reading glasses and scanning the page.

"It's the hair analysis I had done on Libby's remaining hair. Maybe you already know the results of your tests, but mine show thallium. Years ago it was used as rat poison, but it's banned in the US, so exposure to it can't be accidental and based on the timeline they gave me, it shows up right around the time she found out she was pregnant." I waited as he read through it. "Did you get your results yet?"

"Nope, the lab is backed up. I guess you didn't give me all the hair you clipped in the ER."

"Nope," I said, mimicking him.

"Well, I have to say, this puts things in a different light. It isn't what killed her, and I don't see any reason to question whether she committed suicide, but clearly someone was trying to poison her."

"Have you verified the other stuff we talked about? Like Edward's sterility?"

"We talked to him. He was pretty pissed and basically told us to talk to his lawyer and complained to my bosses about harassment." He ran his hand through his hair, a gesture I had come to recognize as frustration. "I can't discuss this with you and nothing I just said goes out of this room, understood?"

I nodded.

"This," he said, shaking the report in my face, "complicates the hell out of things; rich people and politicians are just impossible to deal with. God, I hate cases like this."

He propelled me to the door of his office and over to the elevator. "I can't discuss an ongoing investigation with you, which apparently this has now become, but I really appreciate your bringing this to me."

"Sure, thanks for listening to me," I said as I pushed the elevator call button.

"Okay to keep this report?"

"Yes, I made a copy of it for myself."

"Of course you did," he said as he watched the elevator doors close.

WHEN I got home, I called Libby's GP and told him what had happened and asked if he could get me a copy of her autopsy report. He was taken aback by the hair results and said he'd see if he could get a copy of the report for me. I called Angel then and asked him to find out what the police had on the guy who had been killed under the bridge. He called back several hours later.

"They've got nothing. No idea what he was doing there and the only two people who will admit to seeing anything are homeless and one of them is a pretty unreliable witness. Well, they both are, really; one's just more unreliable than the other. The police can't put Scott at the scene of Jeff's assault, but based on when he had his hand attended to and the wallet and credit card, they're pretty sure he did it. They just don't know who killed him."

"I can't remember, did Jeff have his wallet or cards on him when he was found?"

"I don't think he did, why?"

"I'm just wondering, if the guy had them, why didn't he get rid of them or sell them to someone? Why keep something that would be a dead give-away to your involvement in an assault that turned into a homicide?"

"Nobody ever said criminals were brains."

"No, I suppose not, it just seems like a stupid thing to do."

"It was stupid, but people in these situations can be incredibly stupid. This is looking much more serious than it did originally and I'm sure Frost appreciates your help, although he probably wishes you weren't so helpful, but that's where it needs to stop. Okay, Annie?"

"Okay."

"Listen to me, please?" Angel said before we disconnected.

SEVERAL DAYS later, the autopsy report arrived in the mail with a note from Dr. Kelsey saying he'd edited out the photos, which was a relief; I never wanted to see those.

"Did you read it?" Ian asked when he arrived at the house.

"Yes, and it reads like a suicide. She had ingested about four hundred milligrams of Ambien and two hundred of Valium on top of a blood alcohol level of zero point two. The Ambien might have done the trick, although the dose isn't necessarily a fatal one, but that combined with Valium and alcohol turned out to be a pretty deadly combination. I saw her stash; she had enough on hand to accomplish the task."

I flipped back and forth between pages, reading as I went along. "She had some cuts on the inside of her mouth and some slight bruising on her cheeks. The medical examiner wouldn't speculate about how she'd gotten them. I suppose she could've seized and bitten her cheeks. If I remember right, though, Valium is used to control seizures in an emergency. There aren't any tongue lacerations and I don't see any mention of any other bruising. I wonder if the ones on her cheeks and the cuts on the inside of the mouth could be from someone forcing her to open her mouth."

"Seriously? You watch too much TV. I think you're reaching there. It'd be pretty hard to force someone to take all that medication and drink the alcohol without there being lots of other signs of a struggle," Ian said dismissively.

"Maybe, but Ambien can cause a lot of weird behavior. People have walked in their sleep, eaten, and driven cars on a regular dose and have no memory of it, plus its purpose is to make you sleepy and with that dose you'd hardly be able to resist. Maybe Edward gave her more than her regular dose and then talked her into taking the rest and drinking the alcohol, and maybe at one point she resisted and he forced her mouth open."

"I suppose that's possible, but it seems pretty farfetched."

"Stranger things have happened with the drug, so I think it's possible."

Ian sighed. "Annie, that's quite a leap. You keep coming up with these bizarre ideas; I don't understand why it's so hard for you to accept that Libby committed suicide. She had enough reasons to do it. Please don't tell Frost that; he'll think you've lost your mind."

"I don't plan to. But still, it's a plausible theory."

"Not that plausible and no way to prove it's anything but a theory, and a pretty unlikely one at that," he said irritably.

"I guess." I sat looking at the autopsy report. "I don't think I'm going to mention anything to Frost. The first question out of his mouth would be where did you get hold of the autopsy report? I don't want to have to explain that."

"Thank God."

IT BOTHERED me the police had been unable to find anyone reliable who saw anything the night that Jeff was assaulted or when his alleged assailant was killed. Because the parking lot was pretty much out of view unless that's where you were heading, it wasn't surprising there hadn't been any witnesses. But the homicide under the bridge was different.

There were always people who stood on street corners asking for handouts and on any given day you could see homeless people with their overloaded shopping carts and ratty, overstuffed backpacks flaked out on the banks of the Platte sleeping or recuperating or begging at intersections.

The trees and bushes on the sloping lawns running down to the river had sheltered spots in which people could take refuge overnight. It seemed like there ought to be someone who'd seen something and who wasn't in need of psych meds.

The next day I drove down to Speer and Grant and drove around a two-block area to see who was hanging out there. An older man stood on the corner of one intersection holding up a battered cardboard sign that said Hungry, anything helps. It was cold and he looked miserable and relatively normal. At least he wasn't talking or ranting to himself.

I drove back to the McDonald's on Colfax and bought a large cup of coffee and two Quarter Pounders. I snagged a handful of sugar packets and creamers and drove back to the street corner. I stopped at the stoplight and rolled down my window. I held out a dollar.

As he approached, I said, "If you'll answer some questions, I have a cup of coffee and a couple hamburgers for you. I'll park over there," I said, pointing at the parking lot of the church across the intersection. "If you want, come over and you can sit in the car and eat if you'll let me ask you a few questions."

The light changed and I drove to the church parking lot and waited. He made his way slowly across to the lot and approached my car. His coat was filthy and his face was covered in stubble. I rolled the passenger window down and showed him the food. "I just want to talk."

"What about?"

"About that guy who was killed a few weeks ago under the bridge." Imagining what Ian or Angel would have said, and deciding to ignore it, I unlocked the car. "It's warm in here and there's food."

"You shouldn't let strangers in your car, lady."

"Probably not, but you look like you might be able to help me."

He opened the passenger door and picked up the bag of hamburgers and sat down. He pulled the car door closed, and I was overwhelmed with the smell of unwashed hair and a person who hadn't seen or used soap or deodorant in quite some time. Nurses learn to keep their reactions to themselves, and we can tolerate a lot, but I felt as if the smell had seared my nasal passages and wondered if I would ever get it out of my car.

He opened the bag and took a deep sniff. I offered him the coffee. "There's cream and sugar, if you take it." He took it, doctored the coffee up with enough sugar to make my teeth ache, and used all four creamers before he began eating.

He pretty much inhaled the first burger and drank some coffee, his hands shaking as he brought the cup to his mouth. "Thanks for this, it's really good."

"My name's Annie, what's yours?" I asked, breathing through my mouth.

"Cliff," he said, starting in on the second burger. "Why'd ja wanna to talk to me? Most people won't even look me in the eye. They sit in their cars at the stoplight and pertend there are all sorts of interstin' things to look at so they don' have to see me."

"Because I need some help. Do you hang out around here a lot?"

"Yeah, why?"

"I'm hoping you saw something when that guy was killed a few weeks ago, or maybe you know someone who did."

"What about it? The cops came and talked to me an' mosta the people who hang out in this area, and they din't believe what we told 'em."

"Well, according to the police, of the two people who had information, they felt one wasn't reliable, and no one else claimed to have seen anything." Surprisingly he didn't seem to smell as bad the longer he sat in the car. Perhaps my sense of smell had died, or maybe I'd just gotten used to him at some point.

"Yeah, well, people don' always wanna talk to the police and the police don' always listen."

"That's what I figured. But maybe you'd talk to me?"

"Wadda you wanna know?" He wiped his mouth with the back of his hand, a hand whose fingernails were black with dirt.

"If he's the right person, he hurt a friend of mine. My friend died. I'd like to know what happened the night this guy died. From what I can find out, he wasn't someone who spent time jogging or walking or hanging out under bridges, especially at night, so it seems odd he'd be here."

"Mebbe he was dealin'." He darted his eyes nervously around the car.

"Was he?"

"I din't say I saw 'im dealing, I'm just sayin' mebbe thas why he was there."

"Did you see him at all?"

"I mind my own bizness; safer that way."

"No one else is here, it's just the two of us. Did you see anything, Cliff?"

He sat there for a bit sipping at the coffee, not looking at me, and I wondered if this had been pointless and risky. He didn't look dangerous, but who knew why he was here begging on the street.

"I saw two guys talkin'," he finally said between sips of coffee. "I was holed up on the riverbank by the bridge unner some bushes out of the wind. They woke me up arguin'. Couldn' hear all of it, they was tryin' to keep it quiet."

He laughed a bit, which sent him into a coughing fit. I hoped the cause of the cough wasn't contagious. He smelled like cigarettes so I crossed my fingers that was what caused the cough and continued to listen.

"Weren' too good at it, but they was far enough away it was mos'ly noise from their raised voices. I don' know for sure who he was talkin' to but one a the guys was the dead guy."

"What happened, did you see?"

"Nope, I been drinkin', so I turned over and went back to sleep. Din't wake up 'til the next morning when I heard all the screamin' going on and saw the dead guy."

"Was there anything you remember about the other guy?"

"Had nice clothes. I 'member thinkin' I'd like to get my hands on his coat; looked warm."

"Long coat or short? What kind, like a dress coat or an outdoor-wear type of coat?"

He scratched his head and I had a sudden horrifying thought that maybe he had head lice. It was all I could do not to start scratching my head. God, this probably had been a very bad idea.

"Well, it was late'n dark'n I was drunk, so all I know is it was a dark coat, one a those long fancy coats you see rich guys in."

"And you have no idea what they were arguing about?"

"Seemed like some deal had gone bad. The guy in the long coat said somethin' like 'It's not healthy to threaten me.' Other'n that, I got no idea and I din't wanna know. I din't want anyone to know I was there, neither, so like I said, I turned over and went back to sleep. Stickin' your nose in other people's bizness just gets ya way into trouble. You oughta 'member that."

"Yeah, I probably should." I fished a twenty out of my coat pocket and held it out to him. "Thanks, Cliff, I appreciate you talking to me. Take care of yourself."

He opened the door and got out with his coffee. "Thanks, lady. Wish I had more ta tell ya."

"You've been a big help, thanks. If for some reason you hear anything from anyone else, will you call this number?"

I handed him a piece of paper with my phone number. He took it, shut the car door, and headed back across the intersection with his coffee and his sign. I opened all the windows and sat there for a moment and then drove off. It was cold but I left the windows down for a few blocks to help air things out.

Edward had worn a black dress coat at the funeral, but so had several other men. It wasn't like it was a green plaid coat with gold braid on it; it was a generic black dress coat. Ian had one and Angel probably had one, too. So, I thought, *do I tell Frost?* If I did, I had no idea what he could do with the information. Still, every bit of information helps. Maybe it was just a small detail but if combined with others it could mean something.

I called and asked to talk to him and was greeted with, "What now?"

"Well, you're not in a great mood, are you?"

"Not particularly, no."

"I talked to a homeless guy who was sleeping it off near the bridge where Jimmy Scott was killed. He heard two men arguing, it woke him up, but he wasn't sure what they were arguing about. He is sure that one of them was, as he put it, 'the dead guy.' At one point he heard the other guy say, 'It's not healthy to threaten me,' but he didn't want anyone to know he was there so he rolled over and went back to sleep. He did say that the other guy was in nice clothes, including a long black dress coat."

"You talked to a homeless guy." He seemed to have a habit of repeating what I said. Maybe to convince himself I'd really said it.

"Yes, he hangs out around that intersection of Speer and Grant so I figured maybe he saw or heard something."

"We talked to a bunch of homeless who hang out around there and got nothing useful."

"He said people don't always talk to the police and the police don't always listen. Maybe the information you got isn't as unreliable as you think."

"Did I not ask you to stay out of this?" he asked irritably.

"Yes, but doesn't that help a bit? I saw Edward in a long dark dress coat at the funeral."

"Don't 'yes but' me." I heard a long, heavy sigh and silence before he said, "It's interesting, but not very helpful. There must be thousands of long dark men's dress coats in Denver alone. Plus the killer most likely got blood on the coat when he killed the guy. In which case he would have gotten rid of it. We canvassed a huge area around the murder site and found nothing. We were looking for a murder weapon, but there weren't any coats with blood on them. So we're back at square one. And more to the point you are interfering again, not to mention the risk you took talking to this guy."

He was sounding a little pissed. "I'm sorry."

"Sorry doesn't mean squat if you just keep doing things you've been asked not to do. Now I appreciate that you want to help and that you bring the information to me, but Ms. Collins, I'm not going to say it again, you need to stay out of this. Aside from the risk you place yourself in, information you get could be thrown out if this ever comes to charging someone. You're not the police. Do I have to arrest you and keep you in jail until we solve this?"

"Um, I don't think you can do that." Knowing he was pretty exasperated with me, I said, "I just wanted to help. It feels like this is going nowhere fast."

"It is, but other than the hair analysis, what you've given me is all circumstantial speculation or information like the coat. I can't do anything with any of it. In addition to which, we have no idea whether Jeff Davies' assault was intentional or even connected to Mrs. Matheisen. And we have no idea at this point who killed him."

I was silent waiting to hear more railing against what I had done. When it didn't come, I said, "I guess maybe this will never be solved."

"It'll be solved if I have anything to say about it, but it can take time and you have to be patient."

"I will."

The conversation with the homeless guy was not going to be a topic of conversation with either Angel or Ian. It hadn't amounted to much and I didn't want to get a lecture from both of them again. The problem was I kept getting the sense of Libby or Jeff near me waiting for resolution. I kept seeing images from the dreams, and I felt that they were anxious for me to find out what had happened. It was as bad as having Itchy for a pet.

THIRTY-ONE

A WEEK AFTER TALKING to Cliff, I got a phone call from him. Honestly, I was surprised to hear from him. I wondered how reliable his information had been because it seemed awfully lucky to have stumbled onto a person who had actually seen anything, but he was all I had. When he called he said there were "some people" who were willing to talk to me. He hemmed and hawed around and finally admitted that he'd promised them all twenty bucks and a meal to talk to me. I sighed, knowing it was unlikely I'd get anything useful and would be out money that wasn't worth spending. But I agreed to meet him at the church on the north side of the Platte near the bridge on Grant Street. He suggested we meet in the parking lot and talk, which was a relief. I didn't want to host multiple homeless people in my car. He asked if I'd be willing to bring burgers and coffee and pay him and the six people who had come forward and I reluctantly agreed.

When I arrived with said food, drink, and money, Cliff and his motley crew were waiting up near the church building in a sheltered spot, he with his sign and the rest with signs or ratty backpacks or in the case of the only woman, an overloaded grocery cart.

Cliff made the introductions and seemed to take it as his job to present one person after another to talk to me. It was an experience. I heard the gamut from aliens, to drug dealers, to the CIA being responsible for Scott's murder. I paid them and sent them on their way with food. All this had accomplished was to relieve me of a hundred dollars so far, not counting the price of the food, or the woman who was still waiting, and Cliff. She had held back and not jostled to get ahead of anyone like a couple of the others had done, and she looked reluctant to talk to me.

Cliff took hold of her hand and brought her closer and whispered something in her ear. "This here's a friend a mine, name's Sylvie," he said to me. "I talked to her and she was near where I was, just a diffrent spot. Says she tol' the police what she knew, but they din't seem to believe her. She gets a little worried about things, so you gotta promise you won' try'n take her to the station to talk to 'em."

"Okay, Sylvie, you have my word. It would be helpful to hear what you saw or heard. I'm trying to help some of my friends."

I had given her the burger and coffee in the hopes it would help her feel more comfortable. She looked up for a moment and then went back to her burger. Without looking up, she said, "Friends are good. I like Cliff, he's my friend."

I looked closely at her. I couldn't see any obvious signs of developmental delay, but you never knew, so I took it slow. "Cliff tells me you saw or heard something the night the man was killed under the bridge. Could you tell me about it?"

"I tol' the police. They didden believe me."

"Well, I'm here and I want to listen, if you'll tell me."

"I saw two guys, they were mad. One said the Mad Hatter's son had to give him money to leave." She chewed on a mouthful of burger and I nodded at her, hoping to encourage her to continue.

"He mus' like winter. He said it was so he could leave town 'til it cooled off. It's pretty cold now. I don' like winter. He tol' the Mad Hatter's son that if he didden give him the money, he'd tell on him to the police. The Mad Hatter's son got really mad. He said he'd bring the money the next night, but when the man tried to leave, he hit'm hard on the head. It was scary, so I didden look no more."

"Did you see what he looked like?"

"He was handsome. He was tall with dark hair—and a big coat! I liked that coat it looked warm, it'd cover my whole legs," she said, smiling at me sweetly.

"You didn't see anything else?"

"No, I was scared. I didden want 'im to hurt me."

"I can imagine. Thank you for telling me, Sylvie; you're very brave." I handed them each a $20 bill and I watched Sylvie hide what was left of her burger in her grocery cart and walk away.

"Cliff, there are shelters in town I could take you to and you wouldn't have to sleep outside. Sylvie seems a little fragile to be out on the street."

"Nah, I don' like them shelters. They got too many rules and I don' like being round all those people. I don' like all the religious stuff an Sylvie doesn't like being there, neither. I get antsy, and she gets all wired up, next thing ya know, she's having a meltdown and they take her to the hospital. Just don' seem worth it to me." He finished the last of his coffee and deposited the cup in the trashcan by the church's back door. "'Sides, the priest here is okay with Sylvie an me staying in the church basement when it's bad out and I can keep my stuff there if I want. Sylvie won' part with her cart, so he lets 'er bring it inside. We help out in return; works okay fer us."

"If you get into problems or need anything, please let me know."

"I'm fine. A burger and coffee now and then'd be nice," he said with a shy smile.

"I'll remember that."

WELL, SO much for Sylvie's testimony, or the others for that matter, I thought. Her story seemed to be a mixture of truth and fantasy. The others? Well, there didn't seem to be anything but paranoia and fantasy in those tales. I didn't know what to make of Sylvie's information, though, and if any of it was accurate, it probably wouldn't hold up under legal scrutiny. I could see now why the police dismissed it. Where in the world did the Mad Hatter's son come from? Was the guy wearing a hat? Was it because they were mad at each other? It was anyone's guess. All I could be certain of based on her story and Cliff's, was that these two men had met and one had decided to put an end to the association.

It was frustrating. I figured Frost knew what Cliff and Sylvie had said. In all probability he wouldn't give me much information about the case, but maybe I could get him to tell me something. I never knew whether he was annoyed with everyone or just me. He always sounded frazzled when I called.

"Don't tell me, you've got something else to report," he said when he answered.

"Um, no, I just wondered if you got your hair analysis back."

"We did and it was the same as yours."

"Did you follow up with Edward?"

"Yes."

"Okay," I said, sighing. "I'm sorry to keep bugging you."

"That's okay, but until you sign on with the force, this isn't up for discussion." He paused for a few moments. "Before you go, though, while you were staying there, was there anything Edward Matheisen or anyone else did who could have provided the thallium to Mrs. Matheisen? Anything at all?"

"Well, not really. I suppose it could have been put in her food, although she wasn't eating well at all...." I stopped and remembered the way she seemed to live on tea. "She drank tea like a fish. Cora or Edward was always bringing it to her. I even brought it to her more than once. I suppose it could have been added to that."

"Thanks, you just gave me probable cause to search the place." He sounded much happier. "I gotta go."

THIRTY-TWO

I KNEW I'D GET nothing from Frost about whether he'd found anything during the search, so I pumped Angel. He was more cooperative, but equally annoyed.

Near Thanksgiving Angel said they'd searched Edward's house and seized anything that might be prepared and ingested, but paid special attention to any teas that were there. As it happened there weren't a lot, several small boxes of Celestial Seasonings teas and an elaborately decorated tin of loose tea.

What was more incriminating, they found a suspicious container of powder in the basement of the house identified later as thallium, a spray bottle of water that tested positive for a thallium solution, and a drying rack with traces of the thallium solution on it. The loose tea in the tin they'd seized looked normal but when tested had been saturated with thallium. Based on what had been recovered, they thought the tea had been sprayed with the solution and allowed to dry. The dosage was minimal depending on the scoop used, but if consumed in the quantities Libby did, would produce the symptoms she'd been exhibiting.

Edward and Cora had both prepared the tea and delivered it to Libby. More incriminating was Edward kept the basement storeroom locked. It was old and in his opinion not safe. The key was accessible to Cora and the other staff, but they had no reason to access the room. No fingerprints other than his were found, and no one interviewed claimed to have gone into the basement or known about the thallium.

According to Cora, Edward was in the basement periodically to store or retrieve things and was the only one, as far as she knew, who entered it. She was, however, adamant that Edward would not have hurt Libby and insisted that he was not responsible for the poisoning.

After presenting the case to the DA's office and getting the go-ahead, Frost arrested Edward for the attempted murder of Libby by using the thallium to poison her. Edward continued to proclaim his innocence. While his alibi for the night of Libby's suicide wasn't airtight, neither Frost nor anyone else believed Libby's death was anything other than a suicide. As Angel pointed out, Libby might have killed herself because of what she was experiencing from the thallium, but it hadn't killed her.

Edward was arraigned, charged with attempted murder, and remanded to the Denver county jail until the DA and the defense could either work out a deal that would avoid a trial or his trial occurred. The judge had refused bail, knowing that Edward had the money and the means to disappear.

The news was a relief to me and cheered Ian because he said it meant there was nothing further for me to be involved in. He seemed to relax, and only when he did was I aware how tightly strung we had both been.

The arrest provided some closure for me except for the fact that the dreams continued. When Libby showed up she'd either watch me reproachfully or we'd have weird conversations that were less about her imparting psychic clues as they were about my subconscious struggling with what had happened to her.

She sat on the end of my bed one night, and said, "You should have insisted I get a third opinion, don't you think?"

"Libby, you wouldn't cooperate with anything I asked you to do."

"Well, I was depressed. You're the nurse, you should have known better. I appreciate you pursuing all this, but it might have been better to do it while I was alive."

The woman's words in Estes flitted through my dream—my friend had needed my help; she just hadn't gotten it.

"I'm sure it would have, but I didn't think you were being poisoned. I wish you'd never called me. I didn't help."

"I probably shouldn't have called you, but I'm glad you found out about the thallium. Now you know I wasn't crazy. Are you sure it's Edward?"

"Christ, I don't know anymore."

"Well, this is your dream. I'd tell you but I can't tell you anything you don't already know, can I?"

"If that's the case then go away and let me sleep." And sometimes she would.

Occasionally, Jeff would show up with his battered face. Dreams of him were more peaceful as I had the sense that he was aware of what I had done for him. But he would often caution me to be careful—of what he never said. Sometimes both of them would arrive together and just watch me.

It frustrated me and I remember during one dream saying, "What do you want? We have the person who poisoned you, Libby, and the man who killed Jeff is dead. What more do you want?" They never answered me. They simply came and kept me company. If they wanted something they should damned well say what it was or leave me alone. They didn't seem to agree on either point and continued to visit.

NOW THAT Edward had been charged and the case had been turned over to the DA, I pumped Angel for updates, which he reluctantly provided, reminding me he was risking his job for me.

Edward had refused all deals for a reduced sentence the DA offered or his attorneys came up with.

"Deals? What deals? Why would anyone offer him a deal?" I asked Angel.

"Because nobody wants to go to trial on a case like this. It'd be better if he'd just accept a plea and be done with it, but he pleaded not guilty and is insisting on going to trial," Angel said. "His attorneys and my boss are tearing their hair out."

I was surprised there was any deal on the table.

"And there you would be wrong, *chica*," he said. "Except for premeditated first degree murder, all other charges are up for negotiation."

That was disappointing. At trial, the verdict could go either way...and I would have to testify.

IAN AND I were invited to Angel's parents' house for Thanksgiving. With no family in town, I had no plans. Ian declined. He said he really disliked Thanksgiving and large crowds of people, but for me to go; that surprised me, but he seemed sincere about it, so I went. It was a very different kind of Thanksgiving; there was no turkey, which was a relief. Instead, it was a Mexican feast and a house filled with family members tripping over each other.

When my parents had been alive, Thanksgiving was a big affair with both sets of grandparents attending and the three of us girls inviting whomever the latest boyfriends were. When my grandparents and father passed, Thanksgiving became a quiet and sometimes miserable day. The food would be mediocre, as turkey usually was, regardless who cooked. The best that could be said was dessert was always great. Chip and Maddie had their families to attend to, and now that I lived in Colorado with my parents gone and my sisters living elsewhere, I really had nowhere to go, and I couldn't cook a decent turkey to save my soul.

The sheer number of Angel's family members astounded me. Aunts, uncles, cousins, sisters, brothers, parents, wives, husbands, and assorted other friends were all present. Tables occupied the kitchen, where the kids ate; the dining room, where the older members of the family ate; and the living room, where the rest of us ate at card tables, on the couch or chairs, or on the floor.

It was fun, but at times embarrassing for Angel and me because everyone assumed we were a couple. At one point we looked at each other, shrugged, and quit denying it. No one believed our denials anyway. Truth be told, I felt like we had been a couple for ages, in almost every way except the sex and living together. I thought the lack of those two issues was probably why we got on so well.

After dinner, an elderly woman sat next to me on the couch and took my hand. "I am Angelito's *abuela*. I am so glad he has found a nice girl. He tells me you are a nurse?"

I confirmed it, and she said, "We are so proud of him. The only lawyer in the family, and now a nurse." She smiled and patted my hand. "You must come more often and do not let him get away. He is a good man, a bit frustrating at times, but a good heart."

I agreed, it was a good assessment of him and there was no point in telling her we weren't a couple. She rose and tottered off as Angel brought me dessert.

"I don't think I can eat any more," I protested as he handed me the plate.

"Well, you have to eat this or my grandmother will be very offended. It's her yearly contribution, *tres leches* cake, and it's really good." He sat down next to me with a dish of his own and we began to eat.

"This is good. You know she's practically got us married with kids?"

"Yeah, I know. They want me settled and married."

"You must disappoint them on a regular basis."

He snorted and nodded. "Yeah, I do. One day someone will snag me. But I haven't found the one yet." A mouthful later he amended his statement. "That's not quite right, I have found the one, but she's not interested so I'm playing the field until she is."

I was surprised; it was the only time he had ever indicated anything more than a fleeting interest in anyone. "You sure she'll change her mind?"

"Well, I'm hoping. I've got plenty of time to wait her out." He winked at me. "If I get desperate, I'll take you on."

"Oh, very funny." He could be so annoying, and I felt irrationally slighted by the thought that he'd found someone he was serious about.

AFTER THE holiday I visited Frost, whose expression said my arrival wasn't a surprise and a visit he wasn't looking forward to. I could never tell if he liked me or if he considered me just another cross to bear.

"Didja have a nice Thanksgiving?" he asked, trying to be social.

"I did. How about you?"

"Ah you know, it's Thanksgiving and family, not always the best time, but not bad." He ushered me into what I now thought of as our conference room and closed the door. "What can I do for you?"

"Now that Edward's been arrested I wondered what he said."

He sighed. "You are relentless. How many times do I have to tell you I can't talk about the details?"

"Can't you give me like a synopsis? She's my friend, was my friend. It all seems so pointless."

"Situations like this are never easy and most of the time the reasons behind them are just baffling." He sat back in his chair and ran his hands through his hair, then seemed to make a decision.

"Okay, synopsis. I can't tell you why he did what he did; he denies everything. He says he loved her even though he knew she was cheating." As usual when he seemed frustrated he started tapping a pencil on his desk. "He knew the baby wasn't his and says he was fine with that. The amnio was only to make sure the child was healthy. He thinks she committed suicide because of losing the baby and because of Jeff. So, essentially, he admits to nothing."

He sighed, tossed the pencil on the desk, and ran his hands through his thinning hair. "We have the thallium and the tea, and we have two witnesses who saw him bring her the tea, that's you and Cora. Unfortunately, there were no fingerprints on any of the stuff that was used to contaminate the tea."

"You know it was weird about the tea. A package of it arrived on a monthly basis and Libby claimed it was from an old friend; I think it was the same one who got her started on some of the vitamins she took. She never said who the friend was, but said that it was her favorite tea. It arrived regular as clockwork. Libby said the tea came from Vitamin Cottage or Natural Grocers, although I think those two have merged now, or maybe it was Whole Foods, I can't remember."

"Do you believe that?"

"I have no reason not to. I don't suppose there is any way to prove that Edward put the thallium in the tea?" Frost shook his head. "I wish I knew who was sending it. I just worry the defense will try to create reasonable doubt by claiming the tea arrived contaminated. That's not going to be easy with the thallium in his basement, but you know lawyers."

"You seem to know an awful lot about this investigation. Who's your source?"

"Not saying." He stared at me and looked very annoyed. "I'm not telling you, so you can quit eyeballing me."

"Fine," he said, relenting. "I think I have an idea who it is, but fine. Be glad we at least solved the puzzle of Mrs. Matheisen's health issues. I know this is hard for you, Ms. Collins, but her death was suicide. She had enough reasons to do it."

"Oh for God's sake, call me Annie. Ms. Collins makes me feel like you're talking to my mother." I frowned. "I just find it hard to believe. She was so passionate about her art, she said it was all she really loved."

"Well, people as a rule need more than that to be happy."

"Maybe you're right. Thanks for letting me in on all of this."

"Just keep the information confidential or my head and your secret source's head will be handed to us. It's a relief I don't have to worry about you getting in the middle of this anymore. You will have to testify about the tea, so bear that in mind."

"I will."

THIRTY-THREE

CHRISTMAS, THE SEASON of joy, stress, overspending, depression, disappointment, and suicide, was approaching. My sisters had other plans and apparently so did Ian's family. He said they were all going to Arizona to his parents', so we were on our own. I wasn't sure I could deal with another Angel family affair or continue the charade that we were a couple. The family's assumptions about Angel and me would not sit well if Ian attended. I also knew that most likely Ian would not come, if invited, and I did not want to spend Christmas without him.

The week before Christmas, I stopped at the Vitamin Cottage/ Natural Grocers on Leetsdale to pick up some bath salts and soaps for my sisters. I hadn't come just for Christmas gifts; I'd looked at Whole Foods to see if I could find the tea and then had come to see if Natural Grocers carried it. I cruised the aisles to see if I could find something for my sisters and then made my way to the tea section. I couldn't remember if Libby had said where the tea came from, but I hadn't seen it at Whole Foods, and it didn't look like something your basic grocery store would carry.

I slowly perused the shelves, and sure enough, they carried the tea. I picked up a tin and went to the customer service desk and asked the clerk about whether they made deliveries. If they did, maybe they could tell me who had arranged the deliveries to Libby.

"We don't normally do monthly deliveries," he said. "But I'll look in our order book if you can hang on a second." He rummaged around under the desk and pulled out a battered ring binder. "Nope, no monthly deliveries, like I said, but there was a customer who ordered two dozen tins in May, paid cash when he picked them up."

He wouldn't give out the name or contact information, and I couldn't read the name upside down because of the handwriting, but I could see the phone number. I kept repeating the number in my head as I keyed it into my phone. The clerk didn't know who had taken care of the customer and couldn't give me a description.

After paying for my purchases, I dialed the number. The phone rang several times and the automated recording came on. "The number you have dialed is a non-working number. Please hang up and check the number." Everything turned out to be a dead end.

Maybe the friend who was sending the tea was Libby's other lover. If so, he might have paid cash so the delivery couldn't be traced to him if Edward found out. Two dozen tins seemed over the top to me, even for a friend or former lover, but I didn't know what the point of the deliveries was, so who knew?

I wondered if this friend was the same one who'd called her and thought my providing care was unwise. It seemed like a moot point, she was gone, there was no one who could identify him, and I had no way to find out when or where she'd met the other lover. After four years, I had no idea who her friends were and asking Edward was awkward. Just another dead end.

HAVING THOUGHT about it for a while, I asked Angel if he could get Edward to provide the name of Libby's friend who'd hosted the house-warming. If he would, then perhaps I could ask about who she might have met there.

"Why?" he asked.

"I just want to talk to her. I have a couple of questions she might be able to answer."

He looked at me for a minute, then said, "I wish I knew what the hell you were up to."

"Just trust me, okay? See if you can get the name and phone number for me, please?"

❧

I DRAGGED Ian out to purchase a tree for my place the next night. He had never bothered with decorating as he either spent the holiday with family or traveling, so there didn't seem to be much point. It was snowing outside, and he helped me retrieve the tree stand and the ornament boxes from the garage.

"Who buys real trees anymore?" he asked as he came in the back door with one of the boxes. "Doesn't everybody have a Home Depot special? I don't think I've put up a real tree since I was a kid when the only fake trees available were pink, blue, and white flocked aluminum."

"We could always get an aluminum tree and just put up the pole. Have a 'Festivus for the Rest of Us,' as George's dad on *Seinfeld* would say." I'd found the box with the lights in it and began unraveling them. "I'm not much into feats of strength or telling people how much they've disappointed me in the last year. Although, if we were going to do it, this would be the year."

"Now, come on, no Christmas cynicism, please."

He helped me get the tree in the stand and we spent the evening putting the lights on and decorating it.

"Fake trees are certainly easier, but this turned out very nice," he said when we were done.

"That's why I still do the real trees; they are just so magical."

Quite happy with the results, we settled in for the evening. We ordered in, and while we were eating, he got up and took something from his coat pocket and came back to the table. "Here," he said holding a brochure out to me.

"What's this?"

"Read it and you'll see."

I looked at the brochure, which was for a condo in Aspen that looked really nice. "And you are showing me this, because?"

"Because that's our Christmas present, arrive Friday the twenty-third and return on Monday the twenty-sixth. How does that sound?"

"It sounds absolutely wonderful, but why did you let me put up a tree?"

"As far as the tree goes, we've got almost a week to enjoy it and most people don't take them down right away, so we can still enjoy it when we get back."

"I take it no other presents are required?"

"Nope, I like to keep it simple."

"But you're giving me this, I should give you something."

"You do, you give your company, your affection, and sex, plus you put up with me. What more could a man ask for?"

I took a playful swing at him. "It's lovely, Ian, thanks. It'll be nice to get away. I promise not to find any ghosts or weird psychic women."

"Thank God. I don't think I could take a repeat performance."

WE LEFT at mid-day. The drive, while a long four hours, was uneventful and we arrived around six. The condo was near downtown Aspen and I shuddered to think what he must be paying for it. It had one bedroom and a double-sided fireplace that opened into the living room on one side and the bedroom on the other. It was fully furnished and the complex had a hot tub. It was heaven.

We unpacked and then bundled up to walk to dinner. The town was like a fairyland. Every tree in town looked like it had been dressed with lights. Predictably, Christmas music was playing, which, because Denver radio stations start playing Christmas music the day after Thanksgiving, was getting a little old, but in this setting it seemed enchanting.

We found a bar that served food and didn't require a reservation or have a huge waiting list, and eventually we were escorted to a table near the fireplace, which took the chill off. The streets were plowed, but the snow was deep even in town and it had continued to snow intermittently all day. We placed our drink orders and settled in.

"I checked to see if the pool at Glenwood was open on Christmas Eve," he said. "It's open nine to six; do you want to drive over and spend the day marinating in the hot springs?"

"Yes, please, that would be wonderful."

"We should get some groceries in tomorrow morning; there may not be many restaurants open Christmas Eve or day. We can ask at a couple of the ones we saw coming here on our walk back to the condo. Are you glad you came?"

"Absolutely. What a wonderful way to spend Christmas." It was wonderful. Christmas, no matter what they say, is not always the happiest of holidays, and the chance to be away with him all to myself was the best present he could have given me.

"Thank you, Ian."

"My pleasure."

ON OUR way back to the condo, we found a restaurant that would be open Christmas Eve. None, it seemed, would be open Christmas Day, so we made a reservation. Once back, Ian started a fire and opened one of the bottles of wine we'd brought with us and poured two glasses. As he handed one to me, he wrapped his arm around my waist, pulled me to him, and kissed me. "I've been wanting to do that all day."

"Surely you want more than kisses?" I put my wine down on the breakfast bar we were standing next to and kissed him, running my hands down his back and pulling him up against me.

He broke away to set his glass down and pulled me to him again. It seemed as if the fire burning in the fireplace had ignited something. His kisses were just short of violent as he worked his way down my throat, undoing the buttons on my shirt as he went. He stripped off my shirt and bra and continued kissing my breasts and belly. His face was rough with stubble and left red marks on me as he undid my jeans and shoved them to the floor. He pulled his shirt off, and I struggled to undo his jeans as we clumsily made our way into the living room.

On the floor in front of the fire, he lay next to me and kissed me, letting go and taking my hand and placing it on himself. "God, this is what you do to me," he said breathlessly.

I rolled him over and straddled him, and as he reached up and took hold of my breasts I whispered, "This is what you do to me," as I took him and guided him home.

◌

AS WE lay watching the fire, he groped behind him on the couch and pulled a throw blanket down over us. "I don't think any of my synapses are firing."

"I think they fired just fine, but it may take a while for them to recharge." I chuckled.

"Well, they may recharge but I'm not sure I'll be up to firing them off again."

I got up and retrieved our wine glasses and sat down beside him. "Want yours back?" I asked, holding out his glass. "Maybe we should turn so we can lean up against the couch. We don't want to be charged for wine stain removal."

He took the glass, and we reoriented ourselves and lay back against the couch.

"We may get charged for removal of other fluids from the carpet, but at least they aren't as obvious as the wine would be." He took a drink. "Seriously, I think my brain has short-circuited."

"It was pretty intense, but there are no complaints from me; I enjoyed myself immensely. No pun intended." I laughed.

He looked at me blankly for a moment and then shook his head. "You are incorrigible. Let's sit here for a while and enjoy the fire and the wine, and then I think I might be able to continue what we started in the bedroom."

◌

I SLEPT well for the first time since Libby's death and there were no dreams. We both had a few bony and soft-tissue sore spots the next morning, but after a grocery run, we headed to Glenwood where the hot springs soon took care of the aches and pains.

I think the most enjoyable time at Glenwood is in the winter. Steam rises continually from the two pools, especially the hot one, and you feel lost in a fog of mineral steam. If you happen to be there while it's snowing, it's even better, the snow melts as it falls on your head and shoulders and the rest of you is toasty and content.

The steam is very isolating, too, and after a while, you begin to feel you are in some lost world, alone except for the person immediately near you and the muffled voices of other unseen bathers. Sitting in this warm and private space, Ian and I continued quietly and carefully to reconnect with last night—touching, caressing, and kissing, but never more. It was exquisite and when we could take no more, we drove back to the condo to pick up where we'd left off.

We spent Christmas Day in the condo, with the fire crackling in the fireplace. While dinner was in the oven cooking, we walked out in the snow and returned cold, famished, and happy. Dinner turned out well and we spent the evening cuddled on the couch watching *It's a Wonderful Life*, and working our way through a bottle of wine.

In bed, watching the fire burn low, Ian whispered into my hair, "I'm so happy, Annie, this has been a special Christmas."

"I am, too," I murmured into his shoulder as he held me close. Special was an understatement, but not wrong by any means.

THIRTY-FOUR

I T CONTINUED TO snow the following week and Angel called with a name and phone number for the housewarming host. He asked no further questions, but told me that whatever I was doing, to try to stay out of trouble.

Ian spent more time at my place than he did at his. It seemed as if something had shifted for both of us with Edward's arrest. The tension that I'd felt between us had lifted, and we settled into a more normal life. We spent New Year's Eve at my house with a bottle of champagne to share at midnight. Unfortunately, we both fell asleep on the couch waiting for midnight to arrive.

We both returned to work after the holiday. I called and spoke with the Karen Harris whose name and phone number Edward had provided. She invited me to stop by on my day off. Arriving at her house was a lot like arriving at Libby's for the first time. It was a beautiful home in Cherry Creek north, the latest real estate hot spot. I was as much in awe of the place as I had been when I'd first visited Libby's. We sat in the living room on chairs that were gorgeous, just not all that comfortable.

"So you knew Libby?" She was probably mid-forties, I thought, and had that nipped and tucked look to her and the requisite blond hair. Women in this tax bracket all seemed to look alike to me.

"Yes, we were friends in college and after. She asked me to take care of her for a while."

"Oh, you're the friend she told me about; nice to meet you. It's just so sad what happened to her. I still can't believe it."

I nodded. "I was trying to track down some loose ends and Libby at one point mentioned meeting a friend at a housewarming party you gave."

"Yes, we'd just bought this place. It was a fun party."

"Do you recall her meeting with anyone at the party? Was she with Edward?"

"No, Edward was out of town if I remember right."

"Did you see her connect with anyone at the party?"

"Lord, there were nearly eighty people at that party and it was a year ago. I barely remember everyone who came. My husband invited a lot of people he does business with; I don't remember seeing her with anyone in particular."

"So you weren't aware of her leaving with anyone?"

"No, I'm sorry, I was so busy playing hostess and being introduced to all of Jack's associates, that's my husband, that I just don't know. I remember seeing Libby briefly when she arrived and saying hi to her and I saw her talk to a number of people, but that's about it. I don't think I saw her when she left."

"Well, I appreciate your time," I said, getting up to go. "Would you call me if you remember anything?" I asked, handing her a card with my phone number.

"Of course," she said, taking the card and showing me out.

Dead end after dead end, I thought, walking to my car.

THE TRIAL date was approaching and the whole process of testifying loomed, but work kept me distracted. As I walked past the front desk on my way back to my room after lunch, the charge nurse held out a piece of paper for me, "Annie, you got a call, he asked you to call when you had a chance." I took the piece of paper and saw that it was Angel's number and wondered what he wanted.

He had made himself scarce after Edward's arraignment. I had seen him briefly before Ian and I had left for Aspen when he had brought over some cookies from his grandmother. Calling him back would have to wait until my first break. I was due back in my room, so I tucked the note into my cover jacket, grabbed a new mask, and headed back to work.

When I finally called on my dinner break, he asked, "Did you get what you wanted from Libby's friend?"

"No, unfortunately."

"Sorry I haven't been in touch, I've been pretty busy. My boss is making life miserable for everyone."

"What's up?" I asked. I guessed it was something to do with the case against Edward, which worried me.

"I'm just tired and frustrated and I haven't seen much of you. I just wanted to touch base."

"Are things not going well?" He sounded a little low which was unusual for Angel.

"My boss isn't happy that no one has been able to figure out who sent the tea. He thinks it's a way for the defense to throw enough doubt on Edward's guilt at trial to get an acquittal. As he pointed out, who's to say he doctored the tea?" Angel sounded tired and irritable. "The thallium was in the house, but there's no concrete evidence that he used it, and he claims to know nothing about it. So there's a small chance the tea could have arrived doctored. Frankly, I don't think anyone else is involved; I just thought you'd want to know."

"Is that enough to get him acquitted?"

"Jury trials are a crap shoot. He was charged on the evidence as it stands, but juries are unpredictable. It'd be better if we could pin that down."

"If it helps, the tea was purchased at the Vitamin Cottage/Natural Grocers on Leetsdale and was paid for in cash."

"How the hell do you know that?"

"I didn't actually, but Libby always purchased food and other stuff at Whole Foods or Natural Grocers so I checked both out. Natural Grocers carries the tea. I talked to the customer service guy who said a customer had ordered two dozen tins and paid for them in cash. The clerk couldn't describe the person, and he wouldn't give me any other information. I saw the phone number and called it, but it's a non-working number. So it's another dead end."

I hesitated for a moment, and then confessed, "I'm not sure exactly why Edward would buy two dozen tins of the stuff, but maybe he didn't want anyone to see him buying it repeatedly. That'd up the chances he'd be seen by someone they knew. When I first started working there, she was talking to someone on the phone who wasn't happy about her hiring me. After the call she said he'd bought vitamins for her to help her feel better. Maybe he's the one who was sending the tea and Edward just took advantage of the fact and contaminated it."

"Christ, I don't suppose you have any idea who he might be?"

"Only that she met him at a friend's housewarming party. That's why I asked for her friend's name and number. I thought maybe she would remember who the person was, but she didn't."

"Okay, I'll pass that on. I guess you're still up to your ass in this, correct?"

"Not quite as deep as I was."

"Which, knowing you, means you're up to your neck in it."

I THOUGHT it best, despite my promise to be honest with Ian, not to say anything about the tea or talking to Libby's friend or Angel. We had settled into such a relaxed, happy space that I didn't want to do anything to change it. I wasn't sure there was anything I could do to resolve the who-sent-the-tea issue anyway, and if that turned out to be the case, then it would have been pointless to stir things up.

It occurred to me that there was a lot of stuff during our relationship that I hadn't wanted Ian to know about and that made me uncomfortable. The question was who was in the wrong, me because of my need to figure this out, or Ian because of his insistence that I stop? I thought about how right Libby had been about fatal flaws in relationships, and there were times when I wondered how compatible Ian and I really were. And that made my head hurt.

TWENTY-FOUR HOURS later, I'd been considering and rejecting an idea. The police had turned Edward and Libby's place over when they'd executed the search warrant, and I knew from Angel that they'd searched all the computers and phones and found nothing about the thallium or the tea. I kept thinking, because I had been her friend and was female, that I could perhaps find something at the house if I were to look.

Women tend to keep things that, at times, they would be better off not keeping, like love notes and other personal tokens. Libby knew who sent the tea, so it seemed like she might have gotten a note with the first delivery. If it was from her vitamin friend or her other lover, perhaps she'd kept it.

She had ended her affair with Jeff and the other man abruptly. Faced with pregnancy and her fear of divorce, she might have seen it as her only option, but that didn't preclude feelings for this new lover. I could hear Angel's voice in my head lecturing me about getting involved, but I ignored it.

THINKING ABOUT it, it seemed unlikely that either the lock or the alarm code had remained the same, and I was going to have to talk to Frost about access to the house. I wasn't sure he'd go along with it, but I knew he and the DA were worried and needed to identify who sent the tea.

"Why do you want to get into the house?"

"I've been thinking about the tea. No one knows who actually sent it; maybe it was Edward. Maybe he sent it so it'd look as if it was coming from someone else, or maybe not. I just thought if someone else sent it to her, if that person was important to her, maybe she'd have kept a note or letter. If I went through the place I might be able to find something that would identify the person and then you could talk to them, or maybe I'd find something to indicate that it was actually Edward."

"And why would you be able to find something when we didn't?"

"I may not be able to, but we were friends, I lived with her for quite a while and I know how she thought, and I'm a woman," I said lamely. "I don't know, I'd just like to try, if you'll let me."

He sat and watched me, obviously turning the pros and cons over in his head. "I'm probably going to regret this," he said picking up the phone. He called the evidence storage locker and asked the attendant to find the keys to the house and motioned for one of the uniformed officers who worked as aides to the detectives to go get it. He flipped through a notebook of his and gave me the alarm code.

I HAD convinced Frost to let me go alone, which had taken some talking, but in the end he relented. I was to bring the keys and anything I found directly to him, I was not to pass go, I was not to collect two hundred dollars—although he wasn't that funny about it.

It felt strange to be in Edward and Libby's house. It was cold, the heat was turned down to a temperature that would keep the pipes from freezing, but that wasn't warm. I found the thermostat and boosted the heat up so that I could work without coat and gloves on. It would be a while until the temperature rose, so I left them on while I walked around the main floor re-orienting myself.

It's surprising how quickly a house loses the sense of habitation; there was no scent of perfume, food, furniture polish, or flowers; no sense of anyone having ever lived here.

I sat on the living room couch and wondered where I'd put something special, something I didn't want my husband or anyone else finding. Living alone and never having worried about this before, nothing came to mind immediately. This room, though, was too public, as were the rest of the rooms on the main floor, so it seemed unlikely Libby would have put anything here.

It also didn't seem likely Libby would have concealed anything Edward had sent her, and if he'd sent the tea it was just as unlikely he'd have identified himself, if he were trying to cast blame for it elsewhere. If someone else had sent the tea, it just seemed weird that anyone would go to the trouble to send it monthly. I had never seen the tea arrive, so I didn't know whether it arrived in the mail of how it was delivered. I wondered briefly if it might have been Jeff, as a way to keep in touch. If it was, he surely wasn't the source of the thallium, but it hit the "unlikely" list he'd commit anything to writing. Love makes you do stupid things, though; maybe he'd sent a note or maybe her other lover had. If I could find some proof of who had sent it, then Frost and the DA could investigate further.

I got up and walked up the front stairs as I had months before and wished again, like I will 'til I'm dead, I had not returned Libby's call. It probably wouldn't have prevented her death, but selfishly, I thought it would have kept me out of the whole affair. Based on that thought, no doubt the dreams would be intense tonight. Guilt and grief are powerful emotions.

I stood at the top of the stairs, wondering where to start. I eyed the stairs to Edward's sanctum. I doubted Libby would have put anything there, but this was the perfect opportunity to explore Edward's space, so I turned down the hall and took the stairs to his private quarters. I entered the room and flipped the light on. The police had done a very thorough job of turning it inside out. According to Angel, they had boxed up and taken all his files as well as his computer, CPU, and external backup drives. The desk had been rifled, as had the bookcase.

There was a single bed in the room and a small bath that opened off it; no doubt this was where Edward had moved when Libby became too restless to sleep with. What surprised me were the pictures: An entire wall was filled with pictures of Libby in every mood. They were beautiful. Was this the work of someone who loved his wife or someone who was obsessed with her? I wasn't sure. He had now lost two wives, both to unusual circumstances.

I suddenly felt like a voyeur standing there, so I turned the light off and went back down to the second floor.

I went to her bedroom on the second floor and stood just inside the door. They had gone through it but had had the decency to return it close to its original order. I gazed around and walked into her closet. Her clothes and shoes and all the attendant accessories were still there. I walked up to a rack of clothes and drew them to my face. There was a faint scent of citrus and bergamot from the perfume she'd always worn. I closed my eyes and just breathed it in for a few moments. I fancied I could smell the faint scent of oil paints, linseed oil, and turpentine that I had lived with for four years so long ago.

Releasing the clothes and stepping back, I scanned the closet for likely hiding places. There was an island with drawers for lingerie and I went through each, but again the police had already been there. I'd seen the contents while caring for her; they'd been carefully organized by color. I smiled; so like Libby to make a color wheel of her undies. They were now mixed together in the drawers, so nothing to be found. I went through her dressing table and found nothing.

Those were the only obvious drawers in the closet, so I went methodically through each hanging rack pushing the clothes aside to make sure there wasn't a safe or other cubby hiding behind the clothes. Finding nothing, I went through all the pockets of her jackets and pants, felt inside the toes of her boots, and searched all her purses. Aside from wondering who needed all those purses, I found nothing. I left the closet and went around the room, with similar results. I sat down on the bed, which had been stripped, the mattress and box spring searched and left slightly askew.

I leaned forward with my arms on my knees and could remember her lying on the bed and then on the floor, and my heart clutched and tears started up anew.

"Ah, Libby, this just isn't the way it should have ended. I'm so sorry."

I sat there, my head in my hands, and felt a touch on my shoulder and a peace that eased the grief. Maybe it was Libby, maybe it was an overwhelming need for comfort and forgiveness that made me imagine it, but whatever it was, it was a blessing.

I stood up and checked the bathroom cupboard and drawers, but there was nothing to be found. I left the bedroom and walked down to her studio. Her paintings were gone, no doubt moved to some secure storage facility or perhaps to the gallery for sale. They would be in even more demand now. The artwork in the house was gone as well and all the valuables had been removed and secured. For some reason it annoyed me that he'd left her clothes, as if they had no value, but perhaps he'd been arrested before that had been arranged.

The studio was quiet, the large south-facing windows let in all the light available on this overcast, cold winter's day. The house was warming up, so I removed my coat and gloves and put them by the door. It must have been a delight to work here. I walked over to the cart that contained her oils and acrylics. Her brushes were gathered in several pots by size, ready for her to pick them up and create something beautiful. Pencils, charcoal, brush cleaning jars, and metal containers of solvents sat on the cart. I took two brushes and laid them on my coat. I still wanted something of her.

Her easels stood empty, covered in blobs of paint, as was the floor surrounding them. I went carefully through the drawers of the workbench that contained rags for cleaning up brushes and other things that had paint on them, palette knives, wooden canvas stretchers, and two rolls of raw canvas mounted at the back of the bench. There were other odds and ends whose use I couldn't guess.

I looked through the empty racks where her paintings had stood to dry and remembered the painting she'd given me. The one that had sat in the rack for years because she couldn't part with it. Of all the rooms in the house, this one brought back how much I missed her, missed the friendship we'd had, and I so regretted her loss. Libby had changed, but somewhere in there had been the Libby I loved and this room echoed that.

The racks were empty now and held no surprises, so I moved on. There was a closet that held old jeans and shirts covered in paint—her work clothes. I searched the closet carefully and found no cubbies and no loose floorboards. I began to despair that I would find anything. The only advantage I had over the police was that she had been a friend and a woman… but sometimes that made a difference.

When I'd searched the room and found nothing, I left and walked into the nursery. Since the child was not Edward's, perhaps she had something from Jeff or her unnamed lover she had hidden away in here. The walls of the nursery had been painted a pale yellow, and there was some furniture in place that would never be used. Otherwise, it was bare. I walked around and opened the empty closet, no drawers, no cubbies, another let down.

I turned to the highboy dresser that sat near the crib. It said "Libby" all over it, as did the crib. Both pieces looked handmade. They were contemporary in a pale wood that had been lovingly finished to a high gloss. The highboy had a number of drawers, which I opened and found empty.

In frustration, I sat down on the floor and then lay back on the carpet and let my eyes wander around the room.

"Come on, Libby, help me here. You keep coming to visit and keeping me awake, so surely there's something you want from me."

There was no response; I hadn't really expected one.

My eyes kept drifting back to the highboy with all its drawers. It had probably been made-to-order, and sometimes with special orders artists put little unexpected surprises in their work. It amused them and buyers were attracted to the one-of-a-kind aspect of it. Had the artist who created the piece done that?

I sat up and went over to it and, starting at the bottom, I removed each drawer, turning them over and inspecting all sides and the openings into which they slid. In the top section, which looked as if it had been created separately and set atop the main piece almost as an afterthought, I discovered a space under the bottom drawer when I removed it from the frame. The drawer front cleverly concealed the extra depth; unless you were intentionally looking for it, or viewed it from one side while it was open, you wouldn't know it was there.

The top of the inset piece was tightly joined; there was no latch or button to open the space so it just looked like the floor of the opening where the drawer sat. I pulled out the gloves I'd brought with me from my pants pocket and put them on. I went back to the studio and got a delicate palette knife off Libby's work cart. Back at the highboy I looked closely at the edges of the bottom piece. Almost invisible to the eye, there was a slight indent in the middle of one of the sides. I slipped the knife in carefully and pressed. Nothing happened. So I tried levering it and it popped open. The smell of something familiar rose out of the concealed space. It was so familiar, yet I couldn't name it—aftershave, maybe? In the space was a small packet of letters tied with ribbon and a single unbound letter.

Bingo, I thought, taking them out and sitting on the floor.

I carefully untied the string that bound the stack together. Opening one from the stack I could see it was from Jeff. I scanned it, feeling again like a voyeur, and silently apologized to Libby and Jeff. It was what you'd expect from someone who was in love with another who probably was not as serious as you were. Still, she cared enough to keep them.

I flipped through the remaining letters and there was nothing of interest, so I tied them back together and tackled the remaining letter. Unfolding it, I read:

I'm sorry you feel you have to end what we have. It's been very special. No hard feelings, though, I understand your predicament. I hope you enjoy the tea, think of me when you get it.

Ian

THIRTY-FIVE

I STOPPED BREATHING WHEN I reached the end.
I felt faint.

Ian? My Ian? Was Ian sending the tea, was he the other lover Libby had refused to name?

My mind raced. I couldn't quite catch my breath. If this was my Ian, Libby had ended the relationship only a few months before I met him.

If he knew her, had been sleeping with her, if he was the one on the phone with her that day, then he knew who I was talking about the second I'd told him she'd hired me to care for her.

Why had he said nothing about it? Although the relationship was over, whoever wrote the note still cared enough to send her a gift once a month, perhaps to remind her what she had walked away from each time she received a tin.

I was paralyzed. I didn't want to face having to talk to Ian about it or listen to what had been *very special* about their relationship, or more importantly, why he said nothing when we'd talked about Libby.

For God's sake, it might have been his baby, and he'd given no indication he'd been involved with her. Not even when she died.

Jeff had been distraught about Libby ending things, but Ian had never indicated her death affected him in any way. How could it be him?

Maybe it wasn't, I thought frantically.

The note and the signature were typed on a computer so there was no way for me to tell if it was his handwriting. Maybe that's why he had said nothing—there was nothing to say.

I sat there and breathed deeply, trying to order my thoughts. I had to give the note to Frost or I had to leave it here and walk away. Part of me kept denying that it was the Ian I knew and insisting the letters be put back, sealed up, and left there. And the realist in me knew putting them back wouldn't erase what I'd found or keep me from wondering if it was Ian.

But…who else could it be?

He was so insistent about being truthful and had been so angry when I lied to him, surely he wouldn't lie to me; he wouldn't. *But maybe he would,* that cold rational part of my brain said, *maybe he would.* And if he had, why would he do that?

I couldn't imagine Ian being involved with her and saying nothing about it when she died, however casual the relationship might have been. Maybe he would have said nothing when he found out I was taking care of her. Maybe that's why he wanted me to stop caring for her, to prevent Libby finding out and telling me. But when she died, surely he would have told me.

Then again, if he'd failed to tell me at the start, it would have been much harder to tell me when she died, especially after making such a fuss about my lying about the gallery and the charity event.

I must have paced the nursery for more than an hour, trying to figure out what to do, struggling with the possibility that Ian had deceived me about a number of things and desperately trying to find an explanation for why this couldn't be him. No matter what I came up with, I knew I would have to give the note to Frost and I would have to confront Ian eventually.

It made my stomach burn.

I pulled my phone out and dialed Frost. It rang several times before he picked up.

"What?" he demanded.

"I…I need to talk to you."

"Annie? What's wrong?"

"I found something at the house," was all I could say.

I SAT in front of his desk, sick at heart. "When you get through looking at this stuff, I need to tell you some things."

I put a glove back on, handed the other one to Frost, and pulled the packet of Jeff's letters out of my pocket and put them on his desk, then I pulled the solitary letter from my jacket, and handed it to him reluctantly. He put his reading glasses on and opened the note. His eyes moved across the page and then he stopped and looked up at me.

"Where did you find this?"

"In a concealed compartment in the highboy in the nursery." I sighed. "I don't know if this helps. I mean, who knows who this guy is."

He snorted. "Well, it gives Edward's attorneys more ammunition to present to the jury, not sure it helps the prosecution much. What did you want to tell me?"

I took a deep breath. "Libby told me she was cheating on Edward with Jeff and another man. She would never tell me his name. Her relationship with Jeff was long-standing. I think, that her relationship with this Ian," I stumbled over his name but repeated it more clearly, "with this Ian, was…was more recent." I had struggled as I had driven to meet Frost whether or not to tell him about Ian and could find no way to avoid it. I sat there for several moments and then took a deep breath. "I'm in a relationship with a man named Ian Patterson. He's never spoken about Libby or said anything about being in a relationship with her. I think he would have told me if he knew her, certainly if he was her lover. I didn't know what to do with the note when I found it. I still don't know if I made the right decision." I sat there in misery, and said, "Maybe she knew another man named Ian. If you talk to my Ian, you can't tell him who gave this to you. Please."

"Why don't you want him to know you found this? Are you worried he might have poisoned her?"

"No! No, I am not. He wouldn't do something like that." I watched Frost give me a skeptical look. I felt desperate to defend Ian, and yet I knew the note meant there was a chance he was Libby's lover and a remote possibility he was her poisoner, something I wasn't ready to deal with. "If he sent her the tea, it doesn't mean he was the one who poisoned it."

Frost watched me. "No, it doesn't necessarily, but if he sent it to her, it puts him neck-and-neck with Edward."

"Look, I just don't believe he'd do that. Why would he do that? If it's my Ian, he's got no reason to kill her."

"That we know of."

"God! I should have just burned the damn note. That's one more reason why I don't want him to know I found it. I don't want him thinking I believe that. He may have sent her the tea and been involved with her, but he didn't poison her."

Frost sat on the edge of the desk and watched me as he often did. I could feel the frustration coming off him in waves and watch as he struggled to listen without comment.

"He's been adamant that I stop involving myself since things went south with Libby and particularly after Jeff was assaulted. Things are better now that Edward's been charged and there's nothing left for me to be involved with. He didn't want me getting hurt. If he finds out I did this he's going to be furious, especially if it drags him into the investigation or the trial. The relationship means a lot to me, but if he is the one who wrote the note, I don't know what to do. I wish I'd never found it. At least not telling him I was the one who found it will give me some time to figure out what to do."

"Well, I don't plan to tell anyone *you* found it; it disrupts the chain of custody," he said, placing the packet of letters and the single letter in their own plastic evidence bags, sealing them, and putting them in his jacket pocket. He removed the glove and tossed it in the trashcan and held his hand out for my glove. "I'll need you to go over to the house with me and show me where you found it and how you got to it. You got time to do that now?"

I nodded.

He watched me for a few moments and then continued, "At this point, I have no reason to talk to your Ian. This note has no last name, there's no signature, and no way to know if it was him or not. If I brought him in to talk to, it'd be a dead giveaway that you were involved. How else would I even know him or connect him to this? For now, I wouldn't mention it to him until we can figure out whether it was him or not. This could potentially result in Edward's acquittal. If that happens, the spotlight would be focused on finding this Ian," he said.

I nodded and sat there miserably with a hole burning in my stomach.

AFTER SHOWING Frost where and how I had found the letters, I drove to Wash Park and sat in my car. I had no idea what to do. At the very least, I had to give Ian the benefit of the doubt until Frost could determine whether it was him or not. I had no idea how Frost would do that without incriminating me.

I hoped desperately it wasn't him.

After sitting in the park for nearly an hour, I drove home and called Ian. "I have to work tonight; I'm doing the graveyard shift. Several people called in sick."

"Hmmm, too bad. I was going to suggest a movie or something."

"That would've been nice. I'm going to be pretty wasted when I get home in the morning, but I'll call you when I'm up and we can talk."

"Okay. I've got some work to catch up on anyway. Hope it's a quiet shift and you don't have to work too hard."

"Thanks, Ian. I'll talk to you tomorrow."

Again I wondered if I had done the right thing. I didn't have to work but I couldn't face him. I needed time to figure out what to do.

THIRTY-SIX

I WAS OFF THE next day and at home when there was a knock at the door. I looked through the peephole and saw Angel. He'd been pretty absent and I didn't know what that was about. I figured it was either Edward's rapidly approaching trial, some new love interest, or perhaps he was giving Ian and me some space. Other than the last phone call, I hadn't been in contact with him since before Christmas and he was rarely at home.

"Is Ian here?" he asked as he entered the living room.

"No, he'll probably be here later, though, if you want to talk to him."

"I want to talk to you, privately."

"What about?"

"Were you aware that Frost found a note about the tea at Libby's?"

"When did that happen?" I asked, trying to stall the inevitable.

"Yesterday. He turned the note over to my boss and my boss let those of us on the case know about it this morning. I saw the name Ian on it. I'm wondering if it's the Ian we know." He paced around the living room hands in his coat pockets.

I sighed. This was just getting too complicated. "I found the note and gave it to Frost."

"You found it?" he asked incredulously. "Where?"

"At Libby's."

"Why would you have been in Libby's house?"

"I talked Frost into letting me search it again to see if I could find anything about the tea, and unfortunately, I did."

"Oh, Christ." Angel sat abruptly on the couch and stared at me. "You may have just derailed the whole case. Frost said he found it when he gave it to my boss. If he testifies to that he'll have perjured himself, and if he admits you found it, the chain of custody is totally fucked. It'll get thrown out of evidence or Edward's defense will use it to cast some serious doubt on whether Edward had anything to do with the tea. Jesus, why can't you stay out of things?"

"I thought I could help."

"Well you haven't."

"I guess not." I sat down in the chair across from him and huffed out a breath. "I don't think it's Ian. He would have told me about the affair, if there had been one, when we first discussed Libby." He just stared at me. "Angel, why would he care if people knew it was him, what would it matter, if it was? There's no reason for him to lie about it."

"That's it?" he exclaimed. "That's why you think it isn't him?" He shook his head and looked thoroughly disappointed in me. "You haven't known him long enough to be sure of anything, Annie. People lie all the time. Just because you think it isn't him doesn't mean he didn't have an affair with Libby or send her the tea. He's got no police record or other red flags that I can find, but something's not right."

"You ran a background check on him?"

"Of course I did after I'd seen the note. What'd you expect I'd do?"

"I don't know, not treat him like a criminal? Have some faith in me that I know him and what he'd do?" I stared him down.

"I did what I had to do."

"What are you so worried about? You know him."

"No, I don't, not really. I know the surface Ian, that's all, and I don't particularly like him. I've tried to be friendly because of you, but there's something off about him. It's just too coincidental that the guy who was sending the tea and having an affair with Libby is named Ian. I don't believe in coincidences like that."

He got up and began pacing again. "As to him being a nice guy, he may very well be one, but he may also be a guy who had an affair with a married woman and then sent her tins of tea to remind her of it. If he is, sending her the tea regularly is pretty odd. It borders on stalking." He ran a hand distractedly through his curls. "You can't always judge a person by the way he behaves on the surface, and you don't know him well enough to know how he responds when thwarted or jilted."

"Angel, it almost doesn't matter whether he sent the tea or not; the thallium and everything that was used to contaminate the tea was found in Edward's house. Edward had the motive for using it. What possible reason, assuming he was involved with Libby, would Ian have for poisoning her?"

"Who the fuck knows? It just feels wrong," he snapped irritably. "I'm going to have to talk to Frost and try to figure out what to do about the note. For God's sake, stay out of this, please." He stood up and walked to the door and started to open it, then turned back to me. "I don't want you to be hurt, Annie, either physically or emotionally. We're friends, you're important to me, please be careful. If it turns out I'm wrong, I'll apologize to you and Ian. I have one request: You find out anything that makes you think it's him, you tell me immediately. Swear to me you will."

"Angel, don't worry, I'm fine."

"I know, you tell me that all the time, even when you're not," he said as he left.

The conversation was unsettling, to say the least. Angel, who had never liked Ian, now believed he was some sort of unprincipled gigolo at best or an obsessed stalker or a potential poisoner, at worst. God, I was sick of this situation. I hoped desperately that Ian wasn't involved. The problem was I just couldn't be sure and I didn't know what to do about it.

FROST CALLED me the next day and asked me to come in and talk with him. As he showed me into his office he said, "I talked with Cisneros this morning. Neither of us is very happy with you."

"Yeah, he was pretty pissed off and I guess I've created a huge problem for everyone." I flopped down in the chair and dumped my bag on the floor.

"Well, what's done is done. Angel knows I didn't find the note, but I'm not changing my story. He knows and has agreed not to out me to his boss."

It was no wonder he was losing his hair I thought as I watched him run his hands through it several times.

"I don't know how you'll keep me out of this."

"Angel's going to let his boss know about your connection to Ian, not because of the note but because of your relationship with Angel and Libby. Once he tells the DA about Ian then I'll get the go ahead to talk to him, and it won't involve you 'cause I found the note, not you, so for God's sake don't tell anyone else you found it."

"I won't; I don't want to get either of you into trouble."

"I gotta tell ya my antennae are vibrating."

"What's *that* supposed to mean?"

"It means that I think it is him. If he sent her the tea, what's the big deal? Why be so secretive about it? The fact that he never said anything to you about knowing her makes me wonder. If it was him, then he must have a good reason to not mention it. How do you know he hasn't been lying to you all along?"

That pissed me off. "You are a real jerk, you know that?"

"I do, you're not the first to mention it. But Annie, you've known this guy for less than a year, it takes a while to really know someone and even then they can pull the rug out from under you. I'm just worried about you."

"Why? You make it sound like he's some sort of psychopath or something."

"If it's him, and I'd lay money on it, then you gotta ask yourself why would he send the tea? That's a pretty passive-aggressive unsettling thing to do to someone who's broken up with you. It borders on stalking. That's where I get concerned about you."

"Well, don't be. I can take care of myself. I'd expect him to support me if the tables were turned."

THIRTY-SEVEN

I HELD MY BREATH. Once Angel passed the information to his boss, Frost would be free to talk to Ian without implicating me as the one who found the note. And I knew Ian would be subpoenaed to testify. I wondered what the blowback would be. I didn't know whether the DA would tell Ian Angel had tied him to Libby and me, but I knew Frost would, just to keep me out of the line of fire. Once Ian knew that, it would just jack up the tension between him and Angel.

When I arrived home from work a day after talking to Frost, I found Ian waiting for me, and I could see he was upset.

"I got hauled in to talk to Detective Frost today. He apparently found a note at your friend's house that was signed by an Ian—no last name, printed on a computer—but when Frost handed it over to the DA, Cisneros told the DA that we were involved and presto! I'm now the guy who sent her the tea!" He waved an official-looking paper in front of me. "And then there's this!"

"What is it?"

"A subpoena. I'm *required* to appear in court to testify in Edward's trial. Did you know anything about this?"

"Why would I know?"

"Well, your BFF next door is on the case."

I felt somewhat like I was standing in front of a firing squad as he watched me. "He doesn't discuss the trial with me, and I haven't seen much of him since before Christmas." Well, that wasn't a complete lie. I didn't *know* that Ian had been served with the subpoena and I hadn't seen much of Angel. I wasn't touching the subject of the note with a ten-foot pole.

"Frost grilled me for more than an hour, and now I'll be grilled at trial about a relationship with a woman I never met, and they'll try to pin me with sending the damn tea to her." He slammed the subpoena onto the kitchen table and glared at me. "This is the biggest cluster fuck I have ever seen." He walked to the window and gazed out before returning to the table, snatching up the subpoena and walking out the door as I stood there with my mouth open.

OUR RELATIONSHIP felt fragile. We avoided the subject of Libby and didn't discuss the approaching trial. Ian had made it clear that he was furious with Angel, and Angel had kept his distance. I was edgy about testifying and continued to struggle with my doubts about him. I knew he sensed something was off. As a result, one minute I was withdrawn and anxious, which seemed to make him testy and moody, and the next he'd turn on the charm, I'd put on a normal face, and we'd make an effort to pretend nothing had changed.

I felt as if I were standing on a train track paralyzed, like a deer caught in the headlights of a car, waiting for the train to hit.

THE TRIAL had been scheduled for the middle of February, which was now less than a week away.

The lead prosecutor in the DA's office was handling the trial. Angel would only be peripherally involved because of his connection to me. He helped me prepare for testifying, and we held the practice sessions in his office. The last thing I wanted was a confrontation between Angel and Ian.

The instructions were pretty much the same as he'd given me for talking to the police. Answer the questions, don't elaborate, and don't let the other side piss me off and get me to say something I'd regret. The prosecutor went over my testimony multiple times, the goal being he wanted no surprises when I testified and neither did I.

What I regretted was finding the note. The defense lawyers were delighted that something had turned up to throw doubt on Edward's being the tea supplier. I was warned they'd question me about my relationship with Ian.

Since the discovery of the note, there was this nagging person who lived in my head who kept finding unsettling reasons that implicated Ian at every turn, regardless how ruthlessly I tried not to hear it.

The trial was as unpleasant as I had anticipated, the same questions over and over again in front of a jury who sat and watched my every move. The goal of any good defense attorney is to make the prosecution's witnesses look like unreliable flakes or outright liars. I emerged from the experience feeling like a combination of the two.

It was the usual: How long had I known Libby? Why had we parted as friends? Why didn't I like Edward? Had I actually seen him make the tea or add thallium to it?

"I wouldn't know thallium if I saw it."

"Did you see him add anything to the tea?"

"When I saw him prepare it, he added lemon and sweetener."

"Did anyone else give the tea to the victim?"

"Can you use her name, please?"

"Pardon me, Mrs. Matheisen. Was the defendant the only person who gave her the tea?"

"No the housekeeper, Cora, did, and I also delivered it to her on occasion."

"You were the one who urged the medical examiner to test her hair to see if it showed evidence of any contamination, correct?"

"Yes."

"Why did you do that?"

"I wondered if exposure to a toxin might have been the cause of her illness."

"If that's the case, why wait until she was dead to do that?"

"I asked a physician I know about possible causes for Libby's condition, and one of the things she mentioned was exposure to toxins or heavy metals. I couldn't get Libby to return to her doctors or do much of anything I suggested, and I thought the likelihood of her illness being the result of a toxin or heavy metal was unlikely. I wish I'd done it sooner, but she would have had to agree to it and she wouldn't even agree to see her physician."

Suddenly he switched topics. "You didn't particularly like the defendant, did you?"

"No."

"Why is that?"

"He was cold and standoffish and wasn't someone I could be friends with. Neither of us made any attempt to rectify that."

"And her relationship with him marked the end of your relationship with her, correct?"

"Yes, eventually."

"Did that make you angry?"

"Angry at first, then disappointed and sad."

"Angry enough to set her husband up for a charge of attempted murder?"

"Objection."

"Overruled. Ms. Collins, please answer the question."

"Libby and I hadn't spoken to one another in four years, and the poisoning had begun months before I was hired. I had stopped being angry with Libby or with Edward a long time ago. So to answer your question no, I don't go around setting people up. I didn't know she was being poisoned until after her death."

I saw Angel smile and then hide it behind some paperwork at the prosecution's table.

When the defense attorney didn't get whatever he had been hoping for, he took another tack. Why was I engaged to look after Libby? What did I think about her physical condition, her mental state, her relationship with Edward and Jeff? It was mind-numbing and I felt like I had answered the same questions a hundred different ways.

And then out of the blue he asked, "Would you please explain your relationship with Ian Patterson?"

His lightning question changes kept throwing me off. I glanced at Angel and saw him suddenly on alert. "I…I'm in a personal relationship with him."

"Are you aware that the note that was found was signed Ian?"

"Yes."

"And that didn't concern you?"

"No," I lied.

"Did Mr. Patterson know you were caring for Mrs. Matheisen?"

"He knew I was caring for a friend. I didn't share her name until sometime after we became involved."

"Was he involved with her before he became involved with you?"

"No, not that I'm aware of." I didn't elaborate on all the reasons I had come up with to deny Ian's involvement with her, which were beginning to sound a little lame even to me.

"Are you aware of any connection he may have had with her?"

"No."

"And it didn't concern you that the note was signed Ian?"

"I'm unaware of any connection between Ian Patterson and Libby Matheisen, so I don't believe he had anything to do with the note or Libby." *Well,* I thought, *that's mostly the truth.*

"That's all, the witness is free to go."

"DID YOU know Libby Matheisen?"

"No, I never met her," Ian said.

"And you never had a personal relationship of any kind with her?"

"I just said I didn't know her."

"How do you explain your name on the note about her breaking off with you and then you sending her the tea?"

"I didn't break anything off with her, and I didn't send her any tea. I don't, didn't, know the woman. I have no explanation for the name Ian being on the note other than I am not the only Ian in the world."

"So it wasn't you who sent the note?"

"This is getting a bit tedious…."

"Please answer the question."

"No, I didn't send the note," he said, biting off each word.

Then it was the prosecution's turn.

"Mr. Patterson, you were observed talking to Mrs. Matheisen at a housewarming party. Do you still maintain that you didn't know her?"

"I'm a realtor. I get invited to many of my client's housewarming parties, and I meet a lot of people. Most of the time, at parties especially, it's casual enough that names aren't even exchanged or if they are it's first name only. I don't remember ever meeting anyone named Libby. I think I would if I had carried on an affair with her."

That questioning threw me. Angel had said nothing about it. I was sure someone, most likely Angel, had spoken to Karen Harris. He was the only one who knew about my conversation with her and must have held onto the name he had gotten from Edward. She hadn't remembered anything when I spoke with her. I wondered what had jogged her memory.

I watched Ian's testimony and was a nervous wreck, despite the fact he held up well. The DA and the defense attorney questioned him relentlessly, but he held his temper and stuck to his guns. They had no proof he was the Ian who'd written the note, and finally, they let him go. He left the courtroom without glancing at me. I followed him out, but not before seeing Angel turn around with a frown on his face as he watched Ian leave the courtroom.

I caught up with him outside the courthouse at the bottom of the steps to the City and County building where the courts were. It was freezing and he was pacing, whether from the cold or agitation it was hard to tell.

"You okay?" I asked.

"I'm fine," he said shortly. He turned away from me and then turned back. "Actually, I'm not. I'm pissed. Totally fucking pissed. That was humiliating to be questioned like that by those idiots. Every reporter and person in that courtroom will be talking about it."

"It's over. What does it matter what people think if it wasn't you?"

He glared at me. "'If it wasn't you'? Jesus, do you think I'm lying? *It wasn't me!*" he shouted, attracting stares from a few nearby people. His fist was balled up at his side and it took all my effort not to flinch or retreat a step or two.

"No, I believe you." *Sort of*, I thought and saw him relax his hand. "Ian, all I meant was it doesn't really matter what people think."

"It does matter!" he shouted. "There were people in there who know me, people I've sold property to. They'll believe what they want, not what's true. How do you think this is going to affect my business? What rich son of a bitch is going to use me as a realtor if he thinks I'm going to be screwing his wife behind his back like I supposedly did with Libby?"

I reached out and squeezed his hand. "I'm sorry." I didn't know what else to say, the court of public opinion wasn't a fair one.

He watched me for a moment and then sighed and scrubbed a hand roughly over his mouth. "This is all so fucked up. You don't trust me…." I started to say something and he waved me off. "No, stop, I see it in your eyes. And now everyone thinks I'm lying. I wish I'd never heard of Libby Matheisen or her stupid lovers. I wish you'd never gotten involved with this. I'm royally pissed that Cisneros dragged me into this, and there are days when I wish we'd never met."

That felt like a body blow and I was silent for a moment. "If it's any consolation, I wish I'd never called Libby back. I'm not sorry I met you, though." He didn't reply. I stood in the cold with my hands clenched in the pockets of my coat burrowing my chin into the scarf around my neck and watched him. It seemed seeing how upset he was, hearing how much this whole experience had hurt both of us, helped me come to a decision.

"I do trust you, Ian, I do. We're both stressed out and exhausted. How about we find a restaurant and have some dinner? I could use a drink."

He sighed, took hold of my hand, and said, "Fine." Even though neither of us was.

THIRTY-EIGHT

I T TOOK THE jury four hours to come to a verdict, but they agreed Edward was guilty of Libby's attempted murder. Her affairs, the pregnancy, the fact that the thallium had been found in the basement, and because Edward gave her the tea every morning outweighed the fact that someone else had been sending her the tea. As the prosecutor had noted in his closing argument, the note was computer-generated. Anyone could have written it, including Edward. He couldn't explain the name but neither could he or the defense prove it was Ian.

A week later, the judge sentenced Edward to ten years, after which he'd be eligible for parole. It felt good to have it finally over. It felt as if Libby and Jeff had been given some justice.

The discovery of the note and the trial had unfortunately colored my relationship with both Ian and Angel. Angel had come over after the trial closed and apologized to Ian for bringing him into it, saying he was ethically bound to mention my relationship with Ian to his boss. Ian shrugged it off, but I knew he was still angry. I knew Angel had apologized only for my sake, and he still believed Ian had written the note.

Things changed subtly after that. Angel began popping over more frequently than before, and the visits annoyed Ian no end. It was clear he wanted Angel to stay away and it was equally clear, to me anyway, that Angel was keeping a close eye on me.

No matter what I said, Ian felt like there was more than friendship between us, especially on Angel's part, and that dragging him into the trial had been an attempt by Angel to disrupt our relationship. I kept trying to reassure him, and I tried to discourage Angel from coming over.

"Listen to me, Annie, there shouldn't be any reason for me not to come by and say hi. What's he worried about?"

"He jealous; he thinks we're more to each other than friends. It's as bad as being at your family's house."

"No, it's worse than that, he's really pissed at me about the trial and he wants you to cut off our friendship."

"He's never asked me to do that."

"No, but he's pressuring you by being upset and constantly accusing me and you."

"Well, I've told him it's not true and that you're just a friend. I'm not cutting off our friendship, just asking that you not come over so often for a while 'til things settle down."

"And when he beats the crap out of you because he thinks you're sneaking around behind his back to see me instead of my visiting in front of him, are you going to end our friendship then?"

"What is wrong with you? He's never laid a hand on me."

"I care about you and this isn't going to end well regardless whether he was involved with Libby or not."

"Well, there's nothing for you or for Frost to worry about. The two of you are totally paranoid. Just stay away; I don't need welfare checkups."

"Fine, I'll leave you alone, but if you need me, please ask for help, please, Annie."

"I won't need it. Now just go."

I had almost said, "So Ian won't find you here," but didn't and held the door open for him to leave. I didn't see any way to resolve the issue of whether Ian was lying or whether Angel's suspicions were justified. I kept asking myself if the relationship was worth the trouble. I hadn't found an answer so far and felt trapped in inertia.

I GOT a call from Frost the following day. "Thought you'd want to know we found a coat that may be the one the guy who killed Scott was wearing."

"That's good, right?"

"Yeah, the case on Scott is still open. I'm telling you 'cause your 'confidential source' will probably tell you anyway and I trust you to keep this to yourself. We don't actually know why the assault occurred or whether it was connected to Jeff's relationship with Libby, but we've been continuing to track down loose ends."

He paused. "The search of the immediate area turned up nothing useful. So I've had officers going round to all the thrift stores in Denver and the suburbs on the off chance that whoever killed Scott dumped the coat in one of their collection bins. I figure he burned it or threw it in some dumpster, but I thought it was worth checking out."

"Where was it?"

"The ARC store out in Aurora and the one in Lakewood had a couple of dress coats, the Lakewood store had a black one, so I had an officer pick it up. I've sent it over to the forensic guys for a thorough going-over. No idea whether it's the coat in question, but I'm hoping there'll be some blood traces on it and if we're totally blessed, there may be something from the killer on the coat. Or it could be totally pointless. The only reason the coat was still there, the guy said, was that there isn't much call for dress coats at their stores."

"So why tell me other than to satisfy my curiosity?"

"You said that Ian and your friend Angel had coats like that—" he began.

"Just stop right now. If you want to know whether Ian has a coat like that, ask him yourself and leave me out of it."

There was silence on the line for a long time. "You know I never had a daughter, but I have nieces, and you worry about girls as soon as they're old enough to get involved with guys. You can't really prevent their getting involved, and don't want to necessarily, but it just kills you when the guy is not right or just flat out bad news."

"Look, between you and Angel, I can't take this anymore. At some point you have to trust the person you care about," I yelled at him. "Neither of you have found anything to implicate him."

"Annie, there are a lot of unexplained issues attaching themselves to him. Angel had an interesting conversation with the woman who held the housewarming party. He described Ian to her and asked whether Libby had talked to anyone like that. She said it sounded like her realtor and she'd seen them talking a bit. She insisted both of them left alone some time apart, still, sounds like he lied about never having met her."

"Oh. My. God. So he talked to her at a party, so what?" I asked. "I am not having this conversation with you." I said in frustration as I disconnected and threw the phone on the couch.

I'M NOT a stupid woman, but I was very tired of being alone and dating disappointing men. Unfortunately, I'm not stupid. It was embarrassing to think I wanted a relationship that badly, but it was looking more and more like that was the case.

I couldn't get Angel's conversation or Frost's out of my head. I hadn't seen Angel since we had spoken about his visits. He had been working long hours and was rarely home and I missed him and missed not being able to talk to him.

I didn't know who to believe. I flashed back to the woman in Estes telling me all was not as it seemed and it made me feel like it was three against one, which added to the burning pain in my stomach. But you can only force yourself not to listen for so long.

THAT EVENING at Ian's place when I hung my coat up in his coat closet, I scanned the articles in it and couldn't see his long black dress coat. Later, when I went to use the master bath, I quietly opened his closet and couldn't find it there, either. I did see a suit jacket still in the plastic from a dry cleaner in Cherry Creek. Maybe the coat was there. Maybe to reassure myself I would stop by and see. *Oh God*, I thought, *please let the coat be at the cleaners.*

The next day, I drove to Cherry Creek and parked in the dry cleaner's parking lot. I told the clerk I was Ian Patterson's wife and he had misplaced his dress coat, and asked whether she would check to see if he'd just forgotten to pick it up. The girl came back a few minutes later to say that there was nothing there for him at the moment, and that she had looked through garments that hadn't been picked up after 30 days and there was no coat like I had described. I left and sat in my car. *Where was the coat?*

It was making me insane. My head felt like exploding. I just wanted things to go back to normal. But nothing, not a goddamned thing, had been normal since Libby had called me back in September. The strain was beginning to show and when we got together later that day he asked if I was okay. I would have to talk to him about it at some point, but I couldn't think how to even bring it up.

"Yeah, work's just been hard lately and I'm beat," I said, flopping down on the couch.

"What's been going on?"

"Lots of difficult cases and we're shorthanded. A bunch of people are out sick with some upper respiratory virus. I've had to pick up a ton of shifts lately. They can't work coughing all over the place, so they have to stay home until they're cleared by the hospital's infectious disease bunch."

It was true, people were out sick; it just wasn't the entire truth. It felt like all I did anymore was avoid issues or lie about them.

Edward had been moved to the Colorado State Penitentiary in Cañon City immediately after his sentencing, and Ian wanted to celebrate the entire debacle being over, at his house for a change. He ordered in Indian food, but my stomach had been so tied up in knots since the coat hadn't turned up at the cleaners I could hardly eat. The glass of wine went unfinished.

Jeff visited me in my sleep without Libby this time and stood there with his battered face whispering *Be careful* over and over again. I woke up without startling. His appearances and Libby's had become such a part of my dreams they rarely frightened or upset me now. I lay there for a few minutes and realized I was dying of thirst.

I got up quietly and went down into his kitchen looking for something to drink. I checked the fridge for bottled water and there wasn't any, so I opened the pantry closet where he usually kept them. There weren't any there either and I began nosing around to see if there might be something more appealing than tap water. I had moved some supplies around while looking, and there, at the back of the pantry shelf, sat a tin of tea like the ones sent to Libby.

I heard some movement on the stairs, hurriedly pushed the cans back in front of the tin, and shut the door as quietly as I could. I grabbed a glass from the cupboard and filled it with tap water as Ian entered the kitchen.

"Thirsty?" he asked.

"Yeah, you want some?" I asked, offering him a drink, my mind racing. Ian's missing coat and the tea tin reminded me of Frost and Angel's warnings.

"No, I'm good. I thought I felt you get up. Wondered if you were okay."

"I'm fine. I had another dream that woke me and then I realized how thirsty I was."

"Do you think you should see someone about those dreams? Maybe get some sleeping meds?"

"No, I think it's just the aftershocks of everything that's happened. They'll die down eventually."

"It might help shut them off and let you get some rest."

"Thanks, I think I'll pass for now," I said, putting the empty glass on the counter.

He walked over, wrapped his arms around me, and kissed me. "I'm sorry this has put both of us through such a wringer. Feel sleepy yet?"

"Yeah, a bit."

He led me back to the bedroom and when we got into bed, he said, "I have an idea how to take your mind off this," and began to make love to me.

All I could think of was the note, the tea deliveries, his missing coat, and the tea tin I had just found. I felt cold and kept wondering whether he had lied to the court and me. *Where was his fucking coat?*

I wasn't ready and it was uncomfortable as he pushed into me.

"You don't seem very into this," he said absently as he continued to move.

"I'm exhausted, Ian; I'm just not in the mood."

"It's okay, just relax, it'll take your mind off things."

"Ian, I really don't want to do this right now," I said, hoping he'd stop. I pushed at him but he took my wrists in his hands, held them against the mattress above my head, and continued moving with his eyes shut, his face unreadable. It was a mechanical rhythmic thrusting that didn't include me at all. When he finally finished, he rolled off me and took a few deep breaths and was asleep. I lay there, stunned. It had never been like this; it was almost as if I were just a body for him to do what he wanted with and then discard.

I lay awake and for the first time I wondered who he was and whether Frost and Angel were right and I had been a fool. I had to be up early to go to work and was unable to sleep. I must have dozed off, though, because I was startled by the sound of my phone's alarm at 5:30. Ian mumbled something and I leaned over and said, "Leaving for work in a minute, sleep well." I eased out of bed and dressed. I put my coat on in the living room, grabbed my purse, and left as quickly as I could.

At work, I kept going over and over in my mind his antipathy to Angel, his frustration and anger when I had gotten involved after Jeff's assault and death, the note, the missing coat, the tea, and Angel and Frost's concerns. I felt like a hamster in a wheel until I was so exhausted and my head hurt so badly I couldn't concentrate and left work early to come home.

When I arrived at 6:00 I saw Ian's car across the street from the house, and I wondered briefly why he had parked it there when there were parking spaces in front of the house. My phone rang as I pulled into the driveway. I looked at caller ID and saw Angel's name. I could not deal with him after a day like today, so I sent it to voicemail. I'd find out what he wanted tomorrow.

And tomorrow I would call Frost and set in motion the end to my relationship with Ian and most likely his arrest. Maybe tonight I could convince him to go home and then call Angel back and talk to him about what to do. I closed my eyes for a moment before getting out of the car and walking up to the front door.

"You're home a bit early. Everything okay?" Ian asked as I walked into the house.

"Just a major headache. It was slow, so I came home. I thought I'd take something and go to bed."

He came from the kitchen, took my coat, and hung it up on the coat-track. "I brought over wine and an apology dinner. Can you eat something before you go to bed?" he asked, giving me a kiss. "I'm sorry about last night; I was a bit of a bore about things. Forgive me?"

"Of course. I was out of sorts, so no worries." Memories of the night before chilled me again. *Maybe,* I thought reluctantly, *I should have picked up Angel's call.*

I looked around. He had set the table and opened wine while waiting for me. He began laying out dinner and pouring wine for me; he already had a full glass. The last thing I wanted was to sit and eat dinner and be sociable, but it would appear he wasn't giving me a choice.

I excused myself and went into the bathroom. I swallowed a couple of Advil and stared at myself in the mirror. I looked like hell. I realized just in time, before I used the toilet, that I had my phone in the back pocket of my jeans. I walked into the bedroom and dropped my phone on the end of the bed, took my sweater off and tossed it on the bed. It landed on top of the phone where I left it.

Dinner was good and went some way toward relieving my headache. His conversation was pleasant and once again, I felt the pull of pretending that all was well, the seduction of maintaining a relationship with a man I cared about. But I was also afraid of him now, afraid of who he might be, and that helped clear up the fantasies. I would ask him to leave after dinner and call Angel.

The wine had an odd, bitter taste as it hit the back of my throat, but it was an expensive bottle, and my stomach had been so upset since finding the note that nothing tasted normal anymore, so I said nothing. Ian had sipped at his but wasn't drinking much, I noticed, as he filled my glass for the second time.

"Not indulging tonight?" I asked.

"I may have to meet some clients later. I probably shouldn't worry about it, but it's icy out, and if I drink too much and for some reason need to go out, I don't want to be three sheets to the wind."

We sat and finished the wine, or more specifically, I finished it. He suggested we move to the couch where we could relax. I felt a little weird as I stood up and moved into the living room.

"You okay?" he asked.

"Just a little tired, I guess," I said as I yawned. I felt so sleepy all of a sudden.

"Well, go sit down. Let me clear up dinner and then I'll give you a massage and see if I can make the headache go away."

I sat on the couch and realized that I felt very odd. I was sleepy, but I felt weird, like everything was just slightly out of focus. I let my head fall back and rest against the back of the couch and closed my eyes. I heard Ian tidying up the kitchen and the clinks as he collected the wine bottle and our glasses and took them back to the kitchen. I heard him placing the glasses and the rest of the dishes and silverware in the dishwasher and starting it. Then he put the remaining food and trash in a garbage bag he left in the kitchen.

He came and sat down beside me. "How about that massage?"

I opened my eyes and tried to raise my head, but I was so sleepy and my body felt like lead. I made a serious effort and managed to sit up and lean forward and put my face in my hands. I closed my eyes again to see if I could get the feeling to pass.

"Ian, I don't feel well; there's something wrong." My voice even sounded odd, not quite slurred, but not right.

"Let me help you to the bedroom," he said. "Maybe you should lie down and see if you feel better. Come on, up you go." He pulled me up, wrapped my arm around his neck and held onto it while he put his other arm around my waist and walked me to the bedroom. He helped me into bed and propped me up against the pillows.

"Ian, I really don't feel right, I think I need to go to the hospital or something."

"You're fine, Annie, I just dosed you with some Ambien in your wine."

I opened my eyes and tried to focus on him. "What did you say?"

"I said I put Ambien in your wine. I knew you wouldn't take it voluntarily."

"Why would you do that?" My heart rate escalated and I had a small cold ball of fear in my chest.

"You didn't sleep well last night, and you're very out of sorts today. You seem worried about something." He watched me with a rather flat affect as he reached out and stroked my cheek. "When I dropped some shirts at the cleaners today, imagine my surprise to find out my wife had been looking for a black dress coat of mine. I suppose that, along with the note Frost found, has convinced you that I'm responsible for all this. I can't have that."

"What have you done, Ian?" I was terrified.

"I'm just cleaning up a potential problem, here, like I had to with Libby and with Jeff and with that moron I hired to beat Jeff up." He got up and went into the kitchen and moved the trash bag to the front door.

I tried to sit up and could barely manage to lift my head. I was having trouble staying awake, but my heart was hammering in my chest. I realized this was how Libby had died, Ambien, alcohol, and Valium.

"Have you given me what you gave Libby?" I asked when he reappeared in the bedroom, carrying an old satchel. He set it on the floor next to the bed.

He smiled at me and shook his head as he sat down on the bed next to me. "You're just too clever for your own good; you get something different. You've had a large dose of Ambien to make you more compliant and then you'll get oxycodone mixed with alcohol. That should do the trick, and I wouldn't want anyone to link your suicide to Libby's. Up we go," he said, sliding me up against the headboard.

"Please don't do this, Ian, please." I grabbed ineffectually at his arm.

"I have to." He pushed my hand away. "You just won't stop and you won't forget about the coat, which I'm sure, given half a chance, you'll run and tell Frost about. I don't have a choice. Don't worry, it won't hurt, it'll be like going off to sleep."

I tried to sit up and he caught me and forced me back against the pillows. He rummaged in the satchel and brought out a pair of nitrile gloves he put on and took a nasogastric tube and lubricant out. "Now hold still," he said as if I were an uncooperative child.

He grabbed my face and held my head steady as he threaded the flexible rubber tube into my nose and down into my stomach. I gagged and tried twisting my head away from him, clutching weakly at his hands, but he had a vise grip on my face.

Now I was certain where the bruises on Libby's face and the cuts on the inside of her mouth had come from; I could taste blood in my mouth. It all seemed so surreal and my body felt so heavy. No one would know what had happened. No one would find me in time. How could I have been so stupid?

Once the tube was down, he brought out a large syringe filled with cloudy, wine-colored fluid and attached it to the tube, gently squeezing the plunger until it was empty. He pulled the tube out quickly, making me cough and gag, and put everything in his bag. He put several pill bottles on the bedside table and picked up the bag.

He stood over me and watched me for a moment. "I'm sorry you made me do this; I did enjoy our time together. I would stay and see you off, but I don't want your pain-in-the-ass neighbor to know I was here. Sweet dreams, Annie." He leaned over and kissed my cheek and left the bedroom. I could hear him removing his gloves, washing his hands in the kitchen, opening the front door, and taking the garbage bag with him.

I heard the door shut. I struggled to sit up and couldn't. I was dizzy and nauseated. I was having difficulty keeping my eyes open so I rolled onto my side and tried to reach the bottom of the bed and finally felt my hand close over the phone. Fighting to stay awake, struggling to make my fingers work, I focused as hard as I could to dial 9-1-1.

"Nine-one-one, what is your emergency?"

My lips felt numb and my voice was slurred, "Please...help me."

The phone fell out of my hand onto the floor and as I slid off the bed, I could hear in some distant place the operator saying, "Ma'am, are you all right? Ma'am? What's going on? An ambulance is on the way, just hold on," as I began to lose consciousness.

I was drifting. It wasn't unpleasant; *it was just like he said it would be*, I thought, before my mind went dark.

THIRTY-NINE

I COULD SEE A bright light and I wondered if this was the light people talk about when they relate near-death experiences. It was comforting and inviting. I was drifting toward it, but before I reached it, it disappeared. *Maybe Heaven wasn't willing to take me*, I thought. Then, after what seemed like forever, I saw a light again, but it was moving back and forth quickly, and it, too, went out. I didn't believe in purgatory, but obviously my transition wasn't going to be easy. *It figures*, I thought, *not even dying is going to be easy*. Then I remembered I didn't want to die and realized my throat was sore as I swallowed, and I was cold. I could hear snatches of conversation and had the odd sensation of Libby standing near me with her hand on my shoulder.

"…pumped her stomach…ventilated her…opiates…breathing on her own now."

I tried to focus to determine what they were talking about.

"Good thing she vomited…didn't aspirate, otherwise…DOA…for observation…make sure this wasn't a suicide attempt."

The voice went away and I felt someone pick up my hand.

"I'm cold," I said, surprised I could hardly hear myself speak.

"What do you need, Annie?"

I opened my eyes and looked around and found Angel sitting by the stretcher I was on. "I'm cold and sleepy," I said as my eyes closed.

I felt him put another blanket on me. It didn't help much, but I suspected the coldness wasn't related to lack of blankets.

"Tell me what happened, *chica*."

"Ian," I whispered.

"He's not here." I could hear the dislike in his voice. "I didn't have time to get in touch with him."

I grabbed his hand. "NO! No, don't call him, please."

"Annie, what's wrong?"

"He did this…he did…. Don't let him near me."

"Ian did this to you? Jesus, why?"

"The tea…his…coat."

"What?"

"Don't leave me alone," I pleaded.

"I won't, baby, I'll stay as long as you need me to," he said, stroking my hair.

I knew Angel would be there, and as I began to drift off into sleep, I heard him make a call on his phone and ask someone to let him talk to Detective Frost. And then I slept.

I WOKE up in a hospital room and saw Angel asleep in a recliner that had been pulled up to the bedside. He still held my hand in his and had not let go even as he slept. I lay there and looked around. It felt like a miracle to be able to see and hear normally and not have that overwhelming weight of sleep pressing down on me.

I heard the door open and Angel jolted awake, stood up, and moved between the bed and the doorway. He relaxed when he saw Frost walk in and returned to the recliner and sat down heavily, and yawned. He looked exhausted and had a prominent five o'clock shadow.

"Thanks for coming," he said to Frost.

Frost came to my bedside and scrutinized me. "How are you?"

"Alive."

"That's a good start. Wanna tell me what happened? I assume you didn't try to off yourself, right?"

"No, I didn't." I closed my eyes for a moment. "A few days ago, after you and Angel kept warning me about Ian and told me about the coat you found, I looked for Ian's coat at his house and couldn't find it. Then I found a tin of tea in his cupboard that was like the tea Libby got." I paused, I was still very tired and it hurt to think about what had happened. "I asked his dry cleaner whether his dress coat was there and it wasn't."

"You what?" they both asked simultaneously.

"I couldn't find his dress coat, so I asked at the dry cleaner he uses and they didn't have it," I repeated. "Last night he was at my house when I got home. He had dinner ready and wine open. I had a second glass before I noticed he wasn't drinking anything other than his original glass. He said it was because he might have to meet some clients later."

I stopped and cleared my throat, it hurt when I swallowed, and I guessed it was from Ian's nasogastric tube and the endotracheal tube the EMTs had probably inserted in the ambulance on the way to the hospital.

"When I went to get up and go to the living room, I felt dizzy and weird. By the time he'd cleaned up from dinner and come back to the living room, I was just incredibly sleepy and disoriented." God, I was still tired.

"I told him that and he suggested I go to bed and helped me into the bedroom. When I asked him to take me to the hospital, he told me that he'd dosed my wine with Ambien and he had to silence me because he knew I'd been searching for his coat. He didn't know I'd found the tea. He said he knew I wouldn't let it go or forget about it and I would tell you," I said, looking at Frost.

Frost chuckled, and said, "Well, he got that much right."

I stopped and closed my eyes for a moment, taking deep breaths. "He said he had to 'clean up the problem' like he had with Jeff and Libby and the guy he'd hired to assault Jeff. He put a tube down my throat and pumped a huge syringe full of fluid into my stomach; I think it was filled with crushed pills mixed with wine. And then he left pill bottles on the bedside table and took his bag and the garbage with him so it would look like I was alone."

"Jesus," Angel whispered. "I called you earlier to tell you Frost had gotten a match to Scott's DNA and warn you to stay away from Ian 'til Frost could get DNA from him. Didn't you get that message?"

"I saw your call; I sent it to voicemail. I just couldn't deal with whatever you were calling about and then I never had a chance to listen to it."

Angel spoke to Frost. "Annie didn't return my call, she never does that, and it worried me. I was at work and I tried to call her, and an EMT answered her phone and told me they were transporting her to the hospital. I guess she managed to call 9-1-1 before she lost consciousness."

"Yeah, we have a copy of the 9-1-1 tape and after what you told Angel in the ER, we arrested Patterson. He was at home having a beer and watching TV when we got there." Frost barked a laugh. "He said he'd seen you the day before yesterday and you were very depressed, but he hadn't seen you last night. Very convincing actor, but he was pretty dumbfounded when I told him you'd survived and told us what had happened." He turned to Angel. "With what he told Annie and his attempt to kill her, we have enough to nail him to the wall for Scott and Libby's deaths and for engineering Jeff's beating, so he's been charged with their murders and conspiracy to commit murder for Jeff. After getting a DNA swab from him to compare to the DNA evidence from the coat, that should confirm the coat was his and we have the tea tin on top of that. Annie, you did good." Frost gave me a smile. "I'm glad to see you're on the mend. I'm going to need a full statement when you're released." He seemed ill at ease, but then said, tapping my blanketed foot with his hand, "You take care. Hell, I won't know how to solve a case without your interference, so you need to get better." He smiled and made his goodbyes and left.

I lay there for a few minutes thinking about what happened. "I don't know how I could have been so stupid and so gullible."

"He's a psychopath, Annie. They're charming when they want something and ruthless if you get in their way or you're a threat to them." Angel paused and frowned. "Somehow he found out you were taking care of Libby and got involved with you to keep an eye on what you were doing."

"I think I heard Libby tell him. I overheard her talking to someone she said was a friend and how he'd tried to dissuade her from hiring me like Edward had. You and Frost thought something wasn't right. I was upset and I didn't entirely believe he was being honest, but I couldn't see any reason for him to lie about Libby and I just didn't know what to do."

"I don't understand why he targeted Libby in the first place."

"I can't think straight right now." I sighed. "They were lovers, he was the Ian in the note, and he knew Jeff and Scott. I don't know why he did what he did, and it doesn't make sense."

"It's okay, just rest. There'll be plenty of time to sort this out when you're better."

I WAS dreaming again and I thought, *I shouldn't have to be hounded by dreams, not after what's happened.* It was night in my dream and I seemed to be near a path of some kind. There was a figure in the background that was hard to see. After a moment or two it moved forward a little, and I could see it was Ian with a long black coat on, holding a hat in his hand. The phrase "Mad Hatter's son" echoed in my head. Ian stood there, hat in hand. Ian. It was like a brilliant light went on—Patterson, Mad Hatter's son.

I sat up abruptly, and said, "That's what the Mad Hatter's son meant!"

"What?" Angel asked, confused, sitting up and rubbing his eyes.

"I need to talk to Frost. Can you get him on the phone?"

"I guess. Are you okay?"

"Yes. I have more proof Ian killed the guy who assaulted Jeff."

"Okay, hang on." Angel pulled his phone out of his pocket, punched in the number. "Hey Frost, Annie wants to talk to you. Oh, good, I'll tell her." He hung up.

"I wanted to talk to him."

"He's on his way over. He said he'd talk to you when he got here."

Frost listened to my story patiently. "So despite what I asked, you went back and talked to the homeless guy and friends of his."

"He called me and said he'd found some people who were willing to talk to me, so I met them and listened to what they had to say. Their stories were way out in left field and I blew off all of them. The woman's story, though, stuck with me. She described seeing two men talking and one man hit the other in the head, so that seemed to jibe. But I didn't think her story was totally reliable, either, 'cause she's developmentally delayed or something and she kept talking about a Mad Hatter's son. That's what she called the man who killed Scott. But it just came to me, Mad Hatter's son rhymes with Patterson. She just heard it wrong and they were mad so it makes a certain amount of sense. I bet if she was shown a picture she could identify him."

"Well, keep your shirt on. He's in custody. We're going over his house with a fine-toothed comb, we've got the tea, and we're hoping we can find the bag with the supplies in it or anything else connected to your attack. Because of his arrest, we can compel him to give us DNA to compare to what was on the coat. If it matches then we won't need her testimony. Turns out the car and the townhouse were leased, and the townhouse was leased furnished. His job was legit, but everything else belonged to someone else."

"When we first met, he talked about making yourself up as you go; I guess he did."

Frost eased down to sit on the edge of the bed. "My guess is he was waiting to make sure you were dead, and then, after it wouldn't arouse suspicion, he was planning on disappearing. You sure screwed up his plans." He laughed, a rare sound, and said, "I swear if you weren't such a pain in the ass I'd offer you a job."

FORTY

I WAS HOME AND working again, but restless and depressed. When I could sleep, I was sleeping at Angel's because I couldn't bear to be in my bed or the house. It would have to end; I couldn't keep imposing on him, no matter how comfortable he said the couch was, but I had no idea what I would do when it came to that.

When Angel worked late, Maddie would come and keep me company, and if she were unavailable, Chip filled in. It was clear everyone I knew was worried about me. My sister had offered to come up from Texas and stay with me, but I asked her not to. She had a family and a job to deal with and I didn't want to try to explain what had happened.

No one pressed for details and neither Maddie nor Chip ever questioned me about why I had stayed with Ian and hadn't just ended the relationship when I found the note. I didn't have a good answer, so it was a relief not to have to talk about it.

Ian was in the Denver County Jail awaiting a preliminary hearing. Edward had been released and cleared of the charges. Several days after his release, I drove over to Edward's house. There was a For Sale sign in the yard. I rang the bell and eventually Edward opened the door, which surprised me.

"Anne, I heard what happened, are you okay?"

"Honestly? I'm not sure. May I come in?"

He opened the door and showed me into the living room. I sat on one of the couches and he took a chair opposite. Silence hung in the air for a few minutes.

"I came to apologize for thinking it was you who hurt Libby and Jeff. I was wrong." I took a deep breath as my gaze drifted to the fireplace where a fire was burning and back to him. "In my haste to accuse you, I let the real culprit into my home and into my bed and as a result Libby died and Jeff died and I nearly died." I fiddled with my coat hem. "I just wanted to say I'm sorry to your face and tell you that because she was a friend my only motivation was for whoever hurt her to be punished."

He was quiet for some time and then let out a long sigh. "I would never have hurt her even though she was cheating on me, but you didn't know that. You didn't know me." He got up and walked to the window and looked out on the bare trees in the snow-covered yard. "No one believed me, but I actually wanted the baby. I can't have children, and it would have been a part of Libby, so I was just as sad as she was when we lost it."

He stopped and cleared his throat and when he resumed it as if he were talking to himself. "The problem is I have a very difficult time relating to people or showing affection, and so people think I'm cold or unfriendly. It was why I loved her; she accepted me as I was, at least at first, and brought some joy into my life. In the end, I think I was a disappointment to her, which is why she sought others. But I will always love her."

"I'm so sorry," I said, tears rolling down my cheeks.

"Anne, don't blame yourself. All your actions were because you cared for her, too. There were just forces at work that neither of us could alter."

"You're selling the house?"

"I can't continue to live here, not after what's happened. I let the staff go. Cora offered to stay, but I really didn't want any of them around."

"I'm surprised Cora wanted to stay; she never seemed that connected to you or Libby."

He smiled. "Cora's a lot like me; I think that's why we got along. She cared about both of us in her own odd way. She always insisted that I hadn't done anything to hurt Libby."

"What will you do?"

"I'm not sure, maybe go back to California. I'm renting a townhouse until I decide what to do."

"I won't keep you," I said, rising from the couch. "I'm just very sorry for the way everything turned out. I hope you can forgive me."

"I have. I hope you mend after all this. It's been pretty traumatic for all of us."

I smiled sadly at him and nodded. We walked to the door where he offered his hand and I took it, squeezed it, and left.

*

IAN WAS charged with the premeditated murders of Libby and Jimmy Scott, conspiracy to commit Jeff's murder, and my attempted murder. When his trial finally took place in April, it was an ordeal. It was humiliating admitting that we had been lovers; I felt conned and stupid recounting what had happened.

The prosecuting attorney walked me through the experience on the stand and then the defense took over.

"While you were seeing him, did Mr. Patterson tell you he had any relationship with Mrs. Matheisen or Mr. Davies?"

"No."

"And you expect the court to believe that he killed Mrs. Matheisen, hired someone to assault Mr. Davies, and then killed the person he supposedly hired to assault Mr. Davies?"

"I don't expect you to believe anything. I'm telling you what he told me."

"Isn't it true that Mr. Patterson had broken off your relationship and that on top of the deaths of these people and the difficulties you were having in your relationship you attempted suicide?"

"No, it's not true. I was drugged without my knowledge—"

"Just answer the question."

"Ian shoved a tube down my throat, and pumped narcotics and alcohol into my stomach—!" I shouted over him.

"Your Honor, please instruct the witness to stick to the question as asked."

"You opened the door, Counselor, let the witness finish."

"After pumping me full of drugs and alcohol, he told me he'd killed Libby Matheisen, had arranged for Jeff Davies to be assaulted, and then killed Jimmy Scott, the guy who beat Jeff up. Then he kissed me on the cheek, and left me to die. So, to answer your question," I said, looking him in the eye, "I didn't attempt suicide; Ian Patterson very nearly killed me."

The courtroom was suddenly very quiet.

"No further questions," he huffed, and I was dismissed.

Being interrogated about Libby and Jeff and my last experience with Ian had been nearly unbearable. But the most painful part was thinking about the Ian I had initially known and trying to accept the fact that he never existed.

I moved through the process in a haze, and tried my best not to look at him in court. When I did, he appeared to be the man I had fallen in love with an intense, but normal look on his face, until he looked at me, and then his expression turned frighteningly dead.

I continued to dream about the night Ian had tried to kill me and would jolt awake in a cold sweat, heart thumping but grateful, once I woke, that I was only dreaming. If Angel heard me cry out, he would come sit on the bedside with me until I fell back to sleep and then return to the couch. I took to sleeping with the bedside lamp on so if I awoke and was disoriented at least I wouldn't be in the dark. The memories of it all followed me through the day as well and I began…dissolving.

IAN WAS convicted of two counts of murder, one of conspiracy to murder, and one of attempted murder. The sentencing would be a week later. I had one more item to take care of I hoped would put some of the ordeal to rest. I went to find Frost. He was working behind his desk when I walked in and looked up, surprised.

"Hey, good to see you." He scrutinized me carefully. "You don't look so good."

"Thanks. Are you always this good with women?"

"Unfortunately. What's up?"

"I want to see Ian before he's sent to prison."

He looked at me for several seconds and then said, "I don't think that's a good idea. Why would you want to see him?"

"I want some answers."

"You're not going to hear anything you want to hear, Annie. He'll manipulate you and play with you and you'll come out more confused and upset than you clearly are."

"Trust me, it can't get any worse."

"It can get worse. Talking to him is a very bad idea."

"You've made your point and I understand your concerns. But I want to see him and talk to him. I need to talk to him one last time."

He exhaled in exasperation. "God, you're bullheaded. It's going to take some time. I'll have to clear it with his attorney and the judge first."

"Then please talk to them and let me know."

"What do you want from that head case?" he asked, baffled. "He tried and very nearly succeeded in killing you, aside from the three people he did manage to kill."

"I need to know why."

"I guarantee his reasons won't make sense to you and it isn't going to make you feel better."

"I don't want to feel better, I just want some answers."

FROST CALLED a day later to say Ian's attorney had spoken to him and Ian was agreeable to speaking with me. His only condition was we be alone during the conversation and that no one be listening in. His attorney wasn't happy, but finally agreed to the meeting. Frost wasn't happy nor was Angel. Frost was adamant that it wasn't safe for me to be alone with him, and Angel was so frustrated with me he could hardly talk. I wasn't sure I wanted to be alone with Ian, either, but there was something festering inside me and it needed lancing.

I was admitted to the jail, searched, told to leave my personal belongings, including my phone, in a locker in the visitor's area and was escorted through several rooms and hallways to a locked room with a small, reinforced window in the door. The guard said he would be right outside the door and would be watching through the window. If there were problems, I should stand up and move to the door. I was not to touch the prisoner for any reason. I nodded and looked through the window.

He sat at a small metal table bolted to the floor, as were the chairs. His hands were shackled with cuffs and a chain ran from the cuffs to a waist belt and then to the ankle cuffs, all of which were secured to a bolt in the floor. He had his hands folded on the table and had his head down.

My chest hurt and I could barely breathe. Even in the bright orange jumpsuit, he looked like the man I had fallen in love with, until he heard the door open and raised his head to look at me. His eyes were as expressionless as his face and there seemed to be nothing but coldness in his stare.

"Come to gloat?" he asked.

"No."

"Why, then? I don't see much point in the visit, but I am curious."

"I wanted to talk to you one last time."

"You want to know why, I suppose?" I nodded. He leaned back in the chair and smiled. "It's complicated."

"Explain it to me, then."

"What do you want to know?"

"Why did you kill Libby?"

"For a lot of reasons. I met her at a housewarming party of some clients of mine. She was another of those bored, rich women. But she was hot and appealed to me, so we began seeing each other. I knew she'd been involved with Davies, but I thought she'd cut things off with him."

He sat back in the chair, his shackles making an unpleasant rattling noise. "When she found out she was pregnant she ended it with me. No one ends a relationship with me until I'm ready to end it. Then she went back to that robot she was married to." His lip curled and he looked like he'd tasted something foul.

He watched me for a moment before resuming. "If she had merely ended the affair, I'd have made her life miserable for a while so she understood she shouldn't have treated me that way, and I would have moved on once I felt she'd learned her lesson. But I found out she'd been screwing Davies the whole time she was with me, and that was just not acceptable. So they both had to be dealt with." He watched me, and the eyes I had loved, which had seemed to love me back, held nothing in them but hatred.

"I acted as if ending the affair was fine and then began sending her the tea. I used the thallium to get her to miscarry and then become more and more ill while appearing to be mentally unstable. Thallium's good for that; the symptoms are subtle for a while. Unfortunately, she contacted you. I knew the day she told me about you that you were going to be trouble."

He smiled again, but rather than being friendly it was frightening. "So I watched Libby's house and I followed you to Whole Foods and engineered the encounter in the parking lot so I could start seeing you." He shook his head. "You just kept asking questions and I knew you wouldn't stop. I started to relax when it was clear you thought Edward was responsible. You were very clever when you suggested that Edward might have gotten the thallium off the dark web; it's amazing what's available on it."

He laughed, "Do you know that you can watch a video on You Tube about inserting NG tubes? That was very helpful, I must admit. And there's a lot of information on drugs and dosages. Makes you wonder if you could be a nurse just by watching videos on the Internet. And getting the drugs to use is pretty easy if you know who to ask."

"Did you send me the text?"

"Clever girl. I wanted you to get the text so you'd be convinced it was suicide, but of course you just wouldn't believe it. I took the opportunity when I was through dealing with Libby to leave the thallium and what I used to contaminate the tea with in the basement before I left." He sat there waiting and watching me.

"Was anything between us real?"

"About me or the way I felt about you?"

"Both."

"The family stuff was pure fantasy; I don't have one any more. As for you, I had to keep an eye on what you were up to. I didn't want you figuring out what I was doing, so I had to get close to you. I will say it was fun. The sex was good and you are funny and bright. A little needy and far too forgiving and trusting, but it wasn't unpleasant being with you."

He watched me like the predator he was and smiled. "You latched onto Edward and just wouldn't let go. I almost felt sorry for him, but it was good news for me. Who knew that bitch had kept that stupid note, my one mistake."

He leaned forward and placed his folded hands on the table as if he was trying to teach me something. "The problem with people like you is, you don't know when to stop. If you hadn't kept contacting Frost and hadn't asked about the coat, you would've been fine. After Edward was convicted, I'd have disappeared eventually, when I was through with you. But you didn't and here we are. I have to say I'm impressed you survived; not many have survived my sleep therapy."

"Did you intend for Scott to kill Jeff?"

"I had decided to ignore him at first. After all, it was Libby who was screwing us both and she'd broken off with him and wouldn't talk to him when she found out she was pregnant. Then you got involved and Libby called him and they met and that pissed me off. I hired Scott to assault him and watched it. I made sure Jeff knew why it was happening. I figured if he survived the beating, which was payback for meeting with Libby again, he'd be pretty disabled or he'd die. Either way was fine with me."

I watched him and for the life of me I could not see anything of the Ian I had known and cared about. But that Ian had never existed and what I had known was simply a useful persona to get what he wanted.

"I hope they put you away for the rest of your life."

He smiled and winked at me. "It won't be for the rest of my life, and I will come back and settle the score with you when I get out. You can count on that."

I stood up abruptly and went to the door. When the guard opened it, I fled down the hall to the locked exit door. I pounded on it frantically but had to wait for someone to let me out and collect my belongings.

Frost was right, it had been a mistake to talk to him.

It was freezing outside the jail and I was shivering, but not just from the cold. I found my car and got inside. I sat there for a moment and then opened the door and threw up, retching again and again until there was nothing left to bring up. The shaking got worse for a bit and then began to subside. I started the car and drove home.

For the first time in weeks, I entered my half of the duplex and went into the bedroom. I was so cold and so sick and I felt broken. Frost had been right; it could get worse and it had. I turned back the stale-smelling covers and crawled in, pulling them up around me and closing my eyes as I lay there shivering. I was broken and scared, and I really didn't care if I ever healed.

IN THE intervening days, Angel tried to convince me to return to his side of the duplex and at least continue to sleep there, but I refused. I refused to work, and I stopped returning phone calls or answering the door. At one point, Angel tried to convince me to let him take me to the hospital and I became hysterical. I begged him to just leave me alone and promised him I would get better if he just let me be. Not knowing what else to do, Angel used his key to check on me daily and tried his best to get me to eat and get out of bed, but I couldn't. I felt like I had that night with the Ambien, slow and unable to move.

All I wanted to do was sleep and escape to somewhere Ian would never find me, even if that meant dying. People visited and entered the house without my answering the door. They would sit with me for an hour or two, try to get me to eat something or try to get me up, and then leave discouraged.

Maddie, Chip, and Katy took turns coming every few days to force me out of bed long enough to change the sheets and make me shower and brush my teeth. They treated me like a child and wouldn't take no for an answer. I was always glad when they left; I just wanted everyone to leave me alone.

People left food, some of which I ate when Angel pressed it on me. But mostly, I slept. I didn't see Libby or Jeff in my dreams anymore. I wondered if they were happy with the outcome. Sometimes, I wished they'd come back and keep me company or take me with them.

SIX WEEKS of this and Angel was beside himself with worry. He was visiting twice a day, forcing me to eat at least something at each visit, and trying to work between visits. I was only truly aware of his state of anxiety when his grandmother showed up.

She came into the bedroom and sat on the bed. "*Querida*, you need to listen to me. Turn over and look at me."

She was a formidable old woman, so I turned over toward her.

"My grandson told me what you have been through and my heart breaks for you. I know you are grieving for your friends and yourself, and I know you're afraid." She stroked my face, and said, "We have all been where you are, each for our own reasons, but life goes on and you must, too."

She pulled back the covers and took my hand. "Sit up now and let me help you get cleaned up."

I'd lost the will to protest, so I sat up. So many well-meaning people who just wouldn't leave me alone. Maybe if I let her do what she wanted she'd leave, and I could go back to my cocoon.

She went into the bathroom and turned on the taps to the bathtub. When it was ready she came in and helped me to undress and get into the tub. She washed me like a little child, gently and carefully; washing my hair and rinsing it over and over again, talking to me all the while about how so many people were worried about me. She helped me out of the bath, handed me a towel, and then helped me dress in clothes that now hung on me.

She took me into the living room where, to my surprise, I saw Angel sitting in a chair. He was unshaven and thinner than I had ever seen him and the skin under his eyes looked bruised. She led me to a chair at the kitchen table and had me sit down. She pulled a comb out of her pocket and began slowly combing my hair. Her touch felt wonderful.

I looked at Angel in bewilderment. "Have you been sick?"

He bent forward at the waist and buried his face in his hands, and I could hear him sobbing and I didn't know why. His grandmother leaned over. "He has been sick with worry for you, *querida*, and he is relieved to see you up. Now, I have brought some food that I want you to eat and then we will talk."

Angel sat up at last and rested his head against the back of the chair, running a hand over his face to wipe off the tears. He was breathing raggedly, but had stopped sobbing. His grandmother produced a bowl of soup from a pot on the stove and set it in front of me.

"Eat," she said, and sat down next to me.

There didn't seem to be any way to argue or ignore her dictates about the bath, or the hair, or the food, so I took a spoonful.

"Grandson, you come eat, too, you are both like scarecrows."

He got up and made his way to the table and sat down next to me; apparently even Angel did what his *abuela* said. It didn't seem polite to refuse, and I didn't have the energy to argue about it. We both sat there obediently eating without talking. I made it partway through the bowl when my stomach refused to accept any more. I pushed it away from me. "Thank you, but I can't eat any more."

"You did well, it will give you strength. Grandson, you finish that."

He continued to eat and watched both of us.

"Now," she said, turning to me, "there is a time to withdraw and grieve and there is a time to go on with life. It is hard to do, but time passes and eventually you will be able be put the grief away and remember it less often."

She reached out and stroked my cheek with her soft, wrinkled hand. "It is time for you to return to those who care about you so they can stop worrying about you. You can see the worry it has caused my grandson. I know you did not intend to cause him or your friends pain, but now you need to come back to us so you both can get better."

She picked up the bowls, returned them to the sink, and washed them in hot soapy water, rinsed and dried them, and put them back in the cupboard.

"The first thing you must do is get well," she said as she finished doing the dishes. "You must do it for those who care for you, if you won't do it for yourself. I have left some food in the refrigerator and in the freezer, and I expect you and my grandson to eat it and stop punishing yourselves. I will come and check on both of you. And you are not to go back to bed until evening from now on. If you do, I will take you to the hospital. Do you hear me?"

I nodded.

She got up and gathered her things. "We can talk more another day, but you and my grandson need to talk. My daughter will be waiting outside to take me home. I expect you to eat and get better, *querida*. You too, grandson." She got up from the table and left.

We were silent until Angel said with a sigh, "*Abuela* has spoken and nobody disobeys her." He looked exhausted but produced a half-hearted smile. "She never calls me grandson unless I'm in trouble. I guess we have to get better."

He helped me to the couch where we sat quietly for a few moments before he turned and crushed me to his chest. "Annie, I was so afraid for you. I didn't know what to do. None of your friends could reach you and I could barely get you to eat and you wouldn't get out of bed. I finally called her to help me. I didn't know what else to do." He kept repeating that into my hair.

I didn't quite know what to do, either, but I wrapped my arms around him and told him not to worry, he'd done just fine.

I felt frail and it seemed everything was too much work. He looked just as overwhelmed. We sat quietly for a while, until he said, "I don't think it's a good idea for you to live here. Too much has happened for either of us to stay. If I can find another duplex or some other place we can live near each other, will you let me arrange it and get us moved?"

I thought about it and about remaining here, but he was right, too much had happened and it would never be home or refuge for me again. I nodded. "I'd feel better if you were nearby, not across town. I've gotten pretty used to you being around."

He smiled. "I'm pretty used to you being around, too. With as much trouble as you get into, I don't think I could sleep if I lived too far away. I'll start looking. In the meantime, please come back to my place and stay until we can move. It's not good for you to be here."

"That's going to put a crimp in your social life," I said, making a half-hearted effort to tease him a little. It scared me to think how haggard he looked and how worried he'd obviously been.

He laughed ruefully. "What social life? I barely have a job." He again rested his head against the back of the couch and closed his eyes. "I don't really need a social life right now; all I need is for you to get better."

"Okay," I said, sighing. So many people who wanted me to do something; it was too much work to fend them off. I put my head back against the couch as well and closed my eyes. "I'll stay at your place until then." I reached out and took his hand. "I'm sorry I caused you so much worry."

He squeezed my hand.

I sat there and my last conversation with Ian floated to the surface. I felt a surge of terror start to overwhelm me. "He said he would come back for me," I whispered as if talking out loud would somehow make it real. "I'm afraid of what he'll do, Angel."

With a note of exhaustion still in his voice, he said, "You've been so out of it, I couldn't tell you. The judge sentenced him to two consecutive life sentences, no parole, one for each murder, and gave him another twenty for planning Jeff's assault and thirty years for your attempted murder. He's gone and not coming back."

"I don't believe that. When he comes back it'll be worse." I could feel the panic building. "I wish I hadn't survived."

He sat up and took my face in his hands and turned it so he was looking me in the eyes. "Don't ever say that, you hear me? He's not coming back. He's a monster, but he's human, not some magic creature that can't be destroyed. *He won't get out.*"

I knew Ian wouldn't be paroled, but I couldn't shake the conviction he would get out and find me somehow. Only time would tell, for now all I could do was hope I was wrong.

ACKNOWLEDGMENTS

I'D LIKE TO thank the following people for their help and support while writing this book. My sister Lorelei Starbuck, who has been my muse, my sounding board, and my cheerleader since the beginning. The members of my cheerleading posse: Connie Holtz, Karen Michaud, Lois Miller, Diana Marston, Donna Lefferdo, Carol D'Josey, Erika Zamora, Sandi Parkins, and Donna Parker. In addition, the following professionals graciously provided their knowledge and feedback about puzzling issues: Joe Marino, retired homicide detective, Commerce City, CO; Laurie Cruz Andress, MD; Jenn Brusco; and my editor, Theodora Bryant who was instrumental in helping me tighten up and improve my story. Any mistakes or flights of fancy are my fault entirely. Thanks to Gail Cross of Desert Isle Design, LLC for the great cover art.

ABOUT THE AUTHOR

COLORADO NATIVE, OR nurse, and author of *The Mad Hatter's Son*, Helen Starbuck lives in Arvada, Colorado, and has written stories since junior high. She loves mysteries, thrillers, and books involving strong women. Following the adage to "write what you know," she writes her mysteries from the perspective of Annie Collins an OR nurse.

NO PITY IN DEATH

An Annie Collins Mystery
Be sure to check out the next in the series,
No Pity in Death.

ONE

A
S THE FLASHBACK washed over me, I could feel him gripping my face, pushing the tube down my throat, and forcing the deadly concoction of wine and oxycodone into me while telling me how I had made him do it. How he was just *'cleaning up a problem'* by overdosing me, like he had done when he killed my friend Libby and her lover Jeff. I felt him kiss me on the cheek and tell me, 'Sweet dreams, Annie,' as he left me on my bed to die.

I ended up bent over the grocery cart crying, telling myself I was okay, I was okay, it wasn't real.

"Dear, are you all right? Can I help?" an older woman asked me. Her hand hovered near my shoulder. She seemed hesitant to touch me, but was obviously concerned.

I stood up and wiped the tears off my face trying to still my shaking hands.

"I…I'm fine. I…thank you, I'm fine," I stammered. I grabbed my purse, turned away, left my cart in the aisle, and nearly ran out of the store.

"I WANT you to come see it and let me know what you think," Angel said over the phone. It was toward the end of June, and he'd spent the month looking for a suitable living arrangement for us.

The previous year had been disastrous. Two people I knew had been murdered, in addition to a third person, and I'd nearly died at the hands of someone I thought I knew and loved. Angel and I had lived next to each other for more than four years, but both sides of the duplex we shared seemed poisoned by the experience.

We agreed to go see the place after work.

Angel, known outside his circle of friends and family as Angelo Cisneros, was an assistant DA in Denver. He was appropriately nick-named. Tall, with loosely curled dark hair, and deep brown eyes, he looked like an angel, just one who got into his fair share of trouble. We weren't lovers, although there had always been an undercurrent of attraction between us, which I had steadfastly resisted because of his hit-and-run tactics with women. We were good friends who'd gotten used to living near each other long before the events of last year. He claimed he'd always enjoyed the arrangement because the trouble I got into made life interesting.

It reminded me of the old Chinese curse: *May you live in interesting times.* I was tired of interesting times and desperately wanted life to bore the hell out of me.

He brushed away the curl that always insisted on falling onto his forehead, as he drove to the destination. "It's an older triplex—it's been remodeled. Two bedrooms in each unit, and all three are vacant. I thought if it looked good to you, we can finalize things and get moved in."

I'd spent the last part of April and most of May in what I now thought of as hibernation, following a final conversation with my former lover after he was convicted and before he was sent to prison. Ian's threat to get out of prison and come back to *settle the score* with me for helping put him in prison, left me with an incapacitating terror.

Ian had been sentenced to two consecutive life sentences without parole, twenty years for conspiring to have another person beaten, who ultimately died, and an additional thirty years for my attempted murder. There was no chance he'd get out—at least that's what everyone told me—but I'd seen Ian's face and felt the hatred and I knew if he could find a way to get out he would, and he *would* make good on his promise.

As a result, I think I tried to finish the job he'd started by taking to my bed, not eating, and scaring the hell out of all the people who cared about me.

Multiple conversations with Angel's grandmother, a formidable woman who no one in Angel's family defied, who he called in desperation, had helped me get up and try to go on. I was not doing well; every day felt weighed down. I was, however, performing a reasonable impression of a normal person if you didn't look closely. That seemed to be what everyone expected. Mrs. Sandoval had assured me that, eventually, I would be back to normal.

I had serious doubts about that.

We pulled up in front of a small brick triplex in the Capitol Hill neighborhood, so named because of its proximity to the Colorado State Capitol building. It was one of those 1930s-1940s style, multi-unit, bungalow affairs with a tiny front porch on each unit and fanciful brickwork near the roofline.

"I know it looks old, but it's pretty nicely redone inside. What d'you think so far?" Angel seemed a bit anxious that I like it, and it sounded as if he really did.

"I like the outside. The front yard space needs some work." The grass in front of each unit and a small city-owned strip of grass bordering the street had just given up; not even weeds were growing there.

"Well, yeah, but you like to garden so you could probably get it to looking better. Let's go inside," he said as he fished some keys out of his jacket pocket and opened the door to the end unit.

It was cute inside, but not huge; houses of that vintage rarely were. The living room would accommodate the few pieces of furniture I had left, having sold or given a number of things away because of their connection to Ian and the memories they recalled.

"Nice kitchen," I said, checking out the new cupboards and appliances. "What does the bath look like?" The kitchen had been updated, and I hoped that was true of the bath. I didn't want to deal with old plumbing and moldy tile.

"It's been redone as well, in all the units." He ushered me down the hall, opening the door to one bedroom and then another and finally opening the door to the bath.

"It's really nice. But Angel, the rent on this place is probably through the roof. I don't know if I can afford it."

I wanted desperately to move, but I was short of cash. I had recently returned to the surgery department where I'd worked in the main OR. I was now working in the outpatient surgery pre-op area, easing back into practice. Much to my chagrin, Angel had paid my bills and rent the entire time I had checked out. I owed him money and, although he had yet to ask and might never ask to be repaid, I had to start bringing in a paycheck again.

"No, I worked out a deal, it'll be fifteen hundred a month plus utilities. I think you can manage that, right?"

"Yeah, what kind of deal?"

"I bought the place," he replied with a huge grin on his face.

"You what?"

"I bought it. It's about time I bought something." Angel was pretty much footloose and fancy free, much to the consternation of his family, who thought he should be married and settled by now. I wasn't sure whether buying property constituted being settled to them, but that wasn't my worry.

"We need someplace to live, neither one of us can continue to live where we are. Gabriela and Marisol desperately want to move out and get away from my folks. If my sisters were living next door to me, they'd probably go for it."

"I like it, a lot." I would have liked anything that I could afford, just to move. More embarrassing to me was that I *needed* Angel next door. Although it was something I would never admit to, the thought of living without him close by terrified me. He seemed more than happy to comply.

His face lit up with a smile. "I knew you would! Let's figure out which units we want, then I'll let my sisters know and they can work on my folks."

"I haven't been around your sisters much. They aren't party hearty, loud-music nuisances, are they?"

"Jesus, Annie, you sound about eighty years old; next thing you'll be telling people is to get off the lawn." He laughed. "Well, what there is of it." He opened the door to the middle unit and we took a look around. "They're in school at UCD. They're normal eighteen-to-twenty-year-olds, but with big brother around, it's not likely there'll be any real insanity."

We toured the other end unit, and I finally said, "I'd like one of the end units, I think. I'd prefer you were in the middle one, to give me some buffer from the sibs."

A MONTH into the new living arrangement, I wondered if my choice had been a mistake. The problem was not with Angel's sisters. They kept fairly regular hours, kept their music at a non-ear-drum-puncturing level, and were as pleasant as girls their age usually were. The problem was with the soundproofing between units. Specifically, between Angel's unit and mine—there wasn't any. I heard the occasional laughing, music, and wall bumping, presumably from his headboard, and tried hard to ignore it. Tonight, however, it was driving me crazy.

Once we moved, Angel had jumped enthusiastically back onto the dating bandwagon. He'd given it up for nearly two months while trying to work, check on me, and make sure I hadn't succeeded in offing myself. Now, apparently, he'd decided to make up for it in spades. It was weird; he seemed distracted most of the time and the endless stream of women felt almost frantic to me. I wasn't sure what that was all about; perhaps he was just making up for lost time.

The rhythmic pounding of the headboard against our common wall seemed to go on and on. It was hard not to picture what was going on between him and his latest conquest, and I didn't want to. It pissed me off and, although I rarely slept well anymore, I was tired and it was keeping me awake. At last I sat up and took a shoe and beat on the wall as hard as I could, and yelled, "Give it a rest!"

The thumping stopped immediately. It was very quiet and then I heard some muffled conversation, which escalated considerably in volume. Eventually, his front door opened and slammed shut, and I heard a car start and drive off. Not long afterward, someone, Angel, I presumed, was pounding on my door.

I got up, went to the door, and looked out the peephole. Yep, it was Angel, so I opened the door. He stood there without shirt or shoes, wearing jeans that rested low on his hips; his dark curls in disarray and a bite mark on his neck. I had never seen him without a shirt and I had to admit it was a lovely sight. He had a well-muscled chest and abdomen with a lovely crop of hair across his pecks that met in the middle and drifted in a faint line down to his navel and disappeared into his jeans like an invitation.

"You," he said, pointing a finger at me, "give new meaning to the phrase *coitus interruptus*! She was so upset, she left!"

"And you," I replied, pointing my finger at him, "are incredibly annoying with your headboard banging on the wall. For God's sake, move the damned bed away from the wall. I can't sleep!"

He had the grace to blush, then said, "I'd have thought you'd had enough sleep these last few months to last a lifetime."

"You fucking bastard!" I said, and slammed the door in his face.

"Well, I'm not now, am I? Thanks to you!" he yelled at me through the door.

I heard his door slam shut a minute later. So much for neighborly relations. Neighborly relations, however, were the least of my concerns. Angel and I would sort something out eventually. It was noticeably quieter in the ensuing days; I assumed he had moved the bed.